Cara Colter shares her life in beautiful British Columbia, Canada, with her husband, nine horses and one small Pomeranian with a large attitude. She loves to hear from readers, and you can learn more about her and contact her through Facebook.

Teri Wilson is a novelist for Mills & Boon. She is the author of *Unleashing Mr. Darcy*, now a Hallmark Channel Original Movie. Teri is also a contributing writer at hellogiggles.com, a lifestyle and entertainment website founded by Zooey Deschanel that is now part of the *People* magazine, *Time* magazine and *Entertainment Weekly* family. Teri loves books, travel, animals and dancing every day. Visit Teri at teriwilson.net or on Twitter, @teriwilsonauthr

Also by Cara Colter

Swept into the Tycoon's World
Snowbound with the Single Dad
His Convenient Royal Bride

A Crown by Christmas
Cinderella's Prince Under the Mistletoe

Also by Teri Wilson

How to Rescue a Family
The Ballerina's Secret
How to Romance a Runaway Bride
The Bachelor's Baby Surprise
A Daddy by Christmas
His Ballerina Bride
The Princess Problem
It Started with a Diamond
Unmasking Juliet
Unleashing Mr. Darcy

CINDERELLA'S PRINCE UNDER THE MISTLETOE

CARA COLTER

THE MAVERICK'S SECRET BABY

TERI WILSON

MILLS & BOON

First Published in Great Britain 2019
by Mills & Boon, an imprint of HarperCollinsPublishers,
1 London Bridge Street, London, SE1 9GF

Special thanks and acknowledgement are given to Cara Colter for her contribution to the A Crown by Christmas series.

ISBN: 978-0-263-27263-5

1019

MIX
Paper from responsible sources
FSC™ C007454

This book is produced from independently certified FSC™ paper to ensure responsible forest management.

For more information visit: www.harpercollins.co.uk/green

Printed and bound in Spain
by CPI, Barcelona

CINDERELLA'S PRINCE UNDER THE MISTLETOE

CARA COLTER

To the entire *A Crown by Christmas* team,
editors and writers,
who made the magic happen.

CHAPTER ONE

IMOGEN ALBRIGHT GAVE the perfectly made bed one more completely unnecessary swipe with her hand. The Egyptian cotton sheets, with their one thousand thread count, were soft beneath her fingertips, and a light, deliciously clean fragrance tickled her nostrils.

A little nervously, Imogen tucked a honey-blond strand of her shoulder-length hair behind her ear and glanced around the room. As were all the rooms at the Crystal Lake Lodge, a boutique hotel high in the Canadian Rockies, this room was subtly luxurious and faintly mountain themed with its beautifully hand-hewn wooden furniture and the river rock fireplace at one end of the room.

But was it good enough for a prince?

Ever since she was a little girl and the hotel was managed by her parents, Crystal Lake Lodge, with its promise of luxury in the heart of true wilderness, had attracted an elite clientele. Imogen had grown up with a fuss being made over her and her two sisters, by famous actors, heads of state and sports figures. Some came every year, and a few remained as friends to the family. When they were teenagers, Imogen and her sisters had been the envy of all their friends with their autographed collections of celebrity photos.

But to her knowledge, Crystal Lake Lodge had never hosted royalty before.

One thing about rubbing shoulders with the rich and famous all her life? Imogen knew, better than most, that the fabulously wealthy and well-known were just people. With few exceptions, especially when they came here, they wanted the barriers to come down, to be treated as normal and to be liked for themselves.

Prince Antonio Valenti might have an entirely different attitude, though, if the thick protocol book that had been delivered just yesterday was any indication! There was something so intimidating about that heavy binder that she had not yet opened it.

Was the delivery of the protocol book the reason she felt so nervous? She never felt nervous before guests arrived.

But there was some mystery shrouding this arrival.

For one thing, the Prince was not arriving with an entourage. He was coming by himself with a single bodyguard. For another, the booking had been made with hardly any advance notice.

And for yet another, it was the shoulder season. Imogen wandered to the window and looked out. Even though she had lived here all her life, she felt her breath catch in her throat.

The Lodge was perched high on a mountainside. The views were stunning: from this distance, the town in the narrow valley below looked like one of those Christmas miniature villages that people collected.

The community had been built around the shores of Crystal Lake, which was tranquil and turquoise, reflecting the blaze of fall colors around it. The valley walls were carpeted with emerald green forests that gave way to craggy rock faces. The mountains soared upward to dance with bright blue sky, their pyramid-shaped peaks crowned in brilliant white mounds of snow.

It was October and so the thick stands of pine and fir and balsam were interspersed with larch, the needles spun to stunning gold, lit from within by the late-afternoon autumn sun. Imogen knew if she opened the window, the scents of fall would envelop her: clean and crisp, with the faintest overtones of wood smoke.

Still, as gorgeous as it all was, the question remained: Why would the Prince come now? The summer season—that lake dotted with kayaks and canoes, the air full of the screams of children brave enough to try the mountain waters—was over.

And the ski season was at least a month from beginning.

The mountain trails in this area were world famous for hikers and recreational mountain climbers. When the Lodge had clientele at this time of year, that was who they usually were—outdoor enthusiasts.

And yet when this booking came in and she had asked the reason for the visit, she had been rebuffed as if she had overstepped a line by asking. Then, they had requested she book the whole hotel, though there were only two of them arriving—the Prince and his security man. Thank goodness it *was* the shoulder season, or she would not have been able to accommodate that request.

"Gabi," she said, backing out of the room, giving it one last glance, and then closing the door. "Where are you when I need you?"

"Did you say something?"

One of the local girls, Rachel, who helped at the hotel, popped her head out of the room they were preparing for the security man. Newly married, her baby bump was becoming quite pronounced.

Why did it seem baby season was hitting Crystal Lake in such a big way?

Everywhere Imogen looked there were babies on the way, or people toting brand-new infants. And every single time, she felt that pang of loss and regret.

"Sorry, no, I was talking to myself," Imogen explained.

"I heard you say something about Gabi."

"I was just wondering where she was, that's all."

"Well, everyone is wondering what is up with Gabi, so let me know when you figure it out."

Imogen smiled at the pregnant girl. This was what was lovely—and occasionally aggravating—about small towns. No one could ever have a secret. *Did* Gabi have a secret?

Instead of promising to share gossip, Imogen said, "Rachel, you be careful. No lifting!"

"Ha. My mother was chopping wood when she started having labor with me."

Imogen knew that, despite this assertion, Rachel's pregnancy had not been without complications. She had been going to the city to see a specialist, and the delivery was planned for a hospital there.

Imogen had actually asked the young woman to stop working, but Rachel had brushed off the suggestion with the claim that she was from sturdier stock than that. Imogen was fairly certain Rachel kept working because her young family needed the money, and so she had put her on light duty and told her absolutely no chemicals were to be used for cleaning.

Imogen moved away from Rachel and her thoughts returned to Gabi. Gabriella Ross ran the bookstore in Crystal Lake. They were lifelong friends. They had always been there for each other, but their friendship had deepened even more when Imogen's sisters had accepted jobs overseas and her parents had moved to a warmer climate. When Gabriella's aunt and uncle had passed away, they had become each other's family. They knew each other's secrets and heartbreaks and dreams in the way only closest friends do.

Until recently, that was. Imogen frowned as she went down the wide, curved staircase and headed down a back hallway to the kitchen. Gabi had seemed stressed and preoccupied lately. Normally, she would have been helping Imogen get ready for the arrival of a crown prince. Normally, her friend would have been over the moon with excitement.

Gabi was very bookish, and by now, usually Imogen could have counted on her to have researched all there was to know about the island kingdom of Casavalle. Gabi would have read that protocol book, beginning to end, in about an hour and provided Imogen with a short synopsis of its contents.

"Including what they like to eat," Imogen said, swinging open the door to the huge, stainless steel, industrial fridge in the Lodge kitchen.

But instead of having her nose buried in a book, discerning everything there was to know about the royal family of Casavalle, Gabi had disappeared, with only the vaguest of explanations.

Gabriella *did* have a secret.

Secrecy between the two women was unsettling. It was Gabi who had helped Imogen through the end of her engagement, and it was Gabi who knew, to this day, that tears shone very close to that bright smile Imogen displayed when someone mentioned Kevin to her. Or when she glanced at the engagement picture of the two of them that she could not bring herself to delete as the screen saver on her cell phone.

She felt her heart squeeze, as it always did when she thought of him. He had wanted children so desperately. This was the other thing Gabi knew about her: that Imogen would never have babies.

She had suspected for a number of years, since a serious ski injury, that there might be problems. But after she and Kevin had been dating three years, he had taken her to her favorite Chinese food restaurant, and when she had broken open her fortune cookie, a small diamond ring had winked at her.

"I want you to be my wife. I want us to have babies together."

Of course she had said yes. That picture on her cell phone had been taken by a thrilled waitress seconds after Imogen had put on the ring. But was it the fact that he had included the baby part in his proposal that had made her, finally, investigate further?

Imogen remembered the day she had told Kevin the results of her tests, the distress on his face. He had stammered that of course, it didn't matter, but she had known it had. And she had been right: when she had set him free, he had lost no time in finding a new love. Though he and Imogen had been together for three years and had only just begun to discuss marriage, he had married someone else with appalling speed. They already had a baby on the way. And try as she might to be happy about it…

"Stop it!" Imogen ordered herself, when she felt her throat closing with emotion. She would not ponder endlessly the unfairness of life. She would not! She sorted through a few items in the fridge. They were not what they normally stocked. Instead, tiny individual Cornish game hens, strange sausages, unrecognizable vegetables, tropical fruits and exotic condiment bottles filled the shelves.

Thankfully, she did not have to figure out how to prepare anything. These exotic items had arrived at the request of a retired world-class chef who would be here tomorrow morning in advance of the arrival of Prince Antonio.

Imogen closed the fridge door and cocked her head. The sound of a helicopter—spotting for fires, conducting tourist trips and ferrying heli-skiers—was not uncommon in Crystal Lake. But it was more unusual at this quiet time of year.

She went to the kitchen door and opened it, craning her neck at the skies. Despite the bright sunshine of the day, the air was shockingly cold. She glanced toward Mount Crystal, and sure enough she could see a dark cloud coming to a slow boil over the peak. From long experience with changeable mountain climates, she knew what this meant.

Snow's coming, she thought, just as a small helicopter broke the tree line and then hovered over the Lodge, trees swaying in its backwash, red and orange fall leaves scattering. It tilted, lifted gracefully over the roof, and then the noise intensified.

Imogen went out the back door and quickly followed a stone pathway that wound around the Lodge. She arrived at the front just in time to see the helicopter slowly lowering over the sweeping lawn. Her hair went every which way as the helicopter rocked its way slowly to the ground, until the struts were solidly situated. The noise was deafening for a moment.

It might have only been a two-seater, but the helicopter was silver and sleek, with a dark windshield. It was like something out of a James Bond movie. The roar suddenly went silent as the engines were cut and the rotors drifted to a halt. She saw a crown insignia, gold against silver on the tailpiece of the helicopter.

Her mouth fell open. They were not expecting their royal visitor until tomorrow! They were not expecting an arrival by helicopter.

And, most importantly, she had planned on giving that protocol book a thorough going-over tonight. *Now what?*

As she watched, the pilot got out and held the door. Though he wore no uniform, everything about him, from his bearing to his closely cropped hair, said he was military. He scanned the grounds to the edges of the trees with narrowed eyes. His gaze fell on her, and he squinted long and hard before letting his eyes move on, taking in the building, his watchful gaze resting on doors and windows.

The set of his shoulders relaxed slightly, and he stepped away from the door of the helicopter, holding it open.

Another man stepped out, and the man holding the door bowed slightly and said something to him. She couldn't hear exactly what he said, but she was certain he called the other man Luca.

She might have contemplated the name a bit more—they were expecting a prince named Antonio, after all—but Imogen felt the breath sucked from her body and the autumn mountain glory all around her fade into oblivion.

The man who had been addressed as Luca was astounding. Neat, luxuriously thick hair, as dark as fresh-brewed coffee, touched his brow. His eyes were also the deep brown of coffee, his skin ever so faintly golden, the fullness of his bottom lip and the cleft in his chin absolutely sinful. He was perhaps an inch over six feet, his shoulders broad under a beautifully cut suit jacket. His legs were long under tapered pants pressed to knife-blade sharpness.

He exuded an air of power and self-containment, such as Imogen was not sure she had ever experienced before.

She was also struck by a sense of having seen him before, but of course, in today's world, all royal family members were celebrities. That must be why she felt a tickle of recognition: she had probably seen his face on the front page of a gossip rag. It was, after all, exactly the kind of face that would entice people—especially female people—to buy a copy.

What now? Obviously, even though the temptation was great, she could not run back into the Lodge, as she had a desire to do. She was fairly certain, even without having read the protocol book, that she was probably expected to execute some kind of curtsy. She had planned to practice one. Really, she had!

In fact, she had pictured her and Gabriella, giggling insanely and curtsying to each other.

Apparently nothing about this particular visit was going to go according to plan.

Imogen ran a hand through her scattered hair and lifted her chin. She took a deep breath and stepped forward. No matter what the protocol book said, she wasn't going to go up to the Prince in her work jeans and blue plaid flannel shirt and try to curtsy!

CHAPTER TWO

IMOGEN APPROACHED THE two men. Both swung around to look at her. Both were frowning. This was not the usual reaction of vacationers arriving to the pristine beauty of the mountainside lodge! A bit flustered, she managed to paste a smile on her face.

"Prince Luca?" she said. "I'm sorry, we were expecting Prince Antonio."

Both men looked at her as if it wasn't up to her to tell them who she was expecting.

"Welcome to the Crystal Lake Lodge," she stammered, resisting an impulse to touch her hand to her forehead and bow away!

She extended her hand. Too late, she thought maybe she was not supposed to extend her hand. The soldier type looked at her, dismayed, and as if he might block her from touching the Prince with his own body.

But the Prince stopped him with a barely discernible motion of his head. He took her proffered hand.

His touch was warm and dry and exquisitely strong, subtly but unarguably sensual. His eyes, so dark and deliciously brown, met hers squarely.

Something about his eyes increased that thought that tickled the back of her brain: *I know him.*

But of course she did not know him. And for someone

who had met dozens of celebrities, her next reaction was startling. Ridiculously, she felt like a starstruck teen who had gotten way too close to her rock idol. With all the grace she could muster, she extracted her hand from his grip before she fell under some kind of enchantment. She reminded herself, sternly, that enchantments were over for her.

As if a prince would ever look to a woman like her to be a partner in his enchantment, anyway. Life was not a fairy tale! Fairy tales ended with happily-ever-after. And beyond the final line of the story—beyond the "the end"—was the unwritten expectation of babies. She guessed this was probably even truer for royal families. Weren't they highly focused on heirs? On the continuation of their line?

"Prince Luca," she managed to say. "Or Prince Antonio?"

Neither men offered to clarify who he was, so regaining her composure as quickly as possible, she said, "I'm Imogen Albright. I'm the Lodge manager."

"My pleasure, Miss Albright," he said. "It is Miss?"

The words were said with the deep composure of a man who was very used to meeting people in a variety of circumstances.

There was no need to feel as if his voice—deep, faintly accented, husky—was a caress on the back of her neck.

"Yes, it is," she said, blushing as though it were a failure of some sort. She turned quickly and offered her hand to the other man.

"Cristiano," he said briefly, taking her hand and bowing slightly.

She didn't feel any jolt of electricity from his hand!

For a moment there was silence, and she rushed to fill it. "Obviously, you wouldn't have flown from Casavalle in it, so how does one customize a helicopter with an insignia in such a short time?"

The Prince lifted a shoulder, but Cristiano answered. "It was on order, anyway, from a North American company. We asked the delivery date be pushed up and changed the city of delivery."

It made her very aware of the kind of power and wealth the Prince casually wielded—no wish too great to be granted—and made her even more aware, suddenly, of her own appearance. She was in faded jeans, the lumberjack-style shirt she favored for days with no clients and sneakers with bright pink laces! She didn't have on a speck of makeup and her hair not only wasn't up, but now it was windblown to boot.

She had planned an outfit suited to greeting royalty: a pale blue suit with a tailored jacket and pencil-thin pants, paired with a white silk blouse. She had planned to have her hair up and her makeup done.

"It's a magnificent place," Prince Luca said, glancing at the Lodge.

The two-story building was timber framed and stone fronted, and had a beautifully complicated roofline that made it fit in perfectly with the landscape of towering peaks around it. It *was* magnificent, and coming from someone who was no doubt surrounded with magnificence all the time, it was indeed a compliment.

And yet, even as he said it, she sensed, not insincerity, but a fine tension in him, as if the Prince was preoccupied with matters of significance. Again, his reaction to his surroundings made it seem as if he were not here for a relaxing holiday in the mountains.

When his eyes left the Lodge and returned to her, she glimpsed something in them that took her aback. He didn't just look preoccupied. There was a shadow of something there. Distress?

Which begged the question again: *Why was the Prince*

here? To heal some wound? The thought made him seem all too human. Insanely, it made her want to step toward him, look into the astonishing familiarity of his brown eyes more deeply and assure him everything would be all right.

How silly would that be, especially from her, from someone who had ample evidence everything was not always all right?

"I'm sorry, Your Highness," Imogen said, avoiding a name altogether. "We weren't expecting you today."

"I believe a message was sent," Cristiano said, a bit stiffly, as if she had insulted his competence, "to your cell phone."

Since it felt as if her own competence might be in question, she felt compelled to defend herself. "Our satellite reception here is beyond spotty, so cell phone service can't really be relied on here. It's because of the forests and the mountains. I'm very clear about that when people book." She realized she sounded as if she was justifying herself, so added, "I see it as part of our charm."

The Prince tilted his head at her, considering this. "Is our early arrival a problem, then?"

"No, of course not."

Yes, it was a problem! It was very nearly dinnertime and the chef had done all the meal planning, not Imogen. What was she going to offer them? A peanut butter sandwich? "It's just, um, we aren't quite ready," Imogen said. "The chef won't be arriving until morning. And the cleaning staff isn't quite finished up."

"I trust you'll overcome these difficulties," the Prince said.

His voice was so beautiful it sounded as if he had said something outrageously sexy instead of something extremely mundane.

Of course she would overcome these difficulties. Even though she wasn't the greatest in the kitchen and cooking department, the Lodge was well stocked.

But before she could figure out the specifics of how she was going to *overcome these difficulties*, the crisp mountain air was split with a scream from inside the Lodge. It sounded as if someone was being murdered.

The scream snaked along Imogen's spine. She turned to the Lodge, frozen with shock. Neither of the men experienced that same paralysis.

They both bolted toward the front door, and she snapped out of it and ran after them, even as she registered surprise that the bodyguard would be running, with his Prince, *toward* an unknown situation.

The men, with their long legs, quickly outstripped her. Though neither man had ever been in the Lodge before, they must have followed the sound of wailing, and when she found them, they were squeezed into an upstairs bathroom with Rachel.

"Cristiano?" the Prince asked.

The bodyguard, on the floor with Rachel, looked up. His expression was calm, but his voice when he spoke held urgency.

"She's going to have the baby," he said tersely. "And she's going to have it soon."

"But she's not due for another two weeks," Imogen stammered.

"Where's the nearest hospital?" Prince Luca asked her.

"There's a walk-in clinic in Crystal Lake, but they can handle only very minor emergencies. Rachel's been going to a specialist in the city."

"I have to have the baby at Saint Mary's Hospital," Rachel managed to sob. "They're set up for it. They know—" She couldn't finish the sentence.

"How far to Saint Mary's?" the Prince asked Imogen.

"It's in the city. At least two hours," Imogen said quietly. "If the roads are good." She thought of that storm cloud boiling up over Crystal Mountain with a sinking heart.

"Take her by helicopter," Prince Luca said to Cristiano. "Do it now."

Cristiano gave him a questioning look, and Imogen understood immediately. He was torn. His first duty was to protect his Prince.

"Go now," Prince Luca said, in a tone that brooked no argument.

"Yes, sir," Cristiano said, and scooped up Rachel as if she was a mere child. With the Prince and Imogen on his heels, he raced outside. Imogen noticed the weather had already changed. The wind had picked up and the blue skies were being herded toward the horizon by a wall of ominous gray clouds.

Cristiano made his way to the helicopter with the sobbing woman in his arms. With surprising gentleness, he had Rachel situated in no time.

He turned, saluted the Prince. "I should be back within the hour, sir."

"Miss Albright and I will try and stave off danger until your return," the Prince said drily.

Cristiano turned and got into the pilot's seat. The engines roared to life and the rotors began to move, slowly at first, and then so rapidly they were but a blur. In moments, the helicopter had lifted off the ground and was moving in the same direction as that quickly disappearing ridge of blue sky.

Imogen hugged herself against the sharpness of the wind. A single snowflake drifted down and she tilted her head to it. Knowing these mountains as she did, she was certain of one thing.

Unless he was prepared to fly through a full-blown mountain blizzard, Cristiano was not going to be back in an hour.

"I'm sorry your arrival was so eventful," Imogen said, turning to the Prince. "I can't thank you enough for offering your helicopter."

"It was my pleasure," he said.

"Do you think it was normal labor, or do you think something was wrong?" Imogen asked him.

"I'm afraid I don't know."

She could have kicked herself. How would he know? Dealing with pregnancies was hardly going to be one of his princely duties.

"You're very worried about her," he said with grave understanding.

"Terrified for her," she admitted, and then, even though it might not be allowed, according to the protocol book, she felt driven to expand on that. "While I'm sure your position requires you maintain a certain formality with your staff, it's not like that here. We are a very small hotel, and Crystal Lake is quite an isolated community. In a way, we all become family."

His eyes rested on her very intently for a moment.

"Do you know everyone in the village of Crystal Lake?" he asked.

"Residents, yes. Visitors, no."

He contemplated that for a moment. She was sure he wanted to ask her something, but then he did not. Instead, he put his hands in his trouser pockets. She realized he was very probably getting cold. His tailored suit was obviously custom-made and absolutely gorgeous, but lightweight. The shirt underneath, which had looked white at first glance, was the palest shade of pink, and silk, which was hardly known for its insulating qualities.

"I'm sorry, Prince Luca," she said. "I'm distracted. It's very cold out. I'll show you your room and you can get settled."

Then she realized there was nothing for him to get settled with—his luggage had just gone away with the helicopter.

Still, she showed him the room, chatting about the history of the Lodge as they moved up the sweeping staircase and down the wide hallway to his suite. She was glad she had done this so many times it was second nature to her. She could not get her mind off Rachel, plus there was something about the Prince's presence that could easily tie her tongue in knots.

Finally, she opened the door of the suite she had personally prepared for him. "I hope you'll find the accommodations comfortable," she said.

He barely looked around. He went to the window, and when he turned back to her, he was frowning.

"It's snowing," he said.

She could see the window beyond him, and even though she had been expecting snow, she was a little taken aback by how quickly it was thickening outside the window.

She didn't want to let her alarm show; if this kept up, the helicopter might not be able to return. The chef might not arrive. And what about a replacement for Rachel? Imogen was not certain that she was up to handling a royal visit all on her own.

Where the heck was Gabi when she needed her?

Still, Imogen told herself it was much too soon for alarm. Sometimes these autumn squalls were over almost before they began.

With a calm she was far from feeling, she said, "The weather in these mountains can be very unpredictable. We have a saying here—*if you don't like the weather, wait a minute.*"

"I am from the mountains, too," he said. "Casavalle is in a sheltered valley, but there is quite a formidable range of mountains behind it that acts as a border to the neighboring kingdom, Aguilarez. This actually reminds me of my home. I understand this unpredictable weather."

But if he was from a mountainous region, and if this reminded him of home, why come? Why not choose something less familiar for a getaway?

None of your business, she reminded herself firmly. Her business was to make sure he was comfortable and cared for, for the duration of his stay.

"I'll have dinner ready in about an hour, Prince Luca. Would you prefer I bring it to you, or will you come down?"

"I'll come down, thank you, Miss Albright."

She noticed the Prince looked exhausted. Almost before she had the door closed, he had thrown himself on the bed, and his hand moved to his tie, wrenching it loose from his throat. He looked up at the ceiling, his expression deeply troubled.

She shut the door quickly and made her way down the stairs. She stopped at her office and used the landline to call Rachel's husband, Tom. There was no answer, and so she left a message for him to contact her as soon as possible. And then she tried Gabriella's number.

That same cheerful message she'd been getting for three days came on.

"You've reached Gabi. I must be hiking mountain trails. You know the drill. After the beep."

The beep came, and Imogen said, "I certainly hope

you are not hiking the mountain trails right now, Gabriella Ross! There's a terrible storm hitting. Please let me know you are all right as soon as you can."

But of course, Gabi would be all right. She had, just as Imogen had, grown up in these mountains. She knew what to do in every situation. Tourists might sometimes be caught unaware by the fickle nature of mountain weather, but locals rarely were. Imogen suspected her urgent request for Gabi to call her had an underlying motive that served her.

She was here alone with a prince, a blizzard was setting in and she needed Gabi's help! Plus, she needed to know what the heck was going on with Gabi. What better circumstance than riding out a blizzard together to inspire confidences?

She sighed and went to the window. Night was falling, and between the growing darkness and the thick snow, she could no longer see the tree line at the edge of the lawns.

With worry for both Rachel and Gabi nipping at her mind like a small, yappy dog nipping at her heels, she went to the kitchen and once again investigated the contents of the fridge.

She sighed at all the unfamiliar items, then grabbed a package of mushrooms, some cheese and a few other ingredients. Despite her distress over Rachel's departure and the brewing storm, she had a job to do, and she would do it.

CHAPTER THREE

PRINCE LUCA VALENTI woke to pitch-blackness. He almost wished for the disorientation that came with waking in a different time zone, in a strange bed, but no, he was not so lucky.

He knew exactly where he was and what day it was. He was at the Crystal Lake Lodge in the Rocky Mountains of Canada.

And it was the worst day of his life.

Oddly, since it was the worst day of his life, his thoughts did not go immediately to the sudden onslaught of difficulties he was experiencing.

Instead, for some reason he thought of *her*, Imogen Albright. It wasn't that the wind had tangled her hair, or that she had looked adorable and completely unprofessional in her plaid shirt and faded jeans and those sneakers with the neon pink laces, that made him think of her. It wasn't that she hadn't addressed him correctly, or that she had offered her hand first. It wasn't even the look of distress on her face when they had found the maid in such anguish on the bathroom floor.

No, it wasn't those things that made her, Imogen Albright, his first waking thought.

And it was not really that the fragrance in this room was like her—fresh and light and deliciously clean—and that it had surrounded him while he slept and greeted him when he opened his eyes.

It wasn't any of that.

No, it was the way her eyes had met his and held for that endless moment after he had told her the Lodge was a magnificent building.

When he had glanced back at her, she had been looking at him, those huge blue eyes, an astonishing shade of sapphire, with a look in them that had been deep and unsettling.

He had felt—illogically, he was sure—as if she *knew*, not just how troubled he was, but something of him.

It was as if Miss Albright had easily cast aside all his defenses and seen straight to his soul. For a moment, it had almost looked as if she might step toward him, touch him again—and not his hand this time, either.

Had he actually taken a step away from her? In his mind, he had, if not with his body. It had seemed to him, in that brief encounter, Imogen Albright had seen all too clearly the things he most needed to keep secret.

That this was the worst day of his life.

And there had been something in her eyes that had made him want to lean toward her instead of stepping away.

Something that had suggested she, too, knew of bad days and plans gone awry. That she, somehow, had the power to bring calm to the sea of life that was suddenly stormy. In the endless blue sky of her eyes, in that brief moment, he had glimpsed a resting place.

Still, wasn't *awry* an understatement? His life—strategically planned from birth to death—was veering seriously off the path.

At this very moment, Luca was supposed to be a newly married man, not alone in a bed in some tiny mountain village in Canada, but in the sumptuous honeymoon suite that had been prepared within the Casavalle palace for him and his new bride, Princess Meribel.

Meribel was of the neighboring kingdom of Aguilarez, and years of tension between the two kingdoms were supposed to have been put to rest today with the exchange of nuptials between them. Instead, here they were in chaos. In an attempt to minimize the mess, he had issued a statement this morning.

Irreconcilable differences.

Not the truth, but the truth might have plunged both kingdoms into the thing Luca was most interested in avoiding: scandal.

Meribel's tearful announcement to Luca the night before the wedding had come on the heels of other disturbing news.

His father's first marriage—the one that had ended in the kind of scandal that the Kingdom of Casavalle now avoided at all costs—might have produced a child. A child who would now be an adult. An older sibling to Luca.

Which would mean the role Luca had prepared for his whole life was in jeopardy. The eldest child of the late King Vincenzo would head the monarchy of Casavalle. Was it possible that was not him? It made the ground, which had always felt so solid under his feet, feel as if it was rocking precariously, the shudders that warned of an impending earthquake.

Luca was a man accustomed to control, raised to shoulder the responsibility to his kingdom first, above any personal interests. And yet this whole cursed year had been a horrible series of events that were entirely—maddeningly—out of his control.

Maybe today was, in fact, not the worst day of his life.

Wasn't the worst day of his life that day four months ago when his father, King Vincenzo, had died? With so many things unspoken between them, with Luca needing the gift he would now never receive?

His father's approval.

On the other hand, if one was inclined to look for blessings in terrible situations—which Luca admittedly was not—perhaps it was a good thing his father had died before everything in their carefully controlled world had begun to shift sideways.

The cancellation of his wedding to Princess Meribel meant the cementing of the relationship between Casavalle and Aguilarez was now, once again, in jeopardy.

There was a possibility that the throne—by law—would go to a person unprepared to take it. A person who had not spent their whole life knowing it was coming, every breath and every step leading to this one thing: taking the reins of his nation.

Luca's thoughts drifted to Imogen again.

His brother, Antonio, was supposed to be here at Crystal Lake Lodge. But with the news this morning, Luca had felt a need to deal with these issues himself, as they would have more effect on his life than on anyone else's. Besides, it had felt necessary to get away from Casavalle as the people discovered the wedding they had been joyously anticipating for months was now not to be.

The disappointment would be palpable. Every face he encountered would have a question on it. He would have to say it over and over again—irreconcilable differences—hiding the truth.

Luca had come here armed with a name. He had almost asked Imogen if it was familiar to her. She had said she knew everyone in this village. The village his father's first wife, Sophia, had escaped to, hiding from the world after the disastrous end of her royal marriage. But in the end, Luca had not asked Imogen. He wanted to phrase any questions he asked very carefully. A kingdom relied on how these questions were answered. There would be time to get to the bottom of this.

And speaking of time, he looked at his watch and calculated.

He had obviously missed the dinner Imogen had said she would prepare. He glanced at his cell phone. It was 3:00 a.m. but he was wide-awake. Hello, jet lag. It would be breakfast time in Casavalle, and Luca was aware of hunger, and of the deep quiet around him.

Why hadn't the sound of the helicopter returning woken him? It was unusual that Cristiano had not checked in with him on his return. Unless he had, and Luca, sleeping hard, had missed it?

Was there news of the woman? The baby?

Good *baby news would be refreshing*, Luca thought, not without a trace of bitterness. He was aware of feeling, as well as sour of mood, travel rumpled and gritty. He reached for the bedside light and snapped it on. Nothing happened. He let his eyes adjust to the murkiness and looked for the suitcase Cristiano would have dropped inside the door.

There was none.

He got up and searched the wall for the light switch. He found it and flipped it, but remained in darkness. Still, he made his way to the closet and the adjoining bathroom. No suitcase. And no lights, either. He went to the window, thinking, even in the darkness, he would be able to see the outline of the helicopter on the lawn.

Instead, what he saw was a world of white and black. Pitch-dark skies were overlaid with falling snowflakes so large they could have been feathers drifting to earth.

Mounds of fresh snow were piled halfway up the windowpane, and beyond that, the landscape wore a downy, thick quilt of snow. No wonder the quiet had an unearthly quality to it, every sound muffled by the blanket that covered it.

Even though a mountain range separated Casavalle from Aguilarez, and even though he was, as he had told Imogen, accustomed to the unpredictable weather of such a landscape, he was not sure he had ever seen such a large amount of snowfall in such a short time. It seemed to him well over a foot of snow was piled against the panes of his window.

He had not heard the helicopter return because there had been no helicopter return.

He looked at his cell phone again. No messages. Not surprisingly, as it appeared there was no signal. Miss Albright had warned them the region did not lend itself to good cell phone service.

It was apparent there was no power, no doubt knocked out by the storm, but did that also mean there would be no phone landline, either? He recalled glancing at an old-fashioned phone when he'd entered this room. It was on the desk by the fireplace, and he fumbled his way through the darkness to it and lifted the receiver.

Nothing. He set the phone back down. Luca contemplated what he was feeling.

He was still single when he should have been married.

He was outside of the shadow of protection for perhaps the first time in his entire life.

His cell phone was not working, and his computer was not here.

The snow falling so thickly outside should intensify the feeling that he was a prisoner of the circumstances of the worst day of his life.

Instead, he felt something astonishingly different, so new to him that at first he did not know what it was.

But then he recognized it, and the irony of it. The snow trapping him, his marriage failing before it had begun, the lack of communication with the world, Cristiano being far away, a possible new contender for the throne, all felt as if they were conspiring to give him the one thing he had never known and never even dared to dream of.

Freedom.

He shook off the faintly heady feeling of elation. His father would not have approved of it. The current circumstances of his life required him to be more responsible, not less.

But still, for a little while, it seemed he had been granted this opportunity to experience freedom from his duties and his responsibilities whether he wanted that freedom or not.

He did not know how long the reprieve would last.

And he realized he had no idea what to do with this time he had been granted. Though the first order should be fairly simple. He needed to find something to eat.

He opened his bedroom door and was greeted with a wall of inky darkness. He became aware of a faint chill in the air. Obviously, the heating system was reliant on power. He fished his cell phone back out of his pocket and briefly turned on the flashlight, memorizing the features of the hallway before he turned it back off to conserve the battery. Feeling his way along the wall, and using his memory, he found the sweeping staircase and inched his way down it.

He didn't use the flashlight on his phone again as his eyes began to adjust to the darkness. He saw an arched entry to a room just off the foyer at the base of the stairs. Dining hall?

He entered and paused, letting the room come into focus. Not a dining room, but some kind of office and sitting room combination. There was a large desk by the window, a couch and a fireplace, which it occurred to him they might need.

They.

He could well be stranded here with Miss Albright. He felt a purely masculine need to protect her and keep her safe against the storm, and he went over to investigate the fireplace. Of course, he was not usually the one lighting fires, but he would have to figure it out. Miss Albright protecting him and keeping him safe was embarrassingly out of the question.

He moved deeper into the room, and jostled up against the sofa. A small thump on the floor startled him.

A cell phone was on the floor, and the bump had made it click on, its light faintly illuminating the fact that Miss Albright was fast asleep on the sofa! The cell phone must have fallen from her relaxed hand.

He picked it up, and a photo filled the screen. The picture was of Miss Albright, laughing, her face radiant with joy, as she gazed up at the man she was pressed against. Her left hand was resting against his upper arm, and a ring twinkled on her engagement finger.

It was a small ring, nothing at all like the heirloom Buschetta ring he had given Princess Meribel on the occasion of their formal engagement. That ring had been carefully chosen from the famous Valenti royal collection as the one that would show not just her, but her family and her kingdom, how valued an alliance this one was. The ring, by the famous Casavallian jeweler, had been appraised at fifteen million dollars.

In retrospect, had Meribel accepted that ring with a look that suggested a certain resignation? Had she looked at the ring longer than she had looked at him? Certainly, there had been nothing on her face like what he saw in this picture of Miss Albright.

Carefully, Luca set the phone on a coffee table in front of the sofa. He could taste a strange bitterness in his mouth.

Love.

Obviously, that radiant look on Miss Albright's face came from someone who loved and was loved.

It was the very thing he had trained himself never to desire, the thing that had nearly collapsed the House of Valenti when his father's first marriage, a love match, had ended in abandonment, scandal and near disaster instead of happiness.

Luca had been taught by his father that love was a capricious thing, not to be trusted, not to be experimented with, an unpredictable sprite that beguiled and then created no end of mischief in a well-ordered life.

Meribel's admission of loving another—of carrying another man's baby—total proof that his father's lessons had been correct.

And yet that glance at the photo of Miss Albright and her betrothed had made him feel the faintest pang of weakness, of longing for something he had turned his back on. Something unfamiliar niggled at him, so unfamiliar that at first he could not identify it. But then he knew what it was. He felt jealous of what he saw in the photo of Imogen and her man.

The feeling was unfamiliar to the Prince because, really, he was the man everyone perceived as having everything. Soon to be King, Luca had wealth and power beyond what anyone dared to dream.

And yet, what was the price? A life without love?

What was it like to love as deeply as Meribel loved, so deeply that the future of a nation could be jeopardized? What was it to feel that kind of joy? That kind of abandon? What would it be like to lose control in that way? To give oneself over to a grand passion?

His family's history held the answer: to give one's self over to a grand passion was an invitation to ruin.

And it seemed his father's personal catastrophe, more than thirty years in the past, still had the power to wreak havoc. Had there been a child from the King's brief first marriage? Was the claim real, or in this world so filled with duplicity, was it just a lie, a sophisticated extortion attempt of some sort?

Luca glanced once more at Miss Albright's sleeping face.

He saw sweetness there, and vulnerability. He became aware of that feeling of protectiveness again, especially as he felt the chill deepening in the air. Still, he did not want to risk waking her by lighting the fire.

Instead, he saw a blanket tossed over the back of a wing chair, quietly made his way to it and went back and laid it over her.

Some extraordinary tenderness rose in him as the blanket floated down around her slender shoulders. He reminded himself that she was committed to another. Then he noticed her hand. The ring that had been in the photo was missing.

Not that that necessarily meant anything. Maybe she didn't wear it to do chores.

Luca forced himself to move away from her, and once again went in search of something to eat.

He found a cozy dining room, and on a large plank harvest table, perfectly in keeping with the woodsy atmosphere of the Lodge, sat a single table setting and a bowl of soup—mushrooms clustered in a thick broth and garnished with fresh herbs.

Beside the soup was a plate of cheeses, gone unfortunately dry around the edges, along with strawberries and grapes. All were artfully placed. He considered that for a moment. He wondered if Imogen had been disappointed when he did not come for dinner. He sampled her offering, taking a slice of cheese. Unfortunately, it was as dry as it looked, but it piqued his hunger. He turned his attention to the bowl of soup. It probably only needed heating. Forgetting he would need power to do that, Luca scooped up the bowl and went in search of the kitchen.

CHAPTER FOUR

IMOGEN WOKE WITH a start, struggling to think where she was. Then she remembered. She had frantically come up with a plan for the Prince's dinner, but when he had not come down for the meal she had been somewhat relieved. Her offering had hardly seemed princely!

Then she had come to her office, the place in the Lodge where the cell signal booster was located. She had tried desperately to get news of Rachel, but the thickening storm outside had made even intermittent service impossible. And then the power had gone out completely. It was the reality of life on a mountain, but sometimes nature's reminders of human smallness and powerlessness could be incredibly frustrating.

She must have fallen asleep on the couch. But she didn't recall covering herself with a blanket. She pulled it tighter around herself, until only her nose peeked out. The Lodge was already growing cold. She would have to get up soon and light some fires, but right now…

A crash pulled her from the comfort of the blanket. The unmistakable sound of shattering glass had come from the direction of the kitchen.

Here was another reality of mountain life: the odd creature got inside. On several occasions raccoons had invaded. Once a pack rat, adorable and terrifying, had re-sisted capture. On one particularly memorable occasion—a framed picture in the kitchen giving proof—a small black bear had crashed through a window and terrorized the cook for a full twenty minutes before they had managed to herd it out the door.

Aware of these things, Imogen stood up and looked around, her eyes adjusting to the darkness. There was a very heavy antique brass lamp on the side table beside the sofa. She picked it up and slid off the shade. She tiptoed across the floor and down the short hall, past the dining room, to the kitchen. She took a deep breath and put the lamp base to her shoulder, as if it was a bat she might swing.

She went through the door and saw a dark shape huddled by the fridge. She squinted, her heart thudding crazily. Too big to be a raccoon. Wolverine? Small bear? What had the storm chased in?

"Get out," she cried, and lunged forward.

The dark shape unfolded and stood up. It wasn't a bear! It was a man.

"Oh!" she said, screeching to a halt just before hitting the shape with her heavy brass weapon. She dropped the lamp. The weight of it smashed her toe, and she heard the bulb break. She cried out.

The shape took form in front of her in less time than it took to take a single breath. It was Prince Luca. He took her shoulders in firm hands.

"Miss Albright?"

What kind of dark enchantment was this? Where a bear turned into a prince? Where his crisp scent enveloped her and where his hands on her shoulders felt strong and masterful and like something she could lean into, rely on, surrender some of her own self-sufficiency to? The pain in her foot seemed to be erased entirely.

She bit back a desire to giggle at the absurdity of it. "Oh my gosh. I nearly hit you. I'm so sorry. Your Highness. Prince Luca. I could have caused an international incident!"

He didn't seem to see the humor in it. His handsome face was set in grim lines. His eyes were snapping.

Somebody else had eyes like that when they were annoyed. Who was it?

"What on earth?" he snapped at her. "You were going to attack what you presumed to be an intruder? Who would come through this storm to break into your kitchen?"

"I wasn't thinking a human intruder. I was thinking it might be a bear."

"A bear?" he asked, astounded. He took his hands from her shoulders, but his brow knit in consternation.

"It wouldn't be the first time."

"Seriously?" His face was gorgeous in the near darkness, and his voice was made richer by the slight irritation in it.

"It's not unheard of for them to get inside. Or other creatures. Storms, in particular, seem to disorient our wild neighbors in their search for food and shelter."

His brows lowered over those sinfully dark eyes. "I meant seriously, you were going to attack a bear with—" He bent and picked it up. "What is this?"

"A lamp base."

"It is indeed heavy."

"As I found out when I dropped it on my foot."

"It seems impossibly brave to attack a bear with a lamp. Or anything else for that matter."

"I may not have thought it through completely."

"You think?" He set the lamp base carefully aside.

"On the other hand, I've lived here all my life. I've

learned you have to deal with situations as they arise. You can't just ignore them and hope they go away."

"It was extraordinarily foolish," he said stubbornly.

"You obviously have no idea what a bear can do to a kitchen in just a few minutes."

"No. And even though Casavalle has missed the blessing of a bear population, I have some idea what it could do to a tiny person wielding a lamp as a weapon in the same amount of time."

Did he feel protective of her? Something warm and lovely—suspiciously like weakness—unfolded within her. She saw the wisdom of fighting that particular weakness at all costs.

"Let's make a deal," she said, and heard a touch of snippiness in her tone. "I won't tell you how to do your job, if you don't tell me how to do mine."

He was taken aback by that. Obviously, when he spoke, people generally deferred. Probably when he got that annoyed look on his face, they began scurrying to win back his favor. She just pushed her chin up a little higher.

The Prince shoved his hands in his trouser pockets and rocked back on his heels and regarded her with undisguised exasperation.

"Are you all right, then?" he asked, finally.

"Oh sure," she said, but when she took a step back from him, she crunched down on the broken bulb, and let out a little shriek of pain.

To her shock, with no hesitation at all, Prince Luca scooped her up in his arms. Imogen was awed by the strength of him, by the hardness of his chest, by the beat of their hearts so close together. His scent intensified around her, and it was headier than wine: clean, pure, masculine.

The weakness was back, and worse than ever!

"There's more broken shards over here," he said, in way of explanation, "and it's possibly slippery, as well. I dropped the soup bowl."

"That's the sound that made me think there was a bear in here."

"Ah. Well, let me just find a safe place for you."

As if there could be a safer place than nestled here next to his heart! An illusion—the way she was reacting to his closeness, being nestled next to his heart was not safe at all, but dangerous.

He kicked out a kitchen chair and set her in it. He slipped a cell phone from his pocket and turned on the flashlight, then knelt at her feet.

"You should try and save the battery," she suggested weakly.

He ignored her, a man not accustomed to people giving him directions. "Which foot?"

"Left."

Given the stern look of fierce concentration on his handsome face as he knelt over her foot, he peeled back her sock with exquisite gentleness. He cupped her naked heel in the palm of his hand and lifted her foot. Her heart was thudding more crazily now than when she had thought there was a bear in her kitchen!

"Miss Albright—"

"Imogen, please." Given the thudding of her heart and the melting of her bones, that invitation to more familiarity between them was just plain *dumb*.

"Imogen." His voice was a soft caress, and his tone was one that might be used to reassure a frightened child. Perhaps he could feel the too-hard beating of her heart and had mistaken it for pain and fear instead of acute awareness of him?

"There seems to be a bit of blood here." He leaned in closer, so close that his breath tickled her toes and made her feel slightly faint. "And just a tiny bit of glass. I think I can remove it with tweezers, if you can point me in the direction of some. A first aid kit, perhaps?"

"On the wall over there." Her voice, in her own ears, sounded faintly breathless, as croaky as a frog singing a night song.

He set her foot down carefully, stood and crossed the room. She took this brief respite from his touch to try and marshal herself, to slow down the beat of her heart.

She told herself it was a reaction to the circumstances, to the adrenaline rush of waking to a crash in the night and preparing to do battle with the unknown, and not a reaction to his rather unnervingly masculine touch and presence.

But as soon as he returned with the first aid kit and knelt at her feet again, she knew it had nothing to do with the circumstances. Even in the dark, his hair was shiny. There was a little rooster tail sticking up from where he had slept on it. She had to fight the urge to smooth it back down.

A nervous giggle escaped her as he picked up her foot again, his hand warm, strong, unconsciously sensual.

"Am I tickling?" His voice—deep, and with that faintly exotic accent—was as unconsciously sensual as his touch.

Her giggle deepened, and he smiled quizzically.

Oh, that smile! Though somehow it seemed familiar, she realized it was the first time she had seen it. It changed his entire countenance from faintly stern and unquestionably remote. His smile made him even more handsome. He appeared dangerously approachable, and as if he was quite capable of enchanting people with hidden boyish charm.

"No," she managed to gasp out, "not tickling. It's just this situation strikes me as being preposterous. I have a prince at my feet? Somehow when I got up this morning, I could not have predicted this event in my day."

"Yesterday morning," he corrected her, absently. "It's already a brand-new day."

She contemplated that. It was, indeed, a new day, ripe with potential, full of surprises. When was the last time she had allowed herself to be delighted by the unexpected? A long, long time ago. Since her breakup with Kevin, she realized now, she had tried desperately to keep tight control on everything in her world.

"It's true," he continued, and she detected an unexpected edge of harshness to his voice, "that sometimes we cannot predict the surprises our days will hold."

"Ouch."

"Sorry."

Tentatively, she said, "You said that as if you've had an unpleasant surprise recently." She realized she was being much too forward and was glad for the darkness in the room that hid her sudden blush of insecurity. "Your Highness."

He looked at her. "Shall we just be Luca and Imogen for a little while?"

His invitation to familiarity was quite a bit more stunning than hers had been. It was as stunning as finding a prince at her feet, giving tender loving care to her very minor wounds.

Maybe she was dreaming! If she was dreaming, would she give in to the temptation to reach out and touch the dark silk of his hair? Her fingertips tingled with wanting.

She tucked her hands under her thighs.

"Luca," she said experimentally, and then, "Ouch!"

"It's a bit of disinfectant. It'll just sting for a second."

Had he done that on purpose? To distract her from the question she had asked about his recent unpleasant surprise?

He finished with her foot, cleaning and bandaging it with exquisite sensitivity. Imogen had to steel herself over and over again from gasping, not with pain, but delight.

"That's great," she said, the second he was finished. She started to get up. "Thank you."

His hand on her shoulder stayed her. "Don't get up yet. I have shoes on. Let me find all the broken glass and clean it up."

"No, I'll just—"

"Do as you're told?" he suggested drily.

Despite herself, she giggled again.

He lifted an eyebrow at her. "What?"

"I can clearly see you are used to telling people what to do, but I was just wondering if you've ever cleaned up anything before in your whole life? It doesn't seem very…er…princely somehow."

"Ah, most monarchies have come out of the dark ages," he said, amused. "I might not be quite as pampered as the fairy tales would have you believe."

"Still, I don't think it would be appropriate for you to be mopping up, while I sit here and watch!"

"I think we are stranded here together in this storm, Imogen. Perhaps, for the duration, we could pretend to be just ordinary people?"

She stared at him. Nothing about him was ordinary, and probably never could be. Yes, he would have to *pretend* to be ordinary.

She, on the other hand, possessed that quality of being ordinary quite naturally and in great abundance.

It seemed to her it was a very dangerous game he was inviting her to play. Prince Luca was not ordinary. She was. Their positions in life were completely at odds. Their stations dictated that they could never be friends, never mind the *more* that his exquisite touch on her injured foot had triggered a weak longing for.

And yet life had dealt them a surprise, and they were going to have to get through it together. What if she let go—just a little bit—of that need to be in control?

And was there something ever so faintly wistful in the way he had said that, too? As if he was experiencing a longing of his own? Perhaps to leave his role behind him, however briefly, and try some very ordinary things?

Wasn't that what she had learned in her lifetime of work here at the Lodge? That everyone—no matter how famous, no matter how rich, no matter how successful—needed a place where they could just be themselves. The holiday they needed most, whether they recognized it at first or not, was to have a break from lives that were far from ordinary, where they could be normal, if just for a tiny space in time.

"All right," she agreed slowly. "The broom closet is over there, by the door."

It became evident in seconds that, though he might not have been pampered, his experiences with a broom and dustpan were limited! For a man who exuded grace and confidence, his efforts to clean up were clumsy.

And it was so darned endearing! Was it possible Prince Luca, as an ordinary man, was going to be even more compelling than he was in his royal role?

CHAPTER FIVE

"WHAT BROUGHT YOU to the kitchen in the first place?" Imogen asked, as Luca finished wiping up the spilled soup and used his flashlight on his phone to scan the floor for any remaining glass from the lightbulb.

"I was as hungry as a—"

"Bear!" She finished the sentence for him, and they both laughed. It was such an amazing sensation to share laughter with him. He threw back his head when he laughed, and the sound of it was deep, pure as water bubbling over rocks.

Someone else she knew laughed like that, with a kind of joyous abandon that made the laughter contagious, though she couldn't put her finger on who it was at the moment.

Still, as her laughter joined his, it almost felt as if she had not truly laughed ever before. Or at least for a very, very long time.

"I'm having a bit of jet lag. My schedule is turned around," the Prince explained to her. "I was going to try and reheat the soup you left for me. I'll also chalk it up to jet lag that I forgot I would need power to do that."

"And you're still hungry?"

"Ravenous."

"Well, we can raid the fridge for things that don't need

cooking, or we can find something to cook using the fireplace in the office."

"The latter sounds like the Canadian experience I'm looking for."

She laughed. "Would you like to try a real Canadian experience of the most ordinary kind? Have you ever had a hot dog?"

"A what? You're making me nervous. I didn't know they ate dogs in Canada."

"We don't!"

Then she saw he was teasing her. Of course he knew what a hot dog was! And just like that they were laughing again, the chilly air shimmering with a lovely warmth between them.

"Hot dogs it is. Fast and simple. And some would say delicious. Especially cooked over an open fire." She directed him to where the hot dogs and buns were in the freezer, and she hobbled over and found condiments, which she shoved into a grocery bag.

He took the bag from her and crooked his elbow, and they made their way back down the hallway and to the office with her leaning quite heavily on him. He insisted she go straight to the couch while he figured out the fireplace.

"There's a generator here," she explained to him, "but I'll only want to start it for an hour or so a day, just to keep stuff from spoiling in the fridges and freezers. I don't want to run out of fuel for the generator by running it too much. We can use the fireplaces for our main source of heat and for some cooking and heating water. We might have to chop some wood. I'm not quite sure if that was in your expectation of ordinary."

"You sound as if you're getting ready for a long haul."

The truth was she was feeling quite delirious about the

potential of a long haul, snowed in with the handsome Prince! And she could see from the look on his face, he was feeling anything but!

"I just want to prepare for the worst-case scenario."

"What is the worst-case scenario?" he asked quietly.

"We got snowed in here for a week once, when I was a child."

"A week?" he asked, appalled.

"It was glorious," Imogen told him. "It was at Christmas. We had guests, and we quickly all became family. We made gifts for each other and cooked over the fire. We popped corn and roasted wienies—"

"Wienies?" he asked, clearly trying to hide his horror.

"Another name for hot dogs."

"Go on," he said.

She cast him a glance, and it seemed, impossibly, as if he was genuinely interested.

"We played board games and charades. We sang and played outside in the snow. Christmas is always wonderful up here, but that is my favorite memory ever. It was so simple. Real, somehow."

"You love Christmas," he guessed softly.

"Of course I do! Doesn't everyone?"

He was silent.

"Go on," she encouraged him softly, and then held her breath, because surely a prince, no matter how ordinary he was trying to be, was not going to share details of his private life with her.

But then he began to talk, his voice low and lovely, a voice one could listen to forever without tiring of it.

"Christmas is a huge celebration in Casavalle," Luca said, hesitantly. "Even as we speak, preparations will have begun."

"It's October," she pointed out to him.

"Yes, I know. But it is an absolutely huge undertaking preparing for the season. To begin, there are over six dozen very old, very large live Norway spruce trees lining the drive to the palace. They are all decorated with lights. I think I heard once that there are over a million lights on those trees. When lit, they are so brilliant, no other illumination is used on the driveway.

"The central fountain will be having blocks of ice that weigh in the tons placed in it for the ice-carving competition. We can't always count on cold weather in the valley bottom, so there is a complicated refrigeration system beneath the fountain that prevents melting. A decorated outdoor hedge maze is a favorite with children.

"The head woodsman will be searching the forest for the perfect tree for the castle's grand entrance hall. That tree will be over forty feet high, the angel atop it almost touching the ceiling of the front foyer. The foyer is so large that choirs assemble to sing there, in front of that tree, throughout the holiday."

Imogen wondered if her eyes were growing rounder and rounder.

"Have you heard of the jeweler, Buschetta?"

"I don't think so."

"He was one of my kingdom's most celebrated artisans. His inspiration was Fabergé. He started doing jeweled ornaments for the main entry Christmas tree in the late eighteen-hundreds, and his family continues the tradition. They are wondrous creations—they appear to be one thing, but just as the famous Fabergé eggs, they hold a secret. So a hidden compartment might hold a manger scene of the baby Jesus. It might hold a miniature of an entire town, or a replica of the castle. It might commemorate a special royal event, like a birth or a wedding or a coronation."

What did she hear in his voice when he spoke of special royal events? What great pain? But he moved on quickly, his voice once again even and calm, someone who had given out this particular information many, many times, like a museum tour guide.

"Each year the new ornament is unveiled—its secret revealed in a special ceremony—and it is put on display on a special table. The next year it will be hung in the tree. People come from around the world to see the Buschetta ornaments. The collection is considered priceless. That's part of the reason we start getting ready for Christmas so early in Casavalle—to accommodate the huge crowds, which are quite a boon to our economy."

It all sounded very posh, and while she felt awed by it, she became aware she didn't hear any love for it in his tone.

"Tell me more," she encouraged him.

"The entire palace has to be ready for the unveiling of the tree, so teams of house staff will be hauling decorations—some of them centuries old—from attic spaces and vaults and cellars. The kitchens will be mad with baking.

"Christmas mass is celebrated in the palace cathedral, and the day after Christmas the doors of the palace are thrown open to all the citizens of Casavalle. Huge buffets of all that baking will be set out, along with vats of mulled wines and hot chocolates. It's quite magnificent, really."

It did sound magnificent. She would be totally awed, except what did she hear in his voice?

"Magnificent, but?" she pressed.

He hesitated. "It's not as you described. It's not really warm and fuzzy, but rather magnificent and regal and very formal. The day after Christmas, my brother, Antonio, and I will stand for hours, greeting people at the palace doors. As a child, I dreaded it. My feet would get sore, and I'd be bored out of my head, and I was not allowed to squirm or go off script."

"Off script?" Imogen murmured, distressed at the picture he was painting.

"A quick formal greeting. To the inevitable question about what I had received for Christmas, I answered, 'Everything I had wished for.'"

"And it wasn't true," she guessed quietly from the tone of his voice and his expression.

He shot her a quick, pained look, then made himself busy readying the fire. Was he deliberately turning away from her so she could not read his expression?

"Of course it was true," he said, not looking at her, but crumpling paper, adding kindling and then a log. "I received magnificent gifts. Often I received gifts from other royal families and from around the world. Sometimes, children I did not know sent me things."

She could not stand having his back to her. She could not stand it that she could not see his face when she could so clearly detect something in his voice. She got up off the couch and hobbled over beside him, sank down on her knees in front of the hearth.

A good thing, too, because the fire he was laying was a disaster! Had she really thought a prince would know how to lay a fire?

"Christmas isn't really about the things you get," she said softly, glancing at him and then surreptitiously rearranging his crumpled paper and the too-large bits of kindling he had stacked in a heap.

"I suppose it isn't," he said, his tone stiff.

"It's about the way you feel."

"And how is that?"

"Loved. Surrounded by joy. Giving of your heart to others. Hopeful for the coming year. Having faith somehow, that no matter what is going on, it will all work out."

He snorted with derision. "You sound like one of those films I was enchanted by as a lad. But this is what few people understand about being a royal—it is a role you play all the time. People are looking at you and to you. Sentiment is not appreciated in leadership. In Casavalle, Christmas is about pageantry for the people. It is about giving the subjects of our small nation a memorable and beautiful Christmas."

"Even when you were a boy?" she asked, horrified. "Your own hopes and dreams were usurped by an expectation of you to play a certain role for your subjects?"

He sighed. "Maybe especially when I was a boy. Isn't that the best time to teach such things? That duty, that your responsibility to your nation will always come first? That the pursuit of personal happiness is an invitation to caprice, to calamity?"

She rocked back on her heels, ignoring the pain that caused to her injured foot. She stared at him. "Wanting to be happy is an invitation to calamity?" she sputtered.

He nodded.

"But you must have some happy Christmas memories!"

He contemplated that for way too long, then sighed. "Would you like to know what one of my strongest childhood memories of Christmas is?"

She nodded, but uncertainly. From the look on his face, Imogen was not sure she wanted to know at all.

"My parents had to go away on an official engagement. I don't recall the engagement, precisely, only that that was one of the first times I understood that duty usurped family. Antonio and I spent Christmas with staff.

We unwrapped our gifts by ourselves, ate Christmas dinner at the dining room table by ourselves. I seem to recall we debated the existence of Saint Nick, as the jolly old fellow, along with my parents, was a no-show. We got extra pudding, though."

"But what did your parents say?" she asked, appalled.

"If any explanation was offered, I'm afraid I don't recall."

She said nothing, thinking how sad it was that he could remember extra pudding, but not if he had been offered an apology or explanation. But then, to a young child, what explanation could ever take the sting of Christmas missed by parents away?

She made the mistake of glancing at him. His brows knit together in an intimidating frown.

"Please do not look at me like that," he growled.

"Like what?" she stammered.

"As if you pity me."

She turned quickly away from him. She busied herself striking a match and holding it to the paper, taking satisfaction at the first flicker of flame in her carefully laid hearth.

She could not look at him, because she knew the truth would be naked in her face. And the truth was that she *did* pity him.

And that an audacious plan was forming in her mind. She could tell by the way the snow was piled up outside the window they were going to be here together for a while. Maybe not a week, but a while. She had time.

To give the man who appeared on the surface to have everything—the finest of clothing, a personal helicopter, staff at his beck and call, wealth and power beyond his wildest dream—a sense of the one thing it seemed he had never had.

What Christmas was supposed to be all about.

She was going to give of her heart. To him. Which, if one thought of it sensibly, could turn out to be a very dangerous undertaking, indeed.

Imogen realized that she had not given of her heart for a long time. Protecting herself, nursing its brokenness, feeling fragile.

But suddenly, in the growing light of that dazzling fire, she understood her own healing lay in this direction.

Her healing did not lie in being sensible, in protecting herself from further hurt. If it did, would she not be healed already? No, somehow the key to finding her lost happiness—the happiness she remembered so clearly when she discussed that snowbound Christmas she had experienced as a child—would be found in giving of herself.

Completely, with no thought of what the repercussions of that giving might be, with no expectation of receiving anything in return.

The fire took hard, the flames licking greedily at kindling, and racing up the logs, throwing light and warmth across his face, which she could see was deliberately set into lines of remoteness.

Anyway, how dangerous could it be? Prince Luca would be here for just a short while, and then he would be gone.

On a rack beside the fireplace, with the fire tools, were several forks with long twisted metal stems and wooden handles.

"Luca, may I present to you the very ordinary pleasure of cooking a hot dog?"

She took one from the package, threaded it onto the fork stick and handed it to him, and then took another for herself.

"Not too close to the flame," she told him, demonstrating, "This is the proper open-flame cooking technique for a perfect roast."

As she had hoped, he laughed at her put-on Julia Child accent.

His laughter made her feel warmer than the fire, which would be a good thing for her to remember as she tackled the Prince as her good deed. If she got too close to his particular flame, she was going to get burned.

Doubt suddenly crowded around her.

It was way too early for Christmas.

And yet his kingdom already prepared. Why not give the Lodge over to that Christmas feeling, so that he could experience it?

To be sure, it would be a Christmas feeling that did not involve priceless pageantry, receiving lines, gifts too great to count or appreciate.

This would be Imogen's gift to the Prince for the very short time that he would be here. She would show him how very ordinary things could shine with more hidden delights than a priceless ornament with a secret compartment.

And she would start with a hot dog. She handed him another one threaded onto a stick. An hour later, feeling as full as she had ever felt, not just of hot dogs, but of laughter, they put the sticks down and packed away the remnants of the hot dogs. They sat on the floor, backs braced against the hearth, feet stretched out in front of them.

Her shoulder was touching his. He had removed his suit jacket. Beneath the exquisite, but thin, silk of his shirt, she could feel his skin, heated from being so close to the fire.

"I'm not sure I've ever eaten anything that good," Luca groaned, holding his stomach.

She turned her head to look at him and see if he was serious. He appeared to be!

"You have a little bit of mustard right—" Imogen turned, reached up. She touched his lip with her finger. After the carefree fun of cooking hot dogs together, nothing could have prepared her for the sudden intense sizzle between them. Her hand froze, his lip moved, ever so slightly, as if he might nuzzle that invading finger.

She withdrew her finger from his lip hastily. She made the mistake of licking the mustard off it.

She was aware of his dark eyes sparking on her face with something that was not quite as safe as laughter.

"I'm exhausted," she stammered. She got up hastily from where she had sat shoulder to shoulder with him beside the hearth.

She plunked herself down on the couch, pulled the blanket up to her nose and scrunched her eyelids together, hard.

She was aware he was watching her.

She thought, between the awareness of a full tummy, and the awareness of how his lip had felt beneath her fingertip, and the awareness of Luca's presence in the room with her, she would never sleep.

But her eyes felt suddenly weighted, and an almost delicious exhaustion stole the strength from her limbs and the inhibitions from her lips.

"Luca?" Her voice was husky with near sleep.

"Hmmm?"

"Have you ever built a snowman?"

CHAPTER SIX

EXCEPT FOR THE crackling of the fire, the room had grown very quiet. Luca glanced at his hostess. She was fast asleep on the couch, curled over on her side, the blanket tucked around her. She seemed to have fallen asleep with the ease and speed of a tired child. She had fallen asleep without waiting for his answer.

In the golden light of the fire, she looked extraordinarily beautiful: creamy, perfect skin; unbelievably thick, long lashes; hair a color that made him think of sunlight passing through a jar of syrup.

If he was not mistaken, there was a tiny smear of mustard by the corner of her mouth, just as there had been one at the corner of his.

He frowned. Her mouth was quite lush, that bottom lip full and plump. Since holding her delicate foot in his hand, feeling her shoulder touching his while they cooked and then her finger on his lip, he felt he was aware of Imogen in a very different way than he had been two hours ago. He considered her worst-case scenario that they might be here for a week.

Already, he could feel a dangerous awareness of her, a letting down of his guard almost from that first unfortunate moment when he had suggested they both be ordinary.

And then, one mistake leading to another, he had gone on, quite extensively, about Christmas at Casavalle and seen pity darken her eyes to a shade of navy blue that he might have quite enjoyed under other circumstances rather than her feeling sorry for him!

Imogen Albright, Lodge Manager, feeling sorry for him, Prince Luca of the House of Valenti.

Right before she had slept, she had asked him, her voice thick and unknowingly beguiling, "Have you ever built a snowman?"

"What kind of question is that?" he'd asked, a certain snap in his voice that should have shut her down completely.

Instead, she had said, drowsy and undeterred, "The snow from these early season storms is perfect for it. Heavy and wet."

And then she had been asleep, before he could tell her in no uncertain terms he was not building a snowman with her!

Her easy invitation was his own fault, of course. Jet lag was so disorienting. Luca did not generally let his guard down, and he did not share confidences with strangers. Now she thought they were going to be buddies. Which, admittedly, would have been easier if holding her foot in his hand had not made him so *aware* of her—and not in an *I want to build a snowman with you* kind of way.

Though, if he didn't generally share confidences with strangers, that did beg the question: Who did he share confidences with?

The answer made him feel lonely. And annoyed at his loneliness, and even more annoyed at what he had seen in her eyes as they lit the fire together.

Unless he was mistaken, she was going to make some misguided effort to show him happiness was not a frivolous pursuit, unworthy of any member of the Casavallian royal family. Unless he was mistaken, she was going to try and convince him to build a snowman, as if that was the key to his happiness!

He doubted he would be here a week, even if it kept snowing. Cristiano was going to be beside himself, even now, no doubt, mounting a rescue operation.

Until then, Luca would be in charge. There would be no snowman building, and he would avoid faintly playful moments, like jostling their hot dogs together in the fire! Though, the truth was nothing could have prepared him for the pleasure of a hot dog, nicely blackened over an open flame. Also, Imogen had informed him, referred to as wieners, wienies or tube steaks.

North Americans! They always seemed to want to complicate a dot.

Imogen looked like she might be a very complicated woman.

One who was engaged to another man, thank goodness! Luca had better keep that in mind when he was looking at the mustard-specked temptation of her lips, when he was remembering the slenderness of her wounded foot in his hand, when he was way too aware of the sensation caused by her shoulder touching his as they had cooked those hot dogs.

No, when dawn came, he would set out new rules. He couldn't exactly ask her to stop calling him by his name, but he could make it clear her sympathy was unwanted and overstepped a boundary.

When dawn came, he would make it clear that this was a very serious situation they were in. There would be no time for snowmen! He could use his lack of appropriate winter clothing as an excuse to avoid snow play with her.

Besides, important things needed to be done. From living in a centuries-old palace, he knew about cranky electricity. Though others were designated to look after the frequent problems, he still knew the number one concern of losing power in cold weather was with water freezing.

So firewood would have to be checked and restocked. An inventory of supplies should be made. It would probably be wise to have a plan for getting out of here if they did run out of either wood or supplies.

Fires would have to be started in other rooms or water lines would start to freeze. He would have to familiarize himself with the generator. The palace had several for exactly this situation, and though he had never personally had to run one, it felt good to have tasks to do, important things that would put the barriers, which had slipped a bit last night, firmly back in place between him and Imogen.

These were unfamiliar tasks to him, and yet there was comfort in both having a list of things that needed to be done and in taking charge of the situation.

All that would have to wait, however. Luca was suddenly aware of complete and utter exhaustion.

His sense of being in charge lasted all of two seconds.

This was, currently, the only warm room in the entire Lodge. There was one couch, and she was on it. There appeared to be one blanket and she had it.

Muttering to himself, he made his way through the darkened Lodge, back to his room. Staying in it was out of the question. He could practically see his breath already.

He stripped the blankets off the bed, went back down the steps, glanced at her still-sleeping face and made a bed for himself on the floor in front of the fire.

He thought he would sleep instantly. Instead he listened to her quiet breathing, as contented as the purr of a kitten, and he lay awake until the first light of dawn, leeched of its normal brilliance because of the still heavily falling snow, finally touched the windows.

Imogen woke with a crick in her neck, and a throb in her foot. The air was chilly, and the light was weak and watery, so even before she looked to the window, she knew it was still snowing.

She sat up and swung her feet off the couch. There was a heap of blankets in front of a fire that had died to embers, and it took her a second to realize the heap was a prince!

She was almost certain the royal protocol book would not cover this specific situation, but even so she was pretty sure she was not supposed to be on the couch while His Royal Highness slept on the floor. And yet, when she remembered how protective he had been when she had hurt her foot, she doubted he would have allowed it any other way.

There was something about him that spoke, not of a man who had been pampered, but of a man who had a deeply established sense of honor.

If he was engaged to her, would he have left her when he found out she was infertile?

The question shocked her and she shook it off before she allowed herself an answer. What a ludicrous question to entertain, no matter how briefly. Men like him did not end up engaged to women like her!

She tiptoed across the room so as not to disturb him and added wood to the fire. She blew on it gently until it flared back to life. Then she turned and looked at the Prince.

His hair, so beautifully groomed when he had gotten off the helicopter yesterday, was now faintly rumpled.

The rooster tail stood up endearingly. A shadow of whisker growth darkened his cheeks and chin. It made him look faintly roguish—more like a pirate than a prince—and, unfortunately, more sexy than ever.

But then Imogen noticed, even in his sleep, there was nothing relaxed about him. In fact, he looked faintly troubled, as if he carried a huge weight he could never let go.

Except, Imogen reminded herself, she planned to help him let go of it. Had she really asked him last night if he had ever built a snowman? In the light of day, her plan to show him some normal, good old-fashioned fun seemed altogether too whimsical and faintly ludicrous.

The plan seemed even more ludicrous when his eyes opened. For a split second he looked sleepy and adorable. For a split second, he looked at her as if he felt affection for her. For a split second, she thought *I know you*.

But only for a split second. Then a veil came down quickly over his eyes, making them dark and formidable. Making him both a pirate and a prince. Making her feel as if he was entirely unknowable.

He tossed back the blanket and stood quickly. Despite very wrinkled clothing, he still carried himself with the innate confidence of a man who knew he owned the earth.

"Did you sleep well?" he asked her politely.

"Yes, you?"

He glanced at the heap of blankets and rolled his shoulders. "I'll live. How's your foot this morning?"

"It hurts a bit, but I'll live, also."

"Good. We have a great deal to accomplish this morning." He began to reel off a list. "You need to take care of your foot, so light duty for you. Will you be in charge of breakfast?"

She nodded, though it seemed the question was rhetorical. He had obviously already made the decision.

"And then I'll expect a full inventory of the kitchen supplies," he said. "I'll start putting fires in all the fireplaces, and I'll see to what we need for wood supplies. I've determined the number one priority will be to keep water from freezing."

Of course, he was right. But that tone! He owned the earth—and everything in it, including her—if his bossiness was an indicator! It made it hard to appreciate how much thought he had given this.

"I'll see to breakfast," she agreed, tilting her chin at him. "But I won't be treated like an invalid." Or as a servant to be ordered about! "I'll help you with the wood and fireplaces as soon as I'm done. I already know what we have for inventory."

He looked at her, considering her insubordination with the surprised ill humor of someone who was rarely questioned.

"I told you yesterday," she said, not backing down from the stern downward turn of his mouth, "that I will let you do your job, if you let me do mine."

"As you wish," he said, a bit tightly and as if he had no intention of letting her help him at all.

As he left the room, he seemed as if he was glad to be getting away from her.

"Well, ditto, Your Royal Mightiness," she muttered to herself. She hobbled down the hall to the nearest washroom. She had mustard on her mouth, and her hair was a rat's nest! Her clothes looked very slept in. The water she splashed on her face was jolting, it was so cold.

But it was just the jolt she needed. Luca was just trying to be helpful. He was willingly setting himself tasks that would be completely unfamiliar to him. Why was she being so prickly about it? But she knew exactly why. Last night, he had held her foot with stunning tenderness. Last night, he had confided in her. Last night, there had been warmth between them as they had cooked their hot dogs together, looking for the best position in the fire. Last night, she had decided she had a gift to give him. Now he was trying to reestablish the very barriers that she wanted to keep down, and letting her know that he didn't want any of her gifts!

And wasn't that a good thing, since she was entertaining ridiculous questions like would he have left her if he found out she was infertile?

No, a voice inside her whispered, *he wouldn't have.*

But that really just showed how ill informed she was about the realities of his life. He was a prince. Heirs would be even more important to him than an ordinary man like Kevin.

And Kevin seemed much more ordinary now than he had less than twenty-four hours ago. Imogen splashed more water on her face, needing to stop this flight of fancy right here and right now. You did not compare a prince to your ex-fiancé!

Luca was right. They needed to attend to practical matters first and foremost. Survival—not playing together in the snow, not getting to know each other better—had to be priority one.

What kind of breakfast could she make over the fire?

She settled on a kind of fireside omelet, using the heavy cast-iron skillet. She put a pot of hot chocolate off to one side to heat slowly, and on the other side, a pot of water that they could use for washing up.

"Luca." She went out into the hall and called him. "Breakfast!"

While she waited for him to come, she found her mobile phone, and under the pretense of checking for service, looked at that picture of her and Kevin. She waited for the familiar twist of loss.

How shallow did it make her that after less than twenty-four hours with a prince, it didn't come?

Speaking of the Prince, he'd come into the room. Despite rumpled clothing, there was no denying how his presence—powerful, almost electrical—filled the room.

"Service?" he asked her hopefully, pulling out his own phone.

She shook her head.

"Your boyfriend must be very worried about you."

"I don't have a boyfriend."

"But—" he stopped.

"But what?"

"Your phone dropped on the floor last night. The screen saver came on. I assumed—"

Was that why the barriers had been so firmly back in place this morning? Because Luca had assumed she was in a relationship? She scanned his features.

No, of course not, he looked every bit as remote as before she had announced she didn't have a boyfriend.

The barriers were up because he was a prince and she was a common girl. Because their lives were intertwined under unusual circumstances did not invite friendship or familiarity. She had no gifts to give him and it had been just a moment of madness that had made her think she did.

He looked back at his phone.

"We've had service at some time during the night," he said. "I have a message. From Cristiano."

As she watched, he opened it. His barriers melted. A

light came on in his face that made her want something she had no right to want.

"Look," he said softly. He turned the phone to her.

And she started to weep.

CHAPTER SEVEN

PRINCE LUCA'S RESOLVE to keep his barriers firmly in place dissolved instantly when Imogen began to cry.

"What?" he asked, distressed. He turned his phone back and stared at the picture. "It says they are both well. The baby very thoughtfully put off his arrival until they got to the hospital. Why are you crying?"

And please stop. Immediately.

"It's nothing," Imogen insisted, wiping frantically at the tears. "I'm just so happy. The baby is beautiful. Please show me again."

Luca handed his phone to her and watched her face. He would be the first to admit he was no expert on women. Good grief, he'd had absolutely no idea his own engagement was on such perilous ground. He was so oblivious to emotional language that Meribel's admission of loving another—a baby on the way that was not Luca's—had taken him completely by surprise. He could not think of a single clue that Meribel had dropped that this bombshell was about to explode in his life.

So, an expert at reading the complexities of a woman's mind, he was not.

But even so, there was something in Imogen as she looked at that picture of the maid and her baby that was not entirely happiness. There was a terrible combination of both joy and sorrow on her face.

"It's a boy," she said softly. Her tone, and her eyes—diamond tears still pooling and falling—spoke of a well of sadness that was soul deep.

And yet despite that, yesterday she had wanted to give him the gift of an ordinary experience. She had been willing to overcome whatever this was that haunted her, to give him, a complete stranger, something she had discerned he lacked.

"Let's have breakfast," he suggested. "And then should we venture outdoors? See if the snow is indeed perfect for making a snowman?"

What was he doing? Trying to make another person happy. That was a *good* thing. She was leading with her example. He never wanted to be one of those royals who was indifferent to the pain of others, above it all somehow, privileged to the point of complete insensitivity.

This offer was no different than ministering to her foot yesterday; he felt desperate to take her pain away.

And yet when he saw he had succeeded—when he saw her blue eyes sparkling with anticipation behind the tears—he felt instantly as if his decision could have catastrophic consequences. For both of them. His initial plan—distance and the very serious business of surviving the storm—had been so much better. Reasoned and reasonable.

Of course, *reasoned and reasonable* had gotten him dumped by his bride-to-be on the eve of his wedding. Maybe it was time to experiment with something new?

No!

"Of course, I don't have the right clothing," he said hastily. "I guess it wouldn't be a good idea to get my only clothes wet. Hypothermia and all that."

She went from crying to laughing in one blink of her gorgeous blue eyes. "I'll keep you from getting hypothermia."

He had a sudden forbidden flash of sharing body warmth! "It would be better if we just didn't invite it in the first place."

There was that look in her eyes again: as if she could see right through him.

"We keep plenty of winter clothing here," she said.

"What? Why?"

"All kinds of people arrive thinking they know what a vacation in the mountains entails, but many are ill-prepared for the realities of the Canadian climate. We stock everything so that our guests can have a safe, enjoyable stay, even if they haven't prepared properly."

"Oh," he said. "Snowman making it is, then."

Luca didn't want to admit, even to himself, how he felt he was looking forward to the activity.

To chase any remaining sadness from her eyes, he told himself. But he knew that was not completely it. Maybe it was chasing some all-prevailing somberness from his own soul that he was looking forward to.

And so, after eating a breakfast that was as delicious as it was humble, she led him down the hall to a large storeroom. He noted with relief that she was barely limping.

She held open the door, and they both squeezed into a coatroom made tight with two walls hung with hooks that held winter jackets, sturdy pants, woolen shirts. The far wall was covered with cubbies stuffed with mittens, scarves and toques. Neat shelves above the hooks held rows of boots organized according to size.

"It's like the quartermaster's store," he said. She was

very close. Her scent—sweet and clean and light—tickled his nostrils.

"I know," she said. "We could make snowmen all week long without any risk of hypothermia at all."

She was teasing him. Danger!

"It's not going to be a week," he replied.

She lifted one of those shoulders. "Talk to Mother Nature. It's her plan, not ours."

He was not sure he wanted to be in this tight little closet with Imogen Albright thinking about what Mother Nature might have planned for a man and a woman alone together in the middle of a blizzard.

Without even considering his choices he grabbed things he thought he might need, and with his arms full of clothing, he brushed by her, to the washroom down the hall.

Imogen considered the Prince's departing form. Crazy, but she, a common woman with the most unromantic of jobs, managing a small hotel in the middle of nowhere, seemed to be making the Prince uncomfortable in some way she could not help but delighting in.

Oh, she could feel the discomfort, too. A faint sizzle between them, a primal kind of awareness. It was no doubt the circumstances of being stranded together in a snowstorm, and she should be careful about reading too much into it.

One of them should be putting on the brakes.

But she didn't feel like putting on the brakes. She felt like having some fun, living with spontaneity and verve, for once. She was aware he was turning the tables on her; she could tell he felt sorry for her when she'd reacted—overreacted—to the baby like that.

If she was totally honest about her reaction to the

baby, it wasn't just her own loss that had brought on the unexpected tears.

It was the look on Luca's face, the unguarded tenderness with which he had looked at that photo.

Maybe he didn't even know it, but he was a man who wanted babies of his own. Something she could never give him.

Even if she was fertile, she reasoned with herself, she would never be giving the Prince babies.

So why not just give herself over to giving him what she could?

Her motivation could be very simple: she had felt sorry for him when he revealed details of what seemed as if it might have been a cheerless childhood. Imagine having no fond memories of Christmas.

And so this experience was going to be good for both of them. She was determined about that.

She chose some winter clothes for herself, shut the door of the closet and changed in there. The door had a full-length mirror on the back of it, and she studied herself.

One might hope to be a bit glamorous for a playdate with a prince, but that was a hard look to accomplish in winter clothes. The puffy pink coat and blue pants, padded with insulation, made her seem as if she was quite plump. Her hair was rather messy from sleeping on the couch, but she quickly covered the worst of it with a toque.

With its reindeer dancing around the brim and the too-big pom-pom, the toque hardly seemed an improvement, but there was no point dwelling on it. Still, there was something in her eyes that gave her pause. Despite the fact they were slightly red rimmed from crying, they were now sparkling. There was a look about her of—what?

Excitement. She contemplated that. It was true that it had been a long time since she had felt any excitement about life.

Imogen had not noticed a sparkle in her eyes since the day she had told Kevin she would not be having their baby. Two griefs: the loss of Kevin and the loss of a dream of having children of her own, of forming a family unit so much like the loving one she had grown up in.

Over the past few months, she had not believed this would ever happen. That the light would come back on in her eyes. That she would have hope that she could have happy moments again. To have hope. Was that a good thing or a dangerous thing?

"Oh, Imogen," she whispered to herself. "You don't have to sort out the whole world and its meaning right this second. Lighten up."

With that vow fresh in her heart, she took a deep breath and exited the closet.

When she came out, she could see the Prince was standing outside the front door. She went out, too, and he looked at her, then looked away, faintly sheepish.

She smiled. He wasn't looking away because she didn't look good! Unless she missed her guess, he was entirely self-conscious in his winter getup.

He looked back at her and glowered. "Don't laugh," he warned her.

She chuckled. "Why would I laugh?"

"I look a fool."

She studied him openly. He had made a complete transformation from a prince. He looked like a Canadian lumberjack. Except that nothing quite fit him. The rough woolen pants were too short, as were the sleeves of the colorful plaid jacket. The boots were too big. The toque had a pom-pom on it even larger than the one on hers. Colorful mismatched mittens hid the elegance of his hands. He looked like a boy who had grown too quickly.

"You look quite adorable," she decided.

"Adorable?" he sputtered. "Like a new puppy?"

She cocked her head and studied him. "More like a yard elf. Dressed for Christmas."

"A yard elf?" he asked, aghast. "I don't exactly know what a yard elf is."

"It's—"

"Please." He held up a mittened hand. "Don't edify me."

She laughed.

"I warned you not to laugh."

"Or? Is there some particular punishment saved for the occasion of laughing at the Prince?"

"There is," he said with dark foreboding.

"Do tell." She raised an eyebrow at him.

He jumped from the top step to the bottom one, leaned over and scooped up a handful of snow. "Death by snowball," he said.

"Seems a little harsh." She came down the steps, trying not to wince at the pain in her foot, put her hands on her hips and looked up at him defiantly. Despite his effort at a stern expression, his eyes were glittering with suppressed mirth.

"It's a serious infraction. Laughter." He took the ball he had shaped and tossed it lightly, menacingly, from one mitten to the other.

She could tell his experience with snowballs was limited. The ball was misshapen and did not look like it would survive a flight through the air.

"Yes, Your Highness," she said with pretended meekness. "Please remember I'm injured." Then she swatted his snowball out of his hand. Before he could recover himself, ignoring the pain in her foot, she plowed through a drift of heavy, wet snow. She snatched up a handful of it, shaped a missile, turned back and let fly.

It hit him smack-dab in the middle of his face.

She chortled with glee at his stunned expression. He reached up and brushed the snow away. But her laughter only lasted a moment. His scowl was ferocious. And he was coming after her!

She tried to run, but her foot hurt, and her legs were so much shorter than his in the deep snow. He caught her with incredible swiftness, spun her around into his chest.

"Oh dear," she breathed.

"What would an ordinary guy do?" he growled.

Kiss me. She stared up at him. The tension hissed between them.

"Cat got your tongue?"

She stuck it out at him. "Apparently not." Then she wriggled free of his grasp, turned and ran again. And she suspected her heart beating so hard had very little to do with the exertion of running through the snow, but rather what felt like it was a near miss of a kiss!

With the carefree hearts of children, they soon filled the air with flying snowballs—most of which missed their targets by wide margins—and their laughter. They played until they were both breathless. Imogen finally had to stop as her foot could not take another second of this. Though with her hands on her knees, breathing heavily, she decided it was well worth a little pain.

He took advantage of her vulnerability, pelting her with snowballs, until she collapsed in the snow, laughing so hard her legs would not hold her anymore.

"I surrender," she gasped. "You win."

He collapsed in the snow beside her and a comfortable

silence drifted over them as the huge snowflakes fluttered down and landed on their upturned faces.

Finally, he found his feet and held out his hand to her. "We're both wet. We better get at that snowman."

She took his hand. "Before the dreaded hypothermia sets in."

He tugged and she found her feet and stumbled into him. His hand went around her waist to steady her, and he pulled her closer. She could feel a lovely warmth radiating through the wetness of his jacket. She could feel the strong, sure beat of his heart. His scent filled her nostrils, as heady as the mountain-sweet crispness of the air around them.

She looked up at him: the whisker-roughness of his chin and cheeks, the perfection of his features, the steadiness in the velvet brown warmth of his eyes.

They were back at that question: What would an ordinary guy do?

But despite his clothing, he was not an ordinary guy. A prince! She was chasing through this mountain meadow with a prince.

Would kissing him enhance the sense of enchantment or destroy it?

It was something she was unwilling to find out. She pushed away from him.

"Yes," she said. "Let's see about that snowman."

CHAPTER EIGHT

THE SNOWBALL WAS so big it was taking both of them, their shoulders leaned into it and their legs braced mightily, to move it a single inch.

"I think it's big enough," Imogen gasped. Luca was aware she was favoring one foot, and so he had deliberately taken most of the weight. To be truthful, he was rather enjoying her admiration of his strength!

"Oh, what do you know about building snowmen?" Luca asked her.

She laughed. Luca loved seeing her laugh. It was exactly as he had hoped: the sadness that looking at the picture of that baby had caused her was erased from her eyes. Her cheeks were pink from exertion, her clothes were soaked, and her hair, where it poked out from under her toque, was wet, plastered against the loveliness of her face.

Luca had seen beautiful women in some of the most glamorous situations in the world. He had seen them at balls and concerts and coronations and state functions. He had seen them in the finest designer gowns, in the most priceless of jewelry, in the most exotic settings imaginable.

Princess Meribel, for an example, when dressed up, was like something out of a fairy tale. With a tiara on her head, jewels dripping from her ears, wearing priceless custom-made clothing from designers who vied for her attention, she was the perfect Princess.

There was no "casual"—not in her vocabulary and not in her wardrobe. Even on the deck of a yacht, Meribel was elegant, refined, classic. Her perfectly coiffed hair and perfectly done makeup enhanced beauty that was already unearthly.

And also, Luca reminded himself, cool and untouchable.

For him. Apparently she had been red-hot and quite touchable to someone else.

He shook off that momentarily bitter thought.

Because if he had married Meribel on schedule, he would have never had these glorious, laughter-filled moments, chasing through the snow with Imogen.

Yes, it was true Prince Luca had seen some of the most beautiful women in the world, and yet he was not sure if he had ever seen a woman quite as beautiful as Imogen Albright, in her bulky snowsuit, dusted with snowflakes, happiness shimmering in the air around her.

She seemed natural and spontaneous in a way that made every other thing he had ever experienced artificial and contrived. Imogen was real in a way he was not sure he had ever encountered it before. He found himself wanting to pull the hat from her head, just to watch her hair fall around her face.

He found himself wanting to bend her over his arm and ravish the plumpness of her lips, to find out if kissing her would be as refreshingly wonderful and invigoratingly novel, as awesomely real as the rest of this experience.

He wanted to kiss Imogen as much as he had ever wanted anything in his entire life. He steeled himself against that impulse, waited for it to pass, which it didn't. He took a deep breath.

Instead of kissing her, he inspected the huge snowball, the first for their snowman, with far more intensity than it required. "Okay," he finally managed to say. "This might be a suitable start."

"A suitable start? It's ridiculously large."

He shot her a look.

"What?" she asked.

"People don't generally *correct* me."

"Oh well," she said, with an impish grin and a shrug. "You're the one who wanted to be ordinary."

He had. And the truth was it was surpassing his expectations. Side by side, they began pushing the next ball. When they were done, he could clearly see why she had thought the first ball was big enough. This second one, somehow, had to be hoisted on top of the first one.

It was, again, a total team effort. Finally, grunting, panting, with Imogen giggling so hard she was barely any help at all, they managed to hoist the second ball into place.

The last snowball, the one that would make the snowman's head, was easier to make, thankfully, so that he didn't have to admit she was right—the snowman was too large.

And then they were making eyes out of rocks and arms out of sticks and buttons out of pinecones.

They stood back and eyed their handiwork.

"He's perfect," Luca decided.

"He's not," Imogen argued. She had no idea how refreshing these little disagreements were for him. In his world, when he spoke, everyone deferred to him.

"He's leaning precariously to one side. His eyes are different sizes. He has no nose."

"I think that's part of what I like about him," Luca said. "Perfection, in my world, is expected of everything."

He was not really sure he had realized how utterly exhausting that was until this minute.

Imogen's mittened hand crept into his.

It was unexpected. A gesture of compassion and sympathy.

"I've never felt what I feel right now," he said, encouraged by that small hand in his, or weakened by it, he wasn't sure which.

She held tight to his hand, amazing strength in her touch, turned her eyes away from the snowman and up to his, full of question.

"I feel free," he said slowly, searching for the words. "I feel the enormous freedom of no one watching me. Not meaning you are no one."

"No need to explain, I understand. Completely."

And astonishingly, he knew she did, and just like last night, when he had confessed the disappointment of Christmases past, this felt like another venture into the unknown, and possibly very dangerous territory. Confiding in someone was alien in his world. And yet he could not seem to stop himself from continuing.

"I've never had this freedom—to be able to just gad about, to laugh, to be goofy. You don't know what you've given me."

"You've given me something, too," she said softly.

He watched her face.

"What?" he whispered.

"The hope that I can be happy again."

"Why? What's happened?"

"Let's not spoil this moment," she said. "Our snowman is great, but—"

"But what? He's as perfect as I want him to be."

"What do you know about snowmen?" she teased him.

"Okay. What's missing?"

"A snow woman. He's lonely."

Luca stared at Imogen. Somehow he had the terrifying feeling that she was not talking about a snowman at all. That somehow, now, as from the very beginning, she saw something about him that others did not see.

She saw his soul.

And she saw things there that had been successfully hidden from the rest of the world. Prince Luca, the man with everything, was alone. And he was lonely.

He wondered if marrying Meribel would have assuaged that sense of being lonely. Looking at Imogen, he had a sense his marriage would have been like so much of his life. It would have been exactly like Christmas at his palace home: it would have *looked* perfect, and *felt* empty.

"A snow woman it is," he said, letting go of her hand with all possible haste.

Because he had seen her soul, too. And it promised him something else he had never had before: a resting place, someone to trust with who he really was.

Two hours later, Imogen stood back to admire their handiwork. She and Luca were now thoroughly soaked and exhausted. But an entire snow family of Mama, Papa, two children—a boy and a girl—inhabited the snow-covered front lawn of Crystal Lake Lodge. The snow still drifted down so steadily that the facial features of the snow daddy had already been completely covered by the time the rest of the family was done.

To her delight, Luca reached for her hand naturally as they headed back to the front door of the Lodge.

But then he seemed to realize how naturally it had happened and let go as soon as they were inside.

"Fires to tend to," he said, dropping her hand abruptly. *With relief?*

"We need to get out of these wet clothes first."

His face scrunched up in that barely detectable but funny way that let her know he just wasn't accustomed to someone else telling him what needed to happen first. It goaded her into feeling even more bossy!

"And into something dry as quickly as possible," she said. "Come with me."

"I'll just slip into the washroom and put on—"

"Your clothes from yesterday? Yucky."

His lips twitched. Undoubtedly another first in his world: to be called "yucky."

Still, he followed her, and so they found themselves back in the coat cupboard, going through bins of long johns that were kept for those unprepared guests. He took what she offered him without argument and went and changed.

She changed, too, and regarded herself in the mirror with a rueful shake of her head. If she had to have a pajama party with a prince, was it too much to hope for something a wee bit sexier than long johns that bulged and clung in all the wrong places?

When she saw him in his long johns she realized it was a reprieve. He could not maintain the persona of a prince in a bright red waffle-weave shirt and matching pants, long legs tucked into woolen socks.

He was still her ordinary guy, the one who had played side by side with her all afternoon.

He went off to tend to fires and she found some tinned fish and frozen bread and carried them down to the office. She stoked the fire and then toasted the bread over the flames and made slightly blackened sandwiches.

By the time she finished making sandwiches and setting a pot of hot chocolate in the coals, Imogen was astonished that the light was already fading from the sky. They had played outside the whole day.

When Luca returned, they munched happily on their sandwiches, and then before the light was gone completely, he went and fetched the first aid kit and insisted on looking at her foot.

"I almost totally forgot I had a sore foot," she told him.

"Nonetheless, let's have a look. I could see you favoring it at times. The bandage may have gotten wet today and probably needs to be changed."

As he knelt at her feet unwrapping the old bandage, she contemplated the fact that she had forgotten the injury.

It seemed to her a new realization—this one that bliss was capable of obliterating her pain.

And it seemed to her that applied not just to physical pain, but to emotional pain, as well.

She did what she had wanted to do yesterday.

She reached out and touched his hair. It was still damp from being outside. At first, she just touched it lightly, and then she ran her fingers through it, smoothing down his sweet rooster tail. Then, on pure impulse, she dropped her lips, and kissed the top of his head.

He froze. And then slowly he tilted his head up to her. And then he went back to bandaging her foot. "What was that for?" he asked gruffly.

"I'm not sure," she admitted. "Just this kind of heart-deep gratitude for an amazing day. I feel healed by it, somehow, and not just my foot."

He finished what he was doing, packed away the supplies with more care than might have been completely necessary. He rose, hesitated, and then, in some kind of surrender, came and sat beside her on the couch. They watched the flickering fire. His hand found hers.

"Tell me about it. You wouldn't earlier, but tell me now. What makes you cry when you look at babies?"

She could sense then the absolute command of his presence, because, even though Luca was dressed in long johns and his tone was gentle, it was not an invitation, but an order.

Imogen sighed. She told him everything. She told him about meeting Kevin here at the Lodge, Kevin an instructor at the nearby Crystal Mountain Ski Resort. She told him about a relationship that had felt steady and safe and secure. She told him about how she thought she had found the very steadiness that she had grown up with and had craved since her family had moved away. She told him about wanting nothing more than a family of her own.

Then she stopped, and her voice faltered.

"What happened?" Luca's voice encouraged trust.

She told him about the proposal, and the fortune cookie. "That's the picture you saw on my phone," she said, "of the night Kevin asked me to marry him."

"So why didn't he marry you?"

She sighed. She willed the tears not to fall. "I had a ski accident when I was a teenager. The worst of the injuries healed, but I suspected something that wasn't quite as obvious was wrong. In a way, I didn't want to know, because all my dreams were about family. So I just never followed up on it. But the fact that Kevin's proposal included the mention of babies forced me to find out if what I suspected was true.

"The news wasn't good. I can't have babies."

Luca's hand tightened on hers. "Ah," he said, and she knew he was thinking of her reaction to the photo of Rachel's new baby.

"Of course, Kevin said it didn't matter, and said all the right words. That it was me he loved, and we would figure it out, but right underneath the words, there was some crushing disappointment in his face that I could not bear. So I broke it off. I set him free.

"I'd like to say he seemed heartbroken by the breakup, but his reaction was more one of relief. Even though it had taken him three years to propose to me, he was engaged and married to someone else almost instantly. They're pregnant now."

He was silent for the longest while. When he spoke, his voice was low. She wasn't sure what she expected from him. He struck her as having such an inborn sense of honor, that maybe she expected outrage on her behalf.

She wondered why she had told him any of this. Could it change anything? Of course it could not.

And yet a burden she had carried for months now suddenly felt lighter.

"In time," Luca said, his voice strong and sure, "you will understand what a blessing this was."

"Not to have children?" she said, her voice strangled.

"I was speaking to your broken engagement. Your relationship sounds as if it was as comfortable as an old shoe. I think there are things in you that need better than that. Perhaps he found it—that spark, that passion, that recognition of two souls meeting—perhaps that is why his new life unfolded so quickly. Not as any kind of insult to you.

"As for children," a smile tickled his lips and he touched her chin and lifted it with his finger, so her eyes were forced to meet his, "you will be a beautiful mother one day. We live in an age of miracles. And you will have your miracle. Whether it is through science, or through adoption, or through an act of divinity, of this I am certain—the souls of your children will find their way to you."

Her mouth fell open and tears studded her eyes.

"What an amazing thing to say." Of all the things he could have said, how was it the Prince had said something so perfect?

Luca lifted a shoulder and dropped his finger from her chin.

"I feel it," he said. "Though I consider myself the most pragmatic of men, there are things, sometimes, that intuition knows. I have been trained, even as a child, to respect the gift of intuition as a tool in guiding my kingdom toward a future where sometimes it is hard to know the right answer, where sometimes facts are not enough to arrive at the correct decision."

Imogen felt his voice, his presence, wrapping itself around her.

It had been the most perfect of days, and this was the most perfect of endings. She did not really know how completely she had lived without peace until it was restored to her.

By a prince, sitting beside her in his bright red long johns!

Maybe it was all a dream.

It had to be. Because she drifted off with the deep weariness of one who had traveled a long, long time and had finally arrived at where they wanted—and needed—to be.

CHAPTER NINE

IMOGEN AWOKE. EVEN though she was faintly disoriented, she was aware of a glorious sensation from the bottom of her toes to the top of her head, filling every cell of her being, pumping through her bloodstream with every beat of her heart.

She felt something she had thought that she would never feel again. But then yesterday, building a snow family with the Prince, she had felt it again. Yesterday, just before falling asleep, she had felt it again.

That the feeling remained, even without the laughter ringing in the air between them, even without the quiet contentment of his voice weaving around her, was wondrous indeed.

She realized she had fallen asleep sitting up. Now she found herself nestled against Luca, the steady drum of his heart beneath her ear, his warmth seeping into her, better than a blanket, his tangy masculine scent dancing with her senses.

He had fallen asleep sitting up, too. His arm had found its way around her shoulders. She snuggled deeper against him. And let herself just feel it, that feeling that she had thought she would never have again.

Of being blissfully happy.

After a while, she shifted her position and allowed herself the luxury of studying his face in sleep. The tension she had noticed when she had awoken in the same room with him—could it really be only yesterday?—was gone from his features. How could she feel she knew him so well in such a short period of time?

His features: the whisker-roughened chin and cheeks, his full, sensual lips, his lashes as thick as a sooty chimney brush, filled her with a kind of delight.

His words from last night: spoken with such confidence and so hope-filled that the memory of them made her feel as warm as his body pressed against hers.

Hope.

She had wandered in the desert of despair for so long, unable to find her way out. And the way out had found her.

Taken her completely by surprise.

His words, his sharing his intuition with her, had been an extraordinary gift. Imogen felt a sudden intense desire to give him something in return, something he had never had, a continuation of the ordinary pleasures they had explored yesterday.

But what could she give him that held a candle to the extraordinary sense of hope that he had reawakened in her?

The answer whispered within her, so softly she dismissed it. But then it came again, louder.

Christmas.

She could give him Christmas. Not the trappings of Christmas, but the feeling of it. The delight of it. The sense of the miraculous that was inherent in that day. She could give him not a regal Christmas, where true meaning could become lost in pageantry, and in the pomp and circumstance, but the simplicity of Christmas, where one thing, and one thing alone, shone through.

Shone through as clearly as a star that had led wise men on an incredible journey of faith to a message that had survived over a thousand years, that was still celebrated around the world as intensely as if that babe had been born yesterday.

The message that the babe—and all babies—carried.

The message she had given up on, but that now beat again strongly in her heart.

Love was the true strength, the only way to heal a troubled heart.

Imogen contemplated that for a frightening moment.

Did she really want to be thinking about that—about love—when she was nestled into the safety of his strong, beautiful body? When she could feel the beat of his heart, and his breath stirred her hair?

Of course she did not love him! It was impossible. Despite the fun they had had yesterday—the adventure of survival that they were embarked on together—she could not know him that well. She could not love him.

Except maybe in the greater sense of that word.

The Christmas sense: where love was the force that made you better than you were before, and stronger, and able to give to others from a well of compassion deep within your own soul.

Was not the very spirit of Christmas, somehow, to give joy to a complete stranger, with no thought whatsoever of return, of what was in it for you?

She slipped out from under the protection of his arm, got off the sofa and quietly went and stoked the fire, then tiptoed out of the room so as not to disturb Luca. She had no idea what time it was, but she located her cell phone.

Because it had not been used at all, it still had battery. The time was three in the morning, but Imogen had never felt more awake.

The picture of her and Kevin's engagement had popped up as soon as she had opened the screen to check the time.

She was going to close the phone, but she made herself look at the picture. Then she took a deep breath, and with a new resolve, a sense of extraordinary strength, she deleted the photo. She waited for some feeling—sadness, regret. A feeling came, but it was not the one she expected.

A feeling of newness, of being open to whatever happened next, of not being stuck anymore.

Imogen moved on to see that although there was no cell service at the moment, there had been. A message from Gabi had arrived sometime yesterday. Imogen opened it eagerly.

I am safe. Did not get caught in the snowstorm, though my life is stormy in other ways. I will be in touch soon. Love you, my friend.

Imogen stared at the message. Gabriella's life was stormy? How was that even possible? How could her best friend have a stormy life without her awareness? Had she been that self-involved in her own misery that she had missed some unfolding drama in Gabi's life?

But how? Crystal Lake was too small for the details of people's lives not to be noticed. Everyone knew everything.

But people had suspected something was going on. Imogen had. Rachel had also known something was off with Gabi. But a storm?

Storms usually meant men! And there were no men in Gabi's life, no strangers in town causing tongues to wag.

The only stranger about was the one sleeping in Imogen's office, and no one knew about him.

And it was not as if Gabi ever went anywhere where

she might meet someone. While Imogen sometimes worried Gabi must be lonely, Gabi steadfastly claimed complete contentment with her life. She rarely left Crystal Lake, not even to drive two hours to the city. No, her big event seemed to be the delivery of new books to her store every week.

She loved reading. She loved book club. She loved teaching literacy.

Who was less likely to have a storm in her life than Gabi? Her friend was gorgeous, with her huge brown eyes and her thick chestnut hair that hung midway down her back. She was tall and curvy in the way that made men stop in their tracks and look at her twice, though her innate composure kept most of them from approaching her with their interest.

Gabriella was delightfully unaware of those second looks, of her own extraordinary beauty. She reminded Imogen just a little of Belle, in *Beauty and the Beast*, her nose buried in a book while men floundered at her feet. In fact, Gabi usually forgot she had her reading glasses perched on the end of her nose, making her look like one of those very sexy librarians.

Gabriella Ross was a self-proclaimed hater of excitement.

And yet excitement, of some form, seemed to have found her. But her friend's storm would have to remain a mystery until the storm that raged unabated outside the Lodge subsided.

Terrible, Imogen thought, using up some of her precious battery on her phone to find her way through the darkened Lodge, *to be hoping that the storm would not subside for a long, long time.*

She quickly went about the business of stoking the other fireplaces in the Lodge, and then went to a storage room and unearthed dusty boxes of Christmas decorations. Feeling delightfully like one of Santa's elves, she quietly reentered the office.

While Luca slept, she hung garlands and wreaths. She put out treasured figurines that had been in her family for generations. They might not be Buschetta, but they warmed her heart: reindeer and sleighs, Santa and his missus, a group of carolers. Finally, on the wide sill of the big window, she put out the manger scene. There were dozens of Christmas candles and she put them where, when lit, they would light the figurines. There were candles left over for the mantel. She drizzled shiny tinsel off the door and window frames. Finally, she hung two red socks.

She sat back and took it all in. The room had been transformed to a magic place. It only needed a tree.

And some gifts.

What could she give a man who had everything? How about a memory of a perfect day? Again, she made her way through the darkened lodge, searching out this and that: Ping-Pong balls from the games room, cotton balls from the first aid kit, colorful place mats that she could cut into squares of cloth.

Hardly feeling the cold, Imogen sat down at the kitchen table, and with her tongue caught between her teeth in fierce concentration, she made her gift.

When it was done she regarded it with grave satisfaction, wrapped it carefully in butcher paper and tied it with a piece of string. Then she plundered the cupboards for stocking stuffers: baker's chocolate, a package of pecans, a few pouches of hot chocolate powder.

Tonight, for Christmas dinner, they would have those little chickens that were in the fridge. She would wrap them in tinfoil and slow roast them on the coals of the fire all day.

She went back to the office and put her offerings in one of the socks. And then she went around the room and lit each of the candles.

Luca woke slowly. He could smell hot wax in the air. He opened his eyes to an enchantment.

Candles burned around the room. They lit small figurines and sent a golden glow into a room that had been transformed. Tinsel sparkled like new icicles. There were red-bowed wreaths on the doors. There was a manger scene of figurines in the window. Two bright red socks hung over a fire that blazed merrily.

His eyes found Imogen. She was adorable in her long johns, a red Santa hat with white trim and a huge pom-pom on her head. She was watching him, the smile on her face more enchanting than anything in the room.

"What is this?" he asked.

"It's a gift, for you. It's the gift of Christmas."

He looked at the light in her face and saw her absolute joy in giving this to him. He was not sure a gift—and he had experienced so many of them that were grand—had ever touched him so completely. She must have been up for hours getting this ready.

"It's beautiful," he said softly. What he wanted to say was, *You are beautiful.*

"We just need a tree," she said, suddenly shy, as if he had said those words—*you are beautiful*.

Astonishingly, he could feel the spirit of what she was doing, creeping into him. He couldn't wait to get a tree.

And so they ate a hasty breakfast, donned their now-dry outdoor clothes from yesterday and went outside.

She unearthed an ax from near a woodpile and they

set out across the lawn, past their snow family and into a grove of trees. By the time they got there, they were both breathless with the exertion of plowing through the deep snow.

Luca stopped in the silence of the trees.

He could feel something tightening in his throat as he looked at the sanctuary of beauty and stillness around him.

The moment was made complete when her hand found his. He looked at her to find her gazing into his face, that tiny smile of *knowing* tickling across her mouth.

"What?" he asked her.

"You feel it," she said, her voice low and husky and reverent, as if they were in a church.

"Feel what?" he challenged her. She couldn't really read his mind. And his soul. She couldn't.

"Wonder," she said.

Apparently she could!

He looked down at her and let himself feel it. The absolute wonder of this woman wanting so badly to give him something he had never had.

Luca did something he was pretty sure he had never done, something that was not in the experience of any member of the House of Valenti, something his father would have scorned.

He felt it unfurl inside of him.

A banner.

Of surrender.

He surrendered to what she was doing, and what she was offering. He surrendered himself to the unexpected gift of a perfect day.

Shockingly, it did not feel like a weakness to surrender. Shockingly, Luca felt stronger, and bolder, than he ever had in his entire life.

He felt alive.

He did something he had been dying to do since yesterday. It was part of that complete surrender. Before he could talk himself out of it, he gave in.

He lowered his head over hers and tasted the lushness of her lips.

The warmth of them was absolutely tantalizing in contrast to the cold air. Kissing her was as he had hoped—known—it would be. Real. Her lips told the absolute truth about who she was. And about who he was, too.

Her lips opened eagerly to his mouth, they welcomed him, celebrated him, danced with him. He felt as if he was drinking a wine that he could never get enough of, a sweet elixir from an enchanted land.

He made himself pull away from her, stunned by his own lack of discipline. He felt he should say he was sorry, but he was not in the least sorry, and after she had given him something so real, he could not be insincere with her.

Still, he backed away from her, aware of her wide eyes following his every move, of her breath, quickened, forming little puffs in the cold air. He forced his mind to turn away from her, and it sought desperately for a task to distract.

He went over to a tree with a sense of urgency. It was six feet high and its thick branches were weighed down with snow. He studied it carefully. He walked around it. He was not sure he had ever seen such symmetry in a tree, such vivid color, such headiness of fragrance. But of course, his every sense was heightened. It felt like the very air was shivering around him with newness.

He reached into the trunk and gave it a shake. The

snow cascaded around him, and he was rewarded with her laughter pealing through the stillness.

"This one," he declared. "This will be our Christmas tree."

CHAPTER TEN

IMOGEN WATCHED AS Luca took the ax and swung it powerfully into the trunk of the tree. A fresh bunch of snow fell on top of him, but he shook it off with ease, focused intently on his task.

A few minutes ago, it might have seemed absurd to think the Prince was showing off for her. But that was before he had kissed her.

She took off her mitten and touched her lips. They felt faintly bruised, tingly. Her life felt altered.

Imogen wished he hadn't stopped. But she understood perfectly. A prince could not go about bestowing kisses on commoners!

Still, even though he had backed off on that kiss, she was pretty sure Luca cutting down the tree was for her. Not just to give her a Christmas tree, but as a masculine form of preening.

After a few minutes, he removed the bulky jacket. The view made her mouth go dry—the full broadness of his shoulders revealed, the taut line of his stomach. His arm muscles, outlined by the fabric, tensing, relaxing, tensing again. Somehow, one would not expect a prince to be quite so buff!

Watching him work—easy strength set against this task—was like experiencing visual poetry. She could see the play of his muscles, feel his intensity, smell the faint tang of his exertion mingling with the sharp scent of tree sap.

She had been aware of Luca before. Now that she had tasted the exquisiteness of his lips, the awareness was almost painful, like what she imagined having a tattoo on tender skin might feel like.

The tree finally came down, falling slowly and silently into the snow that surrounded it. He turned and grinned at her, and she allowed herself the satisfaction of having succeeded at what she had originally set out to do.

Luca's face had lost all the sternness and all the tension that had been in it when he had first gotten off that helicopter.

Standing there, leaning on the ax, the fallen tree at his feet, he looked mischievous and boyish, intensely alive, sinfully sexy.

Really, could there be a more humble experience than taking an ax to a tree in the Canadian wilderness? And yet his face was alight with discovery, with an embracing of the spirit of Christmas that was almost childlike.

"It's beautiful," she said softly.

And she didn't just mean the tree. She meant all of it.

He put the ax on his shoulder and picked up the trunk of the tree with his free hand. The tree was huge and heavy, the snow was deep, but he forged ahead.

Imogen leaped to his assistance.

"We're a good team," Luca told her breathlessly as the Lodge came into sight.

"Yeah, a good team of plow horses."

At the stairs of the Lodge, they faced a new challenge. Laughing, gasping, the occasional curse word slipping from the royal lips—which made her laugh all the harder—they finally managed to wrestle the tree up the steps and through the doors.

Once in the office, they had to figure out how to get the tree to stand up. The rough, uneven cuts to the trunk made it nearly impossible, even using the tree stand she had unearthed.

"I think we should tie it to the wall in the corner," Imogen suggested.

"I find that an admission of defeat. Surely, if they can get a forty-foot tree to stand in the foyer at the palace, we can figure this out."

"Well, I hate to break it to you, but we aren't at the palace, and we don't have a team of dozens to help us."

"I find it insulting that you think I need staff to do something so simple."

"Have you ever done something so simple? Set up a Christmas tree?"

"Well, no."

"This has been the yearly challenge in my life since I was a babe, so—" she wagged the string at him "—let me know when you're ready."

An hour later the tree was stuffed in a corner, attached to the walls with nails and string so it wouldn't fall over.

The day unfolded with a delicious combination of ease and tension between them. The smallest decisions seemed tinged with both magic and danger.

"Usually, the first step would be lights," Imogen said, frowning at a box full of light strings, "but is there any point? I guess it would be nice if the power came back on."

But she realized she did not think it would be nice if the power came back on at all, not even if it did make the tree the prettiest thing in the whole Rocky Mountain Range!

They decided on popcorn garlands. Popping corn over a fire was more difficult than they imagined, and soon the room was so filled with the scent of scorched popcorn Luca had to open a window. It was also filled with the sound of their laughter. Finally, they got a batch just right, ate most of it and had to start all over.

When they had enough popcorn to make garlands, Imogen carefully prepared the tiny chickens in tinfoil packets and placed them in a nest of red-hot coals. Soon, the fragrance of the slowly roasting poultry chased even the scorched popcorn smell from the room.

They sat side by side on the sofa, feeling immense enjoyment in the tedious exercise of threading the popcorn onto strings.

"This is what it would have been like for my great-grandparents," she said. "Just taking pleasure in completing very simple, time-consuming tasks."

"Not for mine," he said, and they both laughed quietly, but she heard the wistfulness in his tone.

They chatted about things that existed in that tiny space where their worlds met: what books they had enjoyed, favorite movies, music.

She created a spontaneous game of twenty questions that made getting to know each other fun and surprising and full of discovery.

"Cats or dogs?" she asked him.

"Dogs," he said, and then shot back at her, "Elephants or parrots?"

She laughed. "That would depend on context. Definitely a parrot for a house pet!"

He sighed, "That shows you know nothing of the nature of parrots. Nasty things. My mother was given one for a pet once. Mark that down—worst gift ever. A parrot."

"I'm not sure an elephant would be any better."

"Actually, there's a story about that," he said. "It is said the King of Siam would gift a white elephant to anyone who displeased him. It would seem as if he was being nice, but in actual fact the care and keeping of a ten-ton mammal is extremely onerous."

"Remind me not to displease you!"

"Oh, I will!"

The game continued.

"Beach or ski hill?" she asked him.

It turned out Luca enjoyed skiing, and it proved to be one of the few things they had in common. They talked about that mutual love. Though her career as a ski racer had ended in the accident when she was sixteen, Imogen still loved to cross-country ski the mountain trails around the Lodge.

"Maybe we'll do that tomorrow," she suggested, feeling suddenly shy, as if she was inviting him on a date.

"I've never cross-country skied. I can't wait to try it."

It took a long time to make that garland, but every second of it felt wonderful, an easy companionship between them. Finally, it was ready. With great ceremony, with their shoulders brushing and their hands accidentally touching, they placed their fragrant garland in the tree, then stood back and admired their handiwork.

Finally, they were ready to open the boxes of ornaments. Imogen opened the first one, and smiled.

"Look." She held up her find to show Luca. "These are my two favorites."

Luca took them, one in each hand, turned them over and then passed them back, smiling at her questioningly.

They were reindeer made out of pinecones. They had button eyes and felt ears and tails ratty with age.

"My sisters made them," Imogen said, "when they were just small."

"Will you be with them for Christmas?"

"Of course. My sisters both work overseas, and my parents have settled in Arizona. They loved it here when they lived here, but my mother had a lifelong struggle with asthma. The cold seemed to trigger it and the climate is good for her there. So, we'll meet there again this year."

"For an admitted lover of all things Christmas, you don't sound excited about it."

Imogen hesitated. "Christmas in Arizona never feels quite right. Growing up here, after we opened gifts, Christmas morning, my dad would drive us to town and we'd skate on Crystal Lake. We'd sled on a big hill right beside the lake, and whoosh out onto the ice. It felt as if you were going a million miles an hour when you hit that ice! There was always a big fire going, and tons of hot chocolate and hot dogs. Every kid in town would be there. It was such a sense of community. We were usually so stuffed with hot dogs and marshmallows, we could barely eat Mom's turkey dinner.

"Now my folks have an artificial tree. My dad loves to golf on Christmas Day because there's no lineup on the tees. Last year, my mom refused to cook a turkey because she said it was too hot to get the oven going and the house heated up.

"I miss the way it used to be. I wish they would all come back here for Christmas, instead of me going there."

"Is today the way it used to be?" Luca asked softly.

"Not exactly," she said. "Except for that one year, we always had power."

Not exactly. Because of the kiss part. Not exactly, because of the awareness part. Not exactly, because of the part where Imogen felt as if she might catch on fire every time her hand brushed his.

Though usually people who were afraid of being burned didn't keep inviting it over and over again.

"I understand why you would want to be here," Luca said quietly. "It's magic here."

"What an extraordinary thing to say, given that you are the one who comes from a fairy-tale setting. Tell me about your brother, the one who was supposed to come here. Are you close?"

He contemplated that. "We're close in age. Antonio is only a year younger than I am. In our early years, we were tremendous friends, but as we got older, the expectations on me were different than they were on him. I'd say that the grooming to assume the mantle of leadership began in my early teens and intensified as I got older.

"So, Antonio had way more freedom than I did, and he was quite the rascal at times. I think I envied him his freedom, and he envied me what he saw as our father's favor. Both of us worked hard for the King's approval, and I think Antonio would be surprised to know I feel as if, in Vincenzo's eyes, I never quite measured up, either. I felt close to my father only when I was successful, and of course that drove me to excel at everything I ever did, from sports to lessons.

"We were competitive with each other, as brothers tend to be, but he was also one of the few people I could be myself with, with no worry about keeping up my image. I confided in him, I think, as in no one else, and so it was quite a blow when he announced his decision to join the army.

"I hoped it would be a temporary stop on his career path, but he seems to have found a place where he belongs. He's part of an elite squadron that is posted all over the world. I miss him dreadfully and envy him the camaraderie he enjoys, and the adventures he embraces."

He stopped, frowning.

"But what?"

"He's a brave man, and courageous, but I feel something might have happened to him on his last mission. He was changed by it in some way. And then my father's death followed quickly on the heels of that. But naturally, he's a soldier, so he doesn't talk about *feelings*, or at least not to me."

"It sounds as though you love him very much."

Luca smiled. "That's true, even though I don't think I have ever said those words to him."

"You should."

"Maybe I will."

"What would you be, if you weren't a prince?"

He smiled, a bit sadly. "I've always loved travel and exploring other cultures, but I feel, because of my title, I don't always get to see what's real about a place or about people. The way I have here. It's been a gift."

A companionable silence existed between them as they contemplated their families and the coming of Christmas and unexpected gifts.

And then Luca's eyes drifted to her lips. Her eyes drifted to his. He touched her hand. His fingers stroked the top of it in an unconsciously sensual way.

Magic. If it was really a fairy tale, wasn't this the part where the Prince showed up and saved the day? Rescued the damsel from the dreariness and challenges of her life? With a kiss?

Maybe in this fairy tale, she was also rescuing him. From a life that seemed as if it bore almost unbearable loneliness.

Imogen leaned toward him. Luca leaned toward her.

But instead of kissing her, he cupped the side of her cheek with his hand.

"It's so complicated," he said, his tone gruff with regret.

"Of course it is," she said brightly, slipped away from his hand and went to turn the little chickens in the fire.

Despite the tension, she forced herself to relax, but from then on, Imogen avoided touching his shoulder and hands. They finished hanging ornaments, each one with a story that she shared with him. The little guitar had been a gift from a guest, a classical guitarist. The glass one with the scene painted inside it had been handed down to her family from her grandmother. The ugly handprint, so heavy it made the tree branch droop under its weight, had been made by her in kindergarten.

He studied that one for a long time, a smile on his face, before he hung it by a threadbare ribbon on a sturdy branch of the tree.

"More precious than Buschetta," he told her.

And she had to duck her head from the utter sincerity in his voice, and in his eyes as they rested on her. Only a few days ago, that ornament in particular would have filled her with sadness that she was not going to experience her own children making such things. Now, on the strength of his conviction, she was nursing hope. It made tears smart behind her eyes.

Late in the afternoon, the snow finally stopped. They ventured out into a world so bright and sparkling it almost hurt the eyes. The strength of the sun was already melting the snowmen. It made her feel sad, because the end of the snowstorm, and the melting of their little snow family felt as if it was foreshadowing that their time together, in this magical kingdom of their own making, was coming to a close.

Imogen, despite feeling the sadness of it, knew there was no way a helicopter could land in all that snow, and it would probably be at least one more day before the road to the Lodge opened, possibly two.

Despite her resolve to enjoy the time she had left, to not look to the inevitable goodbye the future held, the mood had already shifted by the time they pulled the little tinfoil-wrapped hens from the fire, and gobbled down their "turkey."

"Possibly the best Christmas dinner I've ever had," Luca declared.

"Don't be silly."

"I'm not. The best Christmas dinner and the best Christmas." His tone was pensive. He, too, was getting ready for the goodbye.

"It's not quite over yet," she said, and got up and took the stuffed sock down from the mantel.

She watched with pleasure as he opened it. He happily shared the chocolate and nuts with her and then carefully opened her package.

One by one he took out the snow family she had made out of Ping-Pong balls and cotton wool.

"They're beautiful," he breathed.

"I know they're clumsy and handmade, but I wanted you to have the memory."

"I will cherish them," he said with sincerity—a prince cherishing her little homemade gift, "but I didn't need them to have the memory. Imogen, I will never forget this time."

He looked at her handmade snow family again and then looked at her.

"I'm sorry. I never thought of a gift for you."

But really? The gift had been these few days. Still…

"There is a gift you can give me," she said slowly.

"Anything."

"When you arrived here, I saw something in you that was troubled. I want you to trust me with it. I want to know why you are here. Are you running away from something?"

She had shared everything with him, her every heartache. And that was the only gift she wanted from him in return. The same level of trust she had placed in him when she had shared her confidences.

Luca could have kicked himself for that *anything*. Of course this woman would require more of him than some bauble that cost the earth financially, but cost nothing emotionally.

He looked at the gift she had given him—that painstakingly crafted snow family—and felt some resistance in him melt away, just like that real snow family outside was melting away.

"I was supposed to be married," he confessed. "Two days ago."

Her mouth fell open. "You ran away?"

He snorted. "No, she did."

How flattering was it that the look on Imogen's face seemed to say, *Impossible, no one would run away from you*?

But then Imogen had coaxed a different side from him, a side that Meribel had never seen, that no one had ever seen. Maybe he hadn't even been aware he had it himself.

"The whole kingdom was preparing for a huge celebration. I wouldn't be surprised if the Buschetta ornament this year will commemorate a royal wedding."

"But what happened to your wedding?"

"I wish I knew. My fiancée, Princess Meribel of Aguilarez, came to me the night before the wedding. She told me she loved another and carried his baby. She confessed she had actually considered marrying me, anyway, passing the baby off as mine."

"But that's awful!"

"And yet she's not an awful person," Luca said. "Like me, she has been raised with the idea that duty came first. She is a princess from the neighboring kingdom. Our fathers signed marriage contracts for us when we were very young. It was to cement a relationship that has not been without its frictions. It was to secure the future of both kingdoms, to strengthen the alliances between them and to give the people peace of mind."

"That is no reason to get married!" Imogen sputtered.

"In my world it is. And in the one Meribel was raised in, it is. But in the end, her heart was stronger than her sense of duty."

"Thank goodness," Imogen muttered.

"Perhaps," he said wearily.

"And so you came here just to escape?"

"I announced the wedding had been called off because of irreconcilable differences, and then decided to take my brother's place on this mission."

"You protected her," Imogen breathed. "At great cost to yourself."

"A prince among men," he said with dry sarcasm.

"You are," she said stubbornly. "She must mean a great deal to you for you to take the brunt of the disappointment of two nations for something that was no fault of your own."

But wasn't it, at least in part, his fault? For not reading anything correctly? For not paying attention? For not noticing that Meribel was deeply dissatisfied with their engagement? Or maybe for not caring?

But for some reason, instead of admitting all that, he wanted to bask in Imogen's admiration.

For just a little while longer. His intuition had been humming since the sun came out. It was nearly over.

If he was honest about it, he felt more unsettled, more despairing, about his time with Imogen ending than he had about the end of his engagement with Meribel.

There, his concerns were largely pragmatic. What kind of chaos could result for the two kingdoms? His pride was wounded, not his heart.

Right now, for the first time in his life, his heart was ruling everything, not his head.

Imogen frowned suddenly. "What mission?" she asked.

"Sorry?"

"You said you were taking your brother's place on a mission. What mission? I can't imagine any kind of royal business that would bring you to Crystal Lake, Canada."

Before he could answer they heard the deep growl of a motor, still in the distance, but the high-pitched, incessant whining growing closer. It was a shocking sound against the deep and complete silence they had experienced for their entire time together.

"Snow machine," Imogen said. "Probably one of the neighbors, or someone from town coming to check on us."

But he suspected it was not. It would be Cristiano, who would have been relentless in his efforts to get back here.

"Gabi probably sent them."

Just like that, he thought, *it is over.* And wasn't that the thing he should have been remembering about an enchantment?

Just like a fairy tale, it came to an end.

But not always a happy one.

And yet, still, his heart ruled above his head. He turned to her.

"Kiss me," he whispered. And to himself he added, *one last time.*

CHAPTER ELEVEN

IMOGEN TOLD HERSELF there was no refusing a royal command, but the truth was, ever since they had kissed this afternoon, every other thing had been overlaid with the awareness of Luca, and of his lips, and of the way tasting them had made her feel.

That kiss had increased her awareness of *him* throughout the day until it was almost painful to be with him. She was intensely aware of the way he moved so gracefully, and of his easy strength, of the way he tossed back his head when he laughed and tilted it toward her when he listened to her. She was intensely aware of the rooster tail that insisted on springing up on the back of his head, inviting her fingers to press it down, and of the scent of him that made her want to bury her nose against his chest, more delicious than the scent of the Christmas tree that filled the room.

But it wasn't just his kiss that had increased her awareness, it was the fact that he had shared his confidences with her. Luca had trusted her.

It had made her see that, despite appearances that he was the man who had everything, he was deeply vulnerable and had led a life of almost unfathomable loneliness. It made her aware that there was a depth in those deep brown eyes, a compassion born of his own unspoken—maybe his totally unacknowledged—suffering.

So when he asked her to kiss him, she forgot his whispered, *it's so complicated.*

She forgot everything: who she had been before this moment and who she would be again after, who he had been before this moment and who he would be again after. She forgot her heartaches and her sorrows.

They melted away, until all that was left was this moment.

Luca leaning in to her, cupping the back of her head with his hand, drawing her to him, closer and closer. She closed her eyes and they connected. His lips were soft but firm; they tasted, incredibly, of wild strawberries, even though that had not ever been on their menu.

They tasted of promises: of winter days chasing through the snow and spring afternoons lying down in meadows of wildflowers. They gave a promise of finding sunlight on gray days and warmth against the cold. They gave a promise of a future full of unexpected adventures, and that included the best adventure of all, which was coming to know another person, deeply and truly.

No wonder when Luca claimed her lips, Imogen forgot his *it's so complicated*, because nothing had ever felt less complicated. In fact, she was not sure she had ever felt anything that had been more simple, more primal, more preordained, more meant to be.

The meeting of their lips, intensifying, breathed life back into her, as though for so long she had been going through the motions, sleepwalking. She tingled after being numb. She became supple after being wooden. Black and white became full glorious color. She was sharp instead of wrapped in cotton. The world was in focus, instead of being fuzzy.

Something softened in her, and Luca sensed instantly she had invited the kiss to deepen yet again between them. He plundered her mouth, and when she was gasping with need and with delight, he shifted his attention to her neck, trailed kisses down it, nuzzled her ears, dropped his head to her neck, explored her ears with his lips, anointed her forehead and her nose with his mouth. With almost frantic need, she put her hands on both sides of his head and guided his mouth back to hers. He moaned and drew her yet closer, his hands tangling in her hair. There was a beautiful savagery between them now, a hunger, a fire.

The background of all of this had been the whine of snowmobile engines, drawing ever closer. It was almost shocking when the engines stopped abruptly, plunging them into silence.

The fury, the urgency, the desperation of the kiss between them intensified. Somewhere in her was the wild thought that this kiss had the power to stop time, that if they focused on nothing else, the moment would never end.

"Your Royal Highness? Miss Albright?"

Neither of them had heard the front door open, but now they sprang apart as they heard footfalls, coming fast down the hall.

They stood, breathing hard, staring at each other. She had a sense of trying to memorize every single thing about this moment: the rapid rise of his chest, the look on his face, the faintly bruised look around his mouth.

Luca put out his hand to her, trying to bridge the gap between them. If she took it, Imogen felt he would run out the back door, escape back to the world that was just them. She reached for it.

"Sir?" The words echoed in the hallway outside the

door. There would be no world of just them. No, his world called for him to come back. The gap between them could not be bridged, because it was time.

And for them, time had just run out.

Luca dropped his hand before her outreached fingers connected with his touch. She stared at his hand, where it had fallen to his side, and then pulled her own away and used it to tuck a strand of hair behind her ear.

Cristiano burst into the room. His relief at seeing Luca was evident, but then his eyes swept the room, and Imogen felt something fragile and private was laid bare to him.

Cristiano took in the leaning Christmas tree, the decorations, the sock on the coffee table, the little snowmen figures she had made, the way Luca and Imogen were dressed, as if they were in their pajamas.

He looked confused. "Are you alone here? Just the two of you?"

Luca nodded, curtly, his eyes never leaving her face. Begging her? Promising her?

"It's just...it looks as if there was a family here. The snowmen out front..." Cristiano's voice drifted away. His eyes went from Luca to her and back again. She felt what had just transpired between them was an open book, puffy lips, mussed hair, heaving chests.

A smooth mask fell over his face. "You're all right, then, sir?"

Luca nodded curtly.

"Another snow machine is coming right behind me so that we can take both you and Miss Albright down to the village. There's power there—I've booked rooms for our meeting. We have to make haste, sir. You are urgently needed in Casavalle. I was able to contact Miss Ross and we can meet her—"

Imogen felt as if she was swimming up from the bottom of a pool. Cristiano's words registered with her as if she was hearing them from under water.

"Wait a minute," Imogen said. "You've contacted who?"

Cristiano went silent.

Imogen turned her attention to Luca. "Who are you meeting with?"

"Gabriella Ross," Luca said quietly.

"*My* Gabriella Ross?" Imogen said, hearing something dangerous in her tone.

"I'm sorry, I don't know what you mean," Luca said uneasily.

"She's my best friend."

Luca strode over to her and gazed down at her, his look stripping, all those promises gone from his eyes as if they had never been.

And really, had they ever been?

"Has she told you about her claim?" he asked, his voice a rasp.

"What claim?" Imogen said, refusing to be intimidated by him, even though he had become a stern stranger before her very eyes.

He searched her face, then turned back to Cristiano, dismissing her. Dismissing every single second they had spent together. He wasn't trudging sadly toward his world, instead of the one they had shared; he was leaping toward it.

"You have news from Casavalle?" Luca asked Cristiano.

Cristiano shot her a look. Was she supposed to bow out so they could have this conversation in private? She wasn't feeling accommodating!

"You can speak in front of her. I trust her completely."

Imogen steeled herself against the compliment. Did he really? Then why was it he had never once mentioned what he was really in Crystal Lake for?

"Unfortunately, there's been a leak about Princess Meribel's pregnancy," Cristiano said, his tone low and uncomfortable. "I'm afraid the mood of the people is not forgiving."

"This is grave news, indeed," Luca said, his brow furrowed with worry.

Imogen thought, again, just as she had when he had first told her about Meribel, that he must care about her very much. Quite frankly, after what he had told her about the Princess's plan to pass off a baby that was not his, Imogen was not at all sure Meribel deserved forgiveness.

"Tensions are quite high," Cristiano said. "Princess Meribel has gone into hiding."

The way he said this made it very clear Luca would be looked to for leadership in this difficult situation.

Imogen watched Luca change as he donned the mantle of his responsibility. Even though he was still dressed in long johns, his authority became very apparent. He went from being an ordinary man to the leader of a people before her very eyes. That remoteness was in him, the unmistakable sense of absolute command.

"Please tell me what Gabriella has to do with any of this?" Imogen demanded.

Luca looked at her coolly, as if he had never kissed her at all, as if the barriers their different worlds erected between them had never been melted away by the heat of their passion.

"I think that would be up to her to tell you," he said.

She felt rebuffed. She felt as if the man she had just kissed with her whole heart and soul, with all the passion she was capable of—the man she had played in the snow with and given the gift of Christmas to, the man who had trusted her with his deepest self—had become an untouchable, unknowable stranger before her very eyes.

She felt as if she wanted to weep.

But she heard the second snowmobile pulling into the yard.

"Get ready," Luca said to her. "We will leave immediately."

"I'm staying here," she said proudly.

"No, you're not."

"It's my job."

"I'll appoint someone to keep things going until the power is restored."

"No, you won't."

Cristiano was staring at her with his mouth open. Obviously, he had never heard anyone argue with the Prince before.

"You're coming with us," Luca said tersely. "I'm not leaving you here to deal with this by yourself."

"The power will be restored shortly."

"And then you can return here."

She straightened her shoulders and lifted her chin. "I am not your serf, Your Highness. You have absolutely no authority over me. I will do whatever I damn well please. I will not spend one more second with a man who deceived me."

Poor Cristiano actually moaned his distress at her tone.

"I never deceived you."

"I mentioned my friend was Gabi. You never said a word about my friend being your *mission,* your reason for being here. You never confided in me *why* you were here at all!"

"I didn't make the association between *Gabi* and Gabriella. We would never use a diminutive in place of the name of someone who is—" he stopped himself, seemed to rethink what he was going to say. "Nicknames are not popular in Casavalle."

"But I just asked you, point blank, what was going on, and you still won't tell me."

But the truth was she wasn't really mad about Gabi, and that wasn't where she felt deceived.

She felt deceived because Prince Luca had just kissed her with what seemed to be his whole heart and soul, and yet he was going to rush back to Casavalle to protect the woman who had betrayed him. You wouldn't do that unless you were nursing some pretty strong feelings.

And maybe even worse, she felt as if she had deceived herself by allowing herself to entertain the notion, no matter how briefly, that she, a woman damaged by both heartbreak and her own infertility, could have a fairytale ending with a prince.

"Gather up your things and go," Imogen said peevishly. "A kingdom awaits you."

"You're coming."

"I'm not."

"You're being particularly obstinate. You'd think you could show a little appreciation for your rescue from this dire situation."

Rescued by a prince. Every girl's dream. Or maybe just every stupidly naive girl's dream!

Imogen was insulted by his use of the term *dire*. In her mind, there had been nothing dire about being snowed in with him. Not. One. Thing.

"Well, I don't need rescuing. And this is not medieval times, where you can throw me over your shoulder and rescue me against my will."

His eyes smoldered with something that suggested he would like nothing better than to do just that.

"You said to remind you not to displease me," he told her.

Already the loveliness of the afternoon of sitting together playing twenty questions was fading.

"Go ahead," she snapped. "Send me a white elephant." Then she turned and left the room before he decided to act on it. What if—under his masterly need to control the situation—she melted instead of remaining defiant?

A few minutes later, she heard both snowmobiles start up and she watched from a chilly upper bedroom as they pulled away, spraying snow behind them.

Prince Luca's entrance had been James Bond worthy, and so was his exit.

She went back to the room they had shared. She had predicted power would be restored, but she was shocked when it picked that moment to flicker on. The overhead light seemed harsh and stripped the room completely of its charm.

Everything looked cheap and tawdry, like a set for a low-budget TV production. The tree was leaning drunkenly against the strings that kept it from falling over. The candles were all burned down and sputtering in deep wax pools. The Christmas decorations made by her sisters seemed old and hokey, and she wanted to smash that little plaster cast handprint that he had declared was more precious than his Buschetta ornaments. The room, and everything in it, seemed to mock her.

Angrily, she took down ornaments off the tree, ripped down garlands, blew out what remained of the candles. Christmas in October. It wasn't magical at all. It was completely ridiculous.

The last thing Imogen did was detach the tree from

the wall. She was so mad that, even though it had taken two of them, struggling mightily, to get the tree into the Lodge, she was able to drag it out and throw it off the stairs with perfect ease.

It was only when she got back inside to the now-naked room, that she realized something.

When Luca had gathered his things with him, even though he had left with haste and urgency, he had taken the little snow family with him.

"I wish he hadn't," she said out loud. "I would have burned them."

But somehow she knew, even though she was hurt, and even though she was angry, that was not true.

CHAPTER TWELVE

LUCA TIGHTENED HIS tie and shrugged on the suit jacket. He adjusted the diamond cuff links and matching tiepin and finally slipped on highly polished custom-made shoes.

He looked at himself in the mirror of the suite Cristiano had procured in a Crystal Lake hotel. The main street hostelry did not have the atmosphere of the Crystal Lake Lodge—not that Luca wanted to make comparisons, or look back at all. He needed to steel himself against what he felt when he thought of Imogen.

Angry, when he thought of her defying him by refusing to be rescued.

Hurt, when he thought of her accusing him of deception.

And something, beyond the anger and hurt, that was the most dangerous thing of all.

The reflection that gazed back at him was a man completely transformed from who he had been two hours ago. From his freshly shaved face to his crisply groomed hair, to the faintly aloof expression on his face, Luca looked every inch a prince.

But he knew himself to be a different man than he had been just a few days ago.

He ordered himself to stop looking back; he quashed the sense of longing. He had urgent responsibilities to tend to, and he had been trained since childhood to put the needs of his kingdom above the longings of his own heart.

Possibly to the point he did not even know what his heart was telling him!

"Thank goodness," he muttered to himself. He looked at his watch. In three minutes, his fate—the one he had moved toward his whole life—would be decided.

Naturally, he hoped it was some kind of trick—a masterful deception that had fooled even his mother, Queen Maria.

Luca recalled well her phone call saying she needed to see him. With the whole kingdom in a frenzied state of overdrive with both a royal wedding and Christmas on the horizon, he had been puzzled by the urgency in his mother's voice during that call, and the distress on her face when he had entered her suite.

Without preamble, she had asked him if he knew who Sophia Ross had been.

At first the name had meant nothing. But then he remembered. "Wasn't that the name of my father's first wife?"

Queen Maria nodded and passed him a letter.

He scanned it quickly, and then, shocked, read it again. It was from a woman, Gabriella Ross, in some tiny hamlet in the middle of the Canadian wilderness, who claimed to have found a letter in the belongings of her deceased mother, Sophia Ross. The contents of the letter had led her to believe King Vincenzo—Luca's father—might be her father.

"How did this get through security to you?" he asked, sorry that the letter had not found its way directly to him.

"It was marked personal and confidential to my attention."

Luca prevented himself from breathing an irritated sigh. Marking an envelope personal and confidential should be a way to gain it more attention in the screening process, not less. He was going to have to speak to Miles Montague, the palace secretary, about that.

"I don't believe it," he said fiercely.

"I didn't at first either. But the tone of it is so innocent. As if she has no idea the repercussions of such a claim."

"These con artists are damnably clever. Anyone who did the slightest bit of research could pose this possibility."

"But the scenario seems quite believable."

"I'm sure no effort would be spared in setting the scene when the stakes are so high. This plot could have been years in the making."

"I called her."

"You what?" Luca allowed himself a moment's more irritation at Montague. His mother should have been protected from this.

"I thought I would be able to tell something from speaking to her."

"And could you?" he had asked, his breathing constricted in his chest.

His mother had lifted a shoulder and looked at him with distressed eyes. "She had no idea the firstborn legitimate child of the King would legally be the ruler of Casavalle."

"She *claimed* she had no idea."

"Yes, that's what she claimed. She was extraordinarily soft-spoken. She owns a bookstore."

"She *says* she owns a bookstore."

"We'll know soon enough. I'm going to ask Antonio to leave immediately following your wedding to meet with her."

"I'll go myself."

"You have other things to attend to. Plus, Antonio has less at stake. You might appear faintly hostile to her."

Luca accepted his mother's judgment, but he wasn't happy about it.

"For now," his mother said, "it might be best if just the three of us know about this."

"Hopefully forever," Luca said firmly.

"In this day and age, no matter how clever the con, my dearest son, there is no way to conceal the facts. Antonio will collect a DNA sample. We'll have it analyzed by our own specialists. It could come to nothing. Of course it could! But I wanted you to know. I didn't want you blindsided by this on your honeymoon."

And then, because the wedding had been canceled and there would be no honeymoon, Luca had decided to come himself. He didn't care if he came across as hostile.

Except, now he did.

Now that he knew this woman, Gabriella Ross, was a friend—a very close friend—of Imogen's, he knew chances of her deliberately setting up such a complex charade were remote. Imogen simply would not have friends like that. And for Gabriella to have grown up here and have a business here was far too complicated a setup, even for the most robust of cons.

But there could still be an error.

Sophia could well have been pregnant by another man's child when she fled her new husband and the kingdom. It was a possibility Luca might not have given so much credence to a few days ago, before Meribel's confession, as he did now.

Cristiano was waiting outside the suite. He fell in, one step behind Luca's shoulder. Their eyes met, Cristiano's full of concern, just before Cristiano stepped in front of him and opened the dining room door.

Luca's first thought was surprise.

Gabriella Ross had come alone. She was sitting at a table by the window, looking out it, her hands curled tensely around a teacup.

While he looked very princely, and he knew it, for someone who was making a try for the throne, she looked extremely humble in an oversize sweater and blue jeans. Who met a prince in blue jeans?

Besides Imogen Albright—but then he had taken her by surprise by arriving early. And this was an arranged meeting.

The most remarkable thing about Miss Ross seemed to be dark chestnut hair, falling in a wave nearly to the small of her back.

And then, hearing the door open, she turned her attention from the window and looked at him.

Slowly, she stood up.

As soon as she stood, the illusion that there was anything humble about her faded. She stood, and it was in the air around her: a certain inherent dignity, a bone-deep grace, a queen-like composure that he knew she had been born with.

In that instant, Luca *knew*.

It was not just his eyes telling him the truth—she did look amazingly like a very beautiful version of his father—it was his heart.

It was that intuition that had kicked in when he had assured Imogen about her future and her future children.

He was in the presence of the next monarch of Casavalle.

What surprised him more than anything as he moved

forward to meet his sister—he did not need the proof of a DNA test—was that he did not feel a sense of loss.

The hostility he had harbored since hearing about the letter faded as her calm and somehow strangely familiar eyes rested on him. He felt, instead, as if he was meeting the future of his kingdom.

And it felt right.

He strode across the room to her. Though she was not petite by any means, he was still much taller than her, and she looked up at him. This close, he could see the nervousness in her.

He did what neither of them had expected.

He got down on one knee and bowed his head to her and covered his heart with his hand. "Your Royal Highness, Princess Gabriella," he said, his voice low with emotion.

"Get up," she said in a strangled voice.

He got up. He took both her hands in his and scanned her face. He kissed both her cheeks.

"My sister," he said, standing back from her.

Her eyes welled up, and he held back the chair for her.

She sank into it, shocked. "I—I—I thought there was to be a DNA test."

"Of course there will be. A formality. I know who you are."

She smiled tentatively. "I do, too. I feel something when I look at you. I feel as if I should be intimidated, but I'm not. I feel the oddest bond, as if I've known you forever. As a child, I wanted this so badly. A family. Of course, I could have never imagined it was going to be a royal family."

"You had no idea?"

She shook her head, her gorgeous hair waving around her lovely features.

"My mom died when I was three. My aunt and uncle raised me. I think they knew, but were sworn to secrecy. Then, I was looking for something else in the attic, and I found a box of my mother's things. Mostly it was baby pictures of me, but there were two letters in it. One was addressed to me, and the other was addressed to your father, to King Vincenzo. I had never even heard of Casavalle. Obviously, she never sent that letter, though it seemed apparent she loved your father very much."

"I wonder why she would love him and not send it?" Luca mused, thinking out loud.

A flicker of a veil dropped over Gabriella's eyes. He had a feeling she knew exactly why the letter had not been sent, but he respected the fact that she might not be willing to tell him, or at least not yet.

"I do hope, someday," he said softly, "I will get to know why a love with such optimistic beginnings had to end with two broken hearts. He never spoke of the failure of his first marriage—at least not to me—for he was not a man accustomed to failure. But there was some sorrow in him that I knew, even as a child, had something to do with the loss of her from his life."

"But didn't he and your mother have a wonderful relationship?"

"It was a good relationship," Luca said carefully, "but it's as if, after your mother, he said goodbye to love, and every decision from there on in was made out of a pragmatic sense of what would be best for our kingdom, including his marriage to my mother."

They both contemplated love gone so terribly wrong for a moment, and then Luca felt a need to correct any misperception he might have given.

"Despite it not being a love match, my mother was perfect for him—strong, pragmatic, loyal."

"I'm glad. Speaking of your mother, Queen Maria mentioned something to me—that as the King's eldest child, I would be next in line for the throne. Let me assure you, there is no need to be threatened by me! I don't want the job!"

"And yet here we are today, looking at the simple truth that despite all that has happened, all the secrets and all the obstacles, here I sit with you. Perhaps you cannot outrun your fate, Gabriella."

She gulped. "Surely I can refuse the obligation."

He tilted his head at her. She was nervous. And she was taken aback. And yet he could see the composure in her, the wisdom.

"Can you?" he challenged her softly. "Do you really think you can refuse what you were born to do?"

"I run a bookstore!"

"I can see it in you, though. I can see it in the way you carry yourself. I can see my father in your eyes. You don't have to decide today. But come. Come to Casavalle. Get to know your family and your kingdom. Give it a chance. If you decide to step into the shoes of the ruler, I will pledge my loyalty to you to my dying breath. I will stand behind you. I will share with you everything I have come to know."

"I just want you to be my brother."

He smiled. "I think that's what I just said. Will you come?"

She was silent, but when she looked at him, he saw the resolve in her eyes.

"Yes."

"Can you be ready to leave quickly? As soon as tomorrow?"

"I'm afraid if we don't leave quickly, I'll change my mind."

"I need one thing from you, before we leave. A favor."

"You need a favor from me? I can't even imagine what that might be."

"I need you to go and talk to Imogen Albright. You need to tell your best friend what is going on."

"Imogen? How do you know about Imogen's friendship with me?"

"I was snowed in with her at the Lodge."

Gabriella covered her mouth with her hand, and her eyes went wide. "When Cristiano contacted me to delay our first meeting because of the snowstorm, he never said you were there, at the Lodge. With Imogen."

"He would never let anyone know where I was, particularly as I was unprotected."

"You and Imogen…"

"Nothing happened!" he said, his tone way too defensive.

"And yet you know we are best friends."

"Well, of course, we conversed."

Gabriella studied him. Her eyebrow went up. She seemed to be hearing quite a lot that he was not saying.

Was that what it was like to have a sister? Of course, one other woman had had the same gift of seeing straight to his heart. And he did not have sisterly feelings toward her at all!

"The road to the Lodge will probably be closed for a few days," Gabriella told him. "I guess I could call her?"

How was Imogen going to feel when she found out her best friend was his sister?

"I can arrange for you to be taken there," he said. "I think the news that you and I are brother and sister will be shocking for her. Not the kind of news one might want to get when they are alone."

Again, Gabriella was watching him with interest. Her

lips twitched. She obviously was finding it quite endearing that he felt so protective of Imogen.

He gave her, his new sister, his most princely glare.

She laughed!

CHAPTER THIRTEEN

IMOGEN AND GABRIELLA sat across from each other at the kitchen table in the Lodge. Imogen had deliberately chosen not to light a fire and have tea in her office when Gabriella had shown up by complete surprise, riding in on the still-closed road by snowmobile.

Gabriella's cheeks were pink from her snowmobile ride, and her hair tumbled out from under her toque in a wild wave of gorgeous color.

Imogen was reeling from what Gabriella had just told her. Luca was Gabriella's brother!

It explained so much. No wonder he had seemed so familiar at times. No wonder she had thought she had recognized him when he had stepped off the helicopter.

And no wonder her friend had been so secretive. This was stunning news, indeed. Dear Gabi, Imogen's lifelong friend, was not just a princess, but the next in line to rule the kingdom of Casavalle!

"And then he tried to convince you to take from him what he has prepared his whole life to do?" Imogen asked softly.

Gabriella nodded. "I'm so sorry I never told you what was going on. It just seemed so unreal. I didn't want to appear the fool—thinking I was some sort of royalty—without confirming it, without knowing the truth."

"What are you going to do?"

"I'm going to go back with him. Just to see. Just to 'give it a chance,' as he suggested. It sounds as if we will be leaving fairly quickly."

"Yes," Imogen said, with faint bitterness. "He has urgent business to attend to." Quickly, she filled her friend in on the Prince's canceled wedding, his intended bride pregnant with another man's child.

"And so," she finished, "he's rushing back there to defend a woman who betrayed him."

Gabi was silent. When she spoke her voice was solemn and quiet. "It seems to me as if Princess Meribel had a very difficult choice to make. Betray him. Or betray herself."

Imogen looked closely at her friend. She had always known this about her. Gabi was unusually wise for someone so young, and almost scarily intuitive. In the new light of who she really was, it begged the question: Were some things ordained? Was it possible the qualities of leadership were genetic?

She sensed both the intuition and wisdom as Gabi met her gaze and held it.

"Tell me what happened between you and Luca," she suggested encouragingly. "There's something about you that's different. I can't quite put my finger on it."

"Oh!" Imogen could feel herself blushing. "Nothing happened!"

"Hmmm. That's what he said, too. Exact words, exact tone of voice."

"I was happy," Imogen admitted in a low voice. She *needed* to tell someone. "I was happy with him." She glanced up to see how Gabi would take that.

Gabi was smiling. "That's what's different! It's not as if you got something back that you lost when you broke up with Kevin. There's something brand-new in you. It sparkles."

"Well, I don't know why it would," Imogen said. "I'm angry right now, not happy."

"The anger is just a thin layer on top of something else."

"Quit being so wise! They will steal you from me to be their Queen, for sure."

They both laughed at that, and Imogen was glad for the laughter. She was not sure she was ready to admit it to Gabi, but she admitted it to herself.

The anger did mask something else. She was aware she would not trade her days with the Prince for any treasure available on earth. There was one thing Imogen was not going to share with Gabriella: in too short a time, she had given her heart to him.

Though it made no sense, though it seemed unreasonable and maybe even impossible, there was a little secret Imogen was nursing.

She had fallen in love with Prince Luca.

Nursing that forbidden love had seemed much easier before her talk with Gabrielle, because then Imogen had thought he was leaving and she would never see him again.

She had thought a quick, clean cut would be for the best.

But now her best friend's life was irrevocably tangled with the House of Valenti. Which meant chances were quite high that Imogen, through her relationship with Gabi, was going to see the Prince again.

And to be completely honest with herself, despite her initial belief that a clean cut would be for the best, now she could not determine if seeing him again would be a good thing or a bad thing.

Although her heart was singing its answer.

* * *

Imogen walked down the hospital corridor happily aware that she had been over-the-top in her selection of gifts for Rachel's new baby, who had been named Ben. She could barely see over the parcels she had loaded up in her arms.

But once she had started shopping, she couldn't stop herself. There were just too many adorable options. And Imogen knew that Rachel and her husband did not have much, so the pleasure of shopping for the new baby had been even more intense.

She had gorgeous sleepers with feet in them in a variety of woodsy themes, a tiny pair of hiking boots, a mobile with blue moose to hang over the crib and a fuzzy receiving blanket with the cutest little bear ears attached to it.

She entered the hospital room and froze. Cristiano was there, standing quietly beside the bed, talking to Rachel. And where Cristiano was… Sure enough, when she looked behind it, Luca was on the other side of the open door.

As if the Prince wasn't devastatingly attractive enough, he was holding the baby!

Imogen's eyes smarted from the beauty of the sight of that strong, capable man holding that vulnerable, tiny baby.

Luca was once again a prince. He was cleanly shaven, his hair was impeccably groomed; he wore a thigh-length belted black woolen jacket that most men could not have carried off. He looked exactly like what he was: a very wealthy, very powerful man, who was sure of himself in every situation.

And yet, despite the rather untouchable look of him, and despite the fact he was apparently urgently needed back in Casavalle, Prince Luca had come personally to the hospital to visit a woman he barely knew.

As she watched, the sleeping baby sighed and snuggled deeper into Luca's chest. The Prince stroked the baby's back and looked at him with such tenderness it felt as if Imogen's heart would break.

For the man she would never have. For the babies she would never have. For the ludicrousness of the dream that looking at the Prince caused in her.

Her mouth went dry as she contemplated that dream. Her. Him. Babies, just as he had promised. Adopted or through some miracle of science.

This was what hope did. It left you wide-open to pain.

Imogen would have backed out the door, but the top box on her mountain of parcels chose that moment to tilt crazily and fall to the floor with a crash. Luca looked up.

For one breathtaking moment, their gazes held. For one breathtaking moment, his eyes were entirely unguarded, soft with welcome.

She could have almost sworn the strength of what she felt for him shone in his eyes, too. But what did it matter?

He had given his heart to another, to Princess Meribel. And when that break healed—as she now knew hearts did, thanks to him—he would need a woman who could give him babies just like the one he held. Wasn't that what she had seen in his expression as he gazed so tenderly at that baby?

Longing?

Royal families, as far as Imogen knew, did not *adopt* babies.

"Imogen," Rachel said. "How lovely of you to come." Cristiano nodded at her, and looked at her a little too long, as if he was trying to puzzle something through. But then he bowed slightly and left the room.

Imogen saw Rachel was surrounded by wrapping paper and boxes. A gigantic teddy bear took up one whole corner of the hospital room. The generosity and obvious expense of the gifts brought by the Prince made her own purchases seem small and redundant.

But you wouldn't think so from Rachel's reaction. She opened each package and was thrilled. She particularly loved the little bear receiving blanket.

"Will you hold him?" Luca had come over to Imogen's side as Rachel unwrapped her parcels.

Imogen had been avoiding looking at him, and maybe avoiding the baby, too. It made her ache for a child of her own.

He carefully held out the baby to her, leaving her no choice but to take him.

She gazed into those small, perfect features and drank in the gorgeous smell of the newborn. She felt the sweet, warm weight of the baby melt into her. The feeling she had was not one of her own loss, but of a beautiful blessing the baby was giving the world with his mere presence.

"He's so beautiful," she breathed.

"Beautiful," Luca agreed, but when she looked up at him, he was not looking at the baby at all, but at her. She felt her heart stop at what she saw in his eyes. She looked back at the baby and cooed.

"Can you believe a prince has come with gifts for my baby?" Rachel giggled.

Imogen looked at Luca, again. Yes, she could believe it.

The baby's face scrunched up. His expression went from serene to furious in the blink of an eye. He stretched out, a tiny fist working free of the blanket and smacking Imogen in the cheek. His eyes opened—slate gray—and so did his mouth. He roared with indignation at finding himself in a stranger's arms.

"He's strong," Luca said with approval.

"And he's hungry," Rachel said, reaching for him. Imogen and Luca left to give her privacy to nurse her baby.

As they left the room, Cristiano gave her that searching look again and then went to the end of the hallway, where he could watch over his Prince but still give them privacy.

"I thought you would be gone already," Imogen stammered.

"I thought you would still be on the mountain."

"The road was finally plowed this morning."

"We're leaving very soon. I wanted to see the baby first, and make sure Rachel was recovering well."

"That was kind of you," Imogen said stiffly.

He cocked his head at her. "Have I done anything to make you think I am unkind?"

"No, of course not," she said hastily. But she felt as if her heart was on her sleeve. It wasn't his fault she had fallen for him when he cared for another.

"I've hurt you in some way," he said.

"No, not at all."

"But you seem angry."

"Do I?"

"Yes."

"Well, I'm not. I mean I do feel as if you tricked me, not letting me know you were here to see Gabi. My best friend is your sister! The news has kind of rocked my world."

"And mine," he said softly.

Of course, his.

"You must be in shock," she said. "Gabi told me that

she, not you, would be heir to a throne that is empty. She told me you want her to give it a chance. Why? She doesn't want the job. She's frightened and just wants to run the other way. Why not let her? Wouldn't that be so much easier?"

"The easy choice is not always the correct one," he told her. "Kingdoms are run by rules and protocol. Centuries-old traditions are the glue that holds them together in a world that changes very rapidly."

"But you've been groomed to be the King of Casavalle for your entire life."

"I will use what I have learned to help her."

She looked at him. She looked at him hard. "Remember when you told me that my fiancé, Kevin, marrying another would be a blessing for me?"

"Yes, I remember."

"This may be the same thing for you. When we had the snowball fight that day and built our snow family, you said to me you had never been as free as you were in those moments. If Gabriella takes the throne, your life will be more your own than it has ever been before."

"That may be true," he said.

"You are so like her, in so many ways. When you said that just now, your tone was exactly like Gabriella's. Your tone and the tilt of your head. If I'd known you were related to Gabi, it would have explained a lot."

He raised an eyebrow at her.

"I mean I felt as if I recognized you from the start. As if I knew you. Now I can see the family resemblance just tricked my subconscious mind. No wonder I felt as if I loved you. I recognized you were very like someone I did love. Barriers were removed that should have stayed in place. That *would* have stayed in place had you just told me the real reason you were at the Lodge in Crystal Lake."

"You felt as if you loved me?" he asked, shocked.

CHAPTER FOURTEEN

IMOGEN REALIZED INSTANTLY that she had said too much. Way too much.

"That came out wrong. I felt as if I cared about you." She was not sure that was an improvement!

"Past tense?"

She wished it was past tense, but she could not lie to him. "No, I suppose not," Imogen said, and then, eager to change the subject, rushed on. "You need to go talk to your Princess," she said.

"Gabriella?"

"Not that Princess!" It showed her what a serious turn her life had taken that she was trying to sort through princesses. "You need to talk to Meribel."

"About?"

"How you feel."

He regarded her thoughtfully. "You do something to me no one else has ever done."

Imogen could feel herself holding her breath.

"You boss me around."

Her disappointment was acute but she smiled with false brightness. She noticed he had managed to dodge the issue about how he felt about Princess Meribel.

"Nice to see you, Your Highness," she said, her tone

formal. "I wish you a safe trip back to your kingdom and a good life."

"Don't say that as though we will never see each other again."

He sounded faintly pleading. It could weaken her resolve. On the other hand, *the thing* she did to him that no one else ever did was not the same *thing* he did to her that no one else had ever done!

"Since you are now related to one of my favorite people in the whole world, it seems likely we will see each other again."

Did he look relieved?

She was entering into very dangerous waters.

Before he could read the turmoil in her face—before he could reach the embarrassing conclusion that she had indeed loved him—she leaned close to him.

"If you do anything—anything at all—to hurt *my* Gabriella you will have to deal with me. It won't be pretty and it won't be fun."

His lips twitched. Annoyance or amusement? Being threatened was probably as new to him as being bossed around.

He nodded, and she still could not read the glint in his eye. Was he humoring her? Or did he understand just how completely she meant business. She turned quickly on her heel and walked away from him.

Even though she wanted to, desperately, she forced herself not to look back.

Luca left Gabriella and Queen Maria together, and exited the room. His mother's grace was matched by his sister's and there was something about the two women together that made the future of Casavalle, despite the unexpected detours—or maybe even because of them—seem as secure as it ever had.

He passed through the front foyer of the palace. As Luca had told Imogen, Casavalle was getting ready for Christmas. The huge tree had been selected for the front foyer.

It soared upward, crowned at the very top with a lit angel. It was, as always, spectacular. Rather than filling him with a sense of the familiar, with homecoming, it made his heart ache for a lopsided tree, held up with strings and nailed to the wall.

Annoyed with himself for thinking so longingly of a much less spectacular tree, Luca shook off his sense of melancholy and headed for the palace secretary, Miles Montague's, office.

Miles looked both pleased and relieved to see him. A mountain of work needed the Prince's immediate attention.

"Prince Antonio has been doing a fine job in difficult circumstances," Miles told him. "But he's not you. We need you."

Ah, to be needed. But for how much longer? Luca could just imagine the adjustment everyone was going to have to make when it was no longer him that they turned to for every decision.

But for right now the work would be a balm—all the stacks of papers that needed to be reviewed, projects awaiting approval, engagements to attend, meetings to be held. It was the very thing he needed to give him back his sense of being grounded in the world.

The secretary looked down at the stack of papers. Off the top he pulled the pink slips that came with phone messages.

"Let's deal with this first. Have you ever heard of Tia Phillips?"

"No, I can't say I have."

"As I thought."

"Who is she?"

"She's been calling, insisting she's friends with Prince Antonio. She says he knew her brother. But my question is, of course, what does *knowing* mean? That he shook his hand once at a ball? That he sat next to him at a charity function? I rebuffed her as kindly as possible, but she doesn't seem to be taking no for an answer."

"Probably Canadian," Luca muttered.

"Sir?"

"Nothing, sorry."

"Sir, do you ever recall your brother mentioning anyone with the last name Phillips, male or female?"

Luca shook his head. "I'm fairly certain I know all Antonio's close friends by name. That one doesn't strike a chord. Have you asked her how Antonio knew her brother?"

"She's particularly unforthcoming in that department. She may have started crying when I asked her."

Luca raised an eyebrow. "Nut?"

"Possibly. Stalker, perhaps? The insistence of her calls made me wary of passing on the message to Prince Antonio, particularly since he has his plate full. We've fielded stalkers before. I'm afraid if I ever put her through to the object of her attentions, we'd have an even bigger problem."

"You didn't think to just ask Antonio?"

"I preferred to ask you. I didn't want to relegate the messages to the bin without running it past you first, sir."

So, there it was. *I preferred to ask you.*

The people of Casavalle, and the staff at the palace,

already saw Luca as King, as the one they could rely on to make decisions both large and small, the one they would turn to.

Of course, Miles not wanting to make the decision himself might also have been because Luca had expressed annoyance with him that Gabriella's letter had made it to his mother simply for being marked Personal and Confidential.

It was obviously making Miles extra vigilant about which messages got through to the royal family and which did not.

Despite having been hard on Miles over the letter to the Queen, Luca knew himself to be more approachable than his father had been. He had thought it would be his signature—what set him apart from his father—when he assumed leadership.

"Just toss them," Luca said of the raft of pink slips clutched in Miles' hand. "We have far bigger things to deal with than some woman who has seen Antonio's picture in a magazine, decided she is in love with him and made up some story to connect the two of them."

"My assessment, exactly," Miles said. He swept the papers into the bin beside his desk with a sigh of relief. "We do, indeed, have larger issues to deal with.

"Sir, since you released the statement calling off the wedding based on what you called irreconcilable differences, the people of Aguilarez seemed quite ready to renew old hostilities in defense of their Princess's honor. They rushed to the conclusion that she had been jilted. By you. On the eve of her wedding!"

"Wars have started for less," Luca said pensively.

"In a way it was a good thing that the truth was leaked, that the betrayal was hers, not yours. But now our people are furious. They feel the insult to you is an insult to

Casavalle and to them, personally. I am getting reports that talk around the kitchen tables and in the pubs is of nothing else. How you've been scorned, and it's a national disgrace that should be avenged.

"Naturally Aguilarez is reeling. I understand Princess Meribel is in hiding and the royal family will be having emergency talks. Her four siblings are en route to Aguilarez now."

"We need to be part of developing a strategy to defuse this situation before it gets out of hand."

"I was hoping you would have a suggestion, sir."

"Arrange a meeting with her family."

"Excellent."

"Both families are going to have to work together to minimize damage. Our relationship with Aguilarez has come so far. We can't risk it all on a matter of the heart."

"No," Miles said approvingly. "Matters of the heart have to be separated from functions of the state."

But when Luca looked back over the history of the two countries, it seemed as often as not, hearts would not be ignored.

Look at his own father, risking everything to follow love.

Now Meribel doing the same thing.

It gave him a headache. *Really?* Could people not put their personal feelings aside for the greater good?

But when he thought of that, he thought of Imogen, and it seemed his own resolve wavered. If he had a decision to make that involved her welfare or the welfare of his kingdom, how pragmatic could he be?

I felt as if I loved you.

For the first time, Luca became shockingly aware that a part of him was answering her.

And it said, *I felt as if I loved you, too.*

And the thing was, that thought of loving Imogen, loving the time they had had together, loving the freedom and the comfort of being with her, didn't make him feel bitter, as he had felt when Meribel had left him behind.

It made him feel better that he had had Imogen in his life even for a short while.

Stronger.

Wiser.

More able to do the right thing.

And suddenly, he knew exactly what the right thing to do was. He had to meet, not just with the royal family of Aguilarez, but with his former fiancée. Just as Imogen had suggested, he needed to talk to Meribel. And not just for the good of both their kingdoms.

He needed to do it for himself.

Piloted expertly by Cristiano, the royal helicopter had made the journey over the rugged mountains that separated the kingdoms of Casavalle and Aguilarez.

From the air, Luca looked down at the royal family's grounds. The palace of the House of Aguilarez was more formidable, and less decorative, than his own home. It was a fortress, its walls incorporating the strength of the mountain that stood directly behind it.

Prince Cesar Asturias was waiting to greet him as Cristiano held open the helicopter door after they landed on the ground. Despite Cesar's reputation as an unapologetic playboy, Luca had always liked him, probably the best of all Meribel's brothers.

"Your Royal Highness, welcome," he said formally, bowing slightly.

"My brother," Luca returned, and saw the immediate relief on Cesar's face.

"I was hoping we would be brothers," Cesar said. "I

don't know what the rest of the family will say today. A formal statement has been prepared and they may stick to it. But I want you to know how sorry I am."

Luca clapped Cesar on the shoulder. "As I am about to tell your family, there is nothing to be sorry for. I am hoping that we can find other ways to resolve some of the growing hostility between our kingdoms. We've been at peace for two hundred years."

"Two hundred and three," Cesar said. "But who's counting?"

Luca laughed. Cesar's quick dry wit was one of the things that Luca enjoyed about him so much.

He was escorted through the palace. He had been here many times, particularly since his engagement to Princess Meribel, but he still noted the differences between this palace and his own home. It wasn't just that there were no Christmas decorations here, yet, that made this palace more formidable, somehow. Even the artwork was darker and more warlike.

He and Cesar entered a conference room. The entire Asturias family had gathered, save for Meribel. But her mother, father and four brothers were all there, seated, their expressions grim.

Formal greetings were exchanged and then Luca was offered a seat. He looked around the table and felt some relief that his future did not hold Christmas dinners with this group of stern-looking warriors.

"Luca," said King Jorge solemnly. "I wish to apologize for the actions of my daughter. She has brought shame to our house."

"I want to suggest we all look at it differently," Luca said.

The men in the room watched him warily. You did not walk into another man's kingdom and disagree with him.

But this was part of Luca's legacy from Imogen: sometimes the heart had to speak, and never mind the pomp and circumstance that could cloak real feelings and keep issues from being resolved satisfactorily.

"This is what I propose."

And he told them the plan.

When he was finished, the brothers looked relieved, and Queen Adriana's eyes, weighted with worry, were sparkling with tears.

Only the King seemed doubtful. "My daughter has brought shame on our family, neglected her royal obligations and broken a promise. I'm not sure your proposal addresses the severity of her transgressions against you, her family and her kingdom."

"Again, Your Majesty, I respectfully disagree."

"What would you propose?" Queen Adriana asked her husband quietly. "I'm afraid the days when you could lock an errant daughter in a tower or ship her off to the convent are well over."

King Jorge mulled that over.

"All right, we will do it your way," the King conceded, and then, lest the concession be seen as weakness, he scowled and added, "In the spirit of Christmas, nothing else."

"Of course, sir," Luca said evenly. King Jorge reminded him of his own father: old-school rulers, being dragged kicking and screaming into a more tolerant modern age.

The formality of the meeting dissolved, and he found himself surrounded by Meribel's brothers, clapping him enthusiastically on the shoulder. Prince Cesar wrapped his arms around Luca and lifted him off his feet.

"We will always be brothers!" he declared.

"I need to see her before I put the plan in place. I need to see Meribel."

"Of course," Cesar said. "I will take you."

King Jorge glared at him. "You know where she is, then?"

"I'm going to hazard a guess," Cesar said, meeting his father's gaze levelly.

"The world is going to hell in a handbasket," Jorge muttered. "There is no respect for authority anymore." His wife patted his arm sympathetically.

CHAPTER FIFTEEN

PRINCESS MERIBEL SCRAMBLED to her feet when her brother Prince Cesar and Prince Luca came through the door of the hotel suite she was in.

"How did you get in here?"

Her brother wagged the key at her. "Have you ever seen two more recognizable mugs than these?" He pointed to himself then Luca. "The innkeeper practically begged us to take the key."

"How did you know where I was?" the Princess demanded.

"Do you really think I wouldn't know where you were?" Cesar said. "I tracked you down the day you moved in here and put protection around the neighborhood and undercover throughout the hotel."

"I can look after myself," she said, proudly. And then more softly, "Dana can look after me."

"Ah, the mystery man is named," her brother said. "Where is he?"

"You mean you don't know?" she said. "You seem to know everything else."

Luca could see this was going to quickly deteriorate into a squabble between the brother and sister, so he stepped in.

"It's good to see you, Meribel," he said.

She rounded on him. "I am terribly sorry I did what I did to you," she said, her voice trembling, "but I won't go with you."

"Yes, I've been reminded fairly recently this is not medieval times," Luca said, and could hear the wryness in his own voice.

"I don't think it's Luca you have to worry about," Cesar chimed in. "It's Father."

"I suppose Father thinks I should be locked in a tower for the rest of my days."

"He does indeed," Cesar said. He wandered over to a fruit basket and chose an apple and bit into it. "Fortunately for you, Luca has come up with another solution."

Luca had told Cesar all the details of his solution on the way here, and Cesar had approved heartily.

"We're not here to make you do anything against your will," Luca assured her. She looked relieved, but wary.

"A solution?" she asked, and faint hope overlaid her wariness.

Luca took her in, this woman he had known since childhood, and saw how truly beautiful she was. Meribel was tiny, and yet delectably curved. Her long, dark hair was piled on top of her head in an elegant twist. Her lovely brown eyes were expertly made-up.

Even in these circumstances, holed up in a hotel room, hiding from the world, she was dressed quite formally, in a skirt and matching jacket, "correct" royal attire for daytime. Rings—minus the engagement ring he had given her—sparkled from every finger, and a diamond pendant hung around her neck.

Like him, Princess Meribel could not easily let go of the notion that you were always on show, always judged—someone was always watching. That made him feel sorry for her.

Other than that feeling, he was aware he felt nothing but relief that he would not have to spend the rest of his days waking up to her. He realized that a marriage to Meribel would have been his "tower," his prison.

"Are you well?" he asked her, crossing the room to her and taking both her hands.

She looked up at him, and her defensive expression crumpled and she began to weep.

He pulled her closer and wrapped his arms around her.

"It's the pregnancy," she said. "I've never been so emotional."

"Just like me," he said, "you've shut down your emotions, almost until it was too late."

She pulled back from him, but did not let go of his hands as she scanned his face. "Is there something different about you?"

"Perhaps I combed my hair differently this morning," Luca said, tired of women suddenly reading him as though he were an open book.

"No," she said tentatively. "It's not that."

"Do you love him?" he asked. "This Dana that you mentioned?"

"It's *that*," she said with a small smile. "That's what is different. I can't even picture you asking me that question a month ago. And the answer is yes, I love him so much."

"And he, you?"

"Yes. Absolutely."

"I'm glad."

"There's that difference again! But how can you be glad? I've wrecked everything. I left you in a humiliating position. I'm so sorry," she sobbed. "I've done a terrible thing to you."

"Shh, now—all this emotion isn't good for the baby, even if it is what's causing all that emotion."

"I tried to make it right. When I could see people were going to blame you, I leaked the news of the pregnancy."

"That was very brave."

"Partly," she admitted. "Partly it was selfish. I didn't want my baby to be born in a web of deceit. I didn't want that baby, someday a teenager, or a young adult, finding old press clippings and thinking I was ashamed of her or him, or that I had tried to hide her or him from the world. People would have eventually found out. I didn't want to feel as if I was harboring a secret."

"That was brave, too," Luca told her.

"Oh, Luca, if I was truly brave, I would have told you all this a long time ago, and not waited until the eve of the wedding to spring it on you. I'm sorry."

"I'm sorry, too."

"You have nothing to be sorry for."

"But I do. I want to own my part of things."

"Your part?" she whispered.

"I've been insensitive. Had I paid any attention to you at all, I would have known something was wrong. If I had *known* you, I would have known immediately when your attention turned to someone else.

"Instead, I allowed all this to happen. I relegated you to roles—my fiancée and my future wife—and then really ceased to see you as a person, appreciate you for who you were and are. We met our formal obligations. We attended functions together. We held hands on cue. We satisfied the hunger of both our kingdoms for a romance, but when I think about the emptiness of it, I'm appalled with myself.

"I don't even know what your favorite movie is. I don't know what music you listen to when you are by yourself. I don't know if you'd prefer a dog, a cat or a parrot for a pet. I don't know how you feel about babies. I've never gone for a walk with you in the snow, or sat with you in front of a fire. For that, I am here to ask your forgiveness."

"You are asking my forgiveness?" Meribel stammered.

"I am."

She mulled that over. She took in his face. A smile began to break out on her mouth. "I forgive you, then."

"Thank you. I did not just come to ask your forgiveness."

"What else, then?"

"I came to thank you," he said quietly. "You've given me the most incredible gift."

She pulled away from him and looked up, her eyes filled with doubt and hope. He took her chin in his hand and scanned her eyes.

"You have shown me what it means to be brave," he told her softly. "You have shown me the lengths one should be willing to go to, to welcome love into their lives."

"Th-then you forgive me, as well?" Meribel asked, fresh tears sliding down her face.

"Not at all," he said. "For me to do that, there would have to be an assumption there is something to forgive."

She had to stand on tiptoe to kiss both his cheeks. "You will always be a prince to me, not just because you were born to the title, but because you have grown into the honor."

"Thank you."

"Whoever she is," she whispered, "she is a very lucky woman."

"I don't know what you mean," Luca said, and heard the stiffness in his voice.

She scanned his face, and she was not put off and she

was not fooled. Princess Meribel laughed, and it was a lovely sound. She said, "Yes, you do."

The frankness of her gaze captured him. The truth of her words wrapped around him.

Yes, he did.

And suddenly nothing in the world seemed as important as what he had experienced whilst snowed in at the Crystal Lake Lodge.

Nothing. Not his obligations, not his kingdom, not all the treasures in the palace vault. With that acknowledgment, something in the heart of Prince Luca flew free and unfettered, like a bird that had been caged, flying toward the sun.

CHAPTER SIXTEEN

IMOGEN FELT EXTRAORDINARILY CROSS. And tired. It had been one of those days! It had begun this morning when she had opened her computer screen to see every single booking had been canceled.

Then, she'd had a call from her boss, demanding a lunch meeting in the city, which was two hours away. The drive there had given her far too much time to think. Her concern should have been getting fired—what had happened to those bookings?

Instead she had grouchily contemplated abject loneliness. Even though they had spoken several times in the few days since Gabriella had departed for Casavalle, Imogen missed her friend acutely.

There was something in Gabriella's voice that she envied. Excitement.

Imogen considered that. Gabriella, who could be counted on to be quiet and calm in any situation, was brimming with excitement and enthusiasm that spilled over into her voice. And her emails. Imogen had never seen this side of her friend before.

Apparently Book Club could not hold a candle to a real-life adventure.

Her thoughts drifted to her own real-life adventure, a helicopter settling on the front lawn while storm clouds brewed over the peaks of the nearby mountains—the day her life had been made new again.

Of course, like a constant hum beneath the surface, she was so aware that she missed someone else, too. Someone she had no right to miss.

On the drive home from her meeting with her boss, her job totally intact, Imogen realized the strangest thing.

Surely she hadn't wanted to get fired?

The Crystal Lake Lodge had been her home her entire life. She had never really been anywhere else; she had never really done anything else.

But the excitement Imogen was hearing in Gabriella's voice was making her wonder if she had not played it too safe her entire life, not just sticking with what was secure and familiar, but trying to re-create the life she had grown up with.

It was as if she had had blinders on, had not been able to see that life held options beyond the Crystal Lake Lodge.

Of course, the Lodge no longer seemed the sanctuary it once had seemed. There seemed to be laughter-filled ghosts there. Out on the front lawn where they had chased each other; in her office where she had introduced Prince Luca to the simple joy of a toasted hot dog. She had refused to put a fire in the hearth since he had left.

If she had gotten fired, she thought, maybe it would have been a good thing. Just as moving on from Kevin was proving to be a good thing.

Those few days with the Prince had shown her there was something else, not as safe, and not as comfortable, and yet a life without it seemed as if it would be empty.

Maybe it would be a good thing, an exciting thing, if her life was made new again.

But would she ever find what she had found with Luca

again? Could any other person, or any other experience, ever fill her the way that one had? Would she ever again feel as if every single moment was shivering with life?

But obviously, there was no sense mooning over a prince—a man so far out of her reach he might as well have been on the moon.

But was there a chance that she could find what she had experienced with him with someone else?

Doubtful, a little voice inside her whispered. *That was one in a billion. He is one in a billion.*

Just a little while ago, she might have been nursing a heartbreak over Kevin, but her life had felt ordered and there had been safety in the predictability of it. And yet, somehow, she wouldn't trade those days with the Prince to go back to that. She felt oddly uncertain if that's what she wanted at all anymore. And that was what was making her feel cranky! That and a four-hour round trip for nothing! To hear about her boss's grandchildren and their trip to Denmark! Not a single mention of Imogen's job being in jeopardy even after she had confessed she thought she had botched the bookings for this week.

It was full dark by the time she turned into the Lodge driveway. Partway up, she met a catering van coming down. Despite her waving her hand to get him to stop so she could find out what business he'd had at the Lodge, the van roared by her. In a few minutes that vehicle was followed by another utility vehicle, which also did not stop when she waved. The driver waved cheerily back at her, but kept going.

She tried to think if she had booked repairs, but nothing came to mind. Still, it felt like just more evidence of how distracted she had become, her tidy little world unraveling out of her control.

More grumpy than ever, Imogen came over the ridge

and arrived at the final curve in the long driveway that led to the Lodge. She went around it and slammed on the brakes.

"What?" she said out loud. She actually blinked to see if the vision went away. She had heard of people pinching themselves to see if they were dreaming, and she considered doing that. If there were any wrong driveways to take, she would have thought she'd taken one, but there was only one road that led to the Lodge.

And she was on it.

But the Lodge had never looked like this.

The Crystal Lake Lodge was absolutely glowing. Every inch of it—rooflines and corners, windowsills and porches—was all outlined with white fairy lights.

Her heart hammering in her throat, not able to take her eyes off her glowing home, Imogen inched up the driveway.

There were no cars in the parking lot, but against a dark sky, she could see smoke chugging out the chimney. She turned off her car and stepped out of it. The smell of wood smoke was tangy in the air.

Though she usually went in the side door, she went around to the front. The porch and front entryway were festooned in garlands.

There was a wreath on the door, a word peeking out from under the fresh, fragrant boughs. *Believe.*

It was an invitation to believe in something—dreams, miracles, fairy tales—and if she hadn't before, she certainly did now. Trembling with shock, with excitement, with anticipation and with hope, Imogen opened the front door.

The entryway had been transformed. Pine garlands wove their way up the staircase, but Imogen took it all in with barely a pause. She raced down the hallway, paused outside her closed office door and then threw it open.

The room was lit by the fire that burned merrily in the hearth, and by candles that burned softly. A huge tree, completely decorated, winking with a thousand brightly colored lights filled one entire corner of the room. Christmas music filled the room.

But she didn't care about any of that. Her eyes adjusted to the dimness, and she saw him, standing there, in the shadows on one side of the hearth, looking across the room at her.

"Luca."

Her lips whispered his name, but her heart cried it.

"Imogen." He pushed out of the shadow, came and stood in the middle of the room. She had seen him dressed as a prince, and she had seen him in long johns. She liked this look: jeans and a sweater with a shirt under it. It made him look ordinary, even as her heart sang there was nothing ordinary about him.

"I—I—I don't understand. What are you doing here?"

She had been frozen in her place; now she moved toward him, helpless, steel to a magnet. She came and stood before him and gazed up into the now so familiar lines of his so handsome face.

"Let me take your jacket."

Helplessly, she let him assist her out of it. Thank goodness, she had dressed nicely and put on a lick of makeup for her lunch engagement with her boss. Still, if she had known she was going to see him again, she might have made more effort to look, well, sexy.

Having dispensed with her jacket, he took her hand and guided her to the couch.

"How on earth did you accomplish this?" she whispered. "The tree isn't even nailed to the wall."

"It took a small army," he admitted, "to get all the reservations canceled and people's vacations rescheduled elsewhere. And it took the cooperation of strangers, like your lovely boss, Mrs. Kennedy, to spirit you away from the place for a day."

"But why?" Imogen asked. "Why have you gone to so much trouble?"

"Gabriella told me she felt bad that she was immersed in Christmas excitement at the palace and that you had been left out."

Imogen should have felt uplifted by her friend's thoughtfulness, but somehow it was not the answer she was hoping for: that Gabriella had sent him.

She tried to hide her disappointment. She would talk about Gabriella, too!

"You know, when I first learned Gabriella's news, I didn't even think she would go to Casavalle. And then when she went, I didn't think she would stay. I felt I knew her well enough to say she would never leave here, Crystal Lake. I certainly never thought she would accept the crown. But when I speak to her lately, I don't know anymore. She sounds happy and excited."

"She has embraced Casavalle like it is a missing part of herself. Which it is."

"You think she's going to accept the crown."

He lifted a shoulder, as if he didn't care about that!

Imogen registered that, happy for her friend and for Gabriella's embracing the adventure life had offered her, and yet achingly aware of her own loss.

"I've always worried about her being lonely," Imogen admitted. "I can't help but think if she accepts the crown it will make it worse."

"She and my mother are already fast friends. She has Antonio and I now. We are her family."

But I'm her family, Imogen wanted to wail. Instead she said, "I was thinking more about a husband for her, and children. I always wanted that for her, but she didn't. She seemed terrified of it, as if she had inherited her mom's sadness and wariness about love. Still, I thought the right person would come along."

"And they will," Luca said.

"Do you think so? Once you are a member of a royal family, how do you ever find someone to love you for you?"

"How indeed?" he asked softly.

Imogen's eyes flew to Luca's face. She should have never let it slip that she had thought she loved him. Because now he seemed to know some truth about her that made her feel vulnerable and faintly pathetic.

Ordinary girl falls hopelessly for Prince.

"I took your advice," he said after a moment. "I went and talked to Princess Meribel."

"And?"

"I told her the truth."

"That you loved her and she had broken your heart?" She forced herself to look at his face.

"Loved Meribel?" He looked puzzled. "What would make you think that?"

"I just felt you must have such strong feelings for her to be so protective of her after she betrayed you. It seemed like love to me."

"It's true that I felt intensely protective of her. Especially since I could see my part in the whole debacle. But love? A kind of love, I suppose, like a brother might have for a younger sister."

"What do you mean, your part?"

"What kind of self-centered jerk doesn't even understand the woman he plans to marry is unhappy? I missed all the cues, and so I felt responsible, at least in part, when the people of Casavalle—and many in Aguilarez, as well—turned on Meribel when they found out her pregnancy was the reason our wedding was canceled.

"So, strong feelings of protection, yes. Love? No. I never loved her, Imogen. I told myself I would in time. I told myself that she would love me, in time. But now I see that was wrong, to think such a marriage could have ever worked, or that any good could come from what would have basically been a charade."

Prince Luca never loved Princess Meribel.

"When I went to see her," he continued, "I thanked her for carrying the most important message of all—to be brave enough to accept the invitation of love if it is presented to you."

She gazed at him, wide-eyed.

"You see, I had my whole life mapped out. My marriage—my entire future—were all decided for me. It's all come crashing down, and you'd think I'd be devastated, but instead I feel this strange elation. And I feel free. For the first time ever, I can make decisions about what I want. I can map out my own life."

Imogen felt almost faint from the way he was looking at her: as if she was the destination on the map of his life, as if she was something he wanted.

"Come," he said. "Let's go to the dining room."

He held out his hand; she took it and allowed herself to be escorted to the dining room. How far did she want to allow herself to be pulled into this enchantment? As wonderful as it had been for Gabriella to set this in place, it was making her ache for things she could not have.

But was that completely true?

She had been mistaken that he loved Meribel. He never had.

And what did it mean for him that he would no longer be King? Did it mean an ordinary girl might be on his radar?

Perhaps, she thought sadly, *but probably not one unable to ever bear his children.* But he already knew that. Why was he here? Surely it wasn't just at the request of Gabriella?

The dining room, like her office, had been transformed into a Christmas fantasy. White and red poinsettias were grouped on the side serving table. The main dining table, laid with a Christmas cloth and beautiful china dishes that she did not recognize, was decorated with lit candles and an ice centerpiece, of snowmen!

"The caterers I passed did this," she deduced.

"I wanted you to think I did it myself!" he teased as he held out a chair for her. She sat down at the table, and he sat at right angles from her and removed the silver tops from serving platters.

Two perfectly roasted Cornish game hens were underneath.

She nibbled on the one he placed on her plate, but her stomach was in knots.

"It's not as good as the one you cooked in the fire," he told her, tasting his own.

"It is so! It has some remarkable sauce on it. No burned places."

He laughed, and some of the knots dissolved in her stomach. Yes, he was the Prince of Casavalle, but he was also *her* Luca, the one she had laughed with and played in the snow with. She had been given the gift of one more encounter with him. Why not embrace it?

"What will happen to you now?" she asked him, suddenly ashamed of herself for her every thought being on herself. Luca had just had the shock of his life: finding out he had a sister and that the job he had prepared for his entire life would not be his. He claimed he was happy, but was he worried, too?

"I can't know what Gabriella's decision will be, but if she chooses the crown, I am superbly qualified to act as an advisor to your friend and I will do that. I find myself feeling quite comfortable with that role. As I said before, I am cautiously relishing the thought of being free in ways I have not yet experienced. I can travel more freely. I can experience other cultures more deeply. Just like Meribel abandoning me for another turned out to be a gift, I am beginning to see that a gift might be hidden in this."

He didn't seem worried at all. They sampled all the exquisite offerings on the table, and when they were finished, Luca said, "Speaking of gifts, I have one other for you."

"I don't need any other gifts, Luca. Just being with you..."

She could feel the blush moving up her cheeks, as if she had said too much. *Way too much. Again!*

"This is what is amazing to me, Imogen, how you see *me*. Not a prince, but *me*. I want you to come back to Casavalle with me."

CHAPTER SEVENTEEN

FOR A MOMENT Imogen's heart stood still. Could she have heard correctly?

"You want me to come back to your kingdom with you?" she asked Luca weakly.

"Yes. You have shown me your world. Now come and see mine."

Suddenly she understood. She nearly laughed out loud at the absurdity of what she had thought! That *he* wanted her to come.

"Is this Gabriella's idea?" she asked quietly. "Is she feeling sorry for me that she is having all the fun, and I've been left behind?"

He regarded her thoughtfully. "If I tell you Gabriella needs you now, more than ever, will you come?"

Would she? It seemed a dangerous thing, indeed, to agree. How would she stop herself from being enchanted? She was already in love with him. What would happen if she accepted an invitation into his world?

Her heart could be broken.

She had to say no.

And yet she thought of the excitement in Gabi's voice, and her new enthusiasm for life. She thought of how, just this morning, she had almost wished she was going to be fired. How she had felt as if life was passing her by, how she had felt envious of life handing her friend an unexpected adventure.

What did it matter why she was being asked to go?

Life was shouting at her to do this. So, even while her head said no, loudly and firmly, her heart said yes.

And somehow it was what her heart said that tumbled off her lips.

A whisper, tentative and frightened.

And then more loudly, more sure, more bold.

"Yes."

"Can we get out? And walk?"

Luca looked at Imogen. She was wide-eyed with wonder, as she had been since the moment she had stepped onto the private jet that had whisked them from Canada and to his world in the blink of an eye.

He probably shouldn't have told her it was Gabriella's idea for her to come to Casavalle, but when he had invited her, she had suddenly looked so terrified.

And then suddenly he had felt terrified, too.

It was the same mistake his father had made with Sophia: jumping in. No, better to say it was Gabriella's idea, to see if they could maintain what he thought they had at the Lodge under these very different circumstances.

Now a royal limousine, as beautifully appointed as the jet, and chauffeur driven, was carrying them to the very gates of the castle.

Just as Luca had told Imogen, preparation for Christmas had begun. It was getting dark and they were just entering the long driveway lined with Norway spruce, the castle awash in light at the end of the tunnel of trees.

Because it was such a huge job, the trees that stood sentinel on both sides of Royal Avenue were always decorated first, and they had been completed.

This year they alternated: one tree completely in white lights, the next one in blue, all the way down the long driveway.

"How many lights do you think?" Imogen breathed. "A million? More? I have to get out. I have to be *in* it. It's a fairy tale come to life."

Luca tapped the driver on the shoulder, gave the quiet command, and the car came to a halt. He exited the car and took Cristiano's place, holding open the door for Imogen.

"Welcome to my home," he said quietly, as Imogen got out of the car, hugged herself tight and turned a slow circle.

She stopped when she was facing the castle. "How can such a place ever feel like home?"

Could it ever feel like her home? He looked at it through her eyes: the castle was constructed of pure white limestone that had been brought, centuries ago, from quarries on the Adriatic Islands. Its soaring spires, walls, wings, towers, were all lit with floodlights, so that the whole place glowed. It did look exactly like the opening illustration for a fairy tale.

It was all so grand compared to the Lodge. Luca felt the oddest thing. He explored the feeling, strangely paralyzed by it. It felt so odd.

He realized he felt something he had never felt before: he felt insecure. But then he looked at her wonder-filled face and remembered, probably for the thousandth time since she had spoken them, the words she had said.

No wonder I felt as if I loved you.

He crooked his elbow to Imogen, inviting her to loop her arm through his. They walked the tree-lined avenue together. It opened, eventually, to a huge front courtyard, a cobblestone driveway circled around a massive fountain. The workings of the fountain had been removed, and huge blocks of ice, weighing several tons each, had been placed there.

"What are these?" Imogen asked, and then her eyes widened. "That's what you told me about, isn't it? The ice that's brought in for the carving competition. It's so mild here. It's magical that you've found a way to keep the ice from melting, to make it happen."

That's what he had hoped for—that beyond the pomp and circumstance, she would see the magic of his world and the beauty.

"Is that the maze over there? The one the children love? It's gorgeous. I couldn't have ever imagined it."

"It's a hedge maze—part of the formal gardens. In the summer it has reflection pools and fountains. It hasn't had its Christmas makeover yet, but it soon will."

"How wonderful to picture children running through it laughing."

He saw her own regret about children flit briefly through her eyes.

"Can you get lost in it?" she asked.

"Oh yes. That's part of the fun. You and I will explore it together," he said. "I'll make sure you don't get lost."

And he meant that. Not just for the maze, but for his world. He would make sure she would not get lost in this strange new place he was asking her to explore.

She seemed to know exactly what he really meant, because she smiled tentatively, and then Imogen turned her attention to the wide granite staircase that led to the massive front doors just as they opened. Two staff members in the simple uniform of the castle—white blouses and black slacks or skirts—held the double doors open for them.

"Is someone going to come out and play the trumpet?"

Imogen whispered, and then, "It's all a little intimidating, isn't it?"

He looked at it through her eyes and felt his heart fall a little bit. The transition he would be asking her to make was indeed huge.

But then Gabriella burst through the open door. Her hair was tumbling around her shoulders, jodhpurs clung to her slender legs, and her shirt was untucked. It was just the moment of informality that was needed!

"Imogen," she called, as she came down the steps, two at a time. She took the smaller woman in her embrace. "Are you totally overwhelmed?"

"Of course I am!"

"Let me get you settled then. You can take tea in my quarters." She giggled. "And wait until you see them."

Just like that, Imogen was whisked away from him. He stared at the two departing women, slightly disgruntled. This wasn't exactly his plan. Luca's lips twitched. Again, these Canadian women just seemed to have a way of disrupting the best-laid plans.

Imogen woke the next morning and felt faintly disoriented. When she remembered where she was, she felt as if she needed to pinch herself.

She sat up in bed—a huge four-poster piece of furniture that centuries' worth of royal people had slept in—and gazed around the room. Not a room, really, but a suite. It was so opulent it took her breath away. The bedclothes were silk. Priceless paintings and wall hangings decorated the walls. When she swung her feet out of the bed, they landed on an ancient Turkish rug.

She padded to the bathroom, which had a huge marble freestanding tub, and she was pretty sure the fixtures were real gold.

She put aside the little voice that tried to tell her she didn't belong here and listened to the other one, which told her to embrace the adventure.

A soft knock came at the door, and she shrugged into the luxurious robe that hung on the back of the door. She wondered if breakfast was going to be delivered on a tray. How did you address the person who delivered it? Did you take it from them or did they set it down?

Imogen, she told herself, *you are in way over your head.*

Just the way Gabriella's mother would have been all those years ago, she thought with sympathy.

She went and opened the door.

Luca stood there. She wasn't sure if she was relieved, or appalled that he was seeing her with messy hair and still in her pajamas.

But of course, he had seen her with messy hair and not exactly as a fashionista before. He looked so good when he gave her a rakish smile.

"Are you going to sleep all day?"

"Have I?" she asked, appalled.

"Welcome to jet lag! Get dressed. I have so much to show you."

"I'm not even sure what I should wear."

"Dress to have fun. I'm going to show you the palace, and then show you the grounds on horseback."

"I don't know how to ride a horse. That's Gabriella's thing."

"Then I'll try not to put you on one that breathes fire, not today."

The tour of the palace began with the dining room, where a delightful breakfast of crunchy, mind-blowingly delicious handmade pastries had been put out. From there Luca took her for a tour of the palace. It was awe inspiring. It might have struck her to intimidated silence, except that Luca was so funny, irreverent and engaging as her personal tour guide.

The palace was truly like something out of a fairy tale.

Luca took her to huge ballrooms, staterooms, the throne room, dining rooms, long galleries and sweeping staircases, as well as kitchens. Amused by her wide-eyed wonder, he let her peek in sumptuous bedrooms and luxury bathrooms. The library took her breath away.

Most magical of all, though, was that Christmas in Casavalle was unfolding exactly as Luca had described it. The palace was being prepared, and it was both breathtaking and awe inspiring.

In a way, it made Imogen feel a little foolish about her humble efforts to create a Christmas for the Prince.

He came from this—beautifully decorated trees in every room, wreaths on every door, real pine and fir garlands lining mantels and staircases. Huge, exotic poinsettias had been imported and brought brightness to every forgotten corner. Priceless ornaments graced side tables and coffee tables that were hundreds of years old.

The last place he took her was the gorgeous tree in the entrance foyer. It was behind ropes, but he opened one and invited her in.

The aroma enveloped her. The Buschetta ornaments were beyond anything she had ever seen before.

"Has this year's been unveiled yet?"

"No, tomorrow. I am hoping you will enjoy the unveiling ceremony."

She really needed to ask questions. How long did he think she could be here? She wasn't going to be able to take leave from her job forever. In the real world there were little issues like needing a paycheck to survive.

But those questions died in her throat when he looked

at her with such warmth. He was truly happy to be showing her his home.

"Are you ready to try riding?" he asked.

She was. In fact, she was surprised to find, she felt ready for just about anything.

CHAPTER EIGHTEEN

IMOGEN SAT WITH Queen Maria and Gabriella on a slightly raised dais in front of that amazing Christmas tree. The unveiling of the ornament was about to begin. She marveled, a little shell-shocked, at the surprise life had given her. A week ago, two, could she have ever imagined this for herself?

Sitting with royalty, in the lavishly decorated front foyer of a palace, waiting for the Buschetta Christmas ornament to be revealed?

The foyer—huge—had almost become an auditorium, with a hundred seats, all of them full, in a semicircle around the dais. There seemed to be a lot of press here, and Imogen tried to look confident and as though she belonged. She had brought her best dress with her and, giggling like two schoolgirls, she and Gabriella had selected hats for this event.

Luca wasn't here yet, and she could feel herself waiting for him. Despite the fact he was a prince, he was her rock, her touchstone, in this gorgeous new world he had introduced her to. His smile was the anchor that kept her from feeling as if she was floating in a dream.

But when he did come in, Imogen's mouth fell open. Could this man really be *her* Luca? The Luca who had donned long underwear and roasted hot dogs over the fire and built snowmen? The Luca who had patiently showed her how to ride yesterday, and who had gotten lost in the maze with her until they were both doubled over with laughter?

The Luca who had kissed her and held her hand? The Luca who had made her heart feel things it had never felt before?

This man was regal in a navy blue uniform, gold braid trimming one shoulder and a peaked cap pulled low over his eyes. His flair for wearing the uniform—the way he absolutely owned it—made Imogen feel suddenly self-conscious, as if her best dress had come from the thrift bin in Crystal Lake. She fought a desire to remove the hat, feeling suddenly as if she was in costume.

But Luca was not in costume in his imposing uniform. He was commanding, and the whole room seemed to ripple with acknowledgment when he walked in.

He nodded at her, his eyes lingered, and for a moment, it seemed as if he was, indeed, *her* Luca, but then his gaze moved on, as if he was preoccupied. He sat with Cristiano, his brother—whom Imogen had only met briefly—and some other very important-looking people on the opposite end of the dais from where his mother, Gabriella and Imogen were seated.

Suddenly, she felt as if she had been seated here by accident. She was probably supposed to have politely refused the invitation to sit with the Queen.

As if sensing she wanted to bolt, Gabriella quietly took her hand and gave her a tiny sideways smile that reminded her of her mantra.

Embrace the adventure.

Imogen took a deep breath and settled more deeply in her chair.

* * *

Luca saw Imogen right away. She looked positively beautiful in a jade-green dress and a showstopper of a hat. She didn't just fit in his world, she dimmed it with her radiance. But he couldn't let himself be distracted, not right now.

The future relations of two kingdoms rested on what he had to say today.

He noted that television, radio, online and print journalists from both Casavalle and Aguilarez were present, as well as a few representatives from media outlets around the world. The unveiling of the ornament was a nice "feel-good" filler piece for slow nights in international news.

Gabriella's presence on the dais was unexplained, for now. It was not unusual for them to have extra people at the opening of the ornament, and indeed, the town mayor was here, as was a member of the Buschetta family.

In front of them was a box, wrapped in plain brown paper. Today they would unveil this year's Buschetta ornament creation for the Christmas tree.

Luca dreaded it.

For one thing, it was the first time his father was not here.

But for another, what if the ornament commemorated the engagement that had ended so badly, or the wedding that had never happened? It could be embarrassing for him, but worse, painful for Imogen.

Queen Maria stood and took the box. She rolled it over in her hand and then turned and motioned Gabriella to come stand beside her.

Luca watched Gabriella and was taken again by her innate grace and her composure. But more, the woman seemed to glow a little more deeply each day, as she was welcomed into the embrace of a family she had not known she had, as she explored the wonders of her new life.

Carefully, Gabriella undid the wrapping.

The ornament was revealed: inside a globe of glass was a baby lying in a manger of straw. It was so lifelike Luca could almost hear it chortling as it reached for the muzzle of the donkey who nuzzled it.

The Buschetta representative came forward and touched a secret switch. The top half of the globe swung open, and he carefully manipulated the manger.

The baby swung away to reveal these words, in tiny perfect calligraphy: *Love makes all the world new again.*

He read them aloud to the audience. There was a collective sigh.

Luca cast a glance at Imogen. She chose that moment to look at him. A brand-new world shivered in the air between them, though she looked hastily away and so did he.

He made himself focus on the ornament, even though he wanted to look back at her and bask in the truth he had seen in her face when those words were revealed.

Luca felt the message in his heart. He waited until the photographers had satisfied their need for pictures.

Then he stood up, took a deep breath and held up his hand for silence and attention.

The silence was almost immediate, people leaning toward what he had to say.

It felt as if he was about to speak the most important words he would ever say.

"It has been suggested to me," he said, "that I forgive Princess Meribel. As all of you know, our engagement ended, not because of irreconcilable differences, but because my fiancée is pregnant with another man's child."

A murmur of outrage went up among the assembled.

"I will not forgive her."

A gasp, laced with a certain delighted sanctimoniousness, went up from the crowd.

"Because," Prince Luca continued, his voice quiet and firm, "there is truly nothing for me to forgive."

This caused muttering, and one reporter shouted, "She left you at the altar, sir."

Another called out, in a voice laced with outrage, "She was with another man behind your back."

"She's pregnant!"

Luca waited patiently for it all to die down. Then he spoke again, his voice strong and calm and sure.

"In fact, I just met with the Princess and I asked for her forgiveness."

This statement was met with stunned silence.

"It takes a great deal of insensitivity to be unable to recognize a relationship is not fulfilling for both parties, and I am guilty of that," he continued.

"In fact, in our meeting, I thanked Meribel Asturias for being the bravest woman I know. I thanked her for teaching me a lesson I desperately need to learn—love is everything.

"Not power. Not wealth. Not influence. Love. Love is the thing worth sacrificing every other thing for—including the promise of a kingdom."

There was complete silence. Luca could have heard a pin drop in that large room. He went on.

"Coming into this Christmas season, that is the message I want you each to hold in your hearts, that love is everything and the only thing. It is the message this beautiful ornament gives the world this year—*love makes the whole world new again.*

"Princess Meribel has brought that reminder to me this season, and I pass on her gift to each of you.

"Do not harbor one acrimonious thought of this woman. She was true to her heart, and it required her to be courageous and determined, and that is what each of us needs to be in pursuit of what is right and what is decent. That is what each of us needs to be in the pursuit of the greatest thing of all, which is love. When her baby is born, I encourage the world to celebrate that wondrous expression of love made manifest.

"Some of you will remember, a long time ago, before Queen Maria, my father loved another. She left my father, and left the kingdom of Casavalle. The circumstances were mysterious. I know the result of her leaving left my father suspicious of love, and maybe some of you felt that way, too.

"And yet I am here to tell you that love always brings a gift with it, even if it takes time for that blessing to be revealed. I promise that my father's long-ago love has left us a precious gift, and soon I hope to be able to share that with all of you.

"Please, I beg of you, go into this Christmas season with your hearts open. Forgive hurts, real and imagined, old and new, small and large. In that forgiveness, you will find you are open to the joy of the simple pleasures of being with your families and loved ones. Build snowmen and warm your hands over fires.

"Take pleasure in the greatest gift we, as human beings, are ever allowed to experience. Embrace love completely."

Luca finished speaking.

Had his words managed to repair anything? To save Meribel from a life of shame? Had his words brought love, as he had hoped?

The gallery was silent. And then one reporter put down her camera, rose to her feet and began to clap.

And then they were all on their feet, clapping with thunderous approval.

His intuition had served him again. He glanced at the people behind him: his brother looked like he was in a state of complete shock, but Gabriella's eyes were shining with tears. His mother looked as pleased with him as she had ever looked. And Imogen looked at him with a pride shining from her eyes that any man would give his life to see.

But didn't that reaction from those women he loved require something of him? Now wasn't there one more challenge? To practice what he had preached? To follow his intuition, his heart, back to the one place and the one person who called him? The place he had felt as free as he had ever felt and as complete as he could ever feel?

Did Prince Luca have it in himself to be as brave as he had just called on others to be?

CHAPTER NINETEEN

IMOGEN WATCHED AS Luca turned and took his seat. She looked around her at the emotion his words had inspired. She had never loved him more.

Or felt as devastated.

She had seen him now, completely. She had seen him as a man and as a prince. She had just witnessed his ability to inspire and lead.

It made her realize how hopeless her feelings for him really were. He was, quite simply, amazing. Everyone in his world knew it, and when this speech got out, the whole world would know it.

Women would be throwing themselves at his feet. Women who came from that same world and would fit easily into it. Women who understood wealth and power. Women who were sophisticated and glamorous.

Imogen understood Gabriella's mother, Sophia Ross. Completely.

As soon as she was able, she slipped away. She went to her room and began hastily putting things in her worn travel bag. Even the bag seemed to mock her; well used and a little frayed, it was exactly the type of thing that would embarrass him about her.

But to be embarrassed by her, he would have to be involved with her. Obviously, he had been kind while she was here. He had shown her the sights and made her laugh and made her love him even more. He had seemed to enjoy spending time with her. She was sure that was genuine.

And yet that man, who had just given that speech…

Imogen felt a shiver run up and down her spine. He was from a different world. In a different league, entirely.

She had to get out of here before she made a total fool of herself. She sank down on the bed. How did one get out of Casavalle? Every single thing about getting here had been organized for her.

There was a tap on the door.

It was more of the same: staff here to tell her something, that dinner was served, or it was time for tea. Or here to deliver freshly laundered items she hadn't asked to be laundered, or new lotions and potions for the bath.

She decided to ignore the knock, but it came again louder. And then, yet again.

She went to the door and opened it.

Luca stood there, resplendent in his uniform, looking tall and strong and sure of himself. Looking like exactly what he was: royalty.

He scanned her face, and she scanned his, wanting to memorize it, memorize what was there: happiness in seeing her.

His smile faded. "What's wrong?"

"Wrong?" she said with forced brightness. "Nothing. It's time for me to go home. I've outstayed my welcome. I know it was Gabriella's idea for me to come and you were a good sport—"

"It wasn't Gabriella's idea," he said softly.

"It wasn't?"

"Will you come outside with me? I have something I want to give you."

She knew she should refuse him. She knew she should pack her bag and get out of here with one shred of her heart intact. But she could not refuse him anything. And that line—*It wasn't Gabriella's idea*—was making something happen to her heart.

She should refuse any more gifts from him, but instead, she let her hand take the one he outstretched to her. One more moment with him, one more memory.

He led her through a labyrinth of passages in the castle and out a side door.

"This is my garden," he said, and his hand tightened on hers. It was a lovely walled space, with vines covering the stones and flowering shrubs giving off a perfumed aroma. The night was beautiful and dark, clear and crisp.

She looked into his face and saw it was just her beloved Luca under all these trappings: the royal uniform, the beautiful spaces. He was still the same Luca who had chased her through the snow, who had kissed her, who had showed her Casavalle with such pleasure.

He was beloved to her. She loved him.

"Look," he said, pointing.

She looked in that direction. It looked for all the world like a huge pile of dirty laundry was sitting in the middle of his pristine garden!

"What is this?" she asked cautiously.

"That's my gift," he said happily.

"Um, what is it?"

"Go down there and stand right in front of it," he instructed her.

She looked at him. He was so light, so filled with mischief, so playful.

So easy to love. So *himself*, somehow.

She did as he asked her.

"Ready?" he called.

She was. She leaped back when the pile of what looked to be fabric in front of her began to hiss and writhe and unfold.

She watched, fascinated, as air rushed into it and it began to inflate. An inflatable snow family took shape before her very eyes. A mama, a papa and two children.

It lit from within. The family's arms began to wave merrily.

Imogen began to laugh. And then he was at her side and they were both laughing until they hurt from it.

She had to lie down on the ground, and he lay down beside her.

"That is just about the cheesiest thing I've ever seen," she said.

"I know. Isn't it great? For me to be cheesy instead of classy is a wonderful feeling."

"Part of being free."

"Yes."

They lay there, side by side, silent, watching the stars dance in the inky skies above them.

Love makes all the world new again, Imogen thought, the message hidden in the ornament today.

It was such a simple message, and yet so profound. And so true. Wasn't she looking at the world in a brand-new way since her days with Luca?

Since her heart could not deny her love for him?

"I let you believe that," Luca confessed softly. "I let you believe it was Gabriella who needed you to come here.

"I was afraid you might not come if you knew the truth. I mean, Gabriella told me she felt bad that she was having all the excitement and that you had been left out. But it was me who couldn't stand the thought of you being left out. It was me who wanted you to see my home."

"You?"

"Imogen, I have missed you so much there are days when it felt as if the air was not enough to fill me anymore. As if I would be left empty and aching for the rest of my life. I missed you.

"And I missed what you can do to ordinary moments like this one. You transform them. You show me what I have been missing my entire life.

"Now that I've had it, I don't feel life would be worth living without it."

"What have you been missing your entire life?"

"Love," he whispered. "That very thing I just spoke of."

"Are you saying—" her voice was barely a whisper "—what I think you are saying?" It felt as if her heart was about to thud out of her chest.

"I don't know how this is possible. To feel so strongly about you after such a short period together. But I want to explore it. I want to see if it's real. I want to spend my life with you."

Imogen swallowed hard.

It was another "pinch me" moment.

And yet, looking at his face—the face she had fallen in love with—she knew he was speaking his truth.

She began to weep.

"You know I can't have your children."

"Oh, my darling Imogen, that causes me distress only because it causes you distress. If we are intended to have children one day, they will find their way to us. I promise you that."

It was the kind of promise you could hang on to. Her tears fell harder.

"And if it was just you and I, forever, I would spend each day with you in total joy, feeling complete, feeling as if not one other thing was necessary."

And then she was gathered up in his arms, and they sat for a long, long time with her nestled against his chest, in the light of the inflatable snow family and of the winking stars.

"It's the best gift ever," Imogen said.

"I'm actually hoping you will think this is the best gift ever."

She turned to him. He held out a box. He lifted the lid and a ring sparkled at her.

"In the last few days, I've lost my bride and lost my throne. Such a small price to pay to find true love and happiness. If you will have me, I would like you to be my wife."

Imogen stared at him, shocked. Logically, she understood they barely knew one another. Logically, she understood that their time together had been underlain with the intensity of being snowed in, and then her visit here, which had seemed about as real as a fairy tale.

But she had been logical her entire life; she had based all her decisions on what was solid and what was sensible. She had planned a safe route through the journey of life.

Not only had all her planning not brought her happiness, she could now clearly see her desire for predictability and safety might have been an obstacle to ever finding the true happiness she felt right now, as exquisitely, as blissfully as she had ever felt it.

She gazed into Luca's eyes.

From the moment he had stepped off the helicopter, she had experienced a sensation of knowing him.

Now she knew it was not because he resembled his sister, and her best friend.

It was not that at all.

Her heart had recognized him.

Her heart had not recognized the impossibility of it. Her heart had never been deterred by the fact she was a common girl and he was a prince.

Her heart had known.

And it knew now.

It knew that others might see it as too soon, or see their worlds as too different, or see them as going up against impossible cultural obstacles.

Her heart cared nothing for any of that. It cared only for the answer that whispered from her lips.

"Yes," she said.

And then stronger, an affirmation of the stunning power and mystery of love, an affirmation of its ability to find you, even when you hid from it.

"Yes!"

He stood up and held out his hand to her. She took it, and he pulled her to her feet and held her tight against him. He tilted her chin, so that her eyes met his. He scanned her face, and he saw the truth of her love there.

"Love has given me what a title never could," he said hoarsely. "Your love has crowned me King."

His lips took hers.

And they became one with it all: with the star-studded sky and the majesty of the mountains, with the life force that breathed through the trees that surrounded them and the earth that they stood on.

They became one with love.

* * * * *

THE MAVERICK'S SECRET BABY

TERI WILSON

This book is dedicated to my writing friends from the Leakey, Texas, writing retreat. From the small-town shop with the meat cleaver door handles to the house on the river and the nighttime campfires, it was the perfect inspiration for writing a Montana romance with a cowboy hero. I love you all.

Chapter One

Finn Crawford was living the dream.

Granted, his father, Maximilian, had gone a little crazy. The old man was intent on paying a matchmaker to marry off all six of his sons. If that wasn't nuts, Finn didn't know what was.

This wasn't the 1800s. It was modern-day Montana, and the Crawfords were...*comfortable.* If that sounded like something a rich man might say about his family, then it was probably because it was true. Finn's family was indeed wealthy, and Finn himself wasn't exactly terrible-looking. Quite the opposite, if the women who'd been ringing Viv Dalton—the matchmaker in question—were to be believed. More important, he was a decent guy. He tried, anyway.

Plus, Finn loved women. Women were typically much more open than men. Kinder and more authentic. He loved their softness and the way they committed so much to everything, whether it was caring for a stray puppy or running a business. Show him a woman who wore a deep red lipstick and her heart on her sleeve, and he was a goner. At the ripe old age of twenty-nine, Finn had already fallen in love more times than he could count.

So the very notion that he'd need any help in the marriage department would have been completely laughable, if he'd had any intention of tying the knot. Which he did *not*.

Why would he, when Viv Dalton was being paid to toss women in his direction? His dad had picked up the entire Crawford ranch—all six of his sons and over a thousand head of cattle—and moved them from Dallas to Rust Creek Falls, Montana, for this asinine pretend version of *The Bachelor*. The way Finn saw it, he'd be a fool not to enjoy the ride.

And enjoying it, he had been. A little too much, according to Viv.

"Finn, honestly. You've dated a different woman nearly every week for the past three months." The wedding planner eyed him from across her desk, which was piled high with bridal magazines and puffy white tulle. Sitting inside her wedding shop was like being in the middle of a cupcake.

"And they've all been lovely." Finn stretched his denim-clad legs out in front of him and crossed his cowboy boots at the ankle. "I have zero complaints."

Beside him, Maximilian sighed. "I have a lot of complaints. Specifically, a million of them where you're concerned, son."

Finn let the words roll right off him. After all, paying someone a million dollars to find wives for all six Crawford brothers hadn't been his genius idea. Maximilian had no one to blame but himself.

"Mr. Crawford, I assure you I'm doing my best to find Finn a bride." Viv tucked a wayward strand of blond hair behind her ear and folded her hands neatly on the surface of her desk. All business. "In fact, I believe I've set him up with every eligible woman in Rust Creek Falls."

"All of them?" Finn arched a brow. This town was even smaller than he'd thought it was. It would have taken him a lifetime to go through the entire dating pool back in Dallas. He should know—he'd tried.

Vivienne gave him a tight smile. "Every. Last. One."

"Okay, then I guess we're done here. You gave it your best shot." Finn stood. He'd miss the girlfriend-of-the-week club, but at least his father would be forced to accept the fact that he wasn't about to get engaged to any of the fine female residents of Rust Creek Falls.

Finn placed his Stetson on his head, set to go. "Thank you, ma'am."

"Sit back down, son." Maximilian didn't raise his voice, but his tone had an edge to it that Finn hadn't heard since the time he'd "borrowed" his father's truck to go mudding with his high school buddies back in tenth grade.

That little escapade had ended with Maximilian's luxury F-150 stuck in a ditch and Finn mucking out stalls every weekend for the rest of the school year.

Of course Finn was an adult now, not a stupid teenager. He made his own choices, certainly when it came to his love life. But he loved his dad, and since the Crawfords were all business partners in addition to family, he didn't want to rock the boat. Not over something as ridiculous as this.

"Sure thing, Dad." He lowered himself back into the frilly white chair with its frilly lace cushion.

Maximilian sat a little straighter and narrowed his gaze at Viv Dalton. "Are you forgetting what's at stake?"

She cleared her throat. "No, sir. I'm not."

A look of warning passed from Finn's father toward the wedding planner, and she gave him a tiny, almost imperceptible nod.

Finn's gut churned. What the hell was that about?

Damn it.

Knowing his dad, he'd gone and upped the ante behind Finn's back. When Maximilian ran into problems, he had a tendency to write a bigger check to make them go away.

Finn sighed. "I'm no longer sure entirely what's going on here, but I think it might be time for this little matchmaking project to end. Half of us are already married."

One by one, Finn's brothers Logan, Xander and Knox had become attached. It was uncanny, really. None of them had ended up with women of Viv's choosing, but they'd coupled up all the same. The way he saw it, his dad should be thrilled. The Crawford legacy would live on, Finn's bachelor status notwithstanding.

Maximilian shook his head. "Absolutely not. We need Viv's help now more than ever. It's not going to be easy to make matches for you, Hunter and Wilder. Hunter hasn't so much as looked at another woman since his wife died. Wilder is just...well, Wilder. And you can't seem to focus on one woman to save your life.

If you're not careful, son, you're going to wind up old, alone and lonely. Just like me."

A bark of laugher escaped Finn before he could stop it. "Please." He rolled his eyes. "You're far from lonely."

His father was rarely, if ever, alone. The business and living arrangements at their sprawling Ambling A Ranch pretty much assured that Maximilian saw each of his six sons on a daily basis. Plus, he was the biggest flirt Finn had ever set eyes on.

His dad had been single for decades. Finn's mother had abandoned the family when all six of her sons had been young. Maximilian might have remained single, but that hardly meant he lacked female companionship. His wallet alone was an aphrodisiac—plus he was something of a silver fox. Being in his sixties didn't stop him from dating nearly as much as Finn did.

Like father, like son.

"Point taken." Maximilian shrugged one shoulder. The corner of his mouth inched up into a half grin. "In any case, we're not here to talk about me. We're here to find you a bride."

"Your son might need to adjust his standards," Viv said, as if Finn wasn't sitting right there in the room. "The sheer number of women he's dated in the past three months should have guaranteed a good match."

"I guess you'll just have to dredge up more women. It seems like the only solution." Finn aimed his best sardonic smile directly at the wedding planner. She was really beginning to annoy him.

Adjust his standards? What the hell was that supposed to mean?

"I've been calling around town to see if I've overlooked any single ladies. This morning alone I've tried all the day-care centers, the veterinary clinic, the medical center and Maverick Manor." Viv tapped a polished fingernail on the pink notepad in front of her. "I thought maybe I could find a few datable, single women working in one of these locations whom I might not be acquainted with, some ladies living in one of the surrounding counties."

So now she was going to import women into town to date him? This whole ordeal was getting more absurd by the minute.

"Any luck?" Maximilian said.

"Not yet. But there's still one place left on my list—Strickland's Boarding House."

An ache took up residence in Finn's temples. "That ramshackle Victorian mansion by the fire station?"

Viv's lips pursed. "It's a town landmark."

"It's purple," Finn retorted.

"Lavender gray, technically." She smiled brightly at him. Jeez, this woman never gave up, did she? *Maybe because your father is offering her a million dollars to marry you off...possibly more.* "Just the sort of place a lovely single woman might choose to stay."

"That actually makes sense, son." Maximilian waved a hand toward Viv's list. "Go ahead and call over to the boarding house. We'll wait."

Finn was on the verge of pulling his Stetson low over his eyes and taking a nap. No one here seemed to care much what he thought, anyway. But once Viv dialed the number, she put her phone on speaker mode, which made napping pretty much impossible.

After two rings, an older man's voice rattled on the other end. "Howdy, Strickland's Boarding House."

Viv smiled. "Hello there, Gene. It's Vivienne Dalton calling."

"Hi there, darlin'. What can Melba and I do for you today?" he said.

In the background, Finn heard a woman—Melba, presumably—asking who'd called. When Old Gene supplied her with the information, she yelled out a greeting to Viv.

Viv and Old Gene exchanged a few more pleasantries. Gene asked about her husband, and she inquired as to the well-being of the baby pygmy goat Gene and Melba were caring for.

Of course there's a baby pygmy goat. Finn suppressed a grin. Maximilian, however, was less charmed. He cleared his throat, prompting Viv to get on with the matter at hand.

She took the hint. "Actually, Gene, I have a rather odd question for you. Do you happen to have any single young women staying at the boarding house who might be interested in a date with a handsome cowboy named Finn Crawford? I'm trying to help out a friend who's new in town."

"Funny you should mention single young women," Old Gene said. "We've had a darling young lady staying with us for a couple weeks now. A bit on the shy side, but sweet as pie."

Viv's eyes lit up. "Really? What's her name?"

"Avery."

Finn narrowed his gaze at Viv's phone.

Avery?

The only Avery he knew would never fit into a place like Rust Creek Falls. She couldn't possibly be talking about…

"Avery who?" Maximilian growled. "Please tell me you're not talking about the daughter of that rat bas—"

"Dad." Finn shook his head. "Chill out."

As usual, Maximilian had a harsh word at the ready for anyone related to his old nemesis, Oscar Ellington.

Finn was certain he didn't need to worry. It just wasn't possible. Oscar Ellington's daughter lived over a thousand miles away, in Texas. Plus, with her pencil skirts, red-soled stilettos and designer handbags, she wasn't exactly what Finn would describe as sweet. Considering they'd only shared one night together, she wasn't exactly *his*, either.

Still, what a night it had been.

"Gene! Stop talking right this minute!" Melba's voice boomed in the background again.

Viv frowned down at her phone. "Is everything okay over there?"

"Fine and dandy," Gene said.

Melba issued a simultaneous "No, it is not. Gene seems to have forgotten we shouldn't be giving out guests' private information."

"But she seems a little lonely," Old Gene countered while Melba continued to balk.

Again, Finn's memory snagged on a sweet, sultry night on an Oklahoma business trip and the most electric kiss he'd ever experienced. The power had gone down, bathing the city in darkness. But when his lips touched Avery Ellington's, they'd created enough sparks to light up the sky.

How long had it been?

Months.

"Excuse me." Finn leaned forward in his chair. He knew he was supposed to be a quiet observer at the moment, but he had to ask. "What exactly does this Avery woman look like?"

The glare Viv aimed his way shot daggers at him.

"Never mind," she said primly. "Sorry to bother you, Gene. We'll chat soon. Give that baby goat a kiss for me. Bye now."

She ended the call, and for a minute, Finn was seriously worried she might throw the phone at his head. "What does she *look like*? You can't be serious."

Maximilian shrugged. "It's a legitimate question."

Finn held up a hand. "Wait. That's not what—"

But Viv wasn't having it. She cut him off before he could explain. "There are far more important things than looks when it comes to a potential life partner."

Agreed.

Finn wasn't looking for a life partner, though. He doubted he'd be looking for one for another decade or so. Besides, he'd simply been trying to figure out if they'd been talking about the same Avery. All Old Gene needed to say was long, lush brown hair and dark, expressive eyes. Then he would have known.

Give it up. This is the opposite end of the country from Texas.

Or Oklahoma, for that matter.

Besides, Avery Ellington would stick out like a sore thumb in Rust Creek Falls. Surely he'd have run into her by now.

"You've found all of Viv's picks attractive so far, son. I'm sure this Avery girl wouldn't be any different," Maximilian said.

Finn let out a long exhale. How shallow could his father possibly make him sound? Maybe it was time to stop humoring the old man and dating every woman Viv Dalton threw at him.

"Thank you for everything, Ms. Dalton, but I think it's time to go." Finn stood and turned toward Maximilian. "Dad?"

His father didn't budge.

Fine. He could waste all the time and money he desired, but Finn was out of there. He tipped his hat to Viv and waded through all the pastel cupcake fluff toward the exit. All the while, his father's words echoed in his head.

I'm sure this Avery girl wouldn't be any different.

That's where he was wrong.

Finn had never met a woman quite like Avery Ellington.

Avery Ellington tucked her yoga mat under her arm and made her way down the curved staircase of the old Victorian house where she'd been living for the past few weeks.

Living? Ha. Hiding is more like it.

Her grip on the banister tightened. She didn't want to dwell on her reasons for tucking herself away at Strickland's Boarding House in Nowheresville, Montana. She had more pressing problems at the moment—like the fact that her Lululemons were practically bursting at the seams.

Even so, instead of heading to the back porch for her early-morning yoga session when she reached the foot of the stairs, she veered toward the kitchen to see what smelled so good in there.

Her appetite had never been so active back in Dallas. She hardly recognized herself. Before, breakfast con-sisted of a skinny triple latte consumed en route to a business meeting. Then again, her entire life had been different *before*. This new *after* was strange…different.

And scary as heck.

"Ah, good morning, dear." Melba wiped her hands on her apron and smiled as Avery entered the boarding house's huge kitchen. "Claire just left to take Bekkah to school, but she made a fresh batch of muffins earlier. Would you like some?"

Claire, the Stricklands' granddaughter, was the official cook for the boarding house. She and her family used to live with the Stricklands, but according to Old Gene, they'd recently moved out, leaving Melba a little out of sorts. Claire still came by regularly to cook, but Melba's empty nest meant Avery got more than her fair share of the older woman's attention.

Not that being doted on was a bad thing, necessarily. Truth be told, Avery was accustomed to it. She'd been doted on her entire life.

"Good morning. And thank you." Avery bit into a muffin and nodded toward her mat. "I'm about to do a little yoga out back. It's such a nice, crisp day."

God, who was she? She sounded like Gwyneth Paltrow on a spa weekend instead of the Avery Ellington she'd been since graduating with honors from the University of Texas and stepping up as the vice president of Ellington Meats.

You're still the same person. This is only temporary. Mostly, anyway.

Right. As soon as she did what she'd come to Rust Creek Falls to do, she'd go straight home and get back to her regular life in Dallas. Her *charmed* life. The life that she loved.

"Here you go." Melba handed her a steaming mug of something that smelled wonderful—nutmeg, brown sugar and warm apple pie. Autumn in a cup. "We've had hot apple cider simmering all morning. This will get you nice and warmed up before you go outside."

"Thank you." Avery took a deep inhale of the fragrant cider and had a sudden urge to curl up and knit by the fire in the boarding house's cozy hearth instead of practicing her downward dog.

Never mind that she'd never held a knitting needle in her life. Clearly she'd been in Montana too long.

She took a sip and glanced at Old Gene, sitting at the kitchen table with a live goat in his lap. "How's the baby this morning?"

Baby.

Her throat went dry, and she took another gulp of cider.

"She's settling in." Old Gene nodded and offered the adorable animal a large baby bottle. The goat wasted no time latching on.

Melba rolled her eyes. "If you call waking up every two hours 'settling in.' Honestly, I don't know what possessed you to bring that thing home."

"My cousin is in the hospital with a broken hip, and he's got a barn full of animals that need tending. What was I supposed to do? Bring home a pig?"

Melba tossed a handful of cinnamon sticks into the pot of cider. "Lord, help me."

Old Gene winked at Avery behind Melba's back, and she smiled into her mug. The morning goat wars had become a regular thing since Gene had returned from his rescue mission to his cousin's farm a week or so ago, goat in hand. Melba was antigoat, particularly indoors, whereas Old Gene doted on the animal like it was a child.

Avery had yet to go anywhere near it. She didn't know a thing about goats. Or baby bottles, for that matter.

"You're really doing your best to get on my last nerve this morning." Melba sighed.

"I was simply trying to do something nice," Old Gene muttered. "You never know. Avery might enjoy going on a date with a nice young man."

"Wait…what?" She blinked.

How had the conversation moved seamlessly and at lightning speed from the goat to her love life?

"Gene." Melba looked like she might hit him over the head with her ladle.

"Can I ask what you two are talking about?" Avery set her mug down on the counter with a *thunk*.

Old Gene shrugged. "Viv Dalton just called. Apparently she knows a lonely cowboy."

"Don't you worry, dear." Melba reached for her hand and gave it a pat. "I made sure Viv knows you're not interested in meeting a man right now. Old Gene had no business even giving her your name."

Avery had no idea who Viv Dalton was, nor did she care. But she cared *very much* about her name floating around town. She might be new to Rust Creek Falls, but she was well aware of how swiftly the rumor mill worked. Case in point: Melba knew her husband was bringing home a goat before he'd even walked through the door. Old Gene had stopped by the general store for supplies on the way back to the boarding house and before his truck had pulled into the driveway, Melba had already gotten half a dozen texts and calls about the furry little kid.

"You gave my name to a stranger?" Avery felt sick.

The goat let loose with a pitiful bleat that perfectly mirrored the panic swirling in her consciousness.

Old Gene and Melba exchanged a worried glance.

"Only your first name." Melba reached for Avery's empty cup and refilled it with another ladleful of fragrant apple cider. A peace offering. "I'm sorry, dear. Old Gene was just trying to help, but I set him straight."

Avery nodded.

She wasn't sure what to say at this point. The day she arrived, she'd made it very clear to Melba that she was in town for a little respite. She'd been in desperate need of peace and quiet.

Avery had a feeling Melba assumed she was on the run from a bad boyfriend—maybe even a not-so-nice husband. She was somewhat ashamed to admit that she'd done nothing to correct this assumption. But it had been the only way to prevent her arrival in Rust Creek Falls from hitting the rumor circuit.

Her time had run out, apparently.

"Apologize to Avery, Gene." Melba pointed at her husband with a wooden spoon.

"I'm sorry," he said.

Avery smiled in return, because it was impossible to be angry at a man bottle-feeding a baby goat. "You're forgiven."

Melba let out a relieved exhale and turned back to the stove. "Go on now and do your yoga in peace. Gene and I both know you're not one bit interested in meeting that Crawford boy, no matter how charming and handsome Viv Dalton says he is."

Avery almost dropped her yoga mat.

That Crawford boy?

She couldn't be talking about Finn. Absolutely not.

Please, please no.

And yet somehow she knew it was true.

Charming? Check.

Handsome? Double check.

She swallowed hard, but bile rose up the back of her throat before she could stop it. She felt like she might be sick to her stomach...again. But that was pretty much par for the course now, just like her crazy new insatiable food cravings and the broken zipper on her favorite pencil skirt.

The goat slurped at the baby bottle, and Avery stared at the tiny animal. So utterly helpless. So sweet.

Tears pricked her eyes, and she blinked them away.

Get a grip.

She had more important things to dwell on than an orphaned goat. *Far* more important, like how on earth she could possibly explain to Melba and Old Gene that the last thing she wanted was to be set up with Finn Crawford when she was already four months pregnant with his child.

Chapter Two

No amount of downward dogs could calm the frantic beating of Avery's heart. She tried. She really did. But after an hour on her yoga mat, she felt more unsettled than ever.

Probably because every time she closed her eyes, she saw Finn Crawford's handsome face and his tilted, cocky smirk that never failed to make her weak in the knees.

She huffed out a distinctly nonyogi breath, scrambled to her feet and rolled up her mat. So much for the quiet, peaceful space she'd managed to carve out for herself in Rust Creek Falls. Her little time-out was over. She could no longer ignore the fact that she'd come here to find her baby's father—not when fate had nearly thrown her right back into his path.

"Finished already, dear?" Melba said when Avery

pushed through the screen door and back into the kitchen of the boarding house. She shook her head. "I don't understand why you young girls enjoy twisting yourselves into pretzels."

Melba's apron was dotted with flour, and a fresh platter of homemade biscuits sat on the kitchen island. The baby goat snoozed quietly on a dog bed in the corner by the window.

"Yes. I think I'm getting a little stir-crazy." She needed a nice distraction, something to completely rid her mind of Finn Crawford until she worked out exactly how to tell him he was going to be a daddy. "Maybe I could help clean some of the guest rooms again?"

Back home in Dallas, Avery typically put in a sixty-hour workweek. Fifty, minimum. She couldn't remember having so much free time on her hands. *Ever.* When she'd first arrived in Montana, all the unprecedented free time had been a dream come true. Pregnancy hormones had been wreaking havoc on her work schedule. The day before she'd left town, she'd actually nodded off in the middle of a marketing meeting. She'd needed a respite. A work cleanse.

Staying at the boarding house had given her just that. And it was lovely…

Until the morning she couldn't force the zipper closed on her favorite jeans—the boyfriend-cut ones that were always so soft and baggy. Faced with such painful evidence of the life growing inside her, Avery had experienced a sudden longing for her old life. She didn't know the first thing about babies or being pregnant, so she'd thrown herself into helping out around the boarding house in an effort to rid herself of her anxiety.

Unfortunately, she knew as much about cleaning as she knew about caring for an infant.

"Oh. Well. That's certainly a kind offer." Melba picked up a dishcloth and scrubbed at an invisible spot on the counter. "But I'm not sure that's such a good idea. Old Gene is upstairs, still trying to unclog the toilet in the big corner room."

Avery's face bloomed with heat. The clogged toilet had been her doing. But what were the odds she'd accidentally flush another sponge?

The baby goat let out a long, warbly bleat. *Meeeeeeehhhhhhh.*

Avery narrowed her gaze at its little ginger head. Was the animal taunting her now?

Melba cleared her throat. "Don't look so sad, dear. If you really want to help out around here, I'm sure we can figure something out."

"I do. Honestly, I'll try anything." Except maybe bottle-feeding the goat. That was a hard no.

Melba consulted the to-do list tacked to the refrigerator with a Fall Mountain magnet. "I need to make a run to the general store. Would you like to come along?"

Avery's heart gave a little leap. She was much better at shopping than cleaning toilets. She *excelled* at it, quite frankly. A closetful of Louboutins didn't lie. "Shopping? Yes, count me in."

"You're sure?" Melba gave her one of the gentle, sympathetic glances that had convinced Avery the older woman thought she was running from some kind of danger. "You haven't wanted to get out much."

Avery nodded. She was going to have to leave the boarding house at some point. Besides, the odds of running into Finn Crawford or his notorious father at the general store were zero. Not a chance. They weren't the sort of men who ran errands. They had employees for that kind of thing. How else would Finn have time to wine and dine every eligible woman in town?

"We're just going to the general store, right? Nowhere else? I have a…um…conference call later, so I shouldn't stay out too long." There was no conference call. At least not that Avery knew of. She hadn't checked in to the office for days. Another first.

If she called in, her father would surely pick up the phone. She'd been a daddy's girl all her life, through and through. That would change once he found out she was carrying Finn's baby. Oscar Ellington would rather she have a child with the devil himself.

"Straight to the general store and back." Melba made a cross-my-heart gesture with her fingertips over the pinafore of her apron.

"Super! I'll run upstairs and change." Avery beamed and scurried up to her corner room on the third floor of the rambling mansion.

Along the way, she heard Old Gene cursing at the clogged toilet, and she winced. The wincing continued as she tried—and failed—to find something presentable that she could still manage to zip or button at the waist.

It was no use—she was going to have to stick with her yoga pants and slip into the oversize light blue button-down shirt she'd borrowed from Old Gene. Lovely. If by some strange twist of fate Finn did turn up at the general store, he probably wouldn't even recognize her.

Any lingering worries she had about running into him were instantly kicked into high gear when she and Melba reached the redbrick building on the corner of

Main and Cedar Streets. Melba said something about the amber and gold autumnal window display, but Avery couldn't form a response. She was too busy gaping at the sign above the front door.

Crawford's General Store.

Did Finn's family *own* this place?

"Avery?" Melba rested gentle fingertips on her forearm. "Are you okay?"

"Yes. Yes, of course." She pasted on a smile. "I just noticed the name of the store—Crawford's. Does it belong to the family you mentioned earlier?"

"Heavens, no. The general store has been here for generations. The Montana Crawfords have lived in Rust Creek Falls for as long as I can remember. The new family is from Texas."

I'm aware.

Seriously, though. Finn's family was huge, and Rust Creek Falls was very small. Quaint and cozy, but rural in every way. Their addition to the population must mean that half the town had the same last name all of a sudden.

"I see," Avery said.

She tore her gaze away from the store's signage long enough to finally take in the window display, with its garland of oak and maple leaves and towering pile of pumpkins. They'd walked a grand total of two blocks, and already she'd seen enough hay bales, woven baskets and gourds to make her wonder if the entire town was drunk on pumpkin spice lattes.

Autumn wasn't such a big thing in Texas. The warm weather back home meant no apple picking, no fall foliage and definitely no need for snuggly oversize sweaters. It was kind of a shame, really.

But here in Montana, fall was ushered in with a lovely and luminous harvest moon, smoky breezes that smelled of wood fire and the crunch of leaves underfoot. Avery had never experienced anything like it.

"Maybe we should get some ingredients for caramel apples and make them for my great-granddaughter Bekkah's kindergarten class. I always bring some to the big Halloween dance, but the children might like an early taste." Melba glanced over her shoulder at Avery as she pushed through the general store's entrance. "What do you think?"

"I think that's a marvelous idea." Avery had never made caramel apples before, but there was a first time for everything.

Apples…autumn…*babies*.

She glanced past the dry goods section near the front of the store and spotted a rack of flannel shirts, quilted jackets and cable-knit cardigans. It wasn't exactly Neiman Marcus, but she was going to have to bite the bullet and invest in a few things that actually fit her changing body.

"Good morning, ladies. Is there anything I can help you with?" A slim woman with dark wavy hair, big brown eyes and a Crawford's General Store bib apron greeted them with a wide smile.

"Yes, please." Melba pulled a lengthy shopping list out of her handbag and plopped it onto the counter. Then she gestured toward Avery. "Nina, I'd like you to meet Avery. She's one of our boarders."

Nina offered Avery her hand. "Welcome to Rust Creek Falls. I'm Nina Crawford Traub."

Seriously. Did *everyone* in this town have the same last name?

"Hello." Avery shook Nina's hand, then dashed off to grab a few warm, roomy items of clothing while the other women tackled Melba's list of supplies.

By the time she returned, the counter was piled high. It looked like Melba was buying out the entire store.

"Wow." Avery's eye widened. She clutched her new flannels close to her chest, because there wasn't enough space to set them down. "This is..."

"Impressive," someone behind her said. There was a smile in his voice, a delicious drawl that Avery felt deep in the pit of her stomach. "Here's hoping you've left some stuff for the rest of us."

Don't turn around, her thoughts screamed. She knew that voice. It was as velvety smooth as hot buttered rum and oh, so familiar.

But just like the last time she'd been in the same room with the bearer of that soulful Texas accent, her body reacted before her brain could kick into gear. Sure enough, when she spun around, she found herself face-to-face with the very man she so desperately needed to speak to—Finn Crawford, the father-to-be, looking hotter than ever wearing a black Stetson and an utterly shocked expression on his handsome face.

Avery realized a second too late what was about to happen. Trouble.

So.

Very.

Much.

Trouble.

Avery?

Finn blinked. Hard.

No way... No possible way.

He was hallucinating. Or more likely, simply mistaken. After all, the brunette beauty who'd just spun around to stare at him might bear more than a passing resemblance to Avery Ellington, but she was hugging a stack of flannel shirts like it was some kind of security blanket. The Avery he knew wouldn't be caught dead in plaid flannel. She might even be allergic to it.

It had to be her, though. On some visceral level, he just *knew*. Plus he'd recognize those big doe eyes anywhere.

Avery Ellington. Warmth filled his chest. *Well, isn't this a fine surprise.*

Finn glanced at the older woman beside her—Melba… Melba *Strickland*, as in the owner of Strickland's Boarding House. So Old Gene's "darling young lady" that Viv Dalton wanted to set him up with was indeed the Avery he knew so well.

He burst out laughing.

Avery's soft brown eyes narrowed. She looked like she might be contemplating dropping the flannel and using her hands to strangle him. "What's so funny?"

"This." He gestured back and forth between Avery and Melba. "I'm not sure you're aware, but an hour or so ago, we were almost set up on a blind date."

"I might have heard something about that," Avery said, clearly failing to find the humor in the situation.

She seemed a little rattled. If Finn didn't know better, he would have thought she was unhappy to run into him. But that couldn't be right. The last time they'd seen one another had been immensely pleasurable.

For both of them.

Finn was certain of it. Plus, they'd parted on good terms.

"It's incredibly good to see you. What on earth are you doing in Rust Creek Falls?" He arched a brow. She was awfully far away from her daddy's ranch in Texas.

Melba interjected before Avery could respond, "Avery is a guest at the boarding house."

Finn nodded, even though they'd already covered Avery's local living arrangements. It still didn't explain what she was doing clear across the country from home.

He swiveled his gaze back to Avery. She looked beautiful, but different somehow. He couldn't quite put his finger on what had changed. Maybe it was the casual clothes or her wind-tossed hair, but her usual cool elegance had been replaced with a warmth that made him acutely aware of his own heartbeat all of a sudden.

"How's the little one?" he said with a smile.

"Um." Avery blinked like an owl. "How did you—"

Finn shrugged. "Everyone in town is talking about it. There's nothing quite as cute as a baby goat."

"The goat. Right." Avery swallowed, and he traced the movement up and down the graceful column of her throat.

Was it his imagination, or did she seem nervous?

"The goat's cute, but she's a handful. I don't know what Old Gene was thinking." Melba rolled her eyes. "She has to be bottle-fed every four to five hours, round the clock. It's almost like having a real baby again, but maybe a little less noisy."

Avery turned toward Melba with an incredulous stare. "*Less* noisy?"

Melba shrugged. "Sure. You know how babies are."

Avery shifted from one foot to the other as she glanced at Finn and then quickly looked away.

Melba's eyes narrowed. "How exactly do you two know each other?"

Why did the question feel like a test of some sort?

Finn gave her an easy smile. He had nothing to hide. "Avery and I are both in the beef business."

"Really?" Melba looked him and up down.

"Absolutely. Our paths used to cross every so often, but we haven't bumped into each other since my family relocated to Montana." A pity, really. "I'd love to take you out while you're in town, Avery."

She bit the swell of her lush bottom lip. "Oh…um, well…"

Not exactly the reaction he was going for. Avery looked as scared as a rabbit, and Melba was once again scrutinizing him as if he were giving off serial killer vibes.

Was he missing something?

His thoughts drifted back to the night they'd spent together in Oklahoma City. It didn't take much effort. The entire encounter was seared in his memory—every perfect, porcelain inch of Avery's skin, every tender brush of her lips.

They'd been in town for a gala dinner of cattle executives, and Finn would be lying if he'd said he hadn't been hoping to run into her. Through their overlapping business connections and a handful of mutual friends, Finn and Avery had been moving in the same orbit for quite a few years. He'd wanted her for every single one of them. How could he not? She was lovely. And smart, too. It took a special kind of woman to hold her own as the vice president of a major company in a business dominated by men. Finn considered himself a Southern gentleman, but that wasn't true of everyone in the beef business. Avery had run into her fair share of chauvinists and good old boys, but she never failed to rise above their nonsense with her head held high.

As much as she fascinated him, he'd respected her too much to make a real move. Their interactions had been limited to a low-key flirtation that he found immensely enjoyable, if somewhat torturous.

But the night in Oklahoma had been different. June in the Sooner State was always a nightmare of blazing heat and suffocating humidity, but that particular weekend had been especially brutal. A heat wave swept through the area, causing widespread power outages as the temperature soared. The gala's luxury hotel was plunged into darkness. Even after they got the generator up and running, the crystal chandeliers were barely illuminated, and heady, scented candles were scattered over every available surface.

He remembered Avery saying something about the animosity between their families, and true, his father had never uttered a kind word about Oscar Ellington. Quite the opposite, actually. There was definitely bad blood between the Crawford and Ellington patriarchs. But Finn and Avery had always managed to get along. And something about the darkness made their little flirtation seem not so low-key anymore, so over laugher and dry martinis at the bar, they'd agreed to set aside any familial difficulty.

She'd looked so damned beautiful in the candlelight, all soft curves and wide, luminous eyes. He'd taken a chance and leaned in…

He swallowed hard at the memory of what came next. It had been like something out of a dream. A perfect night—so perfect he hadn't taken another woman to bed since, despite his popularity in Montana. And now Avery was right here, less than an arm's length away, when he'd thought he'd never see her again.

"Please," he said. "Dinner, or even just coffee? For old times' sake."

He'd been neck-deep in women for the past three months, and now he was begging for an hour of Avery Ellington's time. Wonderful.

Melba cut in again before she could give him an answer. "Look at the time! Sorry to interrupt, but we simply must be going. Avery, how could you let me forget? We have to stop over at the Dalton Law Office to pick up those papers for Gene."

Avery's expression went blank. "What papers?"

"Those very important papers. You know the ones." Melba took the flannel shirts from Avery and handed them to Nina, who shoved them into a bag.

Avery crossed her arms, uncrossed them and crossed them again. Finn's gaze snagged on her oversize blue button-down. Was that a *man's* shirt she was wearing?

His jaw clenched. They hadn't even spoken since that simmering night in June, but Finn didn't like the thought of her with another man. Not one bit.

Overreacting much? It was one night, not an actual relationship. Maybe he wasn't such a fine Southern gentleman, after all.

"Come on, now. We don't want to keep Ben Dalton waiting." Melba shoved one of her five shopping bags at Avery and then linked elbows with her.

"Right. Of course we don't." Avery glanced at him one last time as Melba practically dragged her out of the store. "It was good seeing you, Finn. Goodbye."

He stared after them, wondering what in the hell had just happened.

"Can I help you find anything, Mr. Crawford?" Nina said from behind the counter.

Finn dragged his gaze away from the scene beyond the shop window and Avery's chocolate-hued hair, whipping around her angelic face in the wind like a dark halo.

He smiled, but his heart wasn't in it. "No, thank you."

For some strange reason, he almost felt like he'd already found what he needed. And now he'd just watched her walk away.

Again.

"Where are we going, exactly?" Avery gripped her shopping bag until her knuckles turned white and did her best to resist the overwhelming urge to glance over her shoulder for another glimpse of the general store.

Of Finn.

She almost wanted to believe she'd imagined their entire awkward encounter just now. Since the moment she'd first spotted the two tiny pink lines on the drugstore pregnancy test she'd taken in her posh executive washroom at Ellington Meats, she'd tried to imagine what she'd say to Finn the next time she saw him. Somehow she always imagined she'd be able to utter more than two stuttered words.

Had she managed to string a whole sentence together at all? Nope, she was pretty sure she hadn't. So much for being a strong, independent woman and facing the situation head-on.

"We're not going anywhere, dear. I thought you were going to faint when you saw Finn Crawford. I made something up to get you out of there." Melba gave her hand a comforting pat.

So her panic had been that obvious? Fabulous.

"Oh, thank you. But I was surprised, that's all." Shocked to her core was more like it.

Which was really kind of ridiculous, since the whole reason she'd come to Rust Creek Falls was to tell him about the baby. Get in, drop the baby bomb and get out. That had been the plan. It was just so much harder than she'd imagined. And now here she was, a couple weeks later, still secretly pregnant.

"Finn is an old friend." She stared straight ahead as they walked back to the boarding house. What had just transpired at the general store was a minor setback, not a total disaster. It's not like she could have told him she was pregnant right then and there.

Hey, so great to see you. FYI, I'm having your baby, and I'm planning to raise it on my own. Just wanted to let you know. I've got to pay for my pile of flannel now. Have a nice life.

Beside her, Melba snorted. "Well. He seems to have a lot of friends, if you know what I mean."

Avery's steps slowed as her heart pounded hard in her chest. "I don't, actually."

"It seems pretty obvious that you aren't ready to jump into a relationship. In any event, from what I've heard, Finn Crawford wouldn't be a great candidate."

Avery concentrated hard on putting one foot in front of the other as she turned Melba's words over in her mind. She was almost afraid to ask for more information, but she had to, didn't she? If the father of her baby was an ax murderer or something, that seemed like vital information to have. "Melba, what exactly have you heard?"

The older woman shook her head. "Don't get me wrong. He's a right charming fellow—possibly *too* charming. He's dated practically everyone in Rust Creek Falls since his family moved to town. It's sweet that he asked you to dinner, but Finn isn't right for a nice girl like you."

A nice girl like you.

What on earth would Melba think if she knew the real story?

Avery took a deep breath. The air smelled like cinnamon and nutmeg, courtesy of the decorative cinnamon brooms so many of the local business included in the fall pumpkin displays decorating the sidewalk. But the cozy atmosphere couldn't get her mind off a troubling truth—Finn might not be a serial killer, but apparently, he was a serial *flirt*. Somehow she didn't think a baby would fit neatly into a carefree lifestyle like the one Melba had just described.

But that was fine. More than fine, really. She didn't need Finn's help. If she could run the business division of a Fortune 500 company, she could certainly raise a baby. Her father would blow a gasket once he found out his first grandchild was going to be a Crawford, but he'd get over it. Having Finn out of the picture might even make things easier, where the whole family feud matter was concerned.

She obviously needed to let Finn know it was happening, though. That just seemed like the right thing to do. His reputation around Rust Creek Falls didn't change a thing. It wasn't as if she'd thought she could actually build a life with the man.

Still, the fact that he'd been acting as if Montana was the set of *Bachelor in Paradise* while she was battling morning sickness and freaking out about starting a family with the son of her father's sworn enemy stung a little bit.

Who am I kidding? Avery climbed the steps of Strickland's Boarding House alongside Melba and thought about all the nights she'd spent in this house, secretly wishing Finn would call or text out of the blue so she'd feel less awkward about their situation. Less lonely.

It stings a lot.

Chapter Three

"Mr. Crawford." Melba Strickland stood on the front steps of her big purple house and looked Finn up and down. "This is a surprise."

Was it?

Finn got the feeling she wasn't shocked to see him in the least. The furrow in her brow told him she wasn't pleased about his impromptu visit, either.

"Good morning, Mrs. Strickland." He tipped his hat and smiled, but her frown only deepened.

Once Finn had recovered from the shock of running into Avery at the general store the day before, he'd realized she'd never given his invitation a straight answer. Granted, she hadn't exactly jumped for joy when he'd told her he wanted to take her out while she was in town, but she hadn't turned him down, either. Melba hadn't given her a chance.

After he'd finally collected what he needed at the store, he'd returned to the Ambling A and spent the afternoon making repairs to the ranch's barbed-wire fence. One of the things Finn liked best about Montana was its vast and sweeping sky. He'd always loved the deep blue of the heavens in Texas, but here it almost felt like the sky was stacked on top of itself like a layered cake. A man could do a lot of thinking under a sky like that, and while he'd pounded new fence posts into the rich red earth, he'd managed to convince himself things with Avery hadn't been as awkward as he'd imagined. Old Gene probably had papers waiting to be picked up at the Dalton Law Office, just like Melba said. There was no legitimate reason why Avery should be trying to avoid him.

Now, in the fresh light of day, he wasn't so sure. Melba was definitely giving him the side-eye as he shifted his weight from one foot to the other and tried to see past her to the inside of the boarding house.

Was she even going to let him in?

"I stopped by to see Avery." He nodded toward the bouquet in his hand—sunflowers and velvety wine-colored roses tied with a smooth satin ribbon. "And to give her these."

Melba glanced at the flowers. Her resistance wavered, ever so slightly.

"I'll have to see if Avery is available." She held up a hand. "Wait here."

"Yes, ma'am." He winced as she shut the door in his face.

Finn felt like a teenager again, trying to get permission to take a pretty girl to the school dance. Even back then, he wasn't sure he'd ever run into a protective parent as steadfast as Melba Strickland.

At long last, the door swung open to reveal Avery with her thick brunette waves piled on top of her head and her lips painted red, just like she'd looked that fateful night in Oklahoma. But instead of her usual business attire, she was wearing faded jeans and an oversize cable-knit sweater that slipped off one shoulder as she gripped the doorknob. Finn's attention snagged briefly on the flash of her smooth, bare skin, and when he met her gaze again, her mouth curved into a bashful smile.

"Finn Crawford, whatever are you doing here?" She tilted her head, and a lock of hair curled against her exposed collarbone.

It took every ounce of Finn's willpower not to reach out and wind it around his fingertips. "Shouldn't I be asking you that question?"

What *was* she doing in Montana…in Rust Creek Falls, of all places?

"I had business nearby, and since I was a bit intrigued by the charming town you'd told me all about, I thought I'd check it out while I was in the area." That's right—the last time they'd seen each other, he'd told her all about the plans to relocate the ranch. "It seemed like a nice place to escape for a few days."

Finn nodded, even though her answer raised more questions than it answered, such as what exactly did she need to escape from?

"I actually thought about looking you up, but I wasn't sure if I should," she said.

He arched a brow. "Why not?"

Avery took a deep breath, and for a long, loaded moment, the space between them felt swollen with meaning. But then she just bit her lip and shrugged.

"Are those for me?" She smiled at the bouquet in his hand.

A wave of pleasure surged through him. Whatever her reason for being here, it was great to see her again. "They sure are."

"How very gentlemanly of you. Thank you." She took the flowers and held them close to her chest. Her soft brown eyes seemed lovelier than ever, mirroring the rich, dark centers of the sunflowers. "Do you want to come in while I put these in some water?"

She gestured toward the interior of the boarding house, which was the last place Finn wanted to be while Melba was around.

"Actually, since you seem so interested in the area, why don't I show you around town for a bit? I can even give you a tour of the ranch if you like."

"A tour of the ranch," she echoed. The flowers in her grip trembled. "*Your* ranch?"

Finn paused, remembering what she'd told him in Oklahoma about the supposed feud between their families. Once upon a time, Oscar Ellington and Maximilian Crawford had been friends. Best friends, according to Avery's father. They'd roomed together in college, both majoring in agriculture and ranch management. After graduation, they'd planned to go into business together, but at the last minute, Finn's father had changed his mind. He pulled out of the deal, and the friendship came to its tumultuous end.

"Sure," Finn said. He and Avery weren't their parents. He saw no reason why he couldn't take her to the Ambling A and walk the land with her, show her how the fall colors made the mountainside look as if it were aflame.

Although, if Oscar and Maximilian had turned their youthful dreams into a reality, the ranch wouldn't be his. It would be theirs—his and Avery's both.

Imagine that, he thought. *Being tied to Avery Ellington for life.*

He could think of worse fates.

But that would never happen. Ever. He wasn't even sure why he was entertaining the notion, other than the fact that his dad and Viv Dalton were dead set on putting an end to his independence.

"All right, then," Avery said, but her smile turned bittersweet. "Let's go."

Copper and gold leaves crunched beneath Avery's feet as she and Finn walked from his truck to the grand log cabin overlooking acres and acres of ranch land and glittering sunlit pastures where horses flicked their tails and grazed on shimmering emerald grass.

Calling it a cabin was a bit of a stretch. It looked more like a mansion made of Lincoln Logs, surrounded by a sprawling patio fashioned from artistically arranged river stones. The Rocky Mountains loomed in the background, rugged and golden. Enemy territory was quite lovely, it seemed.

Finn slipped his hand onto the small of her back as he led her toward the main house, and she tried her best to relax. An impossible task, considering that her father would probably disown her if he had any idea where she was right now. Finding out about the baby was going to kill him.

But she couldn't worry about that now. First, she had

to figure out how to tell Finn, and that seemed more difficult than ever now that this little outing was beginning to feel like a date.

Does he have to be so charming?

It was the flowers—they'd completely thrown her off her game. Which was pathetic, considering how active Finn's Montana social life had become. He probably got a bulk discount at the nearest florist.

"This place is gorgeous," she said. "Do all your brothers live out here?"

Finn nodded. "Logan, Knox and Hunter have cottages on the property. Xander and his family just moved into their own ranch house in town. Wilder and I live in the main house with my dad."

His dad.

So Maximilian Crawford was *here* somewhere. Great.

"You look a million miles away all of a sudden." Finn paused on the threshold to study her. "Everything okay?"

No, nothing was okay. She felt huge and overly emotional, and he was still the same ridiculously handsome man, perfectly dashing in all his clueless daddy-to-be glory.

"Actually..." Her mouth went dry. She couldn't swallow, much less form the words she so desperately needed to say.

Tell him. Do it now.

"Yes?" He tilted his head, dark eyes glittering beneath the rim of his black Stetson.

Meeting his gaze felt impossible all of a sudden, so she glanced at his plain black T-shirt instead. But the way it hugged the solid wall of his chest was distracting to say the least.

"I, um…" She let out a lungful of air.

"You're beautiful, that's what you are. A sight for sore eyes. Do you have any idea how glad I am to see you?" Finn reached up and ran his hand along her jaw, caressing her cheek with the pad of his thumb.

It took every ounce of Avery's willpower not to lean into his touch and purr like a kitten. Her body was more than ready to just go with the flow, but her thoughts were screaming.

Tell him, you coward!

"I'm relieved to hear you say that." Butterflies took flight deep in Avery's belly—or maybe it was their baby doing backflips at the sound of its daddy's voice. She swallowed hard. "Because…"

Then all of a sudden, the front door swung open and she was rendered utterly speechless by the sight of her father's mortal enemy standing on the threshold with an enormous orange pumpkin tucked under one arm.

She recognized him in an instant. His picture appeared every year in the Crawford Meats annual report, and he looked exactly the same as his slick corporate portrait. Same deep tan and lined face, same devil-may-care expression.

Maximilian Crawford stared at her for a surprised beat. Then he glanced back and forth between her and Finn until his eyes narrowed into slits. "Well, well. Howdy, you two."

"Dad," Finn said. There was a hint of a warning in his voice, but Maximilian seemed to ignore it.

"Aren't you going to tell me what you're doing keeping company with Avery Ellington?" The older man smiled, but it didn't quite reach his eyes.

Maximilian Crawford had just smiled at her. She

was surprised lightning didn't strike her on the spot. If her father were dead, he'd be spinning in his grave.

"Avery's just here for a friendly visit." Finn's hand moved to the small of her back again, and a shiver snaked its way up her spine. "I'm not sure you two have officially met. Avery, meet my dad, Maximilian."

"Hello, sir." She offered her hand.

He gave it a shake, but instead of letting go, he kept her hand clasped in his. "You're Oscar's little girl."

He was going there. *Okaaaay.*

"One and the same," she said, reminding herself that this man wasn't just her father's nemesis. He was also the grandfather of her unborn child.

"Right." He gave her hand a light squeeze and then finally released it. "I'm not sure if your daddy ever mentioned me, but he and I go way back."

Avery nodded. "I'm aware."

She shot a quick glance at Finn. The night they'd slept together in Oklahoma, he didn't seem to care much about any animosity between their families, but she'd wondered if he'd simply been downplaying things in order to avoid any awkwardness between them.

Not that she'd cared. She'd been more than ready to forget about anything that got in the way of their ongoing flirtation. Besides, they'd been miles away from Dallas. Just like the famous saying—what happens in Oklahoma stays in Oklahoma.

Unless it results in an accidental pregnancy.

"Interesting man, your father." Maximilian's expression turned vaguely nostalgic. "We were roommates back in the day. Almost went into business together. Truth be told, I occasionally miss those times."

Finn sneaked Avery a reassuring grin as his father's attitude softened somewhat.

"How's he doing? And your mom?" Maximilian shifted his pumpkin from one arm to the other. "Good, I hope."

Avery nodded. "They're great."

For now, anyway. Once she started showing, all bets were off.

"Avery's in town for a few days, so I thought I'd show her around a little bit." Finn eyed the pumpkin. "Tell me you're not on the way out here to try to carve that thing into a jack-o'-lantern."

"It's October. Of course that's what I'm going to do."

"Dad, this isn't Dallas. Halloween isn't for a few weeks. If you leave a carved pumpkin outside, it's going to get eaten up long before the thirty-first. The coyotes will probably get it before sunup." Finn shrugged. "If the elk don't get to it first."

"Fine. I'll take it inside after it's done. I've got five more to carve after this one. We can line them up by the fireplace. I just thought the place could use some holiday flair." Maximilian grinned. "Especially since we're welcoming a new little one to the family."

Avery coughed, and both men turned to look at her. "Excuse me. Little one?"

They couldn't possibly know. Could they?

"My brother Logan is a new stepdad. He and his wife have a nine-month-old little girl, and my father suddenly wants us to believe he's transformed from a cattle baron into a doting grandfather." Finn narrowed his gaze at his dad.

"Oh." This seemed promising. It almost made her wish she planned on raising the baby closer to Montana, but that would be insane. She had a job back in Dallas. A family. A life. "How sweet."

Finn held out his hands to his father. "Why don't you leave the pumpkin carving to us? Manual labor of any kind isn't exactly your strong suit."

Maximilian glanced at Avery and lifted a brow. "You're willing to stick around long enough to help Finn with my mini pumpkin patch?"

Avery couldn't help but smile. She wasn't naive enough to believe Maximilian was just a harmless grandpa. He was a far more complicated man than that. On more than one occasion, she'd heard Finn refer to him as manipulative.

Even so, she had a difficult time reconciling the man standing in front of her—the one who wanted to carve half a dozen jack-o'-lanterns for his new baby granddaughter's first Halloween—with the backstabbing monster her father had been describing to her for as long as she could remember.

"I think that can be arranged," she said.

She still planned to tell Finn about the baby today. Of course she did. But what different could a few more hours make?

"I like her," Maximilian said as he handed the pumpkin over to Finn and slapped him hard on the back. "She seems like a keeper, son."

What on earth was she doing here?

A keeper.

Nope. No way, no how. She could have a dozen babies with Finn, but she'd never, ever be a Crawford—not if her daddy had anything to do with it.

Avery set down her paring knife and wiped her hands on a dish towel so she could inspect the pumpkin she'd been attempting to carve. Its triangle-shaped eyes were uneven, and its wide, toothy grin was definitely lopsided. Overall, though, it was a decent effort.

Or at least she though it was until she took a closer look at what Finn had managed to produce in the same amount of time.

"Wait a minute." She frowned at twin jack-o'-lanterns on the table in front of him. "When did you start on the second one?"

He glanced at her pumpkin and stifled a grin. "Somewhere around the time you decided to give yours a square nose."

She swatted at him with the dish towel. The nose had started out as a triangle—she wasn't quite sure how it had ended up as a square.

Finn laughed, ducking out of the way. He managed to catch the towel and snatch it away from her before it made contact with his head. His grin was triumphant, but it softened as he met her gaze.

"You've got a little something." He gestured toward the side of his face. "Right there."

Shocker. Avery wouldn't have been surprised to discover she was covered head to toe in pumpkin guts. The jack-o'-lantern struggle had been very real.

She wiped her cheek, and Finn shook his head, laughter dancing in his eyes.

"I just made it worse, didn't I?" she said, looking down at her orange hands.

"Afraid so. Here, let me." He cupped her face with irritatingly clean fingertips and dabbed at her cheek with the towel.

It was a perfectly innocent gesture. Sweet, really. But Avery's heart felt like it was going to pound right out of her chest, and she had the completely inappropriate urge to kiss him as his gaze collided with hers.

She cleared her throat and backed away. She blamed pregnancy hormones…and the insanely gorgeous surroundings. Finn had set up their pumpkin-carving station on one of the log mansion's covered porches. It had a lovely, unobstructed view of the mountains, plus an enormous outdoor fireplace crafted from stone with a weathered wooden mantel. Any woman would have melted under the circumstances.

Avery kept having to remind herself that half the female population of Rust Creek Falls likely already had.

"You're shockingly good at this." She arched a brow at his two perfectly carved pumpkins in an effort to get her thoughts—and sensitive libido—back under control. "Do you have a degree in festive fall decorating I don't know about?"

"No, but I suppose it's fair to say there are indeed things you don't know about me. After all, our interactions have been pretty limited to business gatherings." Avery waited for Finn to crack a joke about their night together being the exception, but he didn't.

She wasn't altogether sure why that made her happy, but it did. "True."

He seemed different here than he'd been back in Dallas, and it was more than just a switch from tailored business suits to worn jeans and cowboy boots.

"So you like it here in Montana?" she asked.

"I do." Finn nodded and stared thoughtfully at the horizon, where a mist had gathered at the base of the mountain, creating a swirl of smoky autumn colors. "Life is different here. Richer, somehow. I always liked spending time on our ranch back in Texas, but somehow

I never got out there much. I spent more time in boardrooms than I did with the herd. Does that make sense?"

Her face grew warm as he glanced at her. "It does."

Avery couldn't remember the last time she'd been to her own family ranch, much less spent any time with the herd. She'd spent more hours with Excel spreadsheets than she ever had with actual cattle.

Finn's gaze narrowed, and as if he could see straight inside her head, he said, "When was the last time you hand-fed a cow?"

Laughter bubbled up her throat. "Seriously? Never."

"Never?" He clutched his chest. "You're killing me, Princess."

Princess.

She usually hated it when he called her that, but she decided to ignore Finn's pet name for her for the time being, mainly because it sort of fit, as much as she was loath to admit it.

He stood and offered her his hand. "Come on."

She placed her hand in his as if it were the most natural thing in the world, and he hauled her to her feet. "Where are we going?"

"You'll see." He winked, and it seemed to float right through her on butterfly wings. "You trust me, don't you, Princess?"

That was a loaded question if she'd ever heard one. "Should I?"

He gave her hand a squeeze in lieu of an actual answer, then shot her a lazy grin and tugged her in the direction of the barn.

Right. That's what I thought.

Of course she couldn't trust him. He might seem at home here on the farm in a way that made her think there was more to Finn Crawford than met the eye, but just because a man could carve a jack-o'-lantern and went all soft around the edges when he talked about animals didn't mean he was ready for a family.

Avery slipped her hand from his and crossed her arms. "What about the pumpkins? Won't coyotes come and devour them if we leave?"

Her mind had snagged on Finn's casual reference to coyotes earlier, probably because the biggest threat to jack-o'-lanterns in her Dallas neighborhood were mischievous teens.

He glanced over her shoulder toward the porch, where Maximilian had begun cleaning up their mess and hauling the pumpkins inside.

Avery rolled her eyes. "And you call *me* a princess."

He flashed a grin. "Touché."

He took hold of her hand again, and she let him, because his rakish smile and down-home charm were getting to her. And honestly, considering she was pregnant with the man's baby, it was a little late to be worried about hand-holding.

The barn was cool and sweet-smelling, like hay and sunshine. It reminded Avery of the horseback riding lessons she'd had as a little girl. She'd ridden English, of course. No rodeos or trail rides for the daughter of Oscar Ellington. Her childhood and teen years had been about posh country club horse shows and debutante balls.

Her thoughts snagged briefly on what might be in store for her unborn child. If she raised the baby by herself, in Dallas, she'd be setting her son or daughter up for the same type of upbringing she'd had. Her father would see to it.

But was that really what Avery wanted?

She wasn't so sure, and suddenly she couldn't seem to focus on the many difficult decisions she needed to address. She couldn't seem to focus on *anything* except Finn's cocky, lopsided grin and the cozy hayloft in the barn's shady rafters. Wouldn't it be nice to be kissed in a place like that?

For the last time, calm down, pregnancy hormones!

"It's really lovely here," she said, glancing around the sun-dappled space. Horses poked their heads over the tops of stable doors and whinnied as they walked past.

"It's nice. We've got a lot more space than we had in Texas."

"So your move here is permanent, then." She held her breath. What was she saying?

Of course it was permanent. This was Finn's new home.

"Oh, yeah." He nodded and guided her toward the corner of the barn, where a few barrels were lined up along the wall.

Avery wondered how much of his enthusiasm for Rust Creek Falls had to do with his overactive dating life…and just how many women he'd brought out to the Ambling A for this quaint little tour. On second thought, maybe she was better off without that information.

"Here we go." Finn reached into one of the barrels and pulled out a few ears of colorful calico corn—sapphire blues, deep burgundies and ruby reds. It almost looked like he was holding a handful of gemstones.

He offered her a few ears, and she took them. "Pretty. Are we adding a little harvest decor to the jack-o'-lantern display for your niece?"

"No, my dad donated a big batch of harvest corn to the town for the autumn festival, and we've got a few barrels left over. So now what you've got there is a treat for the cattle."

She glanced down at the corn and back up at Finn. He'd been dead serious about spending hands-on time with the herd. "You mean cow treats are a thing?"

"Everyone deserves a little something special now and then, don't you think?" His eyes gleamed.

Avery was a firm believer in this sentiment. It was precisely how she ended up with her most recent Louis Vuitton handbag. It's also how she'd ended up in bed with Finn Crawford on her last business trip.

She blinked up at him and prayed he couldn't read her mind. "Absolutely."

Finn couldn't shake the feeling that there was something different about Avery. When he couldn't figure out exactly what it was, he realized the difference wasn't just one thing. *Everything* about her seemed different somehow.

Then again, he'd never seen her this way before. Finn knew the proper, corporate Avery—Princess Avery, as he liked to call her, much to her irritation. He'd never seen the coppery highlights that fresh sunshine brought out in her tumbling waves of hair. He'd certainly never wrapped his arms around her from behind and held her close in a pasture while she tried to feed an overeager cow an ear of calico corn.

Every time the Hereford's big head got close to her hand, she pulled it back and squealed. The poor confused cow glanced back and forth between Avery and Finn and then stared longingly at the ear of corn.

"Cows seems significantly bigger up close," Avery said.

"This one's harmless, I promise. She's a gentle giant,

wouldn't hurt a fly." He took hold of Avery's hand and guided the corn toward the cow's mouth.

The Hereford snorted in gratitude and wrapped her wide tongue around the corncob.

"Ahh! I'm doing it." Avery laughed, and the cow's ears swiveled to and fro.

The corn was gone within a matter of minutes, and Avery beamed at Finn over her shoulder. "Can I give her another one?"

"Sure." He handed her another ear of the colorful corn.

Avery fed it to the cow all on her own this time, giggling in delight when the animal made happy slurping sounds.

"This is the most hands-on I've ever gotten with cattle." She turned in his arms so she was facing him and shot him a conciliatory look. "You were right. It gives me a whole new appreciation for what we do."

Finn had been a rancher all his life, and he'd never seen anyone take such sheer delight in feeding cattle before. It was a shame Avery's father had never taken the time to teach her the ins and outs of hands-on ranch management in addition to crunching numbers and networking. But he wasn't about to bring up Oscar Ellington and spoil the mood. The man hated him, apparently, although Finn probably never would have known as much if Avery hadn't mentioned it over martinis in the darkened bar in Oklahoma.

"Then it's a good thing I dragged you away from the boarding house," he said.

Avery's hands found their way to his chest, and their eyes met for a beat until she seemed to realize she was touching him.

"Right, but I should probably be getting back." She took a backward step and collided with the cow.

She let out a loud moo, and Avery jumped back into his arms.

He couldn't help but laugh. "Relax, Princess. Everything's fine."

"It's really not." She shook her head, but at the same time melted into him. And this time, when her hands landed on his pecs, they stayed.

Finn could feel her heart beating hard against his chest, and her eyes grew dark…dreamy…as her lips parted ever so slightly.

He'd never wanted to kiss a woman more in his life, but he was still a little thrown by her words.

It's really not.

He had no clue what she meant. Everything certainly seemed fine. She felt so good in his arms. So soft. So warm. And he especially liked the way she was suddenly focusing intently on his mouth.

But he wasn't about to kiss her if it wasn't what she wanted. He inhaled a ragged breath and cast her a questioning glance.

"Honestly, I should go." She lifted her arms and wound them around his neck.

"Avery." He half groaned her name.

If he couldn't kiss her, he was going to have to take her arms and unwind them himself. He wasn't going to last another minute with her pressed against him, looking up at him like she wanted to devour him. He was only human.

But just as his fingers slipped around her wrists, she rose up on her tiptoes and kissed him so hard that she nearly knocked him over. Her mouth was warm and ready, and before he fully grasped what was happening, her fingertips slid into his hair, knocking his Stetson to the ground.

Finn didn't give a damn about the hat. He didn't give a damn about much of anything except the woman in his arms and the way she was murmuring his name against his lips, as if they were suddenly right back in the middle of that surreal, sublime night in Oklahoma.

He'd been thinking about that night for four long months, convinced their paths would never cross again. And now here she was, as beautiful and maddening as ever.

He nipped softly at her bottom lip and she let out a breathy sigh, and somewhere in the back of his mind, he wondered again what exactly she was doing in Montana, so far off the beaten path. He wasn't altogether sure he bought her business trip explanation. No one had business this far out. He didn't dare ask, lest he ruin the moment.

But he didn't have to, because the moment came to an abrupt end, thanks to an earsplitting chorus of hungry moos.

Their eyes flew open, and Avery blinked, horrified. Whether she was more shaken by the sight of half a dozen cows suddenly surrounding them in the pasture or the fact that she'd thrown herself at him, he wasn't entirely sure. He hoped it was the former, but he wouldn't bet his life on it.

"I, um..." She bit her lip. "I'm sorry about that."

"Avery, talk to me. Tell me what's wrong."

One of the cows nudged her, and she shook her head. "Nothing. Nothing's wrong. I'm just... I'm sorry. I should really..."

"It's okay." He nodded, still thoroughly baffled but getting nowhere amid a sea of cattle and half-eaten harvest corn. "I'll take you home."

The look of relief on her face was almost enough to make him think he'd imagined the fact that she'd just kissed him silly. Not quite, though.

Not quite.

Chapter Four

"Tell me again why we're doing this?" Melba's gaze cut toward Avery as she slid one foot to rest alongside her opposite ankle in a wobbly modified version of tree pose. The baby goat bleated in her arms.

Avery had to give Melba credit. She was really being a good sport about the whole goat yoga thing.

"People pay good money to do this in the city. I promise," Avery said as she settled into her own tree pose.

Thanks in part to yoga with animals being all the rage on Instagram, her yoga studio in Dallas had held a special goat yoga fund-raiser after the most recent Texas hurricane and ended up raising thousands for storm relief. How a private fitness boutique in the luxury Highland Park neighborhood procured a dozen tiny goats for the day was a mystery Avery couldn't begin to fathom. But her life in Rust Creek Falls seemed to be teeming with farm animals.

Avery placed her hands in prayer position and closed her eyes. "Think of it as pet therapy and yoga all rolled into one. It's supposed to clear the mind and release loads of feel-good endorphins."

Plus Avery just needed the company. Since her visit to the Ambling A with Finn two days ago, she'd practically been a hermit. She'd shut herself up in her room, poking her head out only for meals and a few speed-yoga sessions, lest Finn turn up at the front door again.

She wasn't ready to see him—not after that kiss. Making out with the father of her baby before he even knew she was pregnant was definitely *not* part of the plan. Nor was making out with him afterward. Her mission was pretty straightforward: face her moral responsibility to tell Finn about the baby, then hightail it back to Dallas and get on with her life as a single-mom-to-be.

The plan involved zero kissing whatsoever.

The trouble was, when Finn dropped her off at the boarding house after she threw herself at him in the pasture, he'd asked if he could see her again and she'd said yes. How could she not? They still needed to have a very important conversation. But she needed some time to get her bearings first, and she definitely didn't need to go back to the Ambling A. It was far too cozy over there, with all the pumpkin carving and the cows munching on harvest corn. What would happen next time? A moonlit hayride?

No.

Because there wouldn't be a next time. She should have never set foot on Crawford property in the first place. Telling him about the pregnancy needed to take place on neutral territory. Someplace safe.

"Is your mind clear yet?" Avery cracked her eyes open to check on Melba.

The older woman gave her a blank look. The baby goat in her arms let out a warbly bleat, and Melba bit back a smile. "Afraid not, dear."

That made two of them.

"Melba!" someone called from inside the house, and before either of them could respond, the door flew open and Old Gene strode onto the porch.

He took in the yoga mats, then glanced back and forth between their tree poses. "What in the world is going on out here?"

"What does it look like?" Melba sniffed. "Avery is teaching me some of her fancy yoga moves."

"You're doing yoga?" He gaped at her as if she'd just sprouted another head. "With the goat?"

"Avery says it's a thing." Melba glanced at her for confirmation.

"Indeed it is." Avery nodded. "Very on trend."

"I'm old, but I'm not dead. I can still learn new things. Besides, you've been gone all morning. Someone had to watch the wee thing." Melba scratched the baby goat behind the ears. When she appeared to realize what she was doing, she stopped.

Her resistance was crumbling where the goat was concerned, much to Avery's amusement. Not that she was surprised. Melba was a natural caretaker. It was what made the boarding house such a nice place to stay.

Avery, however, was still avoiding any and all hands-on interaction with the tiny creature. She knew next to nothing the about farm animals, her recent cattle experience notwithstanding. The one thing she did know, though, was that it should probably have a name by now.

"Have you thought of what you want to call the poor goat yet?" she asked Old Gene.

His gaze darted to his wife. "I thought Melba might want to do the honors."

"Oh, no, you don't." She dumped the baby goat in Gene's arms, where it landed in a heap of tiny hooves, soft bleats and furry orange coat. "If I name her, that means we're keeping her. Nice try, but no."

Melba gave her eyes a mighty roll and huffed off in the direction of the kitchen.

Okay, then. Namaste.

Avery smiled to herself as she bent down to roll up the yoga mats. "Give it a few more days, Gene. I think the little kid is growing on her. Where were you off to this morning?"

Old Gene had been notably absent at breakfast. For once, Claire's homemade cinnamon rolls had lasted past 9:00 a.m. Avery had indulged in seconds, since she was eating for two.

"I was at a planning meeting for the upcoming autumn festival over at the high school, but then the delivery of hay for the hay maze arrived and needed unloading. The last time I tossed a hay bale around, I threw my back out. So I left that to the younger folks and scooted on home." He set the goat on the ground, and the animal teetered toward the grass beyond Avery's makeshift yoga area on the porch.

"That sounds like a wise choice," Avery said. The thought of Melba taking care of an incapacitated Old Gene on top of the boarding house and an orphaned goat was too unnerving to contemplate. "So is this autumn festival a big thing around here?"

Finn had mentioned the festival, and her curiosity was definitely piqued.

Old Gene nodded and crossed his arms as he watched the baby goat bounce around the yard. "Yes, ma'am. It certainly is."

"What's it like?"

"Let's see. The festival starts off with two weeks of fall-themed activities in the evenings and then ends with a Halloween party in the school gym. It's a big family event. The kids dress up in costumes, there are always a lot of Halloween-themed games and Melba brings her famous caramel apples. You'd love it."

Avery grinned.

She'd never been to a small-town festival before. And the last Halloween party she'd attended had been a stuffy masquerade ball at the country club. Adults only. The costumes had all been extravagant rentals and the guests dined on delicate hors d'oeuvres and cocktails. A quaint small-town Halloween did indeed sound lovely.

Old Gene dragged his gaze away from the goat and studied her for a moment. "You'll still be here in two weeks, right?"

"Oh." She straightened and hugged her yoga mat to her chest. "I'm not sure. It kind of depends..."

On how much longer I put off the inevitable.

"I doubt it," she added.

She'd already been away from the office far too long. Her parents thought she was off on a spa getaway with friends. That excuse would wear thin eventually—sooner rather than later.

Old Gene refocused his attention on the goat, and Avery noticed his shoulders sag a little bit. "That's too bad. Melba is going to worry about you when you're gone. She has a soft spot for you, you know."

Guilt nagged at Avery's conscience. She'd known for weeks that Melba suspected she was on the run from a bad relationship, and she'd done nothing to alleviate such worries. Letting her believe in some fictional ex-boyfriend seemed so much easier than trying to explain the truth.

"I know." An ache knotted in her throat.

She liked it here. She liked Melba and Old Gene. She even sort of liked the goat. She would have, anyway, if its very presence didn't remind her of her complete and total lack of maternal instincts. The real reason she'd yet to try to bottle-feed it was because she was afraid she'd mess everything up and the goat would reject her.

How sad was that?

"My wife wouldn't try yoga for just anyone, especially not with this troublemaker." Old Gene scooped the goat into his arms and stuck a foot out in front of him as if he were trying to kick an imaginary soccer ball. "What about me? Am I doing it right?"

Avery snorted with laughter. "You're nailing it, Gene."

"Who says you can't teach an old dog new tricks?" He flashed a triumphant smile and carried the goat inside.

Its little head rested on Old Gene's shoulder, and the animal fluttered its long eyelashes at Avery as they disappeared from view.

She wondered if the sentiment applied to herself, as well. She wasn't exactly old, but aside from the fact that she wasn't in a relationship with her baby's father, she was woefully unprepared for motherhood. She'd never once changed a diaper. As an only child, she'd never spent much time around children, either. She hadn't even babysat for extra money as a teenager. She hadn't needed to. Her parents had always been more than happy to give her everything she wanted, including a job.

There was more truth to Finn's nickname for her than she wanted to admit.

Princess.

She took a shaky inhale of crisp autumn air and tried to ignore the nagging feeling that her charmed existence was about to come to an abrupt end. Maximilian Crawford might have fond memories of her father, but the feeling definitely wasn't mutual. Oscar Ellington was going to hit the roof when he found out she'd slept with Finn.

Ready or not, life as Avery knew it was about to change.

Finn leaned against the vast kitchen counter in the main house of the Ambling A while he stared at the screen of his iPhone and frowned. Four missed calls showed on his display, and not one of them was Avery.

He sighed, put the phone down and then picked it back up again just in case.

Still nothing. Damn it.

He did his best to ignore the fact that he was acting like a lovesick teenager and jabbed at the power button of the high-end espresso machine his father had imported from Europe. You could take Maximilian Crawford out of the big city, but you couldn't take the big city out of Maximilian.

"There you are," the older man said as he strolled into view.

Speak of the devil. "Hello, Dad."

Finn flipped a switch, and dark, aromatic liquid began to fill his cup. Black, like his mood.

"Where have you been, son?" Maximilian jammed his hands on his hips. "Viv Dalton has been trying to get ahold of you all day."

Finn was well aware of the fact that the matchmaker/wedding planner had been trying to reach him. She'd been blowing his phone up all morning, hence the missed call notifications.

"I had meetings all day in Billings. I have a job, remember?" He sipped his coffee, then arched a brow at his father. "And contrary to whatever you've started to believe, it doesn't involve carrying on the family name."

That's what his five brothers were for.

Maximilian glared at Finn's phone, sitting quietly on the marble countertop. "You need to call her back. She's set up a date for you this evening."

Just as Finn suspected. Ordinarily, this bit of news would have taken the edge off his stormy mood. Now, not so much.

"No." Finn shook his head.

"What do you mean, no?" Maximilian looked at him as if he'd just sprouted two heads.

Finn didn't really blame him. He'd nearly surprised himself, as well. "I mean, no. I can't."

Can't was a stretch. *Won't* was more like it. After recently spending the day with Avery, he just didn't have it in him for another date with another total stranger. Frankly, the idea didn't sound appealing at all.

What the heck had gotten into him?

Avery's spur-of-the-moment kiss, that's what.

Finn cleared his throat and took another scalding gulp of coffee.

"Balderdash." Maximilian waved a dismissive hand. "Viv has been going the extra mile to line up these dates for you. Unless you have other plans, you'll go."

Much to his dismay, Finn had zero plans. Avery had agreed to see him again, but he'd been trying to give her some space, since she'd seemed so rattled by the kiss. He thought it best to let her contact him instead of the other way around.

He just hadn't bargained on it taking so long…or that waiting for her call would make him feel like an insecure kid hoping for an invitation to prom.

"I do have other plans, actually." He set down his coffee cup with a little too much force, picked up his phone and tucked it into his pocket as he strode toward the door.

"Since when?" a disbelieving Maximilian said to his back.

Since now.

"Finn." Avery wrapped her arms around her middle and glanced back and forth between the father of her baby and Old Gene, sitting across from one another at the big farm table in the kitchen of the boarding house. "I didn't realize you were here."

"I gave Melba a shout upstairs and asked her to send you down." Old Gene shrugged.

The baby goat was snuggled in his lap with its spindly legs tucked beneath itself. What must Finn think? He lived on that massive log cabin estate out at the Ambling A, and their kitchen looked like a scene out of *Green Acres*.

She blinked.

Their kitchen?

You don't actually live *here, remember. This is temporary.*

"Yes, you did holler for me to send Avery to the kitchen." Melba bustled into the room behind Avery and paused, hands on her sturdy hips. "But you didn't mention we had company."

Finn pushed back from the table and stood. "Hello, Mrs. Strickland." He set amused eyes on Avery. "Hi."

"Hi." Her face went warm, suddenly bashful to be interacting with Finn in front of the Stricklands, which was patently ridiculous. They weren't kids, after all.

But Melba and Old Gene were nurturing in a way that Avery's parents had never been. Not only was it making her think long and hard about what sort of mother she hoped to be, but it was also making her fall more in love with Rust Creek Falls every day.

Of course the fact that there was currently a handsome cowboy smiling at her didn't hurt, either.

"What brings you by, Mr. Crawford?" Melba, apparently the only woman in Montana impervious to Finn's charms, crossed her arms.

"I thought Avery might like to take a ride out to the maple syrup farm." He winked at Avery—just a quick, nearly imperceptible flutter of his lashes, but all the air in the room seemed to gather in her lungs. She was breathless all of a sudden. "If that's okay with you folks, of course."

Avery bit back a smile. He was asking Melba and Old Gene for permission to take her on a date, which was kind of adorable. Too adorable to resist, actually.

"Well, I don't know," Melba said.

"Don't be silly, dear." Old Gene stood. "It's fine. Avery would probably love it out there. It's so colorful this time of year."

The goat bleated its agreement. Melba, outnumbered, sighed.

"I'll go get changed." Avery pulled her T-shirt down in an effort to more fully cover her midsection. She was still wearing yoga pants, and chances were they showed off an entirely different body than the one Finn had seen naked a few months ago.

"It's a farm." Finn tilted his head and looked Avery up and down. "You're not planning on slipping into one of your pencil skirts, are you?"

She laughed a little too loud. Her days of fitting into a pencil skirt were over. For five months, minimum. "No, just something cozy."

Translation: something baggy enough to hide her rapidly expanding baby bump.

She slipped into one of her new flannel purchases, a soft pair of leggings and bouncy sneakers. Melba seemed a little less hostile when she returned to the kitchen. Finn must have really turned on the charm, because when they left for the maple syrup farm, Melba sent them off with a thermos of her special apple cider.

"The Stricklands really seem to enjoy having you around," Finn said as they passed the Welcome to Rust Creek Falls sign on the outskirts of town.

The smells of cinnamon and spice swirled in the cab of Finn's truck, wrapping around them like a plush blanket. Avery closed her eyes and took a deep inhale. "Mmm. Melba and Old Gene are the best, aren't they?"

"They are, but I'm not sure the feeling is mutual, especially where Melba is concerned."

"She's just a little protective, that's all." Avery nearly gasped at how colorful the trees looked as they moved deeper and deeper into the countryside and farther away from Rust Creek Falls.

Finn shot her a mischievous glance. "Do you think you need protecting from me, Princess?"

Avery thought about the warning Melba had given her about Finn after they'd bumped into him at the general store.

Finn isn't right for a nice girl like you.

She arched a brow. "You tell me. Do I?"

Finn responded with a wide grin that told her he definitely hadn't forgotten about the way she thrown herself at him in the pasture at the Ambling A. Maybe Melba had it wrong and he was the one who needed protecting.

Avery straightened in her seat. Finn could smile all he wanted. She intended to take this time together to have a serious discussion with him. There would be no more kissing. Not today, anyway.

Except there was.

Once again, Avery fell completely under the spell of Finn in his natural habitat. Why did he suddenly seem like he belonged on the pages of a hot cowboys calendar rather than in the boardrooms where she usually ran into him back in Texas?

The maple syrup farm was much quieter than she anticipated. She'd expected trees with sap buckets attached and the hum of boilers in the nearby sugarhouse. But as Finn explained, the sapping season usually ran from February until mid-April or so. The farms still had a good number of visitors during autumn, though, due to the spectacular fall colors of the sugar maple trees.

Avery could hardly believe her eyes. After they'd

stopped by the farm's quaint little gift shop and Avery purchased glass bottles of syrup in varying colors of amber, they went for a walk in the sugar bush. The deeper into the woods they wandered, the closer together the trees grew, until she and Finn were surrounded by nothing but blazing red. Crimson leaves floated through the air like radiant snowflakes, and when they came upon a tiny white chapel nestled far into the cluster of maples, Avery was completely and utterly enchanted.

That was her only explanation for what happened next. It was as if the beautiful surroundings had indeed made her fall under a magical spell, because when she looked at Finn in the dappled sunlight of the fiery woods, her canvas bag of maple syrup slipped from her hand and fell to the ground with a soft thud. She wrapped her arms around the father of her baby and kissed him, long and deep. She kissed him so hard that the force of it seemed to shake loose the leaves from the surrounding sugar maples, until at last she had to pull away to catch her breath.

What was happening to her? Why did she keep losing her head like this?

"I'm so sorry," she said, backing away against the solid trunk of a maple tree. Good. Maybe it would knock some sense into her. "I don't know why I keep doing that."

Finn gave her a tender smile that slowly built into a full-wattage grin. Avery's cheeks burned with heat, and she suspected her face had gone as red as the surrounding foliage.

But like the gentleman that he was, her Texas-businessman-turned-Montana-cowboy spared her the embarrassment of saying anything. He simply bent to pick up her discarded bag, then took her by the hand and walked her back down the forest trail, leaving the kiss behind.

Just another of their secrets.

Chapter Five

Finn returned to the Ambling A after taking Avery back to the boarding house to find his dad and his brother Hunter fully immersed in a craft project with Hunter's six-year-old daughter, Wren.

The two men looked woefully out of place in their ranch attire while doing something with paper plates full of paint. Finn wasn't entirely sure what they were trying to accomplish, but Wren seemed as pleased as punch, which he supposed was the objective of the messy affair.

He took it all in with bemused interest and cocked an eyebrow at his father. "This is a surprise. For some reason, I thought you had plans tonight with one of your lady friends."

It was a logical assumption. On any given Friday night, Maximilian typically had a date. Sometimes two.

When he wasn't preoccupied with meddling into his sons' love lives, of course.

"I do." Maximilian ruffled Wren's fair blond hair. "With this little lady right here."

Wren gigged and made jazz hands at Finn, her palms and fingers dripping orange paint onto the copies of the Rust Creek Falls *Gazette* that provided a protective covering for the table. "We're making handprint leaves, Uncle Finn. Do you want to make one, too?"

Large sheets of manila paper were scattered in front of her, decorated with yellow, orange and red handprints that had been fashioned into leaves with the help of stems and leafy veins drawn in brown magic marker.

"It looks like the three of you have got it covered." Finn eyed his brother. "Where on earth did you come up with this?"

Hunter shrugged. "Pinterest."

"Pinterest?" Finn bit back a smile. If anyone actually needed Viv Dalton's dating service, it was Hunter. Most definitely.

"What?" Hunter said, as if perusing Pinterest for kids' craft projects was something all of the Crawford brothers did on a daily basis.

"Nothing." Finn shook his head. It was actually really sweet how his brother had immersed himself into being both a father and mother to Wren. Not that he'd had much of a choice.

Still, it was pretty amusing seeing his rough-and-tumble brother and father sitting around doing arts and crafts on a Friday night. He was used to them doing things like roping calves and cutting hay, not finger-painting.

"I'm going up to bed. See you all in the morning."

Finn faked a yawn and headed toward the stairs, eager to shut himself in his room before Maximilian had a chance to question him about his whereabouts.

"Hold up there, son."

Too late.

"Where have you been off to tonight?" Maximilian frowned down at the mess of paint in front of him. Clearly he'd skipped the Pinterest tutorial. "The young woman Viv wanted to introduce you to called here a little while ago and said she hadn't heard from you."

Finn's jaw clenched shut tight. *Give it a rest, old man. I'm handling my own love life just fine these days.*

And since when had Viv started giving out his phone number?

"I was with Avery Ellington," he said.

There. Maybe if he threw Maximilian a bone, his father would leave him alone for once.

"Is that right?" Maximilian's eyebrows furrowed and then released. "Glad to hear it. The Ellington apple seems to have fallen quite far from the tree. You two make a fine couple."

"Right." Hunter let out a snort as he drew another stem onto one of Wren's handprint leaves. "As if Finn is actually serious about her."

Hunter's casual dismissal of Finn's feelings about Avery rubbed him the wrong way, although he wasn't entirely sure why. She was only in town temporarily, and as Finn himself had reiterated time and again, he wasn't looking for anything serious.

"He's seen her more than once. For your brother, that's serious," Maximilian said.

Hunter nodded. "Point taken."

Finn's chest grew tight. Why had he thought it was

ever a good idea to live under the same roof as his family? "Are you two enjoying yourselves?"

"I am." Wren wiggled in her chair.

"Yes. You are, sweetheart. And I'm glad." Finn narrowed his gaze at his father. "But you need to calm down. Avery and I are just casually seeing each other until she goes back to Texas. It doesn't even qualify as a relationship."

Right... That's why you can't stop thinking about her.

He shifted his weight from one foot to the other, suddenly acutely uncomfortable with the direction this conversation was headed.

"Would it be so awful if she stayed in Montana?" Maximilian pressed his palm into a paper plate full of yellow paint.

Finn couldn't help wishing he'd accidentally spill it down the front of his snap-button Western shirt. "I'm surprised you're pressing the issue. Aren't you and her father are supposed to be mortal enemies?"

"Ellington or not, Avery seems good for you." Maximilian waved a hand, sending yellow paint splatters flying, much to Wren's amusement. "Her daddy and I haven't spoken in years. Maybe all that mess is simply water under the bridge."

Finn somehow doubted Avery's dad saw it that way.

"Regardless, I'm not in a relationship with his daughter." Finn's head hurt all of a sudden. He sighed. "We're just..."

Words failed him.

What *were* they doing? Hell if he knew. Nor did he have any idea why he was still standing around trying to explain it to his meddling father and smart-ass brother.

"You're just what, exactly?" The twinkle in Maximilian's eyes was as brilliant as a three-carat diamond engagement ring from Tiffany.

"Never mind. I'm going to bed." Finn ignored the suggestive smirks aimed his way and headed to his suite.

He didn't have the first clue what he and Avery were doing. One minute she was throwing herself at him, and the next she was knocking her head into a tree. It should have been making him crazy. And it was…

But in a good way—a way that had him counting the minutes until he could see her again. The warmth of Avery's sultry mouth had suddenly become the last thing he thought about before he drifted off to sleep and his first memory upon waking. Because whatever was really going on between them, Finn liked it.

He liked it a whole heck of a lot.

The third time Finn showed up unannounced at Strickland's, Avery was ready.

Call it intuition, or chalk it up to wishful thinking—Avery greatly preferred to think of it as the former. Either way, when he showed up bright and early the morning following their trip to the maple syrup farm, no one was surprised. Not her, not Melba, not Old Gene.

Not even the baby goat. The tiny animal woke from her nap on her dog bed by the back door and kicked her little hooves as Melba escorted Finn into the kitchen.

"Look who's here," she said, wiping her hands on her apron. "Again."

Melba seemed to be doing her best to keep up her general dislike of Finn, but the sparkle in her eye told Avery he was wearing her down. The tote bag full of maple syrup in his hands probably didn't hurt.

"Who wants pancakes?" Finn said, winking at Avery.

The baby goat bleated, and Avery couldn't help but smile.

Melba narrowed her gaze at Finn. "Pancakes aren't on the menu this morning."

Claire had whipped up her famous ham biscuits, which were up for grabs in the dining room. Avery had already eaten one, but she wouldn't turn down pancakes with real maple syrup. Not when she was eating for two

"I thought I'd make them." Finn reached into his bag and extracted a box of organic pancake mix. "Pumpkin spice. Who's in?"

Had Finn Crawford just waltzed into Melba Strickland's home and announced he was going to cook? Oh, this was going to be good. Such a bold move was sure to either win her over or make her an enemy for life.

Old Gene's eyebrows shot clear to his hairline. Avery had to the bite the inside of her cheek to keep from laughing.

"What do you say, Mrs. Strickland?" Finn shot the older woman his most devastating bad-boy grin, and against all odds, it worked.

"Fine." She untied her apron and handed it to Finn. "If you insist. But you'll need to clean up after yourself. Claire and I won't abide a messy kitchen."

She paused a beat, then added, "And call me Melba."

"Yes, ma'am." Finn's grin widened as he tied the frilly apron around his waist.

He looked utterly ridiculous in his boots, jeans and Melba's lacy kitchen attire, but then again, Avery was still snug in her flannel pajamas.

"Come on, dear." Old Gene folded the newspaper he'd been reading into a neat square and pushed back from the kitchen table. "Let's leave these two young things alone for a spell."

Melba cast a questioning glance at Avery, and she nodded. "Go put your feet up. We'll let you know when the pancakes are ready."

The thought of Melba actually putting her feet up was almost laughable, but with a little added encouragement from Gene, she finally vacated the kitchen.

"I think she's starting to like you," Avery said after the swinging door closed behind the Stricklands.

"Good." Finn cocked his head. "Should I be worried about why she didn't like me to begin with?"

That would be due to your reputation as a serial womanizer.

Avery picked up the box of pancake mix and stared intently at the directions. She wasn't about to comment on Finn's overactive social life. Although, since she'd run into him at the general store, he hadn't had time to go on any dates. He seemed to be spending all of his free time with her.

Not that she was complaining. She'd definitely been enjoying his company. Truth be told, she enjoyed it far too much—hence the rather embarrassing habit she'd developed of kissing him whenever the mood struck her. Which was often.

But Avery had to give Finn credit. He still hadn't tried to get her into bed again, which she considered a major point in his favor. Instead of assuming they'd take up right where they'd left off in Oklahoma, he was wooing her.

And it was working. Melba wasn't the only one around the boarding house who'd developed a soft spot for Finn.

You're not supposed to be dating *him. It's a little late for that, isn't it?*

The box of pancake mix slipped through Avery's fingers, and Finn caught it before it hit the floor.

"Whoa there, butterfingers," he said, but affection glowed in his eyes. He gave her a lopsided grin, and her heart pounded with such force that she wondered if he could hear it beneath the thick layer of her flannel pajama top.

If she wasn't careful, she was going to kiss him again, right there in the boarding house kitchen.

She grabbed the first thing she could get her hands on—Claire's favorite cast-iron skillet—and held it in front of her. A shield. "You need some help with those pancakes, cowboy?"

"Not really." He reached toward her and tucked a wayward lock of hair behind her ear. "But I'd never turn down a beautiful woman in pj's."

So I've heard.

She forced a smile. "All right, then. Let's do this."

Even though Finn's hands were occupied pouring batter and flipping pancakes, he was having serious trouble keeping them to himself.

Avery danced around him in her plaid pajamas, giving the batter an extra stir here and there, and there was something about her high, swinging ponytail and slippered feet he found adorably irresistible. He even found himself fantasizing that his mornings could start like this every day if he and Avery were a real couple.

If they were married, for example.

"Oops." Avery winced. "I think you're burning that one."

Finn blinked and refocused his attention on the cast-iron skillet in front of him, where smoke had begun rising from the lopsided circle of batter in its center. Oops indeed.

He scooped up the smoldering remains with a spatula and dumped them in the trash. "We've still got a pretty good stack going."

"Good, because I think there's only enough batter for a few more." She handed him a semi-full measuring cup.

Finn took it, emptied it into the pan and handed it back to her, arching a brow when her fingertips brushed against his. Did she feel it, too? That little jolt of electricity that happened every time they touched?

The sudden flush of color in her peaches-and-cream complexion told him that indeed she did. "If you keep looking at me like that, cowboy, you're going to burn the next one, too."

He didn't much care. He wasn't even hungry, and there was already a towering stack of pumpkin-spiced goodness for Avery and the Stricklands.

The pancakes had been an excuse to see her again. That, and an attempt to get on Melba's good side, since she apparently had decided he wasn't good enough for Avery. When it came right down to it, he tended to agree. Avery was out of his league. She was the kind of woman who deserved to be wined and dined, whisked off to Paris for a romantic weekend getaway, swept off her feet with a surprise proposal.

Finn frowned down at the frying pan. For a man who had absolutely no interest in marriage, the antiquated institution certainly seemed to be occupying a large portion of his thoughts all of a sudden. He blamed his father. And Viv Dalton. And his brothers, three of whom had already fallen like dominoes. Being surrounded by so much marital bliss was messing with his head in a major way.

Things with Avery were exactly as he'd described them to Maximilian earlier. Casual. They were just enjoying each other's company until she went back to Texas.

Sure you are. Because playing house like this is just the sort of thing you usually do with women you're dating.

He flipped the last pancake on top of the stack and tried not to think about what the other Crawford men would say if they could see him now. Truthfully, he didn't much care what they thought. He was enjoying getting to know Avery better.

That didn't mean he wasn't counting down the minutes until she was back in his bed. He definitely was, and the minutes felt like they were getting longer and longer. But he and Avery were under the watchful gaze of Rust Creek Falls now, not on their own in the middle of Oklahoma. The Stricklands were old-fashioned folks, and as much as he wanted to, scooping Avery into his arms and carrying her upstairs to bed simply wasn't an option. Neither was asking her to spend the night at the Ambling A, for obvious reasons.

He wiped his hands on Melba's apron, and before he could stop himself, he said, "Will you go away with me next weekend?"

"Um. You want to go away together?" Avery's eyes went wide. Perhaps he should have removed the frilly apron before suggesting a romantic getaway. "Where?"

Anywhere, damn it.

"A nice B&B someplace. I can take a look around and find someplace special." He ditched the spatula, took a step closer and planted a hand on the counter on either side of her, hemming her in. "What do you say, Princess?"

She narrowed her gaze at him, but he could see the pulse booming at the base of her throat. Could hear the hitch in her breath when his attention strayed to her mouth—so perfectly pink.

"You weren't kidding about the pj's, were you?" she said, her voice suddenly unsteady. "You really do like them."

He ran his fingertips over her cheek. "Princess, where we're going, you won't need flannel."

He leaned closer, so close that her breath fanned across his lips and a surge of heat shot through him, so intense, so molten that he nearly groaned. What the hell was he doing? They were in the Stricklands' kitchen and he was on the verge of kissing her so hard and so deep that she'd forget all about the silly grudge her daddy had against his family.

"Is that a promise?" She lifted her chin ever so slightly, an invitation.

Finn's body hardened instantly. He didn't need to be asked twice. He could practically taste her already—perfectly tempting, perfectly sweet. All sugar and spice and everything nice.

She made a breathy little sound and it was nearly his undoing, but in the instant before his mouth came crashing down on hers, the door to the kitchen flew open.

"It smells delightful in here. Is breakfast ready?" Melba said.

Finn and Avery sprang apart like they were teenagers who'd just been caught behind the bleachers in high school.

"Yes. We were just about to come find you," Finn said, a blatant lie if he'd ever told one.

"That's exactly what it looked like you were about to do," Old Gene deadpanned.

Melba elbowed her husband in the ribs, and he flinched but shot Avery and Finn a wink when she wasn't looking.

Chapter Six

On Friday, Melba sat in the rocking chair on the shaded porch of the boarding house with the baby goat in her lap and eyed Avery's overnight bag.

"You're sure about going off alone for the weekend with Finn?" she said, looking mildly disapproving, as if she suspected that Avery's pajamas were still folded neatly in her dresser upstairs.

"Not the whole weekend." Avery held up a finger. "Just one night."

She had, in fact, packed her pajamas. Because her night away with Finn at the B&B wasn't going to be about sex…not *all* about sex, anyway. The main reason she'd agreed to spend the night with him in the nearby town of Great Gulch was so she could finally tell him she was pregnant.

The secrecy had gone on long enough. It was past

time she told him the truth, and she definitely couldn't go to bed with him until he knew about the baby…no matter how very badly she wanted to.

"Your room will be right here waiting for you when you come back." Melba shifted, and the goat let out one of her loud, warbly bleats.

"The little one sounds hungry," Avery said.

The little one.

Her throat grew dry.

"Doesn't she always?" Melba stood, and the tiny animal's cries grew louder. "Hold on to her while I go get a bottle warmed up, will you, dear?"

"What? I… No…" Avery held up her hands in protest, but before she could come up with a reasonable excuse, she suddenly had an armful of kicking, squirming goat.

"I'll be right back." Melba pushed through the door into the boarding house, seemingly oblivious to Avery's distress.

She stared at the goat, and it stared back.

Meeeeeehhhhhhh.

"Shhh," Avery murmured. "Everything's fine, I promise. Or it will be as soon as Melba gets back."

The goat blinked its long eyelashes as if it was really listening to what she was saying. Its little ears twitched.

"You like it when I talk to you?" Avery smiled tentatively.

This wasn't so bad, really. It was sort of like holding a puppy.

Meeeeeehhhhhhh.

"I know. I heard you the first time," she said, then turned at the sound of a car door slamming shut.

Finn grinned as he strode from his truck toward the

front steps of the porch, a dimple flashing in his left cheek. "Now here's a sight I never thought I'd witness."

"What's that?" she asked, rocking slightly from side to side as the goat relaxed into her arms.

Finn arched a challenging eyebrow. "Corporate princess Avery Ellington holding a goat."

Right. The only thing that might be less likely was the sight of her holding a baby.

Oh, God.

She didn't even know what to do with a baby farm animal. How was she going to succeed as a single mother?

"You should take her." She thrust the animal toward Finn. "I don't think she likes me."

"Don't be silly. Sure she does." He reached to scratch the goat behind one of her ears.

"You think so?"

"Yeah. You just need to relax a little bit." Finn shrugged, as if he'd just suggested the easiest thing in the world.

Relax…while holding a goat and pretending not to be secretly pregnant. No problem.

She took a deep breath. If a goat didn't like her, what hope would she have with a baby? Since the animal seemed to enjoy being rocked, she swayed softly from side to side. Seconds later, she was rewarded with a yawn and then some really sweet snuffling sounds.

"See? There's nothing to it," Finn whispered as the goat's eyes drifted closed.

To her embarrassment, Avery realized she was blinking back tears. She sniffed. "Of course. Easy peasy."

Finn regarded her more closely. "Princess?"

She staunchly avoided his gaze, focusing intently on

the goat's soft, ginger-colored fur with a swirl of white on its forehead. "Hmm?"

"Hey, talk to me." Finn brushed her hair from her eyes, the pad of his thumb coming to rest gently on the side of her face. "What's wrong? Are you having second thoughts about going to Great Gulch?"

"No, not at all." She shook her head. Second thoughts? God, no. She couldn't wait to spend time alone with him, except for the part where she needed to tell him he was going to be a father. But maybe that could wait just a tiny bit longer. "Nothing's wrong, I promise."

Liar.

No more waiting. She was getting weepy over bonding with a goat. Finn clearly knew something was going on.

"Actually..." She cleared her throat. Maybe she should go ahead and tell him right here and right now. Just get it out. "I..."

"Oh, hello, Finn." Melba bustled out onto the porch with a bottle in her hand. She glanced back and forth between them. "I suppose you two are ready to head off on your...adventure."

Finn's lips tugged into a half grin. "Yes, ma'am. But do you want some help with that first?"

Avery went still as he reached for the bottle. What was he doing? She knew he was trying to stay in Melba's good graces, but surely she wasn't going to have to try to operate a baby bottle for the very first time while Finn and Melba watched.

"Be my guest." Melba handed him the bottle and reclaimed her place in the rocking chair. "Gene should be doing this himself, but as usual, he's found something else to do and left me in charge of this troublemaker."

"Do you want to do the honors, or should I?" Finn jiggled the bottle in Avery's direction.

Her heart jumped straight to her throat. She hadn't been this nervous since she'd taken her admissions exam before applying to graduate schools for her MBA.

Her panic must have been obvious, because Finn gently prodded the bottle's nipple toward the baby goat's mouth. "Like this, see?"

Within seconds, the goat was happily sucking at the bottle. Finn winked at her over the animal's fuzzy little head, and slowly, carefully he transitioned the bottle to her hand. Avery held her breath, but the switch didn't seem to bother the goat in the slightest. She felt herself grinning from ear to ear as the kid slurped up the rest of her formula.

"You're a natural," Finn said, and something about the sparkle in his warm brown eyes made her blush.

"That you are." Melba slipped her a curious glance. "You know what, dear? I think you're right. It's high time that wee one had a name."

"Oh, good." Avery handed Finn the empty bottle so she could set the goat down. Her hooves clip-clopped on the wooden planks of the porch. "What name did you choose?"

"I didn't." Melba shook her head. "I thought you might like to pick one."

"Me?" Avery's hand flew to her throat.

Melba shrugged. "If you'd rather not…"

"Pumpkin." It flew out of Avery's mouth almost before she knew what she was going to say.

"Pumpkin?" Finn laughed.

"It fits. Look at her." Avery gestured toward the tiny

animal, kicking and bucking up and down the porch steps on her little orange legs.

"I think it's perfect." Melba nodded. "Pumpkin, it is."

An hour later, Avery stood beside Finn as he slipped the key into their room at the bed-and-breakfast cottage in Great Gulch.

The tiny town was only about thirty miles from Rust Creek Falls, but it may as well have been in a different hemisphere. Avery hadn't spotted a familiar face since they'd crossed the county line, and after spending weeks in a place where everyone knew your name—and a fair amount of your personal business—it was a welcome relief.

She loved Rust Creek Falls. She loved Melba and Old Gene. She'd even developed a soft spot for Pumpkin, much to her own astonishment. But giving Finn such private news in a town where gossip was one of the local pastimes only added to her sense of dread about the whole thing. At least here if he reacted badly to the revelation that he was about to be a father, the only witnesses to his meltdown would be strangers.

But that wouldn't happen. Surely not. He'd been so sweet bottle-feeding the little goat. Avery could suddenly see him helping care for a newborn baby… loving his child.

Maybe even loving her.

"Here we are." Finn smiled down at her as held the door open.

Avery stepped into the room and gasped. A fireplace glowed in the corner of the room, bathing the space in glimmering gold light. The antique furniture was all crafted from dark cherry, the most spectacular piece being the four-poster bed covered in delicate lace bedding. Fairy lights were strung along the canopy, and an array of scented candles covered every available surface.

"Finn, this is lovely." She turned to face him, her head swimming with the rich, dreamy aroma of cinnamon and cloves mixed with something she couldn't quite put her finger on. Vanilla, perhaps.

"So you like it?" He dropped their overnight bags on a luggage rack beside a beautifully crafted armoire that looked like it might hold handmade quilts or chunky knit blankets.

"I love it. It's like something out of fairy tale," she said, suddenly wistful.

"Good." He studied her for a moment, and then his lips curved into a slow smile that gradually built into an expression that took Avery's breath away. "I've wanted to be alone with you, really alone, since the second I spotted you in the general store."

She let out a shuddering breath, and suddenly the air in the room felt thick with promise. Or maybe the intimate hush that had fallen between them was the memory of the night they'd spent in Oklahoma City.

"Avery." Finn held out his hand, and the subtext was clear. He wasn't just offering her his hand—he was offering her himself, body and soul.

But for how long?

She couldn't seem to move a muscle. Even breathing seemed difficult. Her heart was pounding so hard she thought she might choke.

Finn's face fell, and he dropped his hand. "Did I presume too much? If you don't want this..."

"I *do* want this. I want *you*...more than I can possibly

say. This place, this room…it's all so beautiful. I don't want anything to mar our perfect night together." She inhaled a steadying breath before she hyperventilated. Why was this so hard? "I should have been straight with you from the start."

Finn closed the distance between them, wove his fingers through hers and kissed the backs of her hands. First one, then the other. Tenderly. Reverently. "Princess, there's nothing you can tell me that will change the way I feel about you."

She didn't deserve this kind of blind faith—not when she'd been hiding such an enormous secret from him.

"You can't know that," she said, shaking her head from side to side.

"I think I know what you're trying to say." He lifted a hand to her face, drawing his fingertips slowly across her cheek. She closed her eyes and fought the urge to lean into him. Because he couldn't possibly know, could he? "You came here on purpose looking for me."

She opened her eyes and nodded slowly. It was the truth, but not all of it. It was barely even the tip of the iceberg.

"That's great! I'm glad you did. Now come here." He wrapped an arm around her waist and pulled her close until she was pressed flush against him.

Then his mouth was suddenly on hers, and she was opening for him, wanting the warm, wet heat of his kiss—wanting it so badly she could have wept, because she could feel the crash of his heartbeat against hers. Frenzied. Desperate. And she could feel the way his body hardened as the kiss grew deeper, hotter.

Her fists curled around the soft material of his T-shirt, and in one swift move, Finn pulled back, slid the shirt over his head and tossed it onto the floor. In a heartbeat, he was kissing her again, cupping her face and groaning his pleasure into her mouth.

Avery's hands went instantly to the solid, muscular wall of his chest, and he felt so good, so right that she felt like she might die if he didn't take her to bed again. She'd wanted him since Oklahoma...since before she'd even known about the baby.

The baby.

Her eyes flew open and she pulled away, ending their kiss. Her palms, however, stubbornly remained pressed against his pectoral muscles. Was it her imagination, or had he gotten in even better shape since she'd last seen him shirtless? It must be all of the ranch work out at the Ambling A. It hardly seemed fair. He'd gone and made himself hotter while she'd been bursting out of her pencil skirts.

"Finn, wait."

He gave her one of his lazy, seductive smiles that she loved so much and glanced down at her hands, which seemed to be making an exploratory trail over the sculpted ridges of his abdomen. "We'll take it slow, baby. It will be good. So good."

She had no doubt that it would—better than the last time, even.

"We can't." She shook her head, somehow forced herself to stop touching him and crossed her arms.

Finn's gaze flitted to the bed and then back to her. "Why the heck not?"

She couldn't bring herself to say it. How could she? She couldn't even think straight while she was looking at that bare chest of his, much less form a coherent sentence.

But this was it—the moment of truth. One way or another, he was about to find out she was pregnant. He'd see the change in her body the second she undressed.

Slowly, she took his hand and rested it on her belly, telling him the only way she knew how.

His expression went blank for a moment, and then he stared down at his hand covering the slight swell of her tummy. The wait for understanding to fully dawn on him was agonizing. Avery lived and died a thousand deaths in that fraction of a second, until at last he lifted his gaze to hers. A whole array of emotions passed over his face, a lifetime of feelings all at once.

She took a deep breath. Then she let the rest of her secret unravel and laid it at his feet.

"It's yours."

Chapter Seven

Finn's ears rang.

The noise in his head started out as a faint roar—like listening to the inside of a seashell—but it multiplied by the second, drowning out all other sound. Avery's lips were moving, so he knew she hadn't stopped talking. But he couldn't make sense of the sounds coming out of her mouth. Nor could he hear the crackle of the fire in the old stone fireplace, even after he forced his gaze away from Avery and stared at its dancing flame.

He blinked, half tempted to stick his hand in the hearth to jolt himself back to life.

It's yours.

Avery was pregnant…with *his* child. He was going to be a father.

He didn't know whether to be furious or ecstatic.

Somewhere beyond the scathing sense of betrayal, he was delighted at the news. A baby…with *Avery*.

That night in Oklahoma had changed him. Finn had realized that the moment he'd run into her at the general store. All the nonsense he'd put himself through since he'd moved to Montana—all the casual dates with women he didn't even know—reminded him what he was missing without Avery Ellington in his life. It was as if that Oklahoma City blackout had somehow split his life into two parts, before and after. Only now did he fully comprehend why it had felt that way.

But she should have told him sooner. She'd been in town for *weeks* and hadn't said a word.

"It's mine," he said in an aching whisper. And with those two quiet words, the fog in his head cleared.

"Yes." Avery nodded, tears streaming down her face. "Yes, of course it's yours. There hasn't been anyone else. Not for a long, long time."

In the mirror hanging on the calico-papered wall, he saw himself shake his head. She didn't get it. Couldn't she understand? He wasn't questioning her assertion. He was stating a fact. The baby was his. *Theirs*.

Which meant he had a right to know of its existence.

"How could you have kept this from me all this time?" He closed his eyes and thought about all the times in the past few days he'd sensed that something was off. He'd *known*, damn it. He'd asked her time and again to tell him what was on her mind, and she'd refused. Every damn time.

"I tried to tell you. I really did. I just couldn't find the words. Please, you have to understand." She pressed her fingertips to her quivering mouth.

She stood stoically, awaiting his response. But he

could see the hint of tension in her wide brown eyes, then he saw her bite her lip. And even in his fury, Finn hated himself for making her feel that way.

"I asked you to talk to me," he said with measured calmness. But his voice sounded cold and distant, even to his own ears. "I asked you what was wrong, and you looked me straight in the eye and said 'nothing.'"

He sat down on the edge of the bed and dropped his head in his hands.

"There were cows! And your father. And then I couldn't even bottle-feed the goat…and then…" The words caught. A sob escaped her, and when Finn looked up, Avery had wrapped her arms around her middle as if it took every bit of her strength to simply hold herself together. "Finn, I'm sorry. I didn't know how to tell you. I knew it would be a shock. It was for me, too."

He narrowed his gaze. What on earth was she rambling on about? Old Gene's orphaned goat?

She'd been so happy when the tiny thing took a liking to her. She'd beamed like she'd just won a shiny blue ribbon at the state fair. Was this what all that excitement had really been about? The baby?

Not the *baby.* Our *baby.*

"Look, I didn't even realize I was pregnant myself for quite some time. For *months*. I missed my period, and I was so tired all the time, I fell asleep at my desk! But I'd been working such long hours and I just thought…"

Finn flew to his feet. "Are you okay? Is the baby healthy?"

Avery nodded, her eyes still wet with tears.

What had he done? His first thought should have been about the baby, not how long it had taken her to tell him about the pregnancy.

He reached a trembling hand toward her belly and then pulled it back. He had no right to touch her. Not after the way he'd just spoken to her.

"Okay." He swallowed, shame settling in his gut. He couldn't turn back time and change his initial reaction, but he could still make this right. He *had* to make it right. "In the morning we will make the arrangements."

"The arrangements?" The color drained slowly from Avery's crestfallen face. "Surely you're not suggesting I have a…um…procedure?"

Over his dead body. She thought that much of him, did she?

"Princess, you really don't know me very well. Absolutely not." His gaze dropped to her belly again, and he had to ball his hands into fists to stop himself from reaching for her so he could feel the swell of life growing inside her.

The life they'd made *together*.

When he lifted his gaze back to hers, she regarded him with what looked like a cautious mixture of hope and shame. And he hated himself just a little bit more.

He was thoroughly botching this. It was time to make himself clear.

"You and I are getting married," he said flatly.

Avery's jaw dropped. She stared at him for a beat and then had the audacity to laugh in his face. "You can't be serious."

"As a heart attack," he said evenly.

No child of his was going to grow up without a father. Finn knew all too well what it was like to be brought up without two present, supportive parents.

Maximilian was no saint. Finn wasn't fool enough to overlook the fact that his father could be manipulative and somewhat domineering. But he could count on one hand the number of times he'd seen his mother since she'd filed for divorce. She hadn't just walked away from her husband—she'd walked away from her six sons, too. An absence like that left its mark on a boy. A soul-deep wound that took a lifetime to heal.

Possibly longer.

Finn wouldn't do that to an innocent child. He would be there every step of the way, come hell or high water.

"Finn, what you said a few seconds ago is the truth. I don't really know you, and you don't know me, either. Certainly not well enough to entertain the idea of marriage." She shook her head and looked at him like he was as mad as a wet hen.

The only thing his impulsive proposal had accomplished was putting an end to her tears. That was something, at least.

"I won't be shut out of my child's life," he said. His voice broke, and something inside him seemed to break right along with it.

How had he and Avery come to this? They should be in bed together right now, but instead they were suddenly standing on opposite sides of the room as if the past few days hadn't happened at all.

Spending time with Avery in Rust Creek Falls had been fantastic, like something out of a dream. Finn had gone to bed every night thanking his lucky stars that she'd somehow found her way back into his life. He hadn't thought about his dad's ridiculous arrangement with Viv Dalton in days. He'd been too busy figuring out how to see more of Avery before she left town to think about the bounty on his head.

Oh, the irony.

Maximilian was going to be happier than a pig in slop when he heard about this. Avery's dad, not so much.

Just how much did her father despise the Crawfords? Finn hadn't given the matter much thought since he and Avery had agreed to put their family differences aside, but that would no longer be possible.

"I would never prevent you from seeing your child. You know how much I love it in Rust Creek Falls. I'll come visit, and you can come see the baby in Texas as often as you like," Avery said.

She took a step toward him, her hand resting protectively on the slight swell of her abdomen. She looked more beautiful than Finn had ever seen her before—already so attached to the baby they'd made together.

It seemed crazy, but Finn felt that way, too. Even though he'd only known about the pregnancy for a matter of minutes, an intimacy he'd never experienced before drew him closer to both Avery and their unborn child. Despite her words of assurance, a raw panic was clawing its way up his throat, so thick he almost choked on it.

He couldn't be just a visitor in their baby's life. He *wouldn't.*

"Can I ask you a question?" His jaw tightened, because he had a definite feeling he knew why Avery was so dead set on raising the baby on her own.

She blinked. "Of course."

He lifted a brow and fixed his gaze with hers. "How do your parents feel about the fact that you're carrying a Crawford heir?"

Because that's precisely what their child would be—an heir, not only to the Ellington fortune, but to everything the Crawfords had built, as well. The two empires their fathers had created from the ground up would be forever intertwined in a way that neither of them had ever anticipated.

"Um." Avery looked away, and that's all it took for Finn to know the rest of the story.

Oscar Ellington had no idea that his darling princess of a daughter was pregnant with Finn Crawford's baby.

Avery felt sick, and for once, the slight dizziness and nausea that had her sinking onto the B&B's lovely four-poster bed had nothing to do with morning sickness.

She should have told Finn about the baby sooner. That much was obvious. If she could rewind the clock and go back to the very first time she'd seen him in Rust Creek Falls, she would blurt out the news right there in the middle of the general store. Melba would have fainted, and the news would have been all over town faster than she could max out her credit card during a Kate Spade sample sale, but that would have been just fine...because at least Finn would never have looked at her the way he was regarding her right now.

The look of betrayal in his dark eyes was almost enough to bring her to her knees. Her legs wobbled as she sat down, and a coldness settled into her bones, so raw and deep that a shiver ran up and down her spine. She felt more alone than she'd ever been in her entire life.

He wants to marry you, remember?

Weirdly, Finn's abrupt proposal—if you could even call it that, since it was more of a command than a question—only exacerbated the aching loneliness that had swept over her the minute he'd begun looking at her as if she'd inflicted the most terrible pain in the world on him. Probably because she knew his desire to get married had nothing to do with her. He wanted to be close to their baby.

Not her.

"My parents don't know I'm pregnant," she said, heart drumming hard in her chest.

She couldn't even look at Finn as she admitted the truth. When had she become such a coward? It was pathetic. Her baby deserved a mother who could face challenges head-on, like an adult. Not a spoiled princess who'd had everything handed to her on a silver platter.

She squared her shoulders and forced herself to meet Finn's gaze. "I'm going to tell them, obviously. But I wanted to tell you first."

The set of Finn's jaw softened, ever so slightly. But the hurt in his eyes remained.

Avery swallowed hard. "You deserved to know before anyone else. You're the baby's father."

He took a deep breath, and she wondered what would happen if she went to him and wrapped her arms around him. Pressed her lips to his and kissed him with all the aching want she felt every time she looked at him.

Because she did still want him, and a part of her always would. They were tied together for life now. And as scary as that probably should have been, knowing her attraction to him was part of something bigger—something as meaningful as another life—gave her a strange sense of peace.

The only thing keeping her a chaste three feet away from him was stone-cold fear of what he would say or do next. He wanted to *marry* her, for crying out loud.

That was a hard no. This wasn't the 1950s. Besides,

Avery wasn't about to marry a man who wasn't in love with her.

"Where do they think you are? You've been out of the office for weeks. I'm guessing you didn't actually have meetings in the area at all." Finn's brow furrowed, and he looked like he was mentally scrolling through all the little white lies she'd told since she'd rolled into town. She wanted to crawl under the bed's beautiful lace coverlet and hide.

He pinned her with a glare. She wasn't going anywhere.

No more hiding.

"There were no meetings." She shook her head. "Everyone—my mom and dad, the office—thinks I'm at a spa."

She waited for him to make a crack about what a completely believable lie that had been. Was there a soul on earth who would believe Princess Avery had been bottle-feeding a goat and carving pumpkins instead of munching on kale salad and getting daily massages at Canyon Ranch?

For once, he didn't poke fun at her, and for that, she was profoundly grateful. When he came and sat down beside her, she almost wept with relief.

But the feeling was fleeting, because he wasn't finished asking questions.

"I think it's high time your parents, especially your father, know what's going on. Don't you?" He turned to face her, and he was so close that she couldn't help but stare at him and wonder if her baby would have those same features.

Would he or she have those brown eyes with tiny

gold flecks that she loved so much? The same nose? The same dimple that Finn had in his left cheek?

Her face went warm and she nodded. "Yes, I do."

If she was going to come clean, she might as well do a thorough job of it. Besides, telling Finn he was going to be a father had been the most difficult thing she'd ever done. As crazy as it seemed, the prospect of telling her parents seemed easy in comparison. Even talking to her father seemed manageable, especially with Finn sitting beside her.

They weren't an actual couple, and they *certainly* weren't getting married, but was it too much to think they could be something of a team where their baby was concerned?

He crossed the room to collect her handbag from the pile of their untouched luggage and handed it to her. "I'm assuming your phone is in here?"

She nodded. So this was happening now…as in, *right* now.

She could do this. She was a grown woman. Having a baby was a perfectly normal thing to do.

The phone trembled in her hand as she pulled up her parents' contact information, and Finn's gaze seemed to burn straight into her. She knew he fully expected her to chicken out, so she gave the send button a defiant tap of her finger.

The line started ringing, and she glanced at Finn for a little silent encouragement, but he stood in front of her with his arms crossed, stone-faced. Having him tower over her like that made her heart flutter even more rapidly, so she got up so they could stand eye to eye. Technically, they were eye to chest since he was so much taller than she was, but still. It helped.

The phone rang once, twice, three times. Then at last her father picked up. "Hello?"

"Daddy, hi," she said a little too brightly.

"Hello, sweetheart. Are you on your way back from the spa? I was beginning to wonder if you were ever coming home."

"No, not exactly," Avery said. Her gaze flitted again to Finn's serious expression, and she knew the time had come for the truth. All of it. "I actually haven't been to the spa. I've been in Montana."

There was a long stretch of silence before her dad responded.

"Montana," he said. "I don't understand."

"I'm in Rust Creek Falls." She didn't need to elaborate. Her father was well aware the Crawford ranch had picked up and moved away from Texas. He'd practically thrown a party.

Now his voice shifted from daddy mode to CEO mode in an instant. "Avery, what's going on?"

Before she could say anything, her mom picked up the other extension. "Avery? Hello? Are you okay? What's happened?"

Everything. *Everything* had happened. "I'm fine. I'm in Montana with Finn Crawford and, well, I have something I need to tell you."

Her eyes fixed with Finn's, and he took her hand. It was the smallest possible indication that they were a united front, but she seized on it as if it were a lifeline.

"We're having a baby," she blurted.

"Oh, dear," her mother said.

"What?" Oscar Ellington boomed. His voice was so loud that Avery had to hold the phone away from her ear.

"Daddy, calm down," she said, and Finn's brows drew together in concern.

"I don't understand." Avery's mother sounded mystified. "How did this happen?"

The usual way, Mom. Avery wasn't about to get into the details. Her father was already breathing loud enough to make her wonder if he was on the verge of a heart attack. "I'm four months along, and I came up here to let Finn know."

"Is the Crawford boy there right now? Put him on the phone," her father demanded.

The Crawford boy. What were they, twelve years old?

She gripped the phone tighter. "No."

Now wasn't the time for Finn and her dad to have a heart-to-heart, but this was probably the first time Avery had ever willfully refused her father…with the notable exception of sleeping with the enemy.

"Avery, I'm sending a private jet to collect you first thing in the morning. Be on it," her father said. Then he spat, "Alone."

"I can't leave so soon, Daddy. There are things I need to figure out here. But I'll be home soon."

"The hell you will," Finn said with deadly calm. "We're getting married, remember?"

Avery froze. Why in the world would he bring that up now?

She shushed him, but it was too late.

"Honey, I'm not sure getting married is the best idea," her mother said.

Her father was far more insistent. "Avery, I forbid you to marry that man. I won't have a Crawford anywhere near my business. The Ellingtons have the financial means to take care of a child without any help from him."

She wanted to explain that Finn wasn't the horrible person her parents thought he was, despite the fact that he was trying to strong-arm her into marrying him. He was decent. He was kind. Under different circumstances, he might have even been the love of her life.

But she couldn't say any of those things—not while Finn was right there listening to every word she said. She wasn't ready to put her heart on the line like that. Today had been a big enough disaster already. First and foremost, she needed to build a future for her baby. Love was a luxury she couldn't worry about now.

Maybe not ever.

One thing was certain, though. She'd had enough of stubborn men telling her what to do. "Daddy, what exactly are you saying?"

He wanted her to hightail it back to Dallas, but somehow she sensed there was more.

She closed her eyes and concentrated on breathing in and out. No matter what her dad said, she couldn't board a private jet first thing in the morning. She and Finn still needed to hammer out custody arrangements. That might take a while, since he still seemed to think there was a wedding in their future, although she was sure Finn would change his mind once he had time to sleep on it. After all, he'd never much seemed like the marrying type.

Plus, Avery couldn't leave without telling Melba and Old Gene a proper goodbye. The thought of moving out of the boarding house suddenly left her with a lump in her throat. The Stricklands had been so kind to her for weeks now. And what about Pumpkin? She'd miss the sweet little goat.

Once you name an animal, it's yours.

Somehow she doubted her parents would welcome a baby goat any more than they'd welcome the news of her pregnancy.

"I'm telling you to come on home, Avery," her father said.

Just as she'd expected…

Almost.

"But only after you cut Finn Crawford out of your life entirely."

Chapter Eight

Finn felt his throat closing up as he watched Avery's eyes go wide and fill with tears again.

"Daddy, you don't mean that." Her voice was a shaky whisper.

Why had he insisted on the phone call with her parents? Oscar Ellington's disdain for Finn's family was clearly far worse than he'd imagined. So far Avery had done a remarkable job of standing her ground, but something had just changed. Finn wished he knew what.

"I can't deprive my baby of his father." Avery's gaze flew toward his. "It wouldn't be right."

Finn held out his hand. "Give me the phone, Avery."

He couldn't let this continue. She was getting too upset, too shaken. What if it somehow harmed the baby?

Finn wouldn't be able to live with himself if something terrible happened to either Avery or their unborn child all because he'd forced her to confront her parents.

"Avery, please," Finn said, working hard to keep his voice even and failing spectacularly.

At last she dropped the phone in his outstretched hand. "Too late. They hung up."

"Good." He tossed the phone onto the bed and jammed his hands on his hips.

"Good? Are you kidding?" She let out a hysterical laugh. "I just told my parents I'm having a baby and they hung up on me."

We, he wanted to say. *We* are having a baby.

Somehow he managed to bite his tongue. "The important thing is that it's done. They know."

She bit her lip, nodding slowly. "You're right. The worst is over. I'm sure my father will calm down after the news sinks in."

She didn't look sure. The fairy lights wrapped around the delicately carved frame of the romantic four-poster bed brought out the copper highlights in her hair, and Finn fought the urge to bury his hands in her dark waves.

He had the absurd wish that he could kiss her and make everything better. He wanted to lie beside her, take her into his arms and whisper promises that he knew good and well he couldn't keep.

It will all be okay.

Your parents will come around.

We're in this together.

He sat down beside her again, this time close enough for his thigh to press softly against hers. When she didn't pull away, he reached for her hand and wove their fingers together. Progress.

He gave her hand a gentle squeeze and dropped a tender kiss on her shoulder. She turned wide, frightened eyes toward him, but her lips curved into a wobbly smile. Maybe they really were in this together, after all.

He took a calming inhale and said, "We can start planning the wedding as soon as we get back to Rust Creek Falls."

Avery rolled her eyes and dropped his hand abruptly. "Would you stop with the wedding talk?"

And just like that, they were back at square one.

"It's not talk. I'm serious." He stood and started pacing from the bed to the fireplace and back again. "You're going to start showing soon, and everyone in town knows we've been seeing each other. I'll be damned if people start whispering that Finn Crawford has a bastard child. I won't do that to my baby. You shouldn't want that, either."

"You have no right to tell me what I should or shouldn't want. From what I hear, you've never been in any kind of committed relationship." She looked him up and down. "What makes you think you're so ready to jump into marriage?"

"What makes you think I'm not?" he countered.

"Oh, I don't know. Maybe the dozens of women you've dated since our night together in Oklahoma." She marched toward her suitcase while Finn stood, paralyzed.

Of course she knew about all those silly dates Viv Dalton had set him up on. No one could keep a secret in a town as small as Rust Creek Falls.

But it wasn't as if he'd been trying to hide anything. When he and Avery had parted ways in Oklahoma, they'd both thought they'd never see each other again—

other than in the normal course of business. He'd done nothing wrong.

Then why did he suddenly feel like the biggest jerk in the world?

"Those women meant nothing," he said to her back as she gathered her luggage together. "I promise. If I told you the truth about why I'd been going on so many dates, you'd laugh."

She couldn't leave. If she walked out the door, she could be on the next plane to Dallas and he'd never know. He willed her to turn around and stay until they figured things out.

Together.

She dropped her suitcase with a thud and spun around, arms crossed. "Try me. I could use a good laugh."

Finn drew in a long breath. "My dad wants all six of his sons married off. He's offered a matchmaker in town a million dollars—possibly more—to find wives for each of us. Those were all just meaningless setups."

Avery didn't laugh, but she didn't grab her suitcase again, either. A small victory.

Her eyes narrowed. "Because you didn't intend to marry any of them?"

"Exactly. I wasn't looking for a relationship. I was just..."

Having fun.

He couldn't say it, because he could suddenly see how the entire arrangement looked through Avery's eyes, and it certainly didn't seem like the actions of a man who was ready to marry anyone. Not even the mother of his child.

"Things are different now." He held up his hands,

either in an effort to stop her from fleeing or as a gesture of surrender. He wasn't sure which.

"Because I'm pregnant," she said flatly.

Was that the entire reason?

He wasn't sure, so he refrained from answering her. His head was spinning so fast that he couldn't make sense of his thoughts. Avery...a baby...a wedding. Was he ready for all of it?

"Right. That's what I thought." Avery nodded, taking his silence as an admission. "Let's table the marriage talk for now, okay?"

For now.

Finn's jaw clenched. Powerless to press the marriage issue again so soon, he felt an overwhelming emptiness gnaw at him as she continued.

"We can work out a generous visitation schedule while you and I get to know each other better." Avery smiled, but it didn't quite reach her eyes.

Where was that beautiful carefree woman who'd thrown her head back and laughed while one of his cows ate from her outstretched hand? Where was the light that always seemed to shine from somewhere deep within her soul?

Was the prospect of having a baby with him really so awful?

Perhaps, if they did it the way she was describing. She rattled off days of the week and alternating holidays in some crazy, mixed-up fashion that would require a spreadsheet to keep track of. She didn't bother mentioning the fact that if she went back to Dallas, a shared custody arrangement would require multiple flights across the country on a monthly, if not weekly, basis. Maybe it was a good thing her father had a private jet at his disposal.

The thought of Oscar Ellington made Finn grind his teeth so hard that he was in danger of cracking a molar.

"Avery, I..."

Before he could tell her he had no intention of shuttling an infant back and forth between time zones, her cell phone blared to life on the center of the bed. One word lit up the tiny screen: Daddy.

Avery scrambled to pick it up while Finn let out a relieved exhale. Thank God. Surely her parents had come to their senses and Oscar was calling to take back whatever awful things he'd said that had left Avery so shaken. She was the apple of her father's eye. His approval meant a lot to her, and once her dad had gotten over the initial shock, Finn and Avery could stop discussing the baby as if they were two complete strangers and get back to who they'd been in recent days.

And who's that exactly? The future Mr. and Mrs. Finn Crawford?

The thought did seem oddly appealing, despite the fact that he'd been doing everything in his power lately to avoid the altar.

"Daddy," Avery said, smiling faintly as she gripped her phone to her ear. "I'm so glad you called back."

Finn took a tense inhale and reminded himself that the supposed feud between their families wasn't an actual thing.

But apparently hatred was a powerful emotion, even when it was one-sided. Avery's face fell the moment her father started speaking. Finn couldn't make out what was being said, but whatever it was seemed to suck the life right out of her.

Avery's beautiful brown eyes settled into a dull, glassy stare.

"Daddy, be reasonable," she said. Then, in a voice choked with tears, "Daddy, that's not fair."

This time, when her father hung up on her again, she didn't appear panicked or angry or even sad. There was no spark of life in her expression whatsoever. Her hands dropped to her sides, and the phone slipped from her grasp. It bounced off the toe of Finn's left cowboy boot and then skidded beneath the bed.

His gaze snagged on it as it disappeared from view, and when he looked back up, Avery's delicate face had gone ashen.

She shook her head as she blinked back a fresh wave of tears. "I've just been disinherited."

Avery lay in the dark, too exhausted to sleep. Too exhausted to do much of anything, really. Especially too exhausted to keep turning down Finn's marriage proposals.

What had gotten into him? It was as if finding out he was going to be a father had flipped a switch and transported him back to the 1950s. Hadn't he gotten the memo about modern families? Single mothers weren't unheard-of. Families took all shapes and forms nowadays. Just because she was pregnant didn't mean she needed a ring on her finger. She was perfectly capable of raising a baby on her own.

Or she would be, if she wasn't suddenly unemployed.

And homeless.

And alone.

Except she wasn't technically alone. Not entirely. Finn's long, lean form was stretched out beside her, looking more masculine than ever beneath the bed's gauzy white canopy. He'd kicked off his boots but otherwise remained fully dressed on top of the covers. After her big announcement, what was supposed to be a romantic getaway had turned into something much more somber. Any lingering flicker of romance had been fully doused by the most recent phone call from her father.

Now there might as well have been a line drawn straight down the middle of the bed.

She and Finn hadn't discussed the fact that they wouldn't be sleeping together tonight. It had sort of been a given, though. Since she'd told him about the baby, that seemed to be the only thing they'd managed to agree on. Plus, nothing killed the mood like turning down a marriage proposal.

Avery bit the inside of her cheek to stop herself from crying again. Meanwhile, the father of her child was sleeping like a baby. Ugh, it was infuriating.

How could he rest so soundly while her whole world was falling apart? Probably because she was officially stuck in Montana.

He let out a soft snore, and she jabbed him with her elbow. The sharp poke managed to quiet Finn down, but he still didn't crack an eyelid. Avery briefly considered filling the ice bucket with cold water and dousing him with it, but honestly, a wide-awake Finn would be even worse than a snoring Finn at the moment.

She needed time to think. Time to figure out what to do now that she had nothing to return to in Dallas. In the span of one phone call, her entire life had gone up in smoke.

After she'd told Finn her parents had cut her off,

they'd agreed to postpone any more baby talk until tomorrow morning. They'd eaten dinner in silence at a charming little bistro in Great Gulch and then returned to their gorgeous room in the B&B, where they'd been forced to deal with the awkwardness of sleeping in the same bed.

This isn't the way tonight was supposed to turn out.

Avery pulled the lacy comforter up to her neck and sneaked another glance at Finn. Was it possible to be thoroughly angry with a man and yet still want to curl up beside him and burrow against his shoulder? Because she sort of did.

She couldn't help it. It was ridiculous, she knew. But she'd spent the past week and a half wanting him like she'd never wanted another man, and those feelings were impossible to just turn off in an instant. She wished she could. Standing her ground on the whole marriage thing would be so much easier if her heart didn't give a little tug every time he mentioned it.

If she wasn't careful, she might make the critical mistake of falling for the father of her baby. That couldn't happen. She'd lost enough already—losing her heart to Rust Creek Falls' biggest playboy wasn't an option.

She took a deep breath and stared up at the ceiling. The twinkle lights draped from the bedposts bathed the pretty room in glittering starlight. Even in her despair, Avery got a lump in her throat at the beauty of it all.

Finn had chosen well. This would have been the perfect place to rekindle their physical relationship. It was like something out of a fairy tale, except instead of a happily-ever-after ending, she'd just been stripped of everything she'd always known and loved.

Disinherited.

She couldn't wrap her head around the concept. Never in her wildest dreams had she thought her family would turn its back on her under any circumstances, least of all these. She knew her father might be upset to find out she'd been intimate with a Crawford, but cutting her out of his life seemed especially cruel. And the fact that her mother was going along with it was wholly inconceivable.

Avery wasn't technically a mother yet, but she felt like one. In five short months, she'd be able to hold her baby in her arms. Right now, she didn't even know if she was having a boy or a girl, but that didn't matter. She loved her baby, sight unseen. She couldn't imagine ever shunning her child, no matter what. Wasn't that what love was all about—accepting someone unconditionally?

Maybe Avery had it coming, though. She'd been keeping such a big secret for far too long. Finn deserved to feel like a father every bit as much as she felt like a mother. Maybe getting disinherited was some cosmic form of punishment for failing to tell him the truth right away. It was probably a miracle that he wanted to have anything to do with her, much less marry her.

She swallowed around the lump in her throat. Finn wasn't such a terrible person. She knew that. He was a good man, just not exactly marriage material. He went through women like water, and his crazy explanation about why he'd been dating so much was no comfort whatsoever. It made him seem more like a contestant on *The Bachelor* than ever.

And yet…

He was still there, right beside her, when everyone else she knew and loved had disappeared.

Which was why when the sun came up the following morning, casting soft pink light over the lacy white bedding and bathing the room with all the hope of a new day, Finn turned his face toward hers and Avery whispered the precious words he'd been waiting to hear.

"I'll marry you."

They were getting married.

After months of running away from the altar as fast as he could, Finn was elated. He, Avery and their child were going to be a family. His baby would grow up with a real father, one who was there for him or her, every step of the way.

His relief was so palpable that it felt almost like something else. Joy. Maybe even…love.

He swept a lock of hair from Avery's face and pressed his mouth to hers. It was a tender kiss. Gentle and reverent, full of all the things he didn't know how to say. But while his eyes were still closed and his lips still sweet with Avery's warmth and softness, she laid a palm on his chest, covering his heart.

She didn't push him away, though. She didn't have to. He got the message all the same.

"I have a few conditions," she said.

Conditions?

His gut churned, and the sick feeling that had come over him last night as he'd watched Avery's agonizing phone calls with her parents made a rapid return.

He sat up. "Such as?"

Avery propped herself against the headboard next to him and crossed her arms. "For starters, I'd like to keep the pregnancy quiet for a while. Just between us, as long as I can continue getting away with baggy clothes."

He could live with that.

Finn nodded. "Fine. We can tell my family after the wedding. I'm not sure how quickly we can get the church, but once my dad hears we're engaged, I'm sure he'll be more than willing to pull a few strings and—"

She shook her head. Hard. "No."

"I'm not talking about an out-and-out bribe." Although Maximilian wasn't exactly a stranger to that type of behavior. "But we know people in town, and—"

She cut him off again. "I mean no church wedding. I'd like to keep things as simple as possible. A ceremony at the justice of the peace, maybe."

How romantic.

Finn suppressed the urge to sigh. After all, they were getting married for the baby. Why did he keep forgetting that?

He reached for her hand and wove his fingers through hers. "Are you sure that's what you really want?"

"Yes, which brings me to my second condition." She glanced at their intertwined hands and then promptly looked away, taking a deep inhale. "Given the circumstances, I think a marriage of convenience is the best idea."

She let go of his hand and scrambled out of the bed, darting around the room as if she could somehow escape the remainder of the conversation.

No such luck, sweetheart.

"Avery," he said as calmly as he could manage. "What are you talking about?"

She began pulling things out of her suitcase, refusing to make eye contact with him. "I'm just saying that since this marriage is about the baby, we shouldn't muddy the waters by making it personal."

What could possibly be more personal than having a child together?

He arched a brow. "And by personal, I'm guessing you mean sex."

Avery's face went as red as a candy apple. "Exactly. I'm glad you agree."

He did not agree. In fact, he disagreed quite vehemently, but he wasn't about to push the matter.

She was scared.

Scratch that—she was terrified. And Finn couldn't really blame her. He'd always thought Maximilian Crawford was as tough a nut as they came, but clearly he'd been wrong. Avery's father made Maximilian look like a teddy bear.

"I want you to feel safe and secure," he said quietly. "I want that for our baby, too. And if that means no sex for the time being, that's fine."

"Actually, I—"

He held up a hand. "Let's take things one day at a time, okay?"

Surely she didn't think they were going to remain married for the rest of their lives and never make love. They were good together. So good. Once everything calmed down and they were living together as husband and wife, she'd realize he was in this for the long haul. She had to.

"One day at a time." She nodded and shoved her refolded items back into her suitcase. The poor thing was a nervous wreck.

Finn stood, raking a hand through his hair. "Why don't I go get us some coffee? Then we can get ready and head on down to the courthouse."

Her eyes grew wide. *"Today?"*

"Today." His voice was firm. "You have your conditions. This one's mine. There's no waiting period to get married in Montana. We just have to stop by a county office for a license and then we can go straight to the justice of the peace."

Thanks to his father's hobby as matchmaker extraordinaire, Finn knew more about getting married than he'd ever wanted to. For once, all the knowledge he'd picked up in Viv Dalton's wedding boutique was finally coming in handy.

Avery sighed. "Fine."

He crossed the room, intent on getting the coffee he'd mentioned. This conversation was really stretching the limits of his uncaffeinated early-morning state.

But as his hand twisted the doorknob, he paused. "Of course if you'd rather wait and have a church wedding in Rust Creek Falls, we can do that instead."

He could already see it—the little chapel at the corner of Cedar and Main all decked out in tulle and roses. A big fancy dress for Avery and all five of his brothers standing up for him at the altar. Maximilian with a triumphant smile on his face. Funny how the thought of such a spectacle would have made him ill a month ago. Now, it actually sounded nice.

Maybe Avery was right. Maybe he didn't really know what he wanted.

"Nice try, but no." She let out a nervous little laugh and shook her head.

"All right, then. It's settled." He shoved his Stetson on his head and went out in search of coffee, bypassing the free stuff in the lobby in favor of something better.

He thought he remembered seeing a fancy coffeehouse a few blocks away as they'd driven into town.

From the looks of the exterior, it had been the sort of place that served frothy, creamy drinks—lattes and cappuccinos with hearts swirled into the foam. Not his usual preference, but this morning it sounded about right.

After all, this was their wedding day.

Chapter Nine

It was all happening so fast.

Just a few hours ago, Avery had been sipping the cinnamon maple latte Finn had brought back for her—decaf, obviously—and now she was sitting in Great Gulch's justice of the peace court, waiting to officially become a Crawford.

The district clerk's office was situated just below them, in the building's basement. They'd been able to get their marriage license and then headed straight upstairs—one-stop shopping, so to speak. With its rough-hewn wooden posts and quaint clock tower, the small-town Montana courthouse looked like something out of an old Western movie. The judge wore Wranglers and a cowboy hat, while the bailiff's boots jangled with actual spurs, as if he'd arrived at work on his horse and tied the animal to a hitching post right outside.

It was surreal and unique in a way that Avery was sure to remember, even though there was no wedding photographer to capture the moment. No maid of honor or best man. No proud papa walking her down the aisle.

She glanced at Finn sitting beside her in the same hat and snakeskin boots he'd worn on the drive from Rust Creek Falls the day before. He'd changed into a fresh shirt, and she'd found a lovely white eyelet dress with ruffled sleeves in one of the boutiques in Great Gulch's recently revitalized downtown district. Paired with turquoise boots—her "something blue"—she looked more like a Miss Texas contestant than how she'd ever pictured herself on her wedding day, but the wildflower bouquet that trembled in her hands was a colorful reminder that she was indeed about to pledge herself to Finn Crawford for as long as they both should live.

What am I doing?

Her father had disowned her less than twenty-four hours ago. Shouldn't she give him a chance to change his mind?

Then again, why should she? She'd never heard her daddy say a single nice thing about the Crawfords, so he wasn't likely to start anytime soon. And now that she was pregnant with Finn's baby, she'd crossed over to the dark side. There was no going back.

Still, was this really the answer?

"Avery Ellington and Finn Crawford." The judge looked down at the papers in front of him and then peered out at everyone seated in the smooth wooden benches of the courtroom's gallery. "Please step forward."

Finn glanced at her and smiled as he took her hand

and led her toward the bench at the front of the tiny space.

Avery took a deep breath as she walked beside him, inhaling the rich scent of polished wood and the tiny fragrant blooms beyond the opened windows. Finn had told her the flowers were clematis, but most people called them sweet autumn. They climbed the courthouse facade in a shower of snowy white, giving the old building a dreamy, enchanted air, despite its dusty wood floor and the buffalo head mounted above the judge's bench.

Is this really happening?

Avery swallowed. This wasn't the way she'd always pictured her wedding.

Not that she'd been dreaming of getting married anytime soon. But didn't all little girls dream of their wedding day when they were young? Avery always thought she'd be married in a church, surrounded by friends and family. She'd wanted a white princess dress with a train, just like Kate Middleton. Like every other starry-eyed teen, she'd been glued to the television for the royal wedding back then. It seemed so perfect, a real-life fairy tale. Never once had she imagined herself tying the knot already pregnant and dressed like a cowgirl.

"Mr. Crawford and Miss Ellington." The judge's gaze flitted back and forth between them. "You're here to get married?"

Avery tried to answer him, but she couldn't seem to form any words.

Beside her, Finn nodded. "Yes, sir."

"I see you've got your license." Again, the judge sifted through his papers. Satisfied everything was in order, he removed his reading glasses and smiled. "Okay, then. Let's get to it."

Avery gripped her modest little bouquet with both hands as if it was some kind of life preserver. She felt like she might faint.

"We are gathered here in the presence of these witnesses to celebrate the joining of this man and this woman in the unity of marriage," the judge said.

Avery glanced at Finn, but he was staring straight ahead, so she couldn't get a read on his expression. Her pulse raced so fast that her knees were in danger of giving out on her.

It's not too late to change your mind.

No vows had been exchanged yet. She could apologize, turn around and walk right out of the courthouse. It wasn't as if anyone would stop her.

And then what?

She couldn't go home, but she wasn't completely helpless. She had an MBA, for crying out loud. Plus the Stricklands had become true friends. Maybe she could work out some kind of special arrangement to stay at the boarding house indefinitely. Surely she could pay them back eventually.

The more she thought about it, the more she liked the idea of staying with Old Gene and Melba. But if she walked away now, she and Finn would be over for good. There'd be no going back if she left him at the altar… even if the altar was technically a country courthouse with a shaggy buffalo head on the wall.

The judge droned on as her mind reeled, until finally he said, "Please face each other and hold hands."

The bailiff's spurs jangled as he stepped forward to take Avery's bouquet, prompting Finn to bite back a smile. At least he, too, seemed to appreciate the absurdity of the situation.

Once her hands were interlocked with his, though, fleeing seemed like an exceedingly difficult prospect. Could she really bring herself to be a runaway bride when he was holding her hands and looking at her as if she was the most beautiful woman he'd ever seen?

Beneath the amusement dancing in his gaze, there was something else—something that stole the breath from her lungs. Something that made her wonder if the vows they were about to exchange were indeed just words.

She bit her bottom lip to keep it from trembling as the judge said something about marriage being one of life's greatest commitments and a celebration of unconditional love.

Her heart drummed. *Love.* Did she love Finn Crawford? Did *he* love *her*?

Of course not. This wasn't about love. It was about the baby. But a small part of herself wanted it to be real, and that realization scared the life out of her.

"Finn, do you take Avery to be your wife, to have and to hold from this day forward, for better or worse, for richer, for poorer, in sickness and in health, to love, honor and cherish until death do you part?" The judge looked expectantly at Finn, and the moment before he answered seemed to last an eternity.

"I do," he said, and there was a sincerity to his tone that made Avery's fear multiply tenfold.

It's not real, she reminded herself. *It's all just pretend.*

She could do this.

But *should* she?

She placed her free hand on her growing belly to anchor her to the here and now. But when the judge turned his tender gaze on her and began to recite the same question, her throat grew dry and what she suddenly wanted more than anything—more than the wedding she'd dreamed about as a little girl, more than knowing that her father would eventually come around—was a sign. Nothing huge, just a small indication that she was doing the right thing. Everything within her longed for it.

Please.

It was a crazy thing to ask. She knew it was, but she couldn't help wishing…hoping…praying.

And then the most miraculous thing happened. Beneath her fingertips came a tiny nudge. At first she thought she'd imagined it, but then it happened again. The second time it was firmer, more insistent. She looked down at her belly, stunned.

Oh, my gosh.

Her pretty dress fluttered the third time it happened, and that's when she knew for sure—her baby had just kicked. *Their* baby.

"Avery, sweetheart?" Finn prompted.

She looked up and found her husband-to-be and the judge both watching her expectantly, waiting for her to say something.

She inhaled a shaky breath, and for the first time since the awful phone call with her father, she felt like everything might just be okay, after all. She'd needed a sign, and she'd gotten one. A sign more perfect than she could have dreamed of.

She fixed her gaze with the man who'd just pledged to love, honor and cherish her in sickness and in health, for richer and for poorer, and did her best to forget that she was definitely the latter at the moment. She was completely dependent on a man she barely knew, a man who just might have the power to break her heart.

"I do," she whispered.

And against all odds, she meant it, because the moment the baby moved, she'd stopped playing pretend.

They'd done it. After spending the past few months actively avoiding the altar, Finn Crawford was a married man.

He bit back a smile as he maneuvered his truck off Great Gulch's Main Street and onto the highway that led to Rust Creek Falls. There was no logical reason for the swell of elation in his chest. He'd practically been forced to beg Avery to marry him, and according to her terms, the marriage was hardly something to celebrate. Finn had no doubt that if Oscar Ellington hadn't acted like the world's biggest jackass, his daughter wouldn't be wearing Finn's ring.

But there it sat on the third finger of her left hand—rose gold, with a stunner of a center stone. He'd bought it on impulse at an antiques store across the street from the B&B. Avery's eyes had grown wide when he slid it onto her finger in the courthouse, but she'd yet to ask him where it came from. Finn wasn't altogether sure whether her silence was a good thing or a bad one, but every so often he glanced at her in the passenger seat and caught her staring down at the ring, toying with it with the pad of her thumb.

Married.

The beautiful woman sitting beside him was his wife, and she was pregnant with his child. Overnight, he'd gone from being free and single to being a husband with a baby on the way. He should be terrified half out of his mind or, at the very least, somewhat concerned about Avery's sudden insistence on a chaste relationship.

So why wasn't he?

From the moment she'd looked up at him with tears in her eyes and whispered the words *I do*, he'd felt nothing but pure, unadulterated joy. He'd worry about the details tomorrow. For now, he was content to let himself believe that he was ready to be a family man.

"Where are we going?" Avery frowned at the scene beyond the windshield as the truck rolled into Rust Creek Falls. "You just missed the turnoff for the boarding house."

Was she serious?

"That's because we're not going to the Stricklands'. We're going to the Ambling A," Finn said quietly.

Avery said nothing, but instead of toying with her wedding ring, she hid her hand beneath the folds of her dress.

Finn tightened his grip on the steering wheel. "I want to introduce my family to my wife."

Avery blinked at him. *"Now?"*

"Why not? The baby will be here in a matter of months. They may as well get used to the idea."

She shook her head. "We're still keeping the baby news to ourselves for now, right? I'm concerned that once the news is out, it will be all over town."

Finn's shoulders tensed, but she had a point. One thing at a time. Plus, he'd already given Rust Creek Falls enough to gossip about since he'd moved to the Ambling A. If the busybodies in town knew Avery was pregnant, their marriage would be reduced to nothing but a shotgun wedding.

Isn't that what it is?

Yes…no…maybe.

He wasn't sure of anything anymore.

"Okay, we still won't say anything about the baby." He took a measured inhale. "For now."

"Good." Avery nodded, but she was visibly nervous as they turned onto the main road leading to his family's ranch. She wrung her hands until her knuckles turned white.

Finn wanted to comfort her, but he wasn't sure how, especially when he caught sight of the numerous vehicles parked in front of the massive log home. Maximilian's luxury SUV was situated in its usual spot, as was Wilder's truck. But four more automobiles were slotted beside them, which meant Logan, Xander, Hunter and Knox were probably up at the main house, as well. What the heck was going on? Were they having a party in his absence?

He shifted his truck into Park. "It looks like we're about to kill six birds with one stone."

Beside him, Avery closed her eyes and took several deep breaths. When her lashes fluttered open, she glanced at him and shrugged. "Yoga breathing. It reduces stress and anxiety. It's also supposed to be good for the baby."

Finn smiled, then took her hand and gave it a squeeze. He also decided right then and there that they couldn't spend their wedding night at the Ambling A. Avery was right—they needed to be thinking about what was best for the baby. Staying under the same roof as his nutty father and the rest of his nosy family wouldn't be healthy for anyone, much less his unborn child. They'd get in, make their announcement and get out. Maybe they'd even head back to Great Gulch and that beautiful four-poster bed.

No sex, remember?

He sighed as he climbed out of the truck and slammed the driver's-side door shut. No sex. They had a deal. A completely ludicrous deal, but a deal nonetheless.

He had to give Avery credit—she put on a good show. When he pushed open the front door to the big log house, she greeted Maximilian with a big smile and a hug, just like a proper daughter-in-law. As luck would have it, not only were all five of his brothers situated around the big dining room table, but Xander's wife, Lily, and Knox's other half, Genevieve, were there, too. Hunter's daughter, Wren, had a bandanna tucked into the collar of her T-shirt and was digging into a big bowl of chili. Logan's wife, Sarah, sat beside her, bouncing a giggling baby Sophia on her lap.

Finn's attention lingered on the happy nine-month-old, and his chest squeezed into a tight fist.

"Son? Everything okay?"

Finn blinked and dragged his gaze back to Maximilian. "Everything's fine. Great, actually. What's going on? I haven't seen the main house this full in a while."

"We're all about to head down to the fall festival for pumpkin bowling, so Lily put on a pot of chili first." Maximilian planted his hands on his hips. "A few of us tried calling you, but your phone rolled straight to voice mail."

Right. Because he'd been a little busy getting married and all.

"Pumpkin bowling?" Avery grinned. "That's a thing?"

Logan nodded. "Sure it is. It's like regular bowling, only with a pumpkin instead of a bowling ball. It's taking place on the big lawn at Rust Creek Falls Park, and Dad has grand plans to beat us all to smithereens."

"Not going to happen." Genevieve shook her head. "I've been practicing."

"Seriously?" Lily laughed.

"Oh, she's dead serious." Knox slung an arm around his wife and kissed the top of her blond hair. "G never kids about pumpkin bowling."

"Aunt Genevieve has been helping me, too," Wren said around a spoonful of chili. "She said we need to put Grandpa in his place."

"Oh, did she now?" Maximilian crossed his arms while the entire room collapsed into laughter.

"No worries, Dad. We have some news that might take the sting out of the fact that the family has been conspiring against you." Finn slipped his arm around Avery's waist and pulled her close.

The room grew quiet until the only sound was the scraping of Wren's spoon against her bowl and the pounding of Avery's heart as she nestled against Finn's side. Only then, at such close range, could Finn tell that her smile seemed a bit strained around the edges. Forced.

Because after all, they were only pretending to be happy newlyweds. The only thing real about their union was the baby on the way.

"We're married," Finn blurted.

So much for finesse.

He'd intended to say something more poetic, but Avery's stiff smile was messing with his head. What had happened to all the heat that had been swirling between them since she'd thrown herself at him in the pasture? He couldn't look at an ear of calico corn anymore without feeling aroused. He wanted her so much it hurt. And he knew…he just *knew*…that Avery still wanted him, too.

"You're *what*?" Logan glanced back and forth between Finn and Avery.

"Wait. This is a joke, right?" Hunter let out a nervous laugh.

Xander and Knox exchanged stunned glances. Wilder and Hunter just stared, no doubt wondering if they must be next, considering that all of Maximilian's sons seemed to be falling like dominoes, one by one.

"Avery, sweetheart, is this true?" Finn's father set hopeful eyes on Avery. The pumpkin bowling conspiracy had apparently convinced him the entire family had it in for him. Probably because he deserved it after all the meddling he'd done in recent months.

Every head in the grand dining room swiveled in Avery's direction, and Finn's gut churned; he hoped against hope that none of his family members could see through the charade. He wasn't sure he could take it if they could, especially when Logan and Sarah, Xander and Lily, and Knox and Genevieve seemed so blissfully happy.

It was painful enough to know his wife didn't plan to share a bed with him, but it would be beyond humiliating for his brothers and his father to know it, too.

But in answer to Maximilian's question, Avery beamed up at Finn as if he'd hung the moon. Gazing into those warm brown eyes of hers took him right back to Oklahoma—the night that had changed both of their lives for good. And with a lump in his throat, he realized that if he could have gone back in time and done things differently, he wouldn't have changed a thing.

"It's true. Finn asked me to marry him last night, and we just couldn't wait. We went to thc justice of the peace this morning," Avery said, the perfect picture of a blushing bride, radiant with happiness. Finn would have sworn on his life she was telling the truth. "I'm a Crawford!"

Chapter Ten

I'm a Crawford.

The full consequences of what Avery had done didn't fully sink in until she said those words and watched Maximilian's face split into an ecstatic grin.

There was no turning back. The ring was on her finger, and now they'd shared the happy news with Finn's family. She was no longer Avery Ellington. She was Avery Crawford. *Mrs.* Finn Crawford.

"Well, I'll be." Maximilian let out a jubilant whoop that was so loud it shook the rafters of the extravagant log cabin his family called home. "Welcome to the family, darlin'."

He scooped her up in a big bear hug, and before she knew what was happening, Avery was being passed from one Crawford to the next, each one gushing with happiness over the surprise news. They were all so excited, so welcoming, that Avery had to remind herself that she wasn't truly a part of the family, despite the change in her last name. She and Finn were figuring things out, that's all. She'd married him to ensure that he would truly be a part of his baby's life, despite her father's attempts to cut him out entirely. He didn't honestly think of her as his wife, and she certainly wouldn't be standing in the grand main building of the Ambling A with Finn Crawford's ring on her finger if she weren't pregnant with his baby.

Her daddy would see things differently, though. The fact that she'd traded the name Ellington for Crawford would be an unpardonable sin, regardless of the fact that she'd been disinherited. Oscar Ellington had put something terrible in motion when he'd cut her off, but nothing that couldn't have been stopped. One phone call—that's all it would have taken to undo all the pain he'd caused.

But this…

This couldn't be undone.

"I must say, I'm surprised." Wilder narrowed his gaze at Finn. "You swore up and down that wild horses couldn't drag you to the altar."

Avery's ribs constricted, but she glued her smile in place.

"Things change, brother," Finn said, and his gaze found hers and he sent her a knowing grin.

Things change.

Did they? Did they really?

"How adept are you at bowling, Avery?" Genevieve arched a brow. "Do you have much experience handling pumpkins?"

Finn shook his head. "Don't get any ideas. The lot of

you already outnumber Dad by a good amount. You're going to have to trounce him on your own."

He reached for Avery, and his fingertips slid to the back of her neck, leaving a riot of goose bumps in their wake. "Besides, it's our wedding night."

Her stomach immediately went into free fall.

Their wedding night? She hadn't thought that far ahead. Since telling Finn about the baby, she'd pretty much been operating on a minute-by-minute basis.

"Won't you two be taking a honeymoon? I can make a phone call and get the jet down from Helena in two shakes of a lamb's tail." Maximilian dug around in the pocket of his Wranglers for his cell phone.

"Oh, there's no need for that," Avery said before Finn could take him up on the offer. "We're not taking a honeymoon quite yet. Right…darling?"

She cast a pleading glance at Finn.

Darling? She was calling him darling now?

The corner of his mouth quirked into a half grin. "Right, love."

Love. As endearments went, it was a good one. A great one, actually. She practically melted into a puddle right there in the Crawford dining room, because again, she couldn't quite keep track of what was real and what wasn't.

"Maybe it's a good thing we're all heading out, then." Knox bit back a smile.

"Don't be an idiot. We're waiting on the honeymoon, but we're not spending our wedding night under the same roof as all of you." Finn rolled his eyes and punched his brother on the arm.

Knox winced as he rubbed his biceps. "Point taken, but where exactly are you going?"

Finn hesitated, because as Avery knew all too well, he was completely winging it. It was the briefest of pauses, but it gave Maximilian the perfect opening to swoop in with a grand, romantic gesture.

"You'll stay at Maverick Manor. The honeymoon suite!" He jabbed at the screen of his cell phone. "I'll take care of the reservation myself, pull some strings if I have to."

Panic shot through Avery. She couldn't spend the night with Finn in a *honeymoon suite*, of all things. Not if she had any chance of sticking to the arrangement they'd made.

"What's Maverick Manor?" she asked, even though she dreaded the answer.

"It's Rust Creek's newest hotel. Rustic, but upscale." Hunter grabbed a coffee carafe from the marble-topped kitchen counter where a huge blue Le Creuset enamel pot sat, surrounded by bowls of chili fixings. He gave a thoughtful shrug while refilling his cup. "It's quite beautiful, actually. The lobby has a stone fireplace that's so big you can stand upright in it, and the entire back side of the building faces the mountains."

"It's so romantic, Avery. Honestly, it's the perfect place for a wedding night." Sarah sighed. "You'll just love it."

Avery glanced at Finn—at his big broad shoulders, at his capable hands, at the mouth she couldn't seem to stop kissing at the most inappropriate times. Then she shifted her attention back to her father-in-law, grinning from ear to ear.

What bride would turn down the honeymoon suite at the most extravagant hotel in town?

A pretend one. That's who.

Avery was suddenly exhausted. She'd been married all of two hours, and reminding herself not to fall in love with her husband was already becoming a full-time job. Maybe it was a good thing she was unemployed.

"Thank you, Maximilian. That's so kind of you." She took a deep breath. How hard could it be to spend one chaste night in a luxurious room with Finn? It wasn't as if the bed would be heart-shaped. Would it? "Maverick Manor, here we come."

Avery had no idea what Maximilian had said to the staff at Maverick Manor, but whatever it was had everyone falling all over themselves to welcome her and Finn in grand romantic fashion.

"Congratulations, Mr. and Mrs. Crawford," the front desk clerk gushed the instant they'd set foot inside the lobby.

They hadn't even introduced themselves, which had Avery wondering if Maximilian had gone so far as to send photos in preparation of their arrival. Finn's father was definitely over-the-top, so she wouldn't put it past him. Then again, Rust Creek Falls was a small town, and everyone within a one-hundred-mile radius seemed to know precisely who Finn Crawford was… because they'd dated him at some point.

Avery forced a smile and tried not to imagine the effusive blonde with the Maverick Manor badge pinned to her cute denim dress sharing a candlelit meal with her husband.

"We've prepared a lovely stay for you," she said, and to her credit, she didn't seem overly familiar with Finn. *Thank goodness.* She must be new in town. "Tomorrow, we've got you booked for a special couples' massage overlooking the fall foliage on our new pool deck."

"A couples' massage?" Avery blinked. Apparently, a heart-shaped bed was the least of her worries. "That won't be necessary. We're checking out tomorrow morning."

"Are you sure, love?" Finn's hand slipped onto the small of her back, and a rebellious shiver snaked its way up Avery's spine.

"A couples' massage sounds quite—" his gaze flitted toward hers, eyes molten "—nice."

Avery knew that look. It was a look full of heat and promises. The same playfully wicked expression that she'd loved so much that night in Oklahoma. What woman wouldn't?

Damn him.

"Mr. Crawford booked the honeymoon suite for a three-night stay," the clerk oh, so helpfully said.

"If only we could stay that long." Avery batted her lashes at Finn, whose hand remained on her back, where it continued to infuse her with the sort of warmth she most definitely didn't need to be experiencing at the moment. "But we have an appointment tomorrow morning that we simply can't miss. Don't we, darling?"

They did, actually. Finn just didn't know it yet.

He angled his head toward her. "We do?"

Avery's first official prenatal appointment with an obstetrician was scheduled for the following morning at eleven o' clock. Her gynecologist back in Dallas had started her on prenatal vitamins once her pregnancy test had come back positive, but since she no longer delivered babies, she'd given Avery a referral. After a few days in Rust Creek Falls had turned into a week and a week into two, she'd finally broken down and found a doctor in Montana. She'd made the appointment last week, before Finn knew anything about the baby, so she'd chosen a doctor whose practice was situated a half hour away from Rust Creek Falls. That still seemed like a good call, since being in such a small town was like living in a fishbowl.

"Yes, we do." Avery nodded, hopefully putting a firm end to the idea of a couples' massage.

"So, just one night, then?" The clerk glanced back and forth between them.

"Just one night," Finn said with a sudden hint of regret in his gaze that seemed so real that Avery felt it deep in the pit of her stomach.

What were they *doing*?

"Well, the staff at Maverick Manor is here to help you make the most of it. Just let us know if you need anything. Anything at all." The clerk handed two keys to an attendant who looked like he'd arrived fresh off the rodeo circuit. "Kent here will show you to your room."

The congratulatory glint in her eye turned wistful, and it was then that Avery knew the young woman had indeed been one of Finn's many Friday night social engagements. Not to mention the other six days of the week.

She felt sick as she followed Kent, with his perfect felt Stetson and worn cowboy boots, to the top floor of Maverick Manor. The minute Melba had warned her about Finn's overactive social life, she should have turned tail and gone back to Dallas. She could have left him a note about the baby or written him an email. That would have been the chicken's way out, obviously, and

Finn would have no doubt beaten an immediate trail to Texas. But at least then she would have been on her home turf. She might have stood a chance at escaping from their one-night stand with her dignity—and her heart—intact.

Now here she was. In Montana, of all places, with a wedding ring on her finger and her heart in serious danger of cracking into a million pieces.

"Here we are." With a flourish, Kent gestured to the intricately carved door at the end of the hall. Then he unlocked it and held the door open, waiting for the "giddy" newlyweds to step inside.

A heady wave of fragrance drifted from inside the sumptuous room—something floral and sweet. Hyacinths, maybe. They'd always been Avery's favorite flower. And were those *rose petals* strewn on the floor?

God help her, they were. Where was a dust buster when she really needed one?

Avery stared at the petals, terrified to move. As luck would have it, she didn't need to, because before she could register what was happening, Finn scooped her in his arms and swept her clear off her feet.

She squealed in protest, even as her arms wrapped instinctively around Finn's thick neck. He laughed and it vibrated through her, sweet and forbidden.

Avery buried her face in the crook of his neck and whispered again the warmth of his skin. "What are you doing?"

"How would it look if I didn't carry my bride over the threshold? Just go with it, love," he murmured.

They were going to have words about this. They were also going to have words about his new nickname for her, because yes, they needed to put on a good show so their marriage was believable to the outside world, but she was only human. She had feelings, and right now, those feelings were in serious danger of throwing caution to the wind.

She blamed biology. Wasn't she chemically programmed to be attracted to the father of her baby?

Right. That's it. Science. It has nothing to do with his easy sense of humor or how sweet he is around animals or his generous spirit.

Or how he'd turned his entire life inside out for the sake of their baby. Or how he'd been there for her at a time when her own family had turned their backs on her. Or how he looked at her as if he'd simply been biding his time with all those other women, waiting for her to walk back into his life.

The list went on.

And on.

And on…

Kent tucked their bags away in the closet by the door and slipped out of the suite, yet Avery's feet still weren't touching the ground. The heat in Finn's gaze was suddenly infused with a tenderness that made it difficult to breathe. She looked away, determined to collect herself, but it was then that she noticed the trail of rose petals led to a huge bed covered in pristine white bed linens, facing a picture window with a stunning view of the mountains. The sun was just beginning to dip low on the horizon, bathing the yellow aspen trees in glittering light. Their leaves sparkled like pennies, and it was all so beautiful that Avery had to squeeze her eyes closed against the romantic assault on her senses.

When she opened them, she found Finn watching her…waiting. Was he ever going to put her down?

"If you make a crack about my weight right now, I'll never forgive you." She gave him a tremulous smile.

It wasn't a test. She was merely trying to inject some humor into a situation that suddenly seemed far too intimate. Had it been a test, though, Finn would have passed with flying colors.

"I wouldn't dare." His gaze narrowed and swept over her face, settling on her mouth. "You really have no idea how lovely you are, do you? Pregnancy suits you."

She had a sudden flashback of Finn moving over her, looking at her with the same reverence in his eyes as he pushed deep inside her, whispering sweet nothings. At the time, she'd attributed his words to the martinis and the darkness of the blackout, which had a strange way of making everything feel more real, more intense.

But maybe she'd been wrong. Maybe he really had felt those things. Maybe he still did.

"Thank you," she said stiffly, scrambling out of his arms and sliding clumsily to her feet. She took a giant backward step and pretended not to notice when Finn's expression closed like a book. "I'm kind of tired. I should probably get some rest."

"Right. Maybe we should take a nap." He scrubbed at the back of his neck and seemed to look anywhere and everywhere—except at her. "On top of the covers. Fully clothed."

This was the moment when she should have told him the truth—the moment she should have given up the pretense that she didn't have feelings for the father of her child. It would be so easy. She might not need to say anything at all. She could just rise up on tiptoe and kiss him gently on the mouth, and he would *know*. He probably already did.

But she couldn't do it. She couldn't open herself up that way. The past twenty-four hours had been more heartbreaking than she could have ever imagined. She'd lost her job. She'd lost her family. She couldn't lose Finn, too, and that's precisely what would happen if she tried to start something real with him and then realized he didn't love her. If he did, wouldn't he have led with that when he asked her to marry him?

"That sounds good." She nodded. Could this honeymoon get any more awkward? "I have a doctor's appointment tomorrow, at eleven if you'd like to come along. For the baby."

"For the baby," he echoed, and his tone went flat. Lifeless. "Of course I'll be there."

She nodded, because she didn't quite trust herself to speak.

"You okay, Princess?" Finn said, a bit of life creeping back into his tone.

"Yes." She nodded. "Just tired."

So very tired. Tired of dealing with her impossible father, tired of wondering what kind of mother she would be, tired of acting like the night in Oklahoma hadn't meant anything when just the opposite was true. But most of all, she was tired of pretending. Sometimes it seemed like that's all she'd been doing since the day she rolled into Montana—pretending she wasn't pregnant, pretending she didn't have feelings for Finn, and now, pretending they were like any other husband and wife. Suddenly, with Finn's ring on her finger, she wasn't sure she could do it anymore.

"Come on." Finn strode to the bed and gave the mattress a pat. "Lie down. I promise I won't bite."

He smiled, but somehow it was one of the saddest

smiles Avery had ever seen. So she did as he said, kicked off her boots and curled onto her side on the bed with her hands tucked neatly beneath her pillow, lest they get their own improper ideas.

Her eyes drifted shut and just as she began to doze off, she felt the mattress dip with the weight of Finn's body. So solid. So strong.

Tears pricked her eyes, and she wasn't sure why she was crying. She only knew that it was almost physically painful to have him so close without actually touching her. The space between them felt heavy, weighted with all things they couldn't say or do to one another.

When they'd been together in Oklahoma, they'd fallen onto the bed together in a tangle of kisses and heated breath. Despite the martinis, she remembered everything about that night with perfect clarity. The thrill that coursed through her when she'd slid her hands up the back of his dress shirt. The way Finn's eyes had gone dark when looked at her bare body for the first time. His aching groan when he'd pushed his way inside her.

She remembered it all as clearly as if it had just happened yesterday. Did he remember, too?

Was he thinking about it right now, just as she was?

"Princess?" Finn's voice cut through the memories, but the ache in his tone was all too familiar. Too tortured to leave room for any doubt.

Of course he remembers. Of course he's thinking about it.

All she needed to do was turn to face him. She wouldn't even have to say anything. Everything she felt would be clearly written in her eyes—so much longing, and despite the craziness of their circumstances, so much hope.

She bit down hard on her lip to keep herself from answering him. And she didn't dare move. Instead, she squeezed her eyes shut tight and kept her back to her husband.

Then Avery Crawford let the heavy silence and the sweet smell of velvety rose petals lull her to sleep.

Chapter Eleven

Hours later, Finn lay stretched out on the sofa and stared at the ceiling, fully awake. He was either too mad or too turned on to sleep. Probably both, but he couldn't seem to figure out which bothered him most.

Avery wanted him. He knew she did, but something was holding her back. He just couldn't figure out what that *something* was, and he didn't want to push. She was his wife now, and she was pregnant. The burden of patience definitely fell on his shoulders in this scenario, hence his move from the bed to the sofa.

But they'd shared a moment earlier. He thought they had, anyway.

He glared hard at the rough-hewn wood beams overhead, wishing he could ask the room for confirmation. The space itself was glorious, with one wall completely made of stone opposite floor-to-ceiling windows overlooking the rugged Montana landscape. A fire blazed and crackled in the hearth. Hours ago, the air had been thick with longing, and now…

Now, nothing. Surely the walls remembered. Finn sure as hell did.

He sat up and raked his hand through his hair, tugging hard at the ends. Then he sighed, because in that moment, sleep seemed like the most impossible task in the world. He'd be better off spending half an hour under the cold spray of the suite's luxury rainfall shower head than continuing to lie on the sofa listening to the steady breath of his wife as she slept like a baby in the huge four-poster bed. Alone.

He stalked toward the closet, grabbed his duffel bag and slipped as quietly as he could into the grand his-and-hers bathroom. Through his sock feet, he could feel the warmth of the heated stone floor tiles. A Jacuzzi tub overlooked the darkening Montana sky, and like everything else in the suite, the enormous stone shower was built for two. He didn't need to close his eyes to dream of Avery, bare and beautiful, with water streaming down her changing body and droplets glittering on her eyelashes like stars. Sometimes it seemed as if she was all he saw, day or night.

It was making him crazy. They just needed to go ahead and sleep together so they could both get it out of their systems. Then they could go about dealing with the pregnancy with level heads. At least he hoped that's what would happen, because he wasn't sure how much longer he could go on the way things were.

Finn wasn't used to being so wrapped up in a woman like this. He was operating in strange and new territory, and he wasn't sure what to make of it. The baby had changed everything. Obviously.

Although…

Avery had been on his mind ever since Oklahoma, long before he had any idea she was carrying his child. On some primal level, he must have known. It was the only explanation.

The only one he was comfortable admitting to himself, anyway.

Get yourself together.

He glowered at his reflection in the bathroom mirror and hauled his duffel onto the natural marble vanity top. He'd been in such a hurry back at the Ambling A that he'd grabbed the first few articles of clothing he'd seen and stuffed them into his overnight bag along with his dopp kit. He wasn't even sure what all he'd brought.

But he was certain he hadn't packed the jewel-encrusted book that rested on top of his belongings and caught his eye the moment he drew back the zipper on his bag. He picked it up, turning it over in his hands. It was studded with colorful gemstones and looked like something he might see in the windows of one of the antique shops downtown. The jewels formed a swirling letter *A* on the front cover.

He squinted at it. The book definitely looked familiar, but how had it managed to get inside his bag, and what was he supposed to do with it?

Knox.

Finn sighed. He'd thought it was strange when his newlywed brother had insisted on carrying his bag to the truck so Finn could help Avery with her things. He definitely could have managed all their luggage on his own. But apparently Knox's helpful attitude had been a ploy to get his hands on Finn's duffel so he could tuck the book inside. Now that he knew where the gaudy thing had come from, he recognized it as the old diary that he and his brothers had found beneath the floorboards of the Ambling A when they'd been renovating the place a few months ago. Someone had finally managed to pry the lock open—Xander, if Finn was remembering correctly—and since that time, the old book had been making the rounds as each of his brothers had gotten married. Knox had been the most recent to walk down the aisle, so it made sense that the diary would still be in his possession.

Seriously, though? He was supposed to spend his wedding night reading an old book?

It's not like you're busy doing anything else at the moment.

True. So frustratingly true.

His jaw clenched as he moved to sit down, taking the book with him. Mildly surprised to find that the author was a man, he kept reading.

Oddly enough, the diary proved to be a pretty effective way of getting his mind off Avery and the myriad ways he'd rather be spending his wedding night than sitting on the bathroom floor with his legs stretched out in front of him, poring over the details of some poor sod from a different era. But as fate would have it, the author's girlfriend had been pregnant.

A child. A child! Unexpected, unplanned, but not for a moment unwanted. From the second I learned I was going to be a father, nothing else mattered. Only her—only the mother of my baby and the life we're bringing into the world.

Finn's pulse kicked up a notch when he came across

that notable detail. And his heart seemed to make its way to his throat as he read passage after passage about how happy the writer was about the baby. The writer never spelled out his girlfriend's name, but referred to her simply as W throughout the book. As Finn slowly flipped the pages, he realized why.

All this time...all these days we've lived and loved in secret. And now we can't tell anyone about the baby. Not yet. So we continue to go through life pretending, but it's getting more difficult by the hour. W is my whole heart, and I want the world to know how much she and our child mean to me. But as we both know, it's just not possible. Not now. Maybe not ever...

W and her sweetheart were keeping the pregnancy and their relationship under wraps for some reason. He wasn't sure why, but they wanted to keep the baby a secret.

That's when Finn slammed the bejeweled book closed. The similarities were beginning to freak him out a little bit. He felt for the poor guy and W, whoever they were. He really did, but most of all, he wasn't sure he wanted to know how their love story would end.

Avery slept like the dead. The turmoil of the past forty-eight hours had taken its toll, and once her head hit the pillow, she was finally able to escape the craziness that was now her life. She woke the next morning to sunlight streaming through the suite's massive picture window and a scowl on her husband's face.

"Oh." She winced as she sat up and caught her first glimpse of Finn slumped on the sofa. He was already fully dressed, cowboy boots and all. "Did you sleep at all last night?"

Finn looked terrible. He was still the same handsome man who had the annoying habit of making her heart swoop every time she looked at him, but there were new dark circles under his eyes. Even the heavy dose of fresh scruff on his jaw couldn't hide the fact that his complexion was a good shade or two paler than normal.

"Good morning. I'm fine, don't worry about me." His voice was stiff as he closed the strange jeweled book in his hand. "I got you some coffee. It's decaf, so it should be safe."

He nodded toward one of the nightstands flanking the bed, where a steaming latte sat waiting for her with a heart swirled into the foam, and her guilt magnified tenfold.

He really should have stayed in the bed last night. For goodness' sake, it was so large that they each could have easily spread out like starfish and still not even touched one another.

Maybe.

Then again, maybe not. The last time she'd slept all night in a bed with Finn, she'd woken up convinced that she should marry him.

"Thank you." She reached for the latte and took a sip. Pumpkin spice, her favorite. She could still manage to drink it even though the smell of coffee beans sometimes made her nauseous.

But what didn't make her nauseous these days?

Finn stood and tucked the book he'd been reading into his duffel bag, then shifted awkwardly from one booted foot to the other. "You said your doctor's appointment is at eleven, right?"

She nodded.

He picked up his duffel, jammed his Stetson on his

head and strolled toward the door. "We should leave in half an hour. I'll wait for you downstairs."

And then with a quiet click of the suite's carved wooden door, he was gone.

Okay, then. Clearly it hadn't been a magical wedding night.

But she'd been clear about the terms of their marriage from the very beginning. She didn't have a single thing to feel guilty about. Well, other than Finn's serious case of bedhead this morning and the fact that she felt perfectly rested. And maybe, just maybe, that she'd basically run for cover the night before at the first hint of sexual tension between the two of them.

That had been a very necessary moment of self-preservation, though. Surely Finn would get over it. He couldn't stay grumpy forever, could he?

Avery bathed, dressed and met Finn downstairs in half an hour, as requested. He smiled politely at her, carried her luggage and helped her into the truck, but something still seemed off. Despite every effort to dote on her, Finn barely looked at her. Avery should have been thrilled. After all, this was exactly the sort of arrangement she'd wanted. No risk. No pressure. No sex.

Absolutely no sex.

Yet she felt strangely hollow as they drove to her doctor's appointment. When they hit the open highway and Finn relaxed beside her, dropping his right hand to his thigh, she had to stop herself from reaching for it and weaving her fingers through his. She'd grown accustomed to his touch over their time together, and it felt strange now to be so close to him without feeling the brush of his skin against hers. She missed it more than she wanted to admit.

Be careful what you wish for.

The thought spun around and around in her mind as they wound their way past clusters of trees in saffron yellows and fiery reds. Bear's Paw, the town where her obstetrician was located, was situated halfway between Rust Creek Falls and Billings—close enough to a major medical facility in case something went wrong with her pregnancy, but still remote enough to guarantee a modicum of privacy. Avery only hoped Finn had never dated anyone who worked at the practice.

For the first time since their epic argument in Great Gulch, she considered what Finn had told her about his father's efforts to find brides for all six of his sons, to the tune of a million dollars. It sounded crazy. Then again, Maximilian Crawford was definitely the sort of man who got what he wanted, regardless of the cost.

Perhaps she shouldn't be so quick to judge Finn for systematically dating his way through the eligible female population of Montana. As he'd said, they'd been nothing but meaningless setups. Somehow, though, that almost made it worse. He'd been so intent on proving he couldn't be dragged to the altar that he'd acted like a kid in a candy store. And now here he was, right where he'd never wanted to be. Married.

She couldn't help but feel like the consolation prize. And still, all she wanted right then in the world was to hold his hand. Unbelievable.

"Almost there." Finn glanced at her, but his smile was stiff as he exited the highway and turned onto Bear Paw's quaint Main Street.

The town square, with its white gazebo in the center and surrounding mom-and-pop businesses, reminded Avery of both Great Gulch and Rust Creek Falls. There was certainly no shortage of small-town charm in Montana. Raising a family here would be so different than it would in a big city like Dallas. The thought put a lump in Avery's throat, and she wasn't sure why.

Finn's truck slowed to a stop in front of a redbrick building with an arch made of antlers hanging over the entryway.

"Here we are." He nodded.

"Yes, here we are." There was a telltale waver in her voice that had Finn's gaze narrowing in her direction.

For the first time since the night before when she'd leaped out of his arms, he looked at her...*really* looked.

"Hey." He cupped her face in one of his big, warm hands, and the simple contact was such a relief that Avery nearly wept.

Was she in for another five full months of out-of-control emotions? Because it was really getting old.

"You're not nervous about this, are you?" Finn said as his thumb made gentle circular motions on her cheek.

She was most definitely nervous about seeing the doctor. Terrified, actually.

Despite her recent success with the baby goat, she had no clue what she was doing. She'd been such a mess lately. What if the stress of keeping the pregnancy a secret from Finn for so long had somehow harmed the baby?

She'd never forgive herself if that were true. "I'm a little nervous."

"Listen to me." He leaned his forehead against hers, and as his gaze fixed with hers, the new frostiness between them thawed ever so slightly. "Everything is going to be fine. Okay?"

She nodded. "Okay."

With Finn there, it seemed easier to believe. And if anything was indeed wrong, at least she wouldn't have to handle it all on her own.

Her chest grew tight as she climbed out of the truck and walked up the steps leading into building. Being cut off from her family stung now more than ever. If she had a difficult pregnancy or if her baby had health challenges, her parents were willing to let her handle things all by herself. She could hardly believe it. She'd never even set eyes on her son or daughter, and she couldn't imagine ever leaving them in this position. Totally and completely alone.

Except Finn was here, just as he'd promised. And he'd taken a vow to be by her side, no matter what happened.

The gravity of such a promise hit her hard as she checked in with the receptionist and filled out all the necessary medical forms. This was serious. There were pages and pages of questions to be answered and information to process. It all seemed to pass in a worrisome, overwhelming blur until at last she was wearing a paper gown and lying on an examination table beside an ultrasound machine.

After spending most of the morning in the waiting room, Finn now sat, stone-faced, in a chair facing the dark screen. Upon Avery's request, the nurse had gone to find him so they could both catch their first glimpse of the baby at the same time. There was still a layer of tension between them that hadn't been there before their night in the honeymoon suite at Maverick Manor. Although if she was truly being honest with herself, the strain in their relationship had raised its ugly head when she'd first told him about the pregnancy. It was just much more obvious since the tender moment they'd shared when he carried her over the threshold.

He was angry, and Avery could totally understand why. The secret had gotten away from her faster than she could figure out what to do with it, and now she was paying the price. Just because Finn was so eager to put a ring on her finger didn't mean he'd forgiven her.

Nor did it mean that he loved her.

Still, she was so glad to have him sitting there beside her that she could have cried.

"Okay, let's see what we have here." The doctor smiled at Avery and covered her belly with some type of gel.

Then she pressed a device that reminded Avery of a large computer mouse over her abdomen, and the screen lit up with moving shadows in various shades of gray.

The doctor confirmed what they both already knew—Avery's due date lined up perfectly with their night together in Oklahoma as the time of conception. But what Avery wanted most of all was a clear view of the baby, yet she couldn't make sense of the blurry images on the monitor.

And then all the breath in her body seemed to bottle up in her chest as a delicate profile came into view, followed by a glimpse of a tiny foot with five tiny, perfect toes.

"Are you two interested in having one of those trendy gender reveal parties? Or should I go ahead and spill the beans?" the doctor asked.

"Spill," Avery said. "Please."

There'd been enough surprises already. Besides, how could she have a gender reveal party when her own family wasn't even speaking to her?

"In that case, there she is," the doctor said, smiling.

Finn's gaze flew to meet Avery's, and all the things they couldn't seem to say to each other—all the hidden fears and insecurities, all the doubts, tempered by an aching, raw longing for connection—melted away.

There she is.

A little girl. Their daughter—hers and Finn's.

Chapter Twelve

Avery was relieved that seeing the sonogram alleviated some of the tension between her and Finn. A week later, they were still getting along well enough that the Crawfords seemed to genuinely believe they were in love. Even Melba and Old Gene had fallen for the ruse, showering them with congratulations and best wishes upon their return to Rust Creek Falls.

They'd moved into Finn's suite at the Ambling A, which so far had been spacious enough for them to move about in separate orbits. At night, Avery slept in Finn's king-size bed, with its rustic Aspen log frame and sheets that smelled of sandalwood, hay and warm leather. Of Finn.

Her husband camped out on the oversize leather sofa adjacent to the bed, far enough away to avoid any accidental physical contact, but close enough for Avery to grow accustomed to the rhythmic sound of his breathing in the dark. He hadn't touched her at all since she'd taken up residence in his home—not even a casual hug or innocent brush of his fingertips—and somehow hearing him sleep so close by made her feel a little less lonely. A little less like an outsider on Crawford territory.

They weren't going to get away with the lack of physical affection for long—not if everyone was going to remain convinced that they were actual, real newlyweds. But Avery was grateful for a little breathing room.

By the time she and Finn joined the rest of the Crawford clan at the annual Rust Creek Falls Halloween costume party, she'd foolishly begun to believe she had enough of a handle on her emotions to withstand a lengthy public charade.

She was wrong, of course.

So.

Very.

Wrong.

The party was held in the high school gym, which someone had spent a serious amount of effort transforming into a Halloween-themed delight. There was a maze made of hay bales off to the side, swags of twisted orange and black crepe paper and more fake spiderwebs than Avery had ever seen in one place before. As promised, Melba had made her famous caramel apples, and when Avery and Finn arrived, children dressed as ghosts, ballerinas and superheroes had clearly been enjoying the sweet treats, as evidenced by their sticky chins.

Avery couldn't help but smile. She'd never been to a party like this one before, not even when she was a child.

She couldn't remember ever going trick-or-treating, either. Halloween night in Dallas always meant the mayor's posh Masquerade Ball, held at an exclusive hotel overlooking the city skyline. Invitations to the fancy masked ball were coveted, and Avery and her parents were always regulars. When she'd been a little girl, she'd stayed at home with the nanny and watched while her parents headed off to the party, dressed in opulent Halloween finery.

But this, she thought as she looked around the gym, *this is what a Halloween party should look like.*

She loved it all, from the happy children and homemade treats to the makeshift dance floor where an adult dressed as Frankenstein's monster was leading a group in a dance to the "Monster Mash."

"Wait a minute." Avery took a closer look at the face beneath the green makeup. "Is that your father out there on the dance floor?"

Finn shook his head and let out a wry laugh. "It certainly looks that way."

"Hey, it's about time the lovebirds arrived." Wilder, wrapped in bandages to look like a mummy, handed Finn a beer and gave Avery a peck on the cheek. "The gang's all here."

He wasn't kidding. The Crawfords were camped out at two adjoining picnic tables right in the center of the action. All five of Finn's brothers were there, accompanied, of course, by their respective wives and children—Logan and Sarah with baby Sophia, Xander and Lily, Knox and Genevieve, Hunter with Wren. Since Avery's surprise wedding to Finn, Wilder and Hunter were the only two remaining single brothers, and neither had dates for the costume party—unless Hunter's daughter counted. Avery certainly thought so. They looked like the perfect father-daughter Halloween duo, with Wren dressed in a puffy tulle princess gown and Hunter wearing a large cardboard rectangle covered in tinfoil strapped to his chest.

"What are you supposed to be, dude?" Finn cast a dubious glance at Hunter's cardboard accessory. Its tinfoil covering was starting to look a little worse for wear. "A robot?"

Hunter's face fell. "No."

"He's a knight in shining armor," Avery said, winking at Wren. "Obviously. You and your daddy match, don't you?"

"Yes!" Wren giggled and pointed at the plastic crown perched atop her silky blond hair. "I'm a princess, and Daddy is a knight."

"I totally see it," Avery said, struggling to keep a straight face as Finn shook his head at Hunter.

"Nope. That—" he pointed at Hunter's sad silver shield "—is weak. Don't tell me you couldn't come up with a more convincing knight getup."

Hunter glowered at him.

Avery thought it was sweet that Hunter had gone to the effort to try to make a costume.

"Cut your brother some slack." Avery gave Finn a playful little shoulder bump and then froze when she realized what she'd done.

She'd initiated contact—a clear violation of their unspoken agreement not to touch one another, because as they both knew, one thing could very well lead to another. Before the marriage, they'd agreed to no sex. But since the wedding night, they hadn't so much as kissed. Somewhere along the way, the no-sex rule had snowballed into something else. It was as if they were both going out of their way to avoid any physical contact whatsoever.

Avery crossed her arms, uncrossed them and then crossed them again, painfully aware of every part of her body relative to Finn's. Less than inch of space existed between her arm and his chest, and the air in that space felt electric all of a sudden.

A shiver coursed through her while she tried to concentrate on what Hunter was saying.

"I'm doing the best I can." He rested a hand on top of Wren's slender shoulder and gave it a squeeze. "You'll understand one day when you have kids."

Finn practically choked on his beer.

"When's that going to be, anyway?" Wilder grinned at Finn. "You were in such a hurry to put a ring on this lady's finger, I figure you'll be wanting to start a family sooner rather than later."

Avery didn't dare look at Finn. If she did, the truth surely would be written all over her face.

"Give us time" was all he said in response, but when the conversation turned to other, less panic-inducing matters, he slipped his arm around her waist and pulled her close.

Little fires seemed to skitter over her skin everywhere he touched her. Her brain told her to pull away, to save herself. But her body had other ideas. Every cell in her body seemed to sigh with relief at once again being so near to the man she'd married…the man she was afraid she was starting to care for far more than she'd ever intended.

Their eyes met, and then his gaze flitted to her lips. He quickly looked away.

It's all just for show. She needed that reminder. They were newlyweds. His family was watching…the entire town was watching. They needed to make it look real. After all, that's why they'd come to the party dressed in matching bride and groom costumes.

She just wished it didn't *feel* so real.

She did her best to shift her attention elsewhere. Maximilian seemed to be hitting the dance floor with a different partner every time the song changed. His partners ranged from small children he let stand on his feet as he spun them around to women his own age, and everyone else in between. Avery couldn't help but laugh. For a man who seemed so invested in marrying off his sons, he sure was a flirt. The biggest one in Rust Creek Falls, so it seemed.

"Avery." Little Wren tugged on the sleeve of Avery's white dress to get her attention.

"Yes, sweetie?" Avery took a seat on the picnic bench so that they were eye to eye. Finn's fingertips slid casually to the back of her neck, where he toyed languidly with a lock of her hair.

It's only make-believe, no more real than Hunter's tinfoil shield.

"You and Uncle Finn just got married, right?" Wren smoothed down the front of her pink tulle gown. Hunter had chosen the DIY route for his own costume, but he'd obviously steered clear of Pinterest for his daughter's. She looked like a mini Disney princess, all the way down to the petite velvet slippers on her feet.

"We did." Avery nodded, pushing the cheap tulle veil on her head away from her eyes.

Wren's little brow furrowed. "Why didn't you have a fancy wedding with a big white dress?"

"Oh. Well." Avery's heart was in her throat all of a sudden, and her simple bride costume made her feel more like a fraud than ever before. "Not everyone has a fancy wedding. What matters most is finding someone you care about, someone you know you'll love." She swallowed. Hard. "Forever and ever."

"Like happily-ever-after?" Wren said.

Avery nodded, not quite trusting herself to speak.

"Life is perfect when you're a princess or a bride." The little girl spun in a circle with her hands clasped in front of her as if she were holding a bridal bouquet.

Perfect?

Not quite. Avery was a bride, and her life was far from perfect. Sometimes she wished she'd never thought to make her marriage to Finn a business arrangement. Would it really be so terrible to try to make things work? They were having a baby together, after all.

"I can't wait until I'm a bride one day," Wren said, running her tiny fingers over Avery's short costume wedding dress.

And then she skipped away, a vision in tulle, and Avery couldn't help but feel like she'd just had a conversation with her younger self.

Had she really ever been as innocent and starry-eyed as Wren?

Yes, she had. And despite everything, a part of her—the wishful, hopeful part that seemed to rise from the ashes every time she looked at Finn—still was.

But she wasn't a child anymore. It had been years since she'd trusted in fairy-tale endings, and Finn had never tried to pretend he was her Prince Charming. He'd always been up front and honest about what they'd had. Not a lifetime, but a night. Just one…until the baby had come along. It was a shame little girls were set up with such high expectations.

Real life was so seldom as perfect as Wren believed.

Avery was gone.

One minute, she'd been chatting with Wren, and the next time Finn glanced in her direction, she wasn't here.

He frowned into his beer as his brothers continued their running commentary of Maximilian's efforts to charm Melba Strickland onto the dance floor. It wasn't going well for Max. According to town lore, she'd never danced with a man other than Old Gene, and by all appearances, it was going to stay that way.

"Denied." Wilder let out a laugh. "Again."

Finn glanced toward the games area of the gym, where Wren, Lily, Genevieve and Sarah were participating in a race in which they wrapped each other in spools of white gauze to look like mummies. Still no Avery.

"You're missing it." Hunter gave Finn a nudge with his elbow. "I swear Melba is on the verge of conking Dad in the head with one of her caramel apples."

"What?" Finn said absently as he continued scanning the surroundings in search of his wife.

"Hey." Hunter nudged him harder. "What's with you?"

"I can't find Avery."

Hunter shrugged. "She was here a few minutes ago. She probably went to the bar for a beer."

Wrong on both counts. Avery wasn't drinking because of her pregnancy, and it had been longer than a mere few minutes since he'd seen her last.

"I'm going to go look for her." Finn shoved his beer at Hunter.

He took it and shrugged. "Suit yourself, but if you're just looking for an excuse to run off and take your wife to bed, you could have just said so."

Finn grunted a noncommittal response and went to weave his way through the crowd, but he couldn't find Avery anywhere. Panic coiled into a tight knot in the pit of his stomach.

What if something was wrong, either with her or the baby?

She would have said something to him if she wasn't feeling well, wouldn't she?

He didn't want to worry his family or the Stricklands, so instead of asking Melba or one of his female relatives to take a look in the ladies' room, he knocked on the door himself. Still no luck. She wasn't anywhere in the gymnasium.

Adrenaline shot through him, causing a terrible tingle in his chest. He needed to find her. Now.

Finn fled the party without saying goodbye. If he told the other Crawfords why he was so desperate to find Avery, he'd end up outing her pregnancy when he'd promised her they would wait to tell everyone. But if she wasn't in the parking lot or right outside the building, he was going to have to get help from someone. She hadn't just vanished into thin air.

He pushed through the double doors of the gym, squinting into the darkness. The moon hung low in the sky overhead, so big and round it looked swollen. A harvest moon spilling amber light over the horizon.

And in the distance he saw her—Avery, so beautiful in the moonlight—sitting on a playground swing, looking even more like a bride than she had on their wedding day.

Stone-cold relief washed over him. He was too happy to see her to let himself be irritated at her for disappearing like that. He rushed toward her, swallowing the pavement with big strides, but then someone cut into his path. A woman.

"This must be my lucky night," she said, gazing up at him from beneath the brim of a witch's hat.

Finn had no clue as to the woman's identity, other than the generic naughty-witch vibe she was giving off in her skimpy costume. Didn't she know this was an old-fashioned family-friendly party?

"Sorry, I'm on my way..." He gestured vaguely toward the swing set, where Avery lifted her head and met his gaze.

"You're Finn Crawford," the witch said. "At long last. I've been trying to get ahold of you for days."

"What?" He dragged his attention away from Avery to look at the woman again. "I'm sorry. I don't think we've met."

"We haven't, but Viv Dalton assured me you'd be interested in making my acquaintance. I'm Natalie." The witch batted her purple eyelashes at him and laid a hand on his chest.

He gently but firmly removed it. "I think there's been a misunderstanding."

This must be the woman who'd been blowing up his cell a few days ago, the same woman who'd called the Ambling A and spoken to Maximilian.

"I'm not dating anymore," he said. "I actually just got married."

"So that's not just a costume?" The witch blinked in the direction of his tuxedo T-shirt and his adhesive "groom" name tag. Her face fell. "Oh. Too bad."

"Again, sorry. But I really need to go." He looked past her toward the playground, but the swing set was empty now. One empty, lonely swing moved back and forth.

Damn it.

She was gone again.

"Avery?" He called out, jogging toward the playground. She couldn't have gone far. "Avery! Where are you?"

He found her clear around the corner, stomping down North Buckskin Road, her costume bridal veil whipping furiously around her head.

"Avery, thank God," he said, breathing hard as he struggled to catch up. "You had me worried sick."

She rolled her eyes and kept on walking, and it wasn't until she passed beneath a streetlamp that he noticed the dark rings of mascara under her eyes. His gut churned.

She'd been crying.

"Where are you going? What's wrong?"

"Back to the boarding house." She sniffed and kept marching toward Cedar Street, where the old purple Victorian loomed at the intersection.

The panicked knot in the pit of Finn's stomach tightened until he was almost gasping for air. "What? Why?"

"I miss Pumpkin, and I don't want to be anywhere near you right now." She stopped abruptly and glared at him. "I'd much prefer the company of a baby goat to you at the moment."

"Because of the witch?" He glanced over his shoulder toward the high school and then fixed his gaze with Avery's again. She was angry—clearly—but somewhere beneath the glittering fury in her big doe eyes, he saw something else. Hurt.

"Avery." He shook his head and jammed his hands on his hips to stop himself from reaching for her… from plunging his hands in her hair and kissing her full on the lips in flagrant violation of their marital agreement. "Princess, she's no one. Just some woman Viv Dalton wanted to set me up with a while back. But that was after I found out you were here, so obviously I told her no."

Avery glanced up at him for a second, then resumed staring at a spot somewhere to his left. Clearly, she had no interest in even looking at him.

"If you'd stuck around back there, you would have heard me tell Viv's witch that I'd just gotten married and that I couldn't stop for a chat because I'd come outside looking for *you*."

Avery narrowed her gaze at him and squared her shoulders. "I wasn't jealous, if that's what you're thinking."

Liar.

Finn didn't dare laugh, but he was temped. "Is that so, wifey?"

"Okay, maybe I was just a little." She held her pointer finger and thumb a sliver apart. "An infinitesimal amount."

"Got it." He nodded, and the adrenaline flooding his body shifted into something else far more familiar, far more dangerous under the circumstances. Desire. "You're hightailing it back to the boarding house because you were jealous to sec me talking to another woman."

He took a step closer, needing her softness. Her heat. "Even though you have no interest whatsoever in sleeping with me."

Her lips parted, and the tip of her cherry-red tongue darted out to wet them. Finn instantly went hard.

She lifted her chin, determined to stand her ground even though they both knew she'd just showed her hand. She wanted him just as badly as he wanted her. "I already told you why I was going back. I miss Pumpkin."

"So this wild-goose chase you've got me on is about a goat?" He wasn't buying it, not even for a second.

"Yes." She huffed out a sigh. "Mostly. Plus I was talking to Wren and she asked me why we didn't have a big wedding. She told me she couldn't wait to be a bride one day, just like me. And I just… I can't…"

Tears shimmered in her eyes, sparkling like diamonds in the moonlight. "What are we doing, Finn?"

He'd made Avery a promise when she'd agreed to marry him. She'd asked so little of him, and he'd been determined to keep his word, no matter how agonizing that promise turned out to be.

Did she have any idea how many times he'd nearly slipped up and reached for her? A thousand times a day, whether to simply hold her hand, spread his palms over her belly to feel the life growing inside her—the life they'd made together—or to touch her in all the ways he dreamed about every night when he slept alone on his sad leather sofa.

His gaze bored into her as though that's all it would take for her to understand. As if he only needed to look at her hard enough for her to know how badly he ached for her. Then…now…always.

She was his. She'd *been* his all along. Didn't she know that?

Screw it.

He couldn't do it anymore, and from what she was

telling him, neither could she. It was time to forget their silly rules and be honest with each other for a change.

"This," he said, lifting his hand to cup her chin between his thumb and forefinger. "*This* is what we're doing."

Then he touched his lips to hers with a gentleness in stark opposition to the riot taking place inside him. He wouldn't force himself on her—not now, not ever—and he needed some sort of confirmation that this was okay. That this was what she wanted, even though she'd been doing her level best to pretend otherwise.

That confirmation came in the form of a breathy, kittenish sigh and Avery's hands sliding around his neck, her nails digging feverishly into his back. Then she kissed him so hard he saw stars.

There's my girl, he thought. *There's my princess.*

And then there were no more thoughts, no more rules and no more walls as he scooped his wife into his arms and carried her to his truck in plain view of anyone who cared to look. Finn didn't give a damn about appearances. It was time to take his wife to bed.

Chapter Thirteen

We shouldn't be doing this.

Those words kept spinning through Avery's consciousness as she and Finn fumbled their way up the stairs of the log mansion at the Ambling A, kissing and shedding articles of clothing along the way.

Thank goodness the rest of the family was still eating caramel apples and dancing to the "Monster Mash" back in the high school gymnasium. Because as desperately as she ached for her husband right now, she wasn't sure if she could have stopped for anyone or anything. Not even if Frankenstein's actual monster had been blocking their path to the bedroom.

We shouldn't be doing this.

Finn pressed her against the wall just outside his bedroom, and his lips moved away from her mouth, dragging slowly, deliciously down the side of her neck.

She sagged against the cool pine, hands fisting in his hair as he kissed his way from one breast to the other.

They definitely shouldn't be doing *that*.

Stopping wasn't an option, though. It no longer mattered what they should or shouldn't be doing. Desire was moving through her with the force of a freight train, bearing down hard. She needed this. She'd needed this so badly for so long. It felt like forever since the last time Finn had touched her like this, the last time he'd laid her down on the smooth sheets of his bed in Oklahoma and thrust inside her for the very first time.

The only time.

How was that even possible? She was made for this… made for him. They fit together like two halves of the same whole, and after they'd parted on that strange, sad morning in Oklahoma City, she'd never quite felt whole again. All these months it was as if she'd been walking around with a huge piece of herself missing, just out of reach.

And then…

Then she'd realized she was pregnant, and she'd somehow convinced herself that was the reason she'd been feeling so out of sorts. She wasn't in love with Finn Crawford. She couldn't be. They barely knew one another. The only thing she'd known for absolute certain was that he was a Crawford and that her father would probably drop dead on the spot if he ever found out they'd been intimate.

These were the things she'd told herself as she'd put away her pencil skirts, packed her yoga mat and headed to Rust Creek Falls. Love had nothing to do with her messy state of emotional disarray. It all boiled down to science. She was walking around with a piece of

Finn Crawford inside her, his DNA had gone and gotten itself all mixed up with hers, and now her body was confused. It was as simple as that. Three out of four biologists would totally agree with her.

Lies.

Lies, lies and more lies.

Had she really been so foolish as to believe that she could come to the Ambling A and not end up right here, with Finn slowly walking her backward until her knees hit the edge of the bed and they tumbled together, already losing track of where her body ended and his began? Had she honestly thought she could marry him and keep up the whole virgin-bride routine in an effort to spare her heart?

It seemed ludicrous now. Why should she forgo *this*? Finn was her husband, and she was his wife. There was nothing whatsoever wrong with the way he gently parted her thighs and kissed his way down her body, his tongue warm and wicked against the cool of her skin. On the contrary, it was exquisite. She was lost in the moment in a way that she'd never managed to achieve, no matter how many hot yoga classes she'd attended or how often she'd used the meditation app on her phone.

No one existed outside her and Finn. There was no embarrassment, no worry as her hips moved up and down, undulating in perfect rhythm with the stroke of his fingers, searching…seeking the release that only he could give her. She was free and open in a way that she'd never been able to be with anyone else. Because they were special. She could run all she wanted, but she'd always come back to this—to his hands sliding into her hair as his gaze burned into hers, branding her, soul-deep. To the flawless heat of his body perfectly poised over hers and the way he shuddered when he finally slid inside her. To the way she shattered around him instantly, crying out his name.

Finn.

It had always been him, and it always would be. Giving herself to him again changed nothing, because he'd captured her heart a long time ago.

Yet at the same time, it changed everything. Because somewhere beneath the honeyed heat of her desire, she remembered he'd never said it. The one thing she wanted to hear more than anything else in the world. *I love you.*

Her heart ached to hear it, but she managed to push her hunger for it down. Deep down to the place where it had been since the moment Finn slipped the ring on her finger and she realized she wanted it to be real. For *them* to be real.

And she actually thought it would stay there. She believed she could spend her nights in Finn's bed, touching him, loving him, pretending he felt it even though he never said the words. Because sometimes pretending was better than nothing. Sometimes pretending was as good as it got.

But after it was over—after he'd stroked her to climax again and again, after he'd groaned her name and shuddered his release and they lay beside each other with legs and hearts intertwined—he did something that finally broke the pretense beyond repair.

He leaned over and, with the softest brush of his lips imaginable, he kissed her growing belly. And with an ache in his voice that she'd never heard before, he whispered a word. Just one. The most profoundly beautiful one he could have said.

Mine.

If only she could have made herself believe he'd been

talking about her. Or them—her and the baby both. But he hadn't. He'd meant the child, their child, and while it was sweet, it just wasn't enough. And it never would be, because sometimes pretending was better than nothing, but when it wasn't, it was the most devastating heartbreak of all.

I can't stay here anymore.

The thought started as a spark, and in the hours before the sun came up, it exploded into a wildfire, burning out of control and destroying everything in its path—every last hope for a future, charred beyond recognition. She'd repeated it to herself so many times in the night that it became a balm, a way to calm the panic that threatened to eat her alive at the thought of saying goodbye. By the time Finn opened his eyes, she was already dressed, packed and ready to go. All she had to do was tell him.

"I can't stay here anymore."

Finn was dreaming.

No, it wasn't a dream. It was a nightmare—the worst nightmare his unconscious possibly could have conjured.

He closed his eyes and willed the image of Avery, fully clothed with one of her slick designer suitcases in her hand, out of his head. His mind was playing tricks on him. That had to be it. Last night had changed everything. He and Avery had finally stopped pretending and been honest with each other about their feelings. They'd made love.

And that's exactly what it had been, too. Not just sex. Things between him and Avery had never been just physical. He knew that now. On some level, he always had.

But no matter how hard he tried to keep his eyes closed and go back to the world from just hours before—the world where he and his wife were tangled in bedsheets—he couldn't. The space beside him was cold. Empty…

As empty as his heart felt when he opened his eyes and realized the sight in front of him wasn't a dream, after all. It was real.

"Excuse me?" he said, staring hard at Avery's suitcase.

When the hell had she packed it? Had she climbed out of his bed the moment he'd fallen asleep?

"I can't stay here," she repeated, a gut-wrenching echo.

He sat up, and the sheet fell away, exposing him. Avery took a sharp inhale and averted her gaze.

Seriously?

"Look at me, damn it," he growled. "What are talking about? You can't leave, Princess. You just…"

…can't.

What would he say to his family when they woke up and found out she'd left? What would he do? They were a family. She couldn't just leave.

But apparently she could, because she was already walking toward the door.

Out of his bed.

Out of his life.

"No." Finn jumped up and went after her. "Whatever's wrong, we can fix it. Let me fix it, Princess. Please."

He'd never allowed himself to be more vulnerable in his life. He was naked and begging, but he didn't care.

"We can take things slow, if that's what you want," he blurted as her hand gripped the doorknob.

She paused, just long enough to shake her head. "Finn, we..."

"What happened last night doesn't have to happen again. We can wait. We can do whatever you want. Just don't leave."

"Can't you see?" She shook her head again. "I have to. I just need some space. Please."

Space.

He could give her that, couldn't he? Maybe a night or two at the boarding house would do them both some good.

No. Finn glared at her. He wanted her here, with him. He needed his wife and his baby. He needed them as surely as he needed his next breath.

"You're my wife. We had a deal, remember?" he said. Married...till death do them part.

God, what was wrong with him? He sounded as controlling and manipulative as his father.

"You're right." Avery looked past him, toward the bed. "And last night we broke that deal. So now all bets are off."

"Avery." He raked a hand through his hair, tugging hard at the ends. "I'm..."

He couldn't bring himself to say he was sorry. Because he wasn't. Not entirely. What had happened between them last night had been honest and real. Even more authentic than the band of gold around Avery's finger. She knew it as well as he did. Why else would she be running scared?

But even as he prepared to stand his ground stubbornly, he realized that somewhere deep down, he *was*.

He was sorry for anything that made Avery hurt or made her afraid. Because all he wanted was to make her feel loved. And safe in his arms.

He took a deep breath and forced the words out. "I'm sorry."

It didn't matter. Nothing he said mattered, because she'd already made up her mind.

"Me, too," she said quietly.

And then she walked right out the door, taking Finn's baby and every battered beat of his heart with her as she left.

Avery's nonstop flight to Dallas felt like the longest two and a half hours of her life.

She did everything she could to make the time pass as quickly as possible, from her stack of glossy fashion magazines to the vast array of snacks she'd picked up at the airport gift shop. But living at the boarding house for so long had changed Avery's eating habits. She much preferred Melba's and Claire's home cooking to the quick grab-and-go fare and Lean Cuisines she'd lived on while she'd been so busy helping run Ellington Meats. And as it turned out, she'd even lost all enthusiasm for her beloved *Vogue*, *Elle* and *Harper's Bazaar* now that she could no longer wear any of the sleek, fitted clothes featured on their pages.

Or maybe she'd simply developed a sudden fondness for flannel and cowboy boots.

Good grief, what was happening to her? Tastes changed, she supposed. The delicate rose gold ring on her finger was perhaps the most glaringly obvious testament to that fact, from the ring itself to the marriage it represented. Her father would probably have a heart attack the minute he saw it.

She thought about removing the ring before the plane landed, but she just couldn't bring herself to do so. She'd told Finn she was leaving, but she hadn't said a word about ending their marriage. That was a given, though, wasn't it? Part of the condition of coming home had always been cutting Finn out of her life. As welcoming as her parents had been on the phone when she'd broken down and called them from the airport in Montana, she had no reason to believe that had changed.

Taking the ring off seemed so final, though. The ultimate ending to a book she wasn't sure she was capable of closing. She just knew she needed time away from Rust Creek Falls to clear her head and figure out what was truly best for her and her baby. But if sleeping with Finn had confirmed anything, it was that she wasn't built for a marriage of convenience. She'd been fooling herself thinking she could marry a man and not become emotionally attached, especially a man she was already head over heels in love with.

When her flight finally landed in Dallas, she deplaned with nothing but a lump in her throat and her lone carry-on bag. It seemed impossible that she would come home with so little physical evidence of a life-changing month away. Her time in Montana almost felt like a fever dream, too colorful and lush to be real. But that was the whole point, wasn't it? None of it had been real. And now here she was, back on Texas soil with her smallest Louis Vuitton rolling bag and more emotional baggage than she could possibly carry all on her own.

When she saw her mother and father waiting for her just outside the security gate, she braced herself for a flood of emotions. But when her mother gathered her into her arms, Avery didn't even cry. Not a single, solitary tear. She'd come crawling home with her tail between her legs, but at the very least she'd expected to feel a small sense of relief.

After all, she was back in the fold. Her heart was safe now.

Then why did she feel nothing but a horrible numbness and the nagging sense that she'd just made the biggest mistake of her life?

It was a short ride from the airport to the Ellington family home in the moneyed neighborhood of Highland Park, and Avery's parents spent it getting her caught up on everything she'd missed while she'd been away.

Her mother told her about the latest happenings at the country club in lurid detail and suggested now that Avery was back, she might want to help cochair the upcoming Junior League charity fund-raiser. The lawn of the big gothic church on University Drive was a sea of orange now that the annual pumpkin patch was in full swing, and the mayor was throwing his annual Masquerade Ball. Avery had come just in time.

But the Masquerade Ball wouldn't be anything like the sweet Halloween dance she'd attended with the Crawfords. There wouldn't be any costumed children or fake spiderwebs or bobbing for apples. It would be a staid affair, perfectly planned, perfectly decorated and perfectly boring. She missed the small-town charm of Rust Creek Falls already.

Meanwhile, her father filled her in on what she'd missed at the office. He'd promoted one of the project managers in her absence, but her corner office was still ready and waiting for her. She could walk back into her old life just like nothing had ever happened. It would be as if she'd never gone to Rust Creek Falls at all.

Except she had.

She stared blankly ahead as the big iron gate at the foot of the driveway swung open and her father's Cadillac Escalade cruised past the security cameras. Neither of her parents had mentioned her pregnancy. Were they just going to pretend that she wasn't having Finn Crawford's baby in a few months' time? Was that how this strange homecoming was going to play out?

Her hand went instinctively to her baby bump, and a tiny nudge pressed against her palm, just as it had when she'd exchanged vows with Finn in the country courthouse in Great Gulch. Finally, something real she could grasp hold of. Her child. Avery was going to be a mother, and no amount of pretending could prove otherwise.

"I'm married," she said quietly as her father shifted the car into Park.

"Oh, dear." Her mother sighed. Finally she had something more pressing to worry about than the centerpieces for the next country club luncheon.

Her father's gaze locked with hers in the reflection of the rearview mirror. "I saw the ring and figured as much."

She bit her lip and nodded. Good. Perhaps their bizarre sense of denial wasn't as serious as she'd begun to think.

"That's what annulments are for. Our attorney can get this taken care of in a matter of days." Her dad shrugged one shoulder and then got out of the car and shut the door as if the matter had been settled once and for all.

All of Avery's breath bottled up in her throat. An annulment. Could she do that Finn? Did she even want to?

"Honey," her mom said, turning to rest a hand on Avery's knee. "Give your daddy time. We can talk about all of this later. The most important thing is that you're home now."

Avery nodded as she blinked back tears. Only they weren't the tears of relief she'd expected. They were something else, something too horrible and painful to name.

She climbed out of the car and went straight to her childhood bedroom at the top of the home's curved staircase. She passed the grand piano where she'd taken lessons as a little girl and the framed collection of photographs that lined the hallway—Avery as homecoming queen of her private high school, Avery dressed in a white satin gown and elegant elbow-length gloves at her debutante ball, her father spinning her across the dance floor at the father-daughter dance.

It didn't matter how old she was, how well she did at the office or even if she was pregnant, her father would always see her just like those framed images—as his daughter. Just a little girl, barely more than an extension of himself.

How had she never noticed this before? Sure, she'd always been a daddy's girl, following in her father's footsteps and working alongside him at the family business. Daddy's princess. But she'd always thought it had been her choice. *Her* path.

Had it? Had she ever been the one in charge of her own life?

It was all so confusing, and two hours later, once she'd showered, changed and gone back downstairs for dinner, she wasn't any closer to knowing the answer to the many questions spinning around in her head. She was only certain of one thing—the decision whether or not to end her marriage was hers and hers alone.

"Are you feeling better now, dear?" Avery's mom cast a surprised glance at the buffalo-checkered shirt she'd slipped into—one of her purchases from the general store—but refrained from asking why she hadn't dressed for dinner. Mealtime in the Ellington household had always been a rather formal affair.

"A little. I'm really tired." Avery took her seat, the same place she'd sat for every family meal of her life.

As usual, her father was already seated at the head of the table. "You'll feel back to your old self once you get some rest. Leave all the legal details to me. I'll meet with the lawyers first thing tomorrow and get the ball rolling."

Avery picked up her fork but set it back down. "Daddy, no. I'm not ready."

Oscar glanced at his wife, cleared his throat and then spread his napkin carefully in his lap. "Very well. We can discuss the legalities later."

"Absolutely." Her mother beamed. "Avery, I was thinking we could start decorating the bedroom next door to yours for the baby. Won't that be fun?"

Avery blinked. "What about my place?"

She hadn't protested when they'd taken her straight to the big Ellington mansion from the airport, but surely they didn't expect her to *live* here from now on. She was an adult, with her own townhome near the Galleria.

"We can get a crib for there, too, if you like. But

you're going to need help when the baby comes. We just assumed you'd want to stay here for a while." Her mother passed her a bowl of green beans.

Avery scooped some onto her plate and passed it to her father.

"We're just so glad you've finally come to your senses," he said. "Your child will have everything her little heart desires. She'll want for nothing."

Finally, they were talking about the baby. They were saying all the right things, making plans and acting like doting grandparents. Avery's childhood had been a happy one, and if her daughter grew up with the same upbringing, she'd no doubt be a happy, charmed little girl.

She'll want for nothing.

The words echoed in Avery's mind on repeat.

Right, she thought. *But what about what* I *want?*

Chapter Fourteen

Finn parked his rental car at the curb in front of the Georgian-style columned mansion on one of Highland Park's most prestigious streets. The driveway was blocked by a black steel gate with scrolled trim and a crest featuring a single cursive letter. *E* for Ellington.

Was he really going to just walk up to the front door and ring the bell of Oscar Ellington's home when he knew good and well he wasn't welcome here? Hell yes, he was.

Avery had *left* him. And she hadn't simply moved back down the road to Strickland's Boarding House. She'd gone all the way back to Texas, and she hadn't even bothered to give him the news herself. Melba and Old Gene had broken it to him when he'd shown up, desperate to talk to Avery. Melba had even gotten a little teary-eyed. She sat Finn down and tried to feed him some fresh caramel snickerdoodle cookies she'd just made for her boarders, but he couldn't eat. If Avery had gone back to Dallas, it meant only one thing—she'd agreed to her father's ridiculous terms.

Finn hadn't just lost his wife.

He'd lost his daughter, too.

He climbed out of the car and slammed the door. If Avery thought he was going to let her go straight from his bed back to her father without trying to talk some sense into her, she was dead wrong. He had a good idea what this was all about, anyway. They'd broken her sacred no-sex rule. Their fake marriage had suddenly become far too real, and she was running scared.

It would be okay, though. *They* would be okay. They had to be, because if Finn had learned anything in the days since he'd exchanged vows with Avery, it was that he couldn't live without her. Their fake marriage had always been real to him.

He simply needed to talk to her and assure her they could take things as slowly as she needed to. He'd do whatever she wanted, save for one thing—he'd never, ever let her family keep him from seeing his child.

Every damn flight from Montana to Dallas had been booked solid. Avery must have gotten the lone remaining seat on one of the last flights out. Thank God he'd remembered Maximilian's offer to send them off on a private jet for their honeymoon. When Finn told his father why he needed it, he hadn't even hesitated. The plane had been all fueled up, ready and waiting when Finn got to the airport in Billings.

His first stop upon landing had been Avery's town house, but her doorman assured Finn she'd been gone for weeks. There was only one place else she could be—the stately redbrick home in front of him. He gritted his teeth, pressed the doorbell and hoped against hope Avery would come to the door.

No such luck. *No one* came to the door. Instead, an older man's voice boomed through a small speaker situated next to the bell. "Sorry, son. This isn't a good time."

Finn's blood boiled at the sound of Oscar Ellington's condescending tone. He glanced around, trying to figure out how he'd already been identified. Sure enough, there were security cameras stationed in four different corners of the mansion's veranda.

He stared the closest one down. "I've come all the way from Montana. The least you can do is open the door."

"We're in the middle of dinner. Like I said, it's not a good time."

Seriously? He wasn't even going to come to the door?

Finn didn't know why he was surprised. The man had disowned his own daughter—his *pregnant* daughter, who'd always been daddy's little princess until she'd started calling the shots in her own life. Why would he suddenly be reasonable just because Finn had been on a wild-goose chase across the country?

He rang the bell again. Once, twice, three times.

"Am I going to have to call the police?" Oscar bellowed over the intercom.

If he wanted a screaming match, Finn was more than game. He yelled at the intercom, "Call whoever you want. I've come to take my wife home, and I'm not leaving here without her."

Across the street, a security guard's car rolled to a stop. Maybe Oscar wouldn't need to call the cops.

It looked as though the neighborhood watch had that covered.

He beat on the door with a fist. He was done wasting time with the stupid bell and the prissy little intercom. Oscar needed to come outside so they could discuss the situation like men.

But the next voice to come over the intercom wasn't Oscar's. It was Avery's.

"Finn? Is that you?"

He nearly wept with relief at the sound of her soft Texas twang. Less than twelve hours ago, she'd been naked in his bed, and now they were talking through a speaker.

He fixed his gaze on the closest security camera. "Avery, baby. It's me. I've come to take you home. Whatever is wrong, we can fix it. Please, you've got to let me fix it."

"Can't you see that she's made her choice? My daughter wants nothing to do with you. For the last time, I'm ordering you to vacate the premises." Oscar's tone wasn't any more sympathetic than it had been before Avery joined the discussion, and somehow Finn doubted what he was saying was true.

Avery was running scared, but had she really told her father she wanted nothing more to do with him? He didn't want to believe it, but despair had begun to tie itself in knots in the pit of his stomach. He needed to see his wife. He needed to look her in the eye and tell her everything would be all right if she would just come home.

Every muscle in his body tensed. If Oscar didn't open the door, Finn was going to tear it down with his bare hands.

"Daddy, stop," Avery pleaded.

She was crying again, damn it. What was her father thinking? She was pregnant. If he hurt her…if he hurt the baby…

Heat flushed through Finn's body. He felt like he was on the verge of some kind of breakdown, breathing in ragged gulps until he felt like he was choking.

And then, by some miracle, the door swung open.

His head jerked up. He wasn't sure whether to expect Avery or her father as hope and dread danced a terrible duet in his consciousness.

But it was neither of them. Instead, an older woman with Avery's kind eyes stood on the threshold. "You must be Finn. I'm Avery's mother, Marion."

"Hello, ma'am." Finn tipped his hat. "I'm sorry for the…ah…disruption. But—"

She held up her hands. "Don't apologize. I understand this is a volatile situation, and I want to invite you in so we can all discuss this like reasonable adults."

He nodded, wanting to trust her but fully expecting Oscar to appear out of nowhere and slam the door in his face.

"Please, Finn." She held the door open wide, and for better or for worse, he stepped inside.

Avery had never thought she'd see the day Finn Crawford would be standing inside the house where she'd grown up, but here he was…in the flesh. And much to her irritation, that flesh looked even better than she remembered it. Was it possible that her husband had gotten even more handsome in the twelve hours or so since she'd last seen him?

It wasn't, right? Which meant the reason the sight

of him sent shivers through every nerve ending of her body was because she'd missed him. She'd missed him more than she could fathom, but that didn't mean she was going to simply stand by and let the two men in her life argue over her as if she was one of their cattle.

At the moment, Finn and Oscar were staring daggers at each other with nothing but her mother's antique Chippendale coffee table between them to prevent an epic physical altercation. It was beyond ridiculous, and Avery was over it.

"Have you two completely lost your minds?" she spat.

They both started blaming each other at once, her father bellowing on about Maximilian, and Finn insisting that Avery pack her bags immediately and head back to the Ambling A. The crystal chandelier hanging overhead nearly shook from all the yelling.

Avery clamped her hands over her ears as tears streamed down her face. How was she supposed to make sense of anything when they were behaving this way? Maybe she should forget about Montana and Texas altogether and go raise her child on a desert island somewhere.

"Everyone, just settle down," her mother said calmly. "Or *I'll* call the police on *both* of you."

Oscar reared back as if someone had slapped him. Avery probably did as well, seeing as she'd never heard her mother speak to him like that before. Finn cast cautious glances all around.

Marion crossed her arms and continued, "Now that I have everyone's attention, why don't we all sit down? I told Finn we were going to have an adult conversation, and that's exactly what we're going to do."

No one moved a muscle. Finn and Oscar seemed to be engaged in some kind of alpha male contest to see who would comply first.

"That's it." Avery threw up her hands. "I've had enough of both of you."

Finn plopped down on the closest armchair so quickly it looked he was playing a game of musical chairs.

"I'm sitting. I'm ready." He fixed his gaze on her father. "Let's discuss this, Oscar. Man to man."

Her father sat, but not without commentary. "Fine, although there's not much to discuss. Avery left you to come home. I think that says it all."

Finn glanced at Avery, and the pain in his face was visceral. "With all due respect, sir. I'm Avery's husband, and her home is with me."

They were getting nowhere. Avery didn't know whether to cry or knock both their heads together.

"Enough," her mother said sharply. "This isn't for the two of you to decide. It's between Finn and Avery, no one else."

A tiny spark of hope ignited deep in Avery's soul. Finally, someone had said it. Whatever she and Finn felt—or didn't feel—for each other should be between them. She should have never agreed to marry him until the family drama had been sorted out, but she had.

She'd exchanged vows with Finn, all the while thinking she could protect herself from the feelings that came from a genuine relationship. So long as there was a wall between them, she'd be safe. In the end, though, it hadn't mattered how many bricks she stacked—she fell in love, anyway.

She *loved* Finn. Whether or not he loved her back no

longer mattered. Her heart belonged to Finn Crawford, whether he wanted it or not.

Her mother's gaze shifted from Avery to Finn and back again. "You are having a baby together. This baby will bond you together for life."

The vows from their simple country wedding ceremony echoed in her mind, beating in time with her heart.

Until death do you part.

Marion's eyes narrowed, and for a moment, Avery felt as if her mother could see straight into her soul. "I think I know how each of you really feels about the other, but this is not for me to decide. You two need to figure it out…together."

She was right. Of course she was, but they still hadn't tackled the biggest elephant in the room—the angry bull elephant more commonly known as Oscar Ellington.

"As for you." Marion squared her shoulders and turned to face her husband. "I've stood for your nonsense long enough. You had no business cutting Avery off like you did. She's our daughter, our own flesh and blood, and you've been holding on to some silly grudge against Maximilian Crawford for far too long."

Oscar's face went three shades of red. Maybe four. It reminded Avery of the bright leaves back in the maple forest near Rust Creek Falls.

He seemed to know better than to interrupt, though. Marion Ellington rarely criticized her husband. Almost never, as far as Avery could remember. But her patience had finally cracked, and she was apparently finished holding her tongue.

"Either you give Avery back her inheritance—and her job—or I will leave you, Oscar Ellington. This is no idle threat. I will walk right out that door." She pointed to the front door with a trembling hand.

All eyes in the room swiveled toward Oscar. Avery didn't dare breathe while she waited for him to respond.

The silence stretched on for a long, loaded moment until he finally nodded. "As you wish."

Oscar's voice was quiet. Contrite.

When he turned a tender gaze toward Avery, her heart gave a tight squeeze. But what she nearly mistook for heartbreak was something else entirely—it was her heart, and her family, mending back into one unified piece after weeks of shattered silence.

"Your mother is right, sweetheart. I love you no matter what. If you want to stay married to a Crawford, I might not like it, but I'll learn to live with it." With a deep exhale, Oscar faced Finn full-on. "You obviously feel passionately about my daughter. I love her with my whole heart, and if you do, too, then I suppose it's possible for us to find some common ground."

A surreal feeling of euphoria washed over Avery. It started in her chest and spread outward, leaving a tingling surge in its wake.

Her father had just said everything Avery had wanted to hear from the moment she'd first realized she was pregnant. Before she'd even set foot in Rust Creek Falls, she'd lain awake nights, wishing and hoping for something like this to happen. It just seemed so impossible, and once he'd called her with the devastating news that he was cutting her off, she'd given up every last shred of hope.

Thank God for her mother.

If she hadn't intervened, they might never have gotten here. But she had, because that's what mothers did.

They sacrificed all for their children. Avery was only beginning to understand the depth of that kind of unconditional love.

She rested her hand on her belly and fixed her gaze on Finn's. The feud was over. There was no longer anything standing between them. At long last, they could be together—*really* together—without the devastating heartbreak of being cut off from her family.

But now that all the obstacles had finally been torn down, Avery was no longer sure where she and Finn stood. A part of her—a very large, very real part—wanted to cross the room and throw herself at him the same way she had in the pasture at the Ambling A and in the cool quiet of the sugar bush at the syrup farm. Why shouldn't she? What her father thought no longer mattered.

But she'd left.

She'd finally given herself to Finn, and in the heady romance of the afterglow, she'd run away.

They could get past that, though, couldn't they? Everything had turned out for the best. Finn had followed her all the way here. And yet…

Finn was still sitting quietly on the rose damask sofa in the room where her mother threw tea parties. He hadn't uttered a word in response to what her father had just said.

I love her with my whole heart, and if you do, too, then I suppose it's possible for us to find some common ground.

This was the moment where Finn was supposed to confess his feelings. It was the only way to respond to that sort of statement, wasn't it?

I love Avery, too.

That's what Finn should be saying right now. Why wasn't he?

Please. Avery implored him with her gaze. Her feelings had to be written all over her face. Couldn't he see it? *Please, please say it.*

But suddenly Finn couldn't seem to look at her. The passion and fury that had driven him to fly all the way to Texas and practically beat down the door to the Ellington estate seemed to drain right out of him before her eyes.

He frowned down at his hands, folded neatly in his lap. Those hands had touched her in ways no one else ever had before. Those hands knew every inch of her body—every secret place, every soft, silken vulnerability. Avery couldn't look at them anymore without craving the exquisite pleasure of his skin against hers.

When Finn finally spoke, it was in a voice she'd never heard him use before. Quiet. Calm…terrifyingly so. "Can I have a word alone with Avery, please?"

"Of course," her mother said, rising to her feet as she shot a meaningful look at Oscar.

"Yes, yes." He stood as well, pausing to give Avery a kiss on the top of her head before they left the room. "I love you, honey. Remember that, okay? You have our support." He lingered for a moment, shifting awkwardly from foot to foot. "Whatever you decide."

It was strange seeing her father so unsure of himself and only underscored the gravity of what had just occurred. And what might happen next.

"I know." Avery reached out and squeezed his hand. "Thank you."

Finn's expression betrayed little as her parents left the room and closed the French doors, shutting them alone together inside. Avery no longer cared what exact words he uttered; she just wished he would say *something.* Anything.

"I—" She started to apologize for her disappearing act, but at the same exact time, Finn began talking, too.

"Avery—"

They both stopped abruptly and stared at each other. Another day, another time, they probably would have laughed. Neither one of them did so now, though. Avery's chin went wobbly like it always did when she was trying not to cry.

"This changes things," Finn finally said.

She blinked. "What does?"

"This." Finn gestured vaguely at their surroundings—the antique rotary telephone, the gilded wall mirror that had been passed down from generation to generation of Ellingtons, the grandfather clock with its familiar tick-tock that Avery would have recognized blindfolded.

The room they were sitting in hadn't changed a bit since Avery's childhood. She could have drawn a picture of it from memory and not missed a single detail.

"You're back in the fold," he said. There wasn't a drop of bitterness in his tone, and Avery was suddenly unsure whether that was a good sign or a bad one.

"I guess I am." She nodded. "But shouldn't that be a good thing? My father is finally letting go of whatever happened between him and Maximilian. He won't stop you from seeing the baby anymore."

"And you're no longer disinherited," he added with a sad smile. "Which means you no longer need me."

Wait, that wasn't what it meant at all. Was that why he was acting so strangely all of a sudden? He thought the only reason they were together was because she'd had no place else to go?

Isn't it, though?

No.

She tried to swallow, but her throat had gone bone dry. It wasn't the only reason—not anymore. Deep down, it had never been the only reason. Finn was the father of her baby, but it was more than that, too. She'd *wanted* to exchange vows with him in that dusty old courthouse. She'd just been too afraid to admit it because Finn had never been the marrying type.

Oh, no.

Avery's heart plummeted to the soles of her feet. That's what the sudden change in Finn's mood was all about. He didn't want to be married. He never had. He'd just proposed because of the baby and now that there was no feud standing between him and his child, he was trying to let her down gently.

"You don't need me to support you and the baby," he said, spelling things out in a way that hurt more than she ever thought possible. As if all along she'd only been interested in the Crawford money.

"That's not true." She shook her head.

Stop it, she wanted to say. *Just stop saying these things and tell me you love me.*

"I think you need some time alone to figure out what it is you want, sweetheart." The kindness in his voice almost killed her. She'd rather he yell and scream than look at her the way he was looking at her right then… with goodbyes in his eyes.

Sure enough, he unfolded himself from the chair he was sitting in and loomed over her. Just as Avery expected, he already had one foot out the door.

She stood on wobbly legs and forced herself to meet his gaze. Where was the man who'd pounded on the front door with his fists, insisting he wasn't going anywhere without his wife by his side? She needed that man, whether he realized it or not. She *loved* that man.

"You know where to find me when you make up your mind."

They were the last words her husband said to her, followed by a chaste kiss on the cheek and a walk through the foyer to the front door.

And just like that, he was gone.

Chapter Fifteen

Avery couldn't seem to make herself move as the door shut softly yet firmly behind Finn. She wanted to go running after him. She wanted that more than anything in the world, but it was as if a physical force was holding her back, keeping her rooted to the spot.

He'd come all the way to Texas from Montana—for her. When she'd first spotted him on the security camera, she'd nearly wept with relief. If he'd chased her all the way to Texas, that had to mean he loved her.

Right?

She'd seen enough rom-coms to know that at some point, every good love story culminated in a grand romantic gesture. This was it. Finn had followed her to enemy territory so he could win her back.

But now that her mother had finally talked some sense into her father, Finn just up and walked away.

There'd been no declaration of love, no promise of a future together. He'd spoken about their marriage as if it was precisely what she'd set out for it to be.

A business transaction.

And then he'd left her alone to think things through. God, it was humiliating. Avery didn't need to think, and she sure as heck didn't feel like being alone. She wanted Finn, damn it. Couldn't he see that? She was in love with him. She'd been in love with him all along, which was precisely why she'd been acting so crazy—kissing him one minute and running away the next. Even marrying him when they hardly knew each other.

Her behavior had nothing to do with pregnancy hormones. She was head over heels, crazy in love with her husband.

And he'd just walked right out the door.

She'd never felt so alone in her life, not even when her father had so coldly informed her that she'd been disinherited. She pressed a hand to her baby bump, desperate for a reminder that she wasn't completely on her own. She still had her daughter, and she always would.

And she could still have Finn, too. He'd made it perfectly clear that the decision was up to her. But was there really a decision to make if he didn't love her? How could she have been stupid enough to believe that exchanging sacred vows could ever be anything remotely similar to a business deal?

"Avery?" Her mom walked tentatively into the entryway and looked around. "Where's Finn?"

"He's..." *He's gone.* Avery shook her head. She couldn't say it. If she did, she'd break and she wasn't sure she'd ever be whole again.

"Oh, honey." Her mom wrapped her arms around

Avery and hugged her tight. "Don't cry. Everything is going to be okay."

But it wasn't. There'd been no grand gesture, just a quiet goodbye, and now great heaving sobs were racking Avery's body. It was as if she'd been suppressing her real feelings for so long—since that fateful night in Oklahoma City—that she simply couldn't do it any longer. She was feeling everything at once. Joy and pain. Hope and fear. Love and loss.

So much loss that it nearly dragged her to her knees.

Her mother smoothed her hair back from her eyes, then cupped Avery's face in her hands. "Do you love him, sweetheart?"

She nodded as tears kept streaming down her face.

Her mom smiled as if she'd known as much all along. "Then it seems as though you have an important decision to make. Don't worry about your father. I'll handle him. You just do what you need to do."

Avery trembled all over.

Do what you need to do.

She took a ragged inhale as a terrible realization dawned—what she wanted to do and what she needed to do were two entirely different things.

The log mansion at the Ambling A was as quiet as a tomb when Finn walked through the door at three in the morning. He was immensely grateful for Maximilian's access to a private plane, just as he'd been the day before when he was in such a hurry to get to Dallas.

But at the moment, he was even more grateful for the fact that all of his family members were in bed and he wouldn't have to see their disappointed expressions when he walked back through the door without his wife.

The only thing that might have made him feel worse was the more likely possibility that they wouldn't have been surprised at all, that they'd have chalked up his short-lived marriage to Finn just being Finn. He never could commit to anyone or anything. Why should Avery be any different?

But she *was* different, damn it. She'd always been special. She was the one. She always had been, right from the start.

The baby mattered, obviously. Finn would lay down his life for his child, but Avery mattered just as much. He'd only fully realized how much she meant to him after she'd left him. And now…

Now it was too late. She was back in Dallas, back in the loving arms of her family. Finn had his own opinions about what sort of father would ever turn his back on his pregnant adult daughter, but at least Oscar Ellington had done the right thing in the end.

If anyone understood the importance of family, it was Finn. As maddening as Maximilian could be, he'd been the one to raise six boys all on his own after his wife had walked out and left him. There was no denying Finn's father was a difficult man, and there was plenty of blame on both sides where his parents' divorce was concerned, but Maximilian had always been there for his sons. Always would be. Which was why Finn had tolerated his meddling into his sons' love lives as best as he could.

It was also why he'd done an about-face and hadn't insisted Avery return to the Ambling A with him. He couldn't make that choice for her. The last thing he wanted was to come between her and her family yet again. If they had any hope of remaining together, she'd have to make that decision on her own. He didn't want to be the kind of husband and father she'd grown up with. As much as he loved Avery, as much as he wanted her, he refused to bully her back into his home…into his life.

In a way, he'd already strong-armed her into marrying him. Witnessing the effect Oscar's controlling behavior had on the people he loved most in the world had been a wake-up call. Finn loved Maximilian, but he didn't want to grow old and become his father any more than he wanted to become Oscar Ellington. He wanted Avery to come back to him on her own terms, no one else's.

He wanted her to *choose* him.

She would. She had to. They were meant to be together. Finn knew that as surely as he knew the sun would rise over Montana the next morning, filling Big Sky country with endless rays of hope and light.

Finn needed just a hint of that kind of hope right now. Desperately. Somewhere between Texas and Montana, a bone-deep weariness had come over him. He was too tired to think, too tired to hope, too tired to dream.

He just wanted Avery back in his arms and back in his bed. Until that happened, he was lost. He collapsed fully clothed onto his bed and closed his eyes against a darkness so deep that he felt like he was choking on it. And when sleep finally came, he dreamed of his daughter. He dreamed of Avery and the life the three of them could have together—a life filled with love and joy and as many children and baby goats as Avery wanted. He'd give her anything and everything.

But when he woke up, she wasn't there. Of course she wasn't. It was silly to think she'd chase him back to

Montana the moment after he'd left her daddy's mansion. She needed time. Of course she did. But she'd come back—she had to come back. Finn went about his day on autopilot, doing his best to simply get through the hours until Avery returned without breaking down.

For once in his life, Maximilian held his tongue. He must have sensed Finn's need for silence on the matter of his missing wife, because when he strolled into the kitchen to find Finn staring blankly out the big picture window at Pumpkin romping and playing in her new pen, he simply rested a single arm around his shoulder in a tentative one-armed man hug. The unprecedented tenderness of the father-and-son moment caused a lump to lodge firmly in Finn's throat. He nodded, then strode outside to feed the goat to keep the dam of emotions welled up inside him from breaking.

The day wore on, and he busied himself with the daily comfort of ranch work—mending fences, tending to cattle, filling the stalls in the barn with fresh water and hay. His brothers and the ranch hands steered clear, leaving him space and time to brood. In his solitude, Finn worked harder than he had in years, because that's what true cowboys did. They did what needed to be done, no matter what. When they made a promise, they kept it.

He brushed a few stray flakes of hay from his black T-shirt as the air in the barn shifted from soft pink light to the purple shadows of twilight. His back ached, and so did his heart. The day was done, the horses were locked up for the night and the cattle fed, but still there was no sign whatsoever of Avery.

Finn pulled his Stetson low over his eyes and pressed his fist into his lower back, seeking relief. Then, for the first time all day, he allowed himself to consider the possibility that he'd been wrong, that maybe Avery wasn't coming back to the Ambling A. Not today… not ever.

His throat grew thick again, and just like this morning when Maximilian had given him the closest thing to a true embrace they'd ever shared, he felt as if he was on the verge of tears for the first time in his adult life. But then he heard something that gave him pause—an excited little bleat coming from the direction of Pumpkin's pen. Finn's heart stuttered to a stop.

It was silly, really. Baby kids got excited about anything and everything. Just because Pumpkin was suddenly making a ruckus didn't mean the goat's—and Finn's—favorite person in the world had suddenly reappeared.

But hope welled up in his chest nonetheless. And when he bolted out the barn door and saw Avery's familiar silhouette framed by a perfect autumn sunset, he nearly fell to his knees in relief.

"Avery," he said, his voice rusty and raw. "Thank God."

He held out his arms, but instead of running toward him, Avery slowed to a stop and gave him a watery smile. It was the saddest, most lonely smile he'd ever seen, and that's when Finn knew. He knew it with every desperate beat of his battered heart.

His wife had come home to say goodbye.

The relief in Finn's weary face nearly shattered Avery's resolve.

Clearly he was happy to see her. Elated, even after she'd spent the duration of her travel day—two flights, one three-hour layover and the winding drive to Rust Creek Falls from Billings—convincing herself that she was doing the right thing. The *only* thing. As hard as walking away from Finn would be, it wouldn't be as torturous as building a life with a man who didn't love her, constantly waiting for the shoe to drop and everything she held most dear to crumble to the ground.

She was sure she couldn't do that to herself, and she was positive she couldn't do it to her baby. Better to develop some sort of reasonable, platonic co-parenting arrangement now than end up having to try to find her way once Finn remembered he'd never had any interest in marriage in the first place…to anyone, least of all her.

But she couldn't tell Finn what she needed to say over the phone. He'd been by her side since the moment she'd told him she was pregnant, which was more than she could say for her own flesh and blood. In the end, she'd been the one to run, not him. So he deserved to hear the news face-to-face.

First, though…

She sent a gentle smile to the baby goat bleating excitedly and butting her furry head against the hay bale in the center of her pen. "What is Pumpkin doing here?"

Finn removed his Stetson, raked a hand through his hair and replaced it. Avery tried, and failed, not to stare at the flex of his biceps as he did so. "You said you missed her, so when I went looking for you at the boarding house, I asked Melba and Old Gene if I could bring her to the Ambling A."

Oh. Wow. He'd gone looking for her at the boarding house? "I'm guessing Melba was delighted with that arrangement."

Finn nodded. "She said something about Pumpkin belonging to you already."

Once you name an animal, it's yours.

Avery could hear Melba's voice in her head as clearly as if she were standing right beside her.

How was she going to do this? She loved life in Rust Creek Falls. She loved everything about it.

"I think we should get an annulment," she said without any sort of prelude. If she didn't say it now, she never would. "Or if we don't qualify for one of those, then a divorce."

The *D* word. She barely forced it out. Her voice cracked midway through, turning it into three or four syllables instead of two.

Finn said nothing.

He just stood there staring at her as if she'd kicked him in the stomach. Behind him, the mountains shimmered in shades of red and gold. Never in her life had she thought complete and utter heartbreak could be surrounded by so much beauty.

She cleared her throat and forced herself to finish the speech she'd been mentally rehearsing for hours. "This is all my fault. I take full responsibility. I should have told you about the baby from the very beginning, and I never should have suggested our marriage be one of convenience."

It seemed so absurd now. How could she have ever thought a fake marriage was a good idea when, all along, her feelings for Finn had been heart-stoppingly real?

"It was just..." she continued while nearby, Pumpkin bounced on and off a bale of hay. *It was just the worst mistake I've ever made.* Avery swallowed hard. "It was wrong."

The set of Finn's jaw hardened. His soft brown eyes—eyes that usually danced with laughter and Finn's trademark devilish charm—darkened to black. "*Wrong?* That's the word you'd use to describe our marriage?"

Avery shook her head. This wasn't going at all how she'd planned. "Please, Finn. You know what I mean."

She was referring to the agreement they'd made not to become intimate, and he knew it. But neither of them could seem to acknowledge it out loud, probably because that arrangement had been nothing short of impossible. She'd fallen into bed with Finn almost instantaneously, and despite all the hurt feelings swirling between them, she still wanted him. She craved the weight of his body on top of hers, the velvety warmth of his skin, his searing kiss. She always would.

"I appreciate everything you were willing to do for me—" she paused for a breath, then forced the rest of the words out "—for the baby. But I should have never agreed to rely on you for money, no matter the circumstances. That's all sorted out now, and I'm not going to hold you to an agreement we never should have made in the first place."

There, it was done. Almost.

Finn deserved to know the whole truth before she walked away for good. "What the baby and I both need isn't money or security. It's love. *Real* love. And I can't let myself settle for a knockoff."

"What the heck are you talking about?" Finn's voice boomed louder than Avery had ever heard it before. It even startled poor Pumpkin into inactivity. She let out a mournful bleat. “Are you crazy? Of course I love you. Why would you think otherwise?”

Avery opened her mouth to yell right back at him, and then blinked, trying to wrap her mind around what he’d just said.

Surely she’d heard him wrong.

“But you...” She shook her head, and hot tears filled her eyes.

He couldn’t be serious, but Avery didn’t think he’d toy with her emotions. Not at a time like this. Finn had never once told her he loved her, though. How was she supposed to know?

“I love you, Avery! I fell in love with you the first night we were together back in Oklahoma!” He yelled it so loud that there was no way she could misunderstand. The entire population of Rust Creek Falls probably knew Finn Crawford loved her now.

Avery didn’t know how to process it, though. It was too much, more than her fragile heart could handle after all she’d been through in recent weeks.

She burst into tears.

“Don’t cry, love,” Finn said, closing the distance between them and taking her into his arms. “I’m sorry for yelling. It’s just that I’ve been tied up in knots, worried you weren’t coming back.”

He pressed a tender kiss to the top of her head as she buried her face in his shoulder. He smelled like hay and horses, farm and family...like all the things she’d come to love so much about life here in this wild, beautiful place.

“I love you,” he said, gently this time. Like a whisper.

Avery closed her eyes, wanting to believe, but needing to be sure. What if this was still just about the baby?

She shook her head against the soft fabric of his T-shirt, fighting as hard as she could. But falling for Finn Crawford had always been as easy and sweet as falling onto a feather bed.

"You love me, or the baby?" she managed to murmur, even as she felt her heart beating hard in perfect harmony against his.

Finn pulled away slightly, took her face in his hands and forced her to meet his gaze. "I love both of you, Princess. I'll admit it threw me when you told me you were pregnant, and I definitely could have handled the news better. Our relationship hasn't exactly been traditional."

He sighed, and the corner of his mouth tugged into a familiar half smile.

Had Rust Creek Falls' most notoriously single Crawford just used the word *relationship*?

"But, darlin', there was always a part of me that connected with you right from the start. Didn't you feel it, too, Princess?" His gaze dropped to her mouth as the pad of his thumb brushed a tender trail along her bottom lip. "Don't you feel it now?"

Then her husband dipped his head and kissed her as the sun fell on another autumnal day in Montana, and while the horses whinnied in the barn and the trees on the horizon blazed ruby red, the last bit of Avery's resistance faded away.

She felt it, too—with every breath, every kiss, every captivated beat of her heart. She felt it.

This kiss, this place…this man she loved so much. Finn Crawford wasn't just the father of her baby. He was her home, and at long last, Avery Ellington Crawford was home to stay.

Epilogue

Hours later, Avery lay in Finn's bed, naked and sated. Once again, he'd scooped her off her feet and carried her upstairs, where he'd made love to her in the same bed where she'd somehow managed to convince herself that he didn't love her.

How could she have been so wrong?

The question nagged at her in the afterglow. Finn had told her why he'd been going on so many dates. He'd even admitted he hadn't slept with anyone since their night together in Oklahoma. How had she taken the beautiful moment when he'd kissed her belly and whispered *mine* as something else—something frightening and lonely? Something to run away from.

She wondered if the answer was somehow tangled up in the ugly episode of her disinheritance. She thought maybe so, but she didn't want to think about that now. She'd made peace with her father, and in the end, her mother had stood up for her in a way she never could have imagined. On some level, she was glad it had happened. Being cut off from her family had taught her some important truths. It taught her she was capable of standing on her own two feet and making her own decisions. It taught her what kind of parent she wanted to be to her baby. And most of all, it taught her she could trust Finn Crawford. He was a keeper, and she had no intention of running again. Ever.

He ran tender fingertips across her baby bump, then pressed a hand to her heart and whispered her favorite word.

"Mine."

Her heart was his, now and forever. Past, present and always.

"I have an idea," he said, shooting her one of his boyish grins.

"Oh, yeah? Does this idea involve a goat?" She kind of wanted another one. Another baby, too, now that she was thinking about it. The more, the merrier. After all, the Ambling A had plenty of room.

"It does not." He arched a brow. "Unless you want Pumpkin to be part of our wedding. That could be arranged. Maybe she could be the ring bearer. Don't people do that with dogs?"

Avery shifted so she could get a better look at his expression. Was he serious? "Aren't you forgetting something, cowboy? We're already married."

He picked up her hand and toyed with the rose gold band on her finger. Someday Avery might pass it on to their daughter and tell her the story of how she'd married her father in tiny country courthouse in Great Gulch where the bailiff wore spurs. And then maybe her daughter would pass it on to her own child, and so on and so on, so that generations of Crawfords would remember the fine man who'd won her heart against all odds.

"I know we're already married, but I'd like to have another wedding—a ceremony like the one Wren asked you about. A big celebration that both our families could attend." He bent to kiss her, warm and tender. "Think about it. How does that sound, Princess?"

She smiled at her husband. She didn't need to think about anything. The answer fell right off her tongue. "Perfect."

Just like a fairy tale.

* * * * *

MILLS & BOON

Coming next month

THEIR FESTIVE ISLAND ESCAPE
Nina Singh

An appealing, successful, handsome man was asking to spend time with her on various island adventures but his only objective was her business acumen.

That shouldn't have bothered her as much as it did. But that was a silly notion, it wasn't like she and Reid were friends or anything. In fact, a few short days ago, she would have listed him as one of the few people on earth who actually may not even like her.

"Why me?" Celeste asked. There had to be other individuals he could ask. A man like Reid was unlikely to be lacking in female companionship.

She imagined what it would be like to date a man like him. What it would mean if he was sitting here asking her to do these things with her simply because he wanted to spend time with her.

What his lips would feel against hers if he ever were to kiss her.

Dear saints! What in the world was wrong with her? Was it simply because she'd been without a man for so long? Perhaps it was the romantic, exotic location. Something had to be causing such uncharacteristic behavior on her part.

Why hadn't she just said no already? Was she really even entertaining the idea?

She wasn't exactly the outdoors type. Or much of an

athlete for that matter. Sure, she'd scaled countless fences during her youth trying to outrun the latest neighborhood bully after defending her younger sister. And she'd developed some really quick reflexes averting touchy men in city shelters. But that was about the extent of it.

Reid answered her, breaking into the dangerous thoughts. "Think about it. Between your professional credentials and the fact that you take frequent tropical vacations, you're actually the perfect person to accompany me."

Again, nothing but logic behind his reasoning. On the surface, she'd be a fool to turn down such an exciting opportunity; the chance to experience so much more of what the island had to offer and, in the process, acquire a host of memories she'd hold for a lifetime. It was as if he really was Santa and he had just handed her a gift most women would jump at.

Continue reading
THEIR FESTIVE ISLAND ESCAPE
Nina Singh

Available next month
www.millsandboon.co.uk